When Dead Ain't Dead Enough

Dead Enough

Book 1 of
The Dead Among Us

The dead should ever rest in peace, but when dead ain't dead enough, the living should fear for their mortal souls.

by

J. L. Doty

TELEMACHUS PRESS

Cover Designed by Telemachus Press, LLC

Cover Art:
Copyright © Thinkstockphoto/138180607/iStockPhoto
Copyright © Thinkstockphoto/138183983/iStockPhoto
Copyright © @GettyImages/Thinkstockphoto/87628950/photos.com
Copyright © Thinkstockphoto/100549058/Hemera

Published by Telemachus Press, LLC
http://www.telemachuspress.com

Visit the author website:
http://www.jldoty.com

Follow the author on Twitter:
http://www.twitter.com/@JL_Doty

ISBN: 978-1-938135-29-3 (eBook)
ISBN: 978-1-953757-05-0 (paperback)
ISBN: 978-1-953757-16-6 (hardcover)

Version 2023.11.08

KEpuz!po!KJNEFTLUPQ:
Formatted using eTools for Writers 3.8.8, Nov 08 2023, 10:49:32
Copyright © 2013-2016 by J. L. Doty

Printed in the United States of America

10 9 8 7 6 5 4 3 2 1

When Dead Ain't Dead Enough

Book 1 of
The Dead Among Us

Prologue:
Reunion

IT WAS JUST a mirror, but when Paul looked into it a bat-like monster glared back at him with blood-red goat-slitted eyes. It screamed out a cry from hell, exposing a mouth full of razor sharp teeth. Then it reached out, its arm extending from the glass like the smooth surface of a still pond. It tried to seize him with a clawed hand, talons the length of his fingers grasping for his throat. And though it couldn't reach him, and he wanted to run screaming like a child, he stood paralyzed, unable to utter a word or move a muscle.

Looking into its eyes had been a mistake, he now realized, for he felt an overwhelming compulsion to come to the monster, to step within its grasp and embrace it. It loved him, cherished him like no one else had since Suzanna. All he needed to do was return that love, just walk toward the mirror and lose himself in its desire. He was about to do so when something inside him snapped and he came to his senses. The vision in the mirror was a monster from hell, not a lover. He lifted a foot to back-step away from it, but the foot stepped forward of its own volition, and in the monster's eyes he saw greedy satisfaction, the joyful knowledge that it would have him, that it would devour him. He was powerless to defy it.

Little by little he advanced across the room, each step an agonizing struggle, each step a failure as it drew him closer, a puppet ruled by the strings of those blood-red eyes. Then suddenly he was within its grasp and the hand gripped his throat. It dug razor sharp talons into his larynx and pulled him toward the mirror. He thought his face would smash against the glass, but when his cheek touched the surface his head sank into it. And as he was drawn into the realm that spawned the monster, he screamed—

Paul slammed awake and sat up in bed. "Fucking dream," he growled, gasping for air, beads of sweat rolling down his cheek. He switched on the light next to his bed and snarled, "Just a fucking dream."

He told himself that, time and again, every time he woke from that nightmare— just a dream. He knew this evil, this darkness that stalked him inside the mirror, and a piece of him feared *he* might be this evil, that it was some darkness in his own soul that stalked him. After all, the monster in his dream was his own reflection.

"Just a dream," he said. "Just a dream."

Suzanna's ghost walked into the room. *But it wasn't a dream,* she said. *It's waiting for you, Paulie-boy. And I don't think you can escape it.*

••••

Paul sat at the kitchen table watching Suzanna bustling about preparing dinner. It was his favorite time of day, to sit there at the end of the day with a glass of wine and chat with her while she put the finishing touches on their meal. It had been his favorite time of day back when she was alive, and he was so happy she'd come back to him, even if only as a ghostly specter.

Cloe bounced into the kitchen in her school uniform. Well, like Suzanna it wasn't really Cloe, just Cloe's ghost. *Can I help with dinner?*

Suzanna looked over her shoulder and winked at Paul as she said, *Not until you finish your homework.*

Oh please, mommy! Please, please, please! I hate homework! Homework's so boooooring.

Paul decided to intervene. "Sorry, munchkin, it's the rule. Homework before you get to help with dinner."

Cloe skipped across the kitchen and stopped just a foot or so short of Paul. The real Cloe, the living Cloe, would've jumped into his lap, but they both knew that wouldn't work for this Cloe. *Daddy, homework's too hard.*

Suzanna turned toward them, a plate of steaming food in each hand. *Well, since dinner's ready anyway, sweetheart, tonight you get a reprieve.*

••••

He was an older man, distinguished looking, standing on a street corner in the gathering twilight in the quiet San Francisco neighborhood. Gray hair, clean shaven, dressed in a tweed jacket, slacks, pale-blue shirt and conservative tie, anyone walking by might assume he was a professor at one of the local universities, and that was exactly the image Walter McGowan wanted to project. He leaned casually against the brick front of the brownstone behind him, lowered his barriers and let his senses expand into the oncoming night.

He was getting closer, but working alone was a long, drawn-out process of slowly triangulating on the source. It helped that the idiot broadcast the conjuration on a regular time schedule: every morning and evening without fail; one might think breakfast and dinner. He wasn't sure why he hadn't called in help, but, while the conjuration was powerful, and broadcasting it without wards and precautions was sloppy, the fool hadn't done anything truly dangerous, at least not yet. Some of McGowan's colleagues didn't feel the need to understand a situation before acting, tended to assume the worst and overreact. They might decide to kill the poor fool before determining if he was truly dangerous, so McGowan had decided he should work alone. What was most frustrating was the fellow's uncanny ability to snap the old man's locator spell, to do so almost casually as if the act of cutting it was a mere afterthought. That took strength, and the kind of control of which few were capable. Well, maybe he wasn't such an idiot after all.

This evening it followed the normal pattern, starting near sunset with a steady background that was some sort of spirit interaction. It wasn't strong enough for him to pin down a precise direction, and certainly not strong enough to note distance. But, if the fellow was true to form, the material conjuration, when it came, would be powerful, distinct, and well defined. So he waited, eyes closed, sensing the vague, easterly direction of the source, waiting . . . waiting . . . waiting . . .

There! A powerful conjuration, powerful and dangerous, dangerous beyond imagining. Maybe he should call in his colleagues, stop playing with misguided compassion, just kill the idiot and be done with it.

••••

The conjuration hit Vasily Karpov like a slap and he started visibly. Vladimir, his cold-hearted, blond killer, noticed his reaction immediately, while Alexei, his dark, big, dumb bear, continued to lean on the lamp post, as always oblivious to anything short of a lightning bolt.

"Wake up, idiot," Karpov snarled as he gave Alexei a shove.

Alexei stumbled, and he and Vladimir looked fearfully at Karpov, both dreading his wrath. It was unfair to treat them so. After all, they were just big, dumb muscle, and while both did have some arcane capacity, their capabilities were just too limited to be of any value in that respect. Karpov kept them around purely for the brawn.

"Follow me, you idiots."

Karpov marched down the street, heading west toward the conjuration. He needed to move quickly while some residue of the invocation remained. It was dwindling, and the spell he'd cast to help him locate arcane activity was dissipating rapidly.

"Mr. Karpov," Vladimir said in Russian.

"Shut up," Karpov growled. "I'm trying to concentrate."

Vladimir cringed and wisely remained silent.

Karpov led them two blocks west, then one north, and there, his ability to sense the conjuration's direction dissipated completely. "Blast," he snarled in frustration.

He turned to the two thugs. "We're closer. And we'll get closer tomorrow, and the next day. And when we find this wizard, we kill him, no hesitation, no questions asked."

The big, dumb bear and the hulking Slav nodded vacantly and grinned.

••••

Paul knew that sharing his apartment with the ghosts of his wife and daughter was anything but normal. He knew they didn't really exist, knew they were just hallucinations, knew he should probably get help. Still, he loved watching Suzanna cook, and watching Cloe sitting at the coffee table in her school uniform struggling with her homework, her little face scrunched up in confusion at some problem she couldn't solve. And though they were both dead and buried, and all he had now were shadows of what they'd once been, that was all he could have, so he accepted the situation.

Suzanna looked over her shoulder at him and smiled. She was translucent in a ghostly, apparition-like way, and he could see the stove and cupboards through her. Cloe skipped into the room carrying some toy, and like her mother was little more than a translucent specter.

He knew that seeing them had to be some sort of traumatic reaction to their deaths, one right after the other, Suzanna in a car accident, a few months later Cloe in a hit-and-run. It had been a real one-two punch, and Paul had crashed hard, lost his job as an architect, stopped eating regularly, lost weight, bathed only a couple times a week, shaved only here and there. He'd looked so scruffy a stranger on the street had offered him a few bucks for a meal.

Then a little more than a year after they'd been taken from him, he'd been sitting at the kitchen table one morning, drinking reheated, two-day-old coffee, thinking of how Suzanna used to cook breakfast before he went to work. That too had been one of his favorite times of day, to just sit there and watch her work while Cloe bounced around with the energy of a seven year old girl, trying to get ready for school.

That was the first time Suzanna had appeared, just walked into the kitchen as if she'd never been gone. She'd paused, looked at him, smiled and said something; at least her lips moved, though no sound emerged. But he knew she said, *Bacon and eggs, Paulie-boy?*

"Ya," he said, and smiled back at her, putting down the two-day-old coffee. "That sounds great."

She'd given him a wink and bathed him in that glorious smile of hers, turned to the stove and pulled a couple of pans out of the cupboard. She had brownish-blond hair cut chin length, and wore one of his T-shirts as she often did in the morning. Since she had small breasts she could get away without wearing a bra, and when she bent over he got a little enticing hint of bikini panties. She'd looked over her shoulder at him that first morning, grinned knowingly and said, *Always the letch in the morning, eh Paulie-boy?*

Cloe had then raced into the room and said, *Hi daddy.* She'd had on her school uniform, and his heart swelled that day to know they'd both come back.

He'd said, "Hi, munchkin."

Cloe had tugged on the hem of her mother's T-shirt, dancing from one foot to the other expectantly. Suzanna had looked down at her and smiled with so much love. *Don't dawdle. You have to get ready for school.*

But I don't want to go to school. Can't I be sick today?

But school's good for you, darling. And you want your mom and dad to be proud of you, don't you?

Yeeesssss . . .

Come on, off with you now. I have to finish your dad's breakfast.

Paul knew he was hallucinating, but damn, the bacon and eggs were good.

1

Discovery

HIGH CHANCELLOR CADILUS knelt before the Seelie throne and lowered his eyes to look at the stone floor. That it was cold, lifeless stone was a reflection of the ill humor of Magreth, the Summer Queen. Cadilus spoke softly, "You summoned me, Your Majesty?"

Her voice rang through his thoughts. "Rise, Cadilus, and look upon us."

He stood and raised his eyes slowly, and only now realized the depths to which trouble had touched the heart of the Seelie Court. His queen's eyes blazed with fire, the pupils no longer visible, while the shadows of undeveloped, primordial Sidhe spirits danced around her flame-red hair. "There's a stirring on the Mortal Plane, Cadilus, a restlessness the like of which I've not felt in centuries."

"I too have sensed a certain disquiet, Your Majesty. And I believe it extends to the Netherworld as well."

She stood, and the shadows of the ancient spirits scattered to the far corners of the room like a flock of starlings startled by a hawk. "Yes, the Netherworld is troubled, and it looks hungrily upon the Mortal Plane. It looks with greed and desire. I feel that in my heart."

She tensed, and with a visible effort the flames in her eyes died. The emerald green pupils she turned on Cadilus bored deep into his soulless heart. "Come. Walk with me. We'll discuss this in private."

With no more than a whim, the walls of the Seelie palace disappeared, and she and Cadilus now strolled down a path in a sumptuous garden, ripe with spring blossoms. Magreth spoke without emotion, "Portents have manifested."

Cadilus looked at her carefully. "Portents, Your Majesty?"

"Yes. The Morrigan has taken notice."

Cadilus made no effort to hide his surprise. "That is indeed dire news, Your Majesty. Which aspect has the triple goddess assumed?"

"I fear she's assumed all three: sovereignty, prophecy and war."

"Indeed, a most auspicious portent. We must be facing a time of change."

She stopped in her tracks and turned to face him. She'd taken on the aspect of a young Sidhe girl, a child with ancient and troubled eyes. And the shadows of the old Sidhe spirits had returned, perhaps drawn to her to seek comfort in some way. "After centuries of weakening, the pathways between the Three Realms have strengthened, and increased in number. And the Morrigan has roused the non-aligned fey from their complacency."

Her eyes radiated her anger and frustration, and beneath that gaze Cadilus would have flinched had he been a weaker mage. "Unaroused, the non-aligned fey are at worst a nuisance, Your Majesty, with their little tricks and games. But aroused to a common cause by the Morrigan, they could be a danger to all of Faerie. Tell me she hasn't given them common cause."

"I cannot say one way or another, Cadilus. I cannot tell you why she's stirred the non-aligned. So I bid you—I task you—keep a close eye on this most unusual of developments. Watch closely all three Realms, and tell me of any change."

Cadilus bowed deeply. "As you wish, Your Majesty."

••••

Old man Strath met him personally. "Paul, you're looking good." The surprise on his face was evident as he gripped both of Paul's shoulders and held him at arm's length. He looked him up and down with obvious joy. "You've gained back some weight." Strath gave his shoulders a fatherly squeeze. "And you've put back on some of that muscle."

"Ya," Paul said. "I'm working out a bit, a little bit, and eating regular again—" He'd almost added, *now that Suzanna's cooking for me again,* but he knew better than to say that. Strath wouldn't understand.

"Come on in, Paul. Come on in."

Paul followed Strath into his office. Strath offered him a seat on the couch he kept in the corner of his office and joined him there. "I gotta say, Paul. Last time I saw you—what, three months ago? You didn't look too good. Looked like you needed a shave, and a bath, and you were damn near anemic. You really had me worried. But look at you now."

"I just needed time. And it really helped that—" He bit back his words, clamped down on that thought viciously. He'd almost said, . . . *that Suzanna and Cloe are back.*

Strath missed the hesitation, looked him over again and grinned. "Well whatever it took, I'm glad to see the old Paul's back."

"I'm not completely the old Paul, but close enough."

Strath shook his head sadly. "Nothing'll ever bring back Suzanna and Cloe."

"Ya, you can't bring 'em back," Paul lied. "You can't bring 'em back."

"So what can I do for you, son? What brings you here?"

"Well . . ." Paul hesitated. "I need to ask a favor. It took me a while, but I'm no longer buried under a mountain of self-pity. I still miss them, and it still hurts, but I'm functioning again, as you can see, and I need to go back to work, and I was hoping . . . well . . . that . . . maybe . . ."

As Paul spoke, the look on Strath's face slowly morphed from happiness to concern, then an almost painful grimace. "You want your old job back, huh?" Paul could see it coming. "Damn, I'm sorry, son, but I've already replaced you, and we're a small firm, so I can't carry any fat."

At the pain on Strath's face Paul said, "I'm sorry. I shouldn't have asked." He started to stand.

Strath pushed him back down and said, "Wait a minute." He stood and paced across the room, a thoughtful look on his face. "But, you know, I heard Carry's looking for someone. And if not him, there'll be someone else hiring. The industry's picking up, and you're a talented guy, and I can give you a great recommendation. I hate to see you go to the competition, but let me make some calls. I bet I've got something for you before you get home."

They spent another half hour just chatting and catching up, though Paul was careful not to speak of Suzanna and Cloe in the present tense. Then Paul took his leave.

Out on the street Paul decided to get a sandwich for lunch. He turned down Geary, and as he walked he scanned the street ahead for a place to eat, but that Suzanna-feeling came over him suddenly. It was hard to describe, but after Suzanna had died, whenever she came to him she brought with her an odd sense of comfort and a little tickle in the back of his soul, and he felt that now, on the street in broad daylight.

Stunned, he stopped and scanned the street again. A typical lunch-hour crowd jammed the San Francisco sidewalks with pedestrians, but up ahead near the corner he spotted a woman that, from behind, looked like she might be Suzanna. And as she turned the corner he caught a glimpse of her profile, and now he was almost certain it was her. He raced after her.

••••

The Summer Knight of the Winter Court stood on the street corner impatiently. He wore a glamour that gave him the appearance of a young mortal dressed fashionably in a business suit. It wouldn't do to have people wondering why an immortal Seelie Warrior with pointed ears stalked the streets of a mundane city in broad daylight.

The Morrigan, the triple goddess, the goddess of sovereignty, prophecy and war, had summoned Anogh in a dream, and he knew well that only a fool ignored such a demand. For some reason she'd wanted him on this street, on this corner, at this place and time, though, as is always the way of a goddess, she hadn't enlightened him as to her reasons. It was a very ordinary day on a busy San Francisco street, and he stood there waiting, wondering what he was waiting for. And then the ghost of a pretty young woman walked past him, though ghosts didn't ordinarily haunt city streets in the light of day. The apparition paused next to him, looked at him directly and smiled at him in the oddest way, then walked on.

Of course, he could see her only because he was a powerful Sidhe mage, and, until the young man bumped into him, he would've sworn that no one else on the street was aware of the specter walking in their midst. The young fellow apologized quickly and rushed on, chasing the ghost. Anogh knew the young man, or rather, had known him a long time ago but couldn't recall how or when. And since a Sidhe mage never forgets such details, he knew the goddess was clouding his mind for some unknown godly reason. Anogh followed the fellow.

The ghost led the young man a merry chase. As he turned each street corner she was always a city block ahead of him, glimpsed for just an instant as she turned and vanished down another street. She was clearly guiding the young fellow to a destination of her choice, and only after he'd followed her for several city blocks did she turn into a store that sold expensive shoes to young mortal women.

••••

Katherine McGowan paced back and forth in front of the mirror, admiring the new pair of Pradas. It wasn't as if she couldn't afford them. She wasn't wealthy, but she had plenty of money, and she already had a closet full of nice shoes, though only a few pairs this expensive. One more pair was just an impractical extravagance, and if she bought them they'd constantly remind her of her ex-husband Eric, and how much he'd disapproved of her frivolous expenditures, even though it was her own money earned by her own efforts. She was a grown woman, and he'd never stopped treating her like a child.

"They look good on you, Dr. McGowan," the clerk said. "They go nicely with that suit."

Yes, they do look good, she thought, looking at her reflection in the mirror. The Pradas were a nice touch, and they complimented the Vera Wang suit. And it wasn't as if she had anything else to spend her money on, especially since she no longer needed to support that deadbeat ex-husband of hers. Eric would've been quite angry to see her buy these, so she turned to the clerk and said, "I'll take them. And the matching purse, too."

The clerk smiled and turned to ring up the sale, and it was at that moment that the ghost walked through Katherine's aura. She gasped as a sensation of cold yearning washed through her; she reached out and clutched at a display table to keep from col-lapsing to the floor. The ghost wasn't visible, but she could feel it hovering around her. She sensed its anticipation and realized it had sought her out purposefully.

"Is something wrong?" the clerk asked. "Are you ok?"

The moment passed, the ghost was gone and Katherine said, "Ya, I'm fine." She made up a little lie, though it was actually the truth. "Just had one of those moments that felt like a ghost walked over my grave."

"Oh, I get those all the time," the clerk said. She leaned close and whispered, "With me it's usually a PMS thing."

"I know what you mean," Katherine lied, thinking, *But you don't get them the way I do.*

A tinkling bell drew her attention to the front door. A fellow about her own age walked in and let the door swing shut behind him. He was handsome and dressed well. More out of reflex than anything else she glanced down at his left hand, and saw he wore no wedding ring. She looked into his eyes and liked what she saw so she smiled, and as he smiled back she caught herself involuntarily twirling a lock of her hair with her finger.

She pulled her eyes away from his and dropped her hand to her side, disgusted with herself for reacting that way. She'd actually twirled a lock of hair, like some horny little schoolgirl. She wasn't about to hit on some guy in a shoe store. Shoe stores and grocery stores were Eric's style.

The clerk smiled at the fellow and said, "Feel free to look around, and I'll be with you as soon as I'm done here."

She looked at Katherine. "Will there be anything else, Dr. McGowan?"

"No," Katherine said, "That'll be all." For some reason she couldn't take her eyes off the young man, and started to fantasize about him in her bed. She had to clamp down and end that train of thought quickly.

He ignored the two women and scanned the store with his eyes. He was searching for something, and there was just a hint of desperation about him. Suddenly Katherine realized he was looking for the ghost. Her arcane senses warned her that he too was a practitioner of the magical arts, and now she understood that he'd followed the ghost into the store.

He stepped further into the store, and when he was close enough Katherine whis-pered, "You don't have to worry. It's gone now."

He started and looked at her, and his eyes narrowed with distrust. "She's gone?" he asked.

She, Katherine thought, the ghost of some woman who'd probably meant some-thing to this man.

"Yes," she said. "She's gone."

He nodded, turned and walked toward the entrance, but paused there and looked back at Katherine. Their eyes met for a long moment, then he turned and stepped out of the store without a word.

•••

Katherine McGowan, Anogh thought, *the Old Wizard's daughter. Amazing!*

Anogh had assumed a glamour of invisibility and slipped into the shop on the young man's heels. He might've completely missed the connection had not the clerk called her by name: *Dr. McGowan.* He knew the old man's daughter was a mortal physician of some kind, and he'd heard a vague description: thirtyish, pretty, brunette, nice figure. But merely the name and a description would not have been enough. Her arcane scent branded her, for she reeked of the Old Wizard as only family would. And the ghost had led the young man straight to her, purposefully, with single-minded determination.

The triple goddess had wanted Anogh to see this, the young man and the Old Wizard's daughter. They were connected in some way, and since Anogh could easily find the young witch, he stayed close to this unknown young man as he left the shop, and he followed him all the way back to his apartment.

2

Connections

"OLD MAN STRATH was as good as his word," Paul told Suzanna. He was sitting in the kitchen watching her prepare dinner, sipping on a glass of wine. "He called me on my cell before I got home. Carry is hiring, and he got me an interview. And he's got calls into a couple of other firms, says he thinks he can get me interviews even if they're not hiring right at the moment. You know, plant the seed for when they are."

That's wonderful, sweetheart, Suzanna said, looking over her shoulder, giving him that big smile of hers. She wore one of those lightweight summer dresses, more like a sleeveless T-shirt that extended to just below her knees. But unlike a T-shirt it was cut to hug her gorgeous figure, to emphasize it, and that made Paul long to touch her again, to hold her in his arms once more. That could never be.

"I saw you on the street today," he said again, and again she ignored him. That was the third time he'd tried that, and the third time he'd gotten no response. Maybe it hadn't been her and he'd just imagined the whole thing. Certainly there was no reason for his Suzanna to lead him to a shoe store where that pretty young woman was trying on some sort of fancy shoes. He recalled that she was quite attractive, auburn hair down to her shoulders, wearing a smart business suit with a skirt cut just above the knees, a nice figure, with nice legs ending in the fancy shoes.

Guilt washed over him as he thought of Suzanna, and he said, "Smells like you're making Suzanna's famous pot roast."

And it's ready right now. She popped open the over door, cringed back from the heat for a moment. She pulled on big hot-pad mittens and lifted the pan out of the oven, gave the oven door a quick tap with her heel to close it, and laid the pan on the counter. She called out, *Cloe, dinner's ready.*

Coming, mom.

She looked at Paul and smiled contentedly. *It's serve yourself, Paulie-boy, so grab a plate and dive in.*

"Damn," Paul said, "you make good pot roast."

••••

He had him, or at least close enough, direction and distance. Two blocks east, maybe one block south. The idiot had finished the conjuration so he wouldn't find him tonight. Still, the fellow's pattern was unwavering, and he'd do it again around breakfast-time tomorrow morning. McGowan was reasonably confident that would be enough to narrow it down to a single building. Tomorrow night he'd have him, and hopefully end this safely before the fellow hurt someone.

He considered that carefully for a moment, decided it would be wise to bring in some backup, just in case.

••••

"Stay hidden," Karpov hissed as he watched the old fellow walk down the street.

"Yes, Mr. Karpov," Alexei grumbled.

"And stay silent."

"Yes, Mr. Kar . . ."

"Idiot. Silence."

Standing in the shadows one block west of the old fellow, Karpov considered the situation carefully. "The Old Wizard is hunting the same prey. But he's too soft. Probably find some excuse not to kill the fool. So we'll take care of that for him. We'll let him do the work, let him find this rogue for us."

Vladimir asked, "Do you want me to follow him?"

Vladimir and Alexei were pure muscle, couldn't follow each other without being spotted. "No. We'll bring in Mikhail for that."

••••

Paul used his fork to peel off a big slab of pot roast and shovel it onto his plate. He speared a couple of carrots and a big hunk of potato, its flesh having taken on that brownish cast that comes from simmering in the gravy for so long. Then he scooped gravy over everything, and it was a real balancing act to keep the gravy from sloshing off his plate onto the floor as he crossed the kitchen. He put the full plate down carefully on the dinner table and sat down. A moment later Suzanna and Cloe joined him, each carrying their own plate, though neither of them had been as piggish as Paul.

He speared a bite of potato, swirled it in the gravy and tossed it in his mouth, rolled it from cheek to cheek and sucked air to keep it from burning his tongue. "Great pot roast, honey."

Both Suzanna and Cloe smiled at him.

"Cloe," he said. "Tell me what you did at school today."

••••

In the early morning hours Anogh waited outside the building for the young man to leave. When the fellow emerged wearing a business suit and carrying a briefcase, Anogh knew he'd be gone for several hours.

Anogh climbed the steps to the door of Paul Conklin's apartment building. The lock on the door meant nothing to a Sidhe mage; a few words and a gesture of power and the door popped open. Anogh stepped through it, closed and relocked it.

He took the lift to the fourth floor, and the door to Conklin's apartment was no more trouble than that at the front of the building. Anogh didn't know what he was looking for exactly and had been careful to avoid forming any expectations. He just wanted to know more about this young man who was in some way connected to the Old Wizard's daughter. Such connections were never coincidental, and as far as the triple goddess was concerned, they certainly weren't accidental. So he had no expectations as he stepped into Conklin's apartment, and was struck by six hundred years of grief. He could never mistake the arcane scent that permeated the place, and he cringed and staggered across the room as that scent lifted the fog the triple goddess had woven through his thoughts.

He'd known grief for centuries, but not this grief. This pain was new, and yet it was old. The triple goddess had let him grieve in ignorance, and had chosen this moment to let him understand the true depth of his loss.

With tears streaming down his cheeks he turned and left the apartment, for there was no more to be learned there.

••••

It had been a busy day, starting with the interview with Carry, which was early, so Paul had rushed there right after breakfast. Then there were two phone interviews with other firms, all thanks to old man Strath, and Paul had wanted to do his homework beforehand, check out the firms carefully so he could sound knowledgeable.

As he walked into the kitchen he wanted to tell Suzanna about the interview, but as had been happening recently she wasn't there at first, and there was something in the way, something that prevented him from seeing her. He wasn't concerned, however, because he'd quickly learned how to break through it. Nothing was going to stop him from seeing his Suzanna. He just had to push against it a little; not too hard, just a little, and then it popped like a soap bubble and went away.

Suzanna was there, waiting for him. *It's just sandwiches tonight, Paulie-boy.*

••••

Standing on the street outside the apartment building, McGowan staggered and reached out to a streetlight, gripped it tightly for a moment until the vertigo passed. A nicely dressed, middle-aged woman passing by looked at him oddly, as if he was drunk, or something.

That had hurt. He should've known better than to try using the locator spell again. The idiot—no, he had to stop thinking of him as an idiot. He clearly wasn't an idiot, just foolish, then. The fool had snapped his locator spell with no effort whatsoever, just casually shrugged it aside like someone brushing an annoying fly out of their face. There were few, if any, who were capable of doing that with such little effort. But while the spell itself hadn't located his quarry, the power the fellow had expended to break it had provided all he needed.

He let go of the streetlight, straightened and crossed the street. The front door of the building was locked, residents only. But a quick rune spell would take care of that. He looked up and down the street to ensure he'd be unobserved, then bent down and used his index finger to trace the rune carefully on the surface of the door lock. It was an elder rune, used by ancient wizards to seal tombs, grimoires and their arcane work-shops. Here he traced it backwards, did so seven times, each time invoking his own power and spilling a bit into it. After the seventh pass the rune glowed momentarily and the lock clicked open.

He was now close enough that the low background of the spirit interaction was enough to guide him. He didn't take the elevator because he didn't yet know what floor. He'd learn that as he got closer. He started up the stairs moving slowly. If this fool was as dangerous as he suspected, he didn't want to alert the fellow to his presence inadvertently.

It wasn't the second floor, or the third, but on the fourth the source of the broadcast was no longer above him, so he walked down the hall, stopping at each apartment door and extending his arcane senses into the apartment, then moving on to the next. When he found it there was no question. Only then, with just the wood of a single door separating them, did he sense that the fellow had not summoned some sort of spirit. Only then did he understand the true danger the poor fool had summoned into this life, a demon from the Netherworld, a succubus, and it was that that prompted the impulse to knock.

••••

The knock on the door startled Paul. He hadn't had any visitors in more than a year, the last being a steady stream of friends coming to console him for Suzanna's death, and then two months later again for Cloe's death—

No. Don't think about that. That was the past, a past that didn't exist anymore. They weren't dead, not any more, not completely dead, not truly dead.

He looked up from his plate. Suzanna and Cloe had vanished and were no longer seated at the table. And gone too were their plates and utensils. In fact, the table in front of their seats was completely bare. Paul looked down at his own plate, stared for a moment at the half-finished ham and cheese sandwich Suzanna had made.

The doorbell rang, followed by a repeat of the knocking. He stood, hastily swallowing the bite of sandwich he'd taken before the first knock, dropped his napkin on the table and headed for the living room. At the front door he paused and peered through the peephole, was surprised to see an older man whom he didn't recognize standing in the hall. He wasn't a neighbor Paul had seen before, and he didn't look like a salesman. But then perhaps he was a new neighbor who'd recently moved in.

••••

At the first knock his sense of the demon vanished. He waited for several seconds, then rang the doorbell and knocked again. He could be patient now; his sense of urgency had fled with the demon. The lens of the peephole darkened as the occupant looked him over. Then the door opened slowly to reveal a young man looking at him inquisitively. "What can I do for you?" the young man asked politely.

The knock had been an impulse and McGowan hesitated. The young man appeared to be thirtyish, dressed in slacks and a nice shirt, handsome, well-groomed with neatly trimmed brownish hair, broad shoulders and a trim waist—perhaps even a bit too trim, as if he'd lost weight recently. And he didn't look like a fool, or an idiot, but he was a sorcerer—there was no doubt of that—and he was summoning demons without the proper protections. At a loss for words, the old man spoke haltingly. "I'm . . . Walter McGowan."

The young man's eyes narrowed. "And again, what can I do for you, Mr. McGowan?"

Walter didn't know the young man's name. "I . . . just wanted to . . . talk to you about . . ."

"Listen, I don't mean to be rude, but whatever you're selling, I'm not interested."

McGowan had to make this young fellow understand. "But what you were doing is dangerous, very dangerous."

"What I was doing was having dinner with my family. And I don't see how that's dangerous, nor is it really any of your business. Now, forgive me, but I'm going to go back to that." The young man closed the door carefully, almost softly.

On the way out, now that he knew the apartment number, McGowan stopped and checked the mailboxes: Conklin, something Conklin. At least he knew the young man's name.

••••

Paul returned to the dinner table and sat down. Suzanna and Cloe were gone. And they wouldn't have just left, not vanished like that, not if they'd truly been there. It was a blatant reminder of what he already knew but sometimes forgot: he was nuts, bug-fuck nuts, and getting worse by the day.

He finished the ham and cheese sandwich, alone and in silence.

••••

Mikhail stood in the shadows and almost held his breath as the Old Wizard walked out of the apartment building and up the street. Like a small animal in the presence of a dangerous predator, he remained still and motionless long after the old man had strolled out of sight. Mikhail knew his own limitations, and following the powerful old wizard was a dangerous undertaking. But the instructions he'd been given were quite specific, and it would be even more dangerous to fail to follow those orders.

After the street had been silent and empty for several minutes, he retrieved his cell phone and dialed a number he knew well. His boss answered the call. "Karpov here."

Karpov had chosen to speak English, so Mikhail did the same in a thick Russian accent. "Mr. Karpov, it's Mikhail. I followed the old man to an apartment building. He did exactly as you said, he appeared to be tracking something."

"Ah," Karpov said. "He's done our work for us, found the rogue and led us to him. That was much faster than trying to track him ourselves."

"Do you want me to go into the building, sniff out the rogue and kill him?"

"No, Mikhail. He's probably out of your league, too dangerous to kill without preparation. Just remember the address and you can come in off the street. We'll kill the rogue another night."

3

Convergence

THE TWO GUARDS standing at the entrance to the queen's apartments were just ceremonial, for while Magreth walked the halls of the Seelie Court, none could hope to harm her. They both wore the ceremonial armor of their ancestral houses, layered scales of silver and topaz and lapis lazuli, with masked helms that hid their faces completely, swords made of the finest silver strapped to their sides. They had competed for the honor to stand guard at the Summer Queen's residence.

Cadilus stopped between them, facing the tall doors to the residence. There was no need to knock, for Magreth and her attendants would know he awaited admittance. After only a heartbeat the doors opened slowly to reveal one of Magreth's ladies-in-waiting, a pretty, young thing, probably no more than a hundred years old. Cadilus nodded politely and said, "Please tell Her Majesty I have news regarding developments on the Mortal Plane."

She smiled warmly; she was still too young to have acquired the cold and hardened exterior of the more experienced Seelie. "She is already aware of your desire for audience. You may enter."

The walls of the palace began to dissolve, to shift and shimmer, to change and realign in a different form. Beneath his feet he stood on a path of crushed, white gravel in a sumptuous garden of spring blossoms. He was now walking, and beside him walked Magreth.

"You have news?"

"Yes, Your Majesty, though no developments of great import. Merely bits of information that begin to form a picture, though, as yet, an incomplete one."

"And?" she asked impatiently, her tone flat and hard.

"The Old Wizard is involved in some way, along with some of his colleagues. And it appears the unpleasant Russians are putting their fingers in the pie as well. They're looking for someone, some sort of young wizard, and I think that when they find him they're going to kill him."

"Should we intervene?"

"I think not, Your Majesty. It's a wholly mortal affair, probably only loosely connected to our concerns regarding the uneasiness in the Three Realms. And what's one dead mortal wizard to us?"

As they strolled down the gravel strewn path she looked his way and flames danced in her eyes again. "Perhaps we should take this young wizard captive before they kill him. We might learn something."

"That's an option, Your Majesty. But first we must locate him, and I'm afraid the Old Wizard and those Russians are ahead of us there. It's probably impossible to get to him before they kill him. They are, after all, more powerful in their own Realm, while we are weaker there."

She stopped and turned to face him. "I understand. But see what you can do."

He bowed lightly. "As you wish, Your Majesty."

The walls of the garden dissolved and he was now strolling away from the queen's apartments.

••••

Paul paused for a moment in the lobby of the office building on Market Street, looked at his reflection in one of the floor-to-ceiling windows separating him from the sidewalk outside. His tie was straight, suit neatly pressed; appropriate for an interview, though perhaps a bit more formal than day-to-day attire. But he didn't know this Dayandalous fellow so he wanted to err on the side of proper and conservative. He headed for the elevators, got one right away and pressed the button for the forty-fourth floor.

Dayandalous had called him yesterday, said he'd spoken with Strath; said Strath had given Paul an excellent recommendation. Paul had called Strath, and at first Strath claimed to have no knowledge of any Dayandalous, didn't recall having had such a conversation.

"That's odd," Paul said. "I'm sure I got the name right: Dayandalous. Fellow said he spoke with you yesterday, spoke at some length."

"Oh, yes, yes!" Strath said. "That's right. We did talk. I just forgot, one of those senior moments. You know?"

What Paul knew was that Strath didn't have senior moments. The old fellow was as sharp as a tack. Paul chalked it up to the fact that Strath was quite busy, and Paul's job search wasn't the highest priority on his list.

Like Paul, Strath had not previously heard of this Dayandalous fellow. He clearly wasn't part of the local architectural community, and Paul had been unable to learn anything about him prior to this interview. Strange, but nevertheless, an interview was better than no interview at all. He figured he could learn a bit about the fellow's firm during the process.

Suite 4401, Dayandalous had told him. When the elevator doors opened it was obvious suite 4401 occupied the entire forty-fourth floor. There was no hallway leading to other suites; the elevator opened directly into a large and luxurious lobby for Dayandalous's firm. Behind a darkly wooded desk sat a receptionist that could've made it into any modeling agency in the world. As Paul approached her she smiled.

"I'm Paul Conklin. I have an appointment with Mr. Dayandalous."

Her smile widened. "Yes, Mr. Conklin. Dayandalous is expecting you. Please have a seat"—she waved her hand at a couch against one wall—"and I'll let him know you're here."

Paul sat down, picked up a magazine and started leafing through it, not really paying attention to anything in it. He didn't have to wait more than a minute or two before a tall black man in a dark business suit approached him. Paul stood. "Paul Conklin?" the man asked politely, sticking out his hand. "I'm Dayandalous." The fellow had the deep and resonant voice of a Shakespearean actor.

"It's nice to meet you, Mr. Dayandalous," Paul said, shaking his hand. Dayandalous was tall, six-four, six-five, broad shouldered, trim waist, early middle age, wearing a suit that must've cost a month of Paul's wages, probably Armani or something like that. And Dayandalous was black. Not the black of an African American man whose skin is actually brown, but real black, true black, carbon black. Paul looked into Dayandalous's eyes, and for a moment he thought they were amber, like the eyes of a cat, with oddly shaped pupils. But when he blinked and looked again they were simple, ordinary blue, with normal round pupils. As Dayandalous ushered Paul into his office he thought, *No hallucinations now, Paulie-boy. Save that for the privacy of your own home.*

Dayandalous sat Paul in a comfortable chair facing a desk the size of an aircraft carrier, then sat down behind the desk. Dayandalous held up a couple of sheets of paper. "You've got a nice resume, Mr. Conklin."

"Thank you, Mr. Dayandalous."

"It's just Dayandalous. No mister."

"Certainly, sir." Paul had a hundred questions, but interviews don't go that way. The interviewer gets to ask questions first, and the interviewee answers, tries to be polite and make a good impression. If Paul did make a good impression, then he'd get a chance to ask some questions of his own, and if Dayandalous was truly interested, maybe a lot of questions. So Paul had to be patient.

Dayandalous questioned him rather thoroughly, though in a nice way. In addition to Paul's architectural credentials he was quite interested in Suzanna and Cloe's deaths, not asking for crude, impolite details, but focusing more on Paul's reaction. And that was understandable, since everyone knew Paul had gone into a funk for an overly long time, and anyone would want some reassurance before hiring him. But at one point Dayandalous raised an eyebrow and said, "Well it's good to know you're not seeing things that aren't there."

It startled Paul so much that before he could stop he blurted out angrily, "What do you mean by that?"

Dayandalous's expression turned stony, and again Paul had the impression of amber eyes with vertically slit pupils, but this time the pupils flared dark red instead of black. Paul blinked, and when he looked again Dayandalous's eyes were once again blue, simple blue with simple black pupils. Dayandalous smiled warmly.

Paul felt suddenly calm, couldn't recall what had upset him so, and since Dayandalous seemed unconcerned he let it go.

Dayandalous stood. "Well thank you for coming in, Paul."

Paul also stood, because that was what he was supposed to do. He was certain of it. Dayandalous escorted him back to the elevators, personally called an elevator for him, kept up a polite and charming banter while they waited for it. But in the back of Paul's thoughts he kept thinking there was something he'd forgotten, and it wasn't until he stepped into the lobby back on the ground floor that he realized he hadn't learned anything about Dayandalous's firm, hadn't asked even one question.

He turned around, went back to the elevators and called one, thinking he could at least get a brochure or something from the receptionist. When the elevator arrived he stepped into it, and was going to press the button for the forty-fourth floor, but there was no such button. He stood there for a moment staring at the buttons, and they ended at thirty-eight. Perhaps one of the other elevators went all the way to the top. There were six elevators, and he patiently waited for each, but not one went beyond the thirty-eighth floor. He searched the lobby, thinking he'd taken a wrong turn and there was another bank of elevators. But that wasn't the case.

Paul asked the security guard in the lobby, "How do I get to the forty-fourth floor?"

The guard looked at him oddly and said, "There's no forty-fourth floor in this building, sir. The top floor is thirty-eight."

"But I was just on the forty-fourth floor." Paul decided to mention the name of the firm and the man he'd just spoken to on the forty-fourth floor, but he couldn't remember anything about either.

The guard's expression changed to concern, perhaps wondering if he'd have to deal with a nut-case, hopefully not a violent nut-case. He spoke as if speaking to a child. "I said no forty-fourth floor. If you have business on the forty-fourth floor, then you got the wrong building."

He ushered Paul out to the street. Paul stood there for a moment, then turned back to the building and looked at it carefully. It was like any of a dozen other buildings on

Market Street, and for the life of him he couldn't remember why he'd wasted his time coming here.

••••

Baalthelmass had hunted and fed on the Mortal Plane for more than a century before It could disguise Its true nature with a glamour and appear human. And it had taken another century of feeding on mortal souls before It could actually control Its shape and walk freely among them. And now, after four centuries It had built Its power to the point where It need fear only the most powerful of mortal wizards.

Wearing the shape of a handsome, wealthy American aristocrat, It sat in the study of Its mansion, and with no more than a thought summoned Its most important thrall. She responded instantly, but the size of the mansion was such that it took her several seconds to make her way to Its study. When the door opened a beautiful young woman stepped into the room. She had exotic eastern features, olive skin, luscious red lips, and when she lowered herself to her knees and bowed her head, a cascade of long, black tresses hid her face behind a curtain of untamed curls. She waited for Baalthelmass to speak.

"Belinda, my dear," It said, gesturing casually with a hand. "Come. Join me."

She rose, crossed the room and sat down on the floor at Its feet, placed her hands on Its knee and rested her chin there. She looked into Its eyes with unbridled desire.

"I have a task for you," It said. "A Lord of the Unliving has come among us, here in my own feeding grounds."

"Really, my lord," she said, and her eyes widened with fear. "Are we in danger?"

Baalthelmass shrugged. "Ordinarily I would say, 'Yes.' I would hide, find a new city, a new continent, a new identity, and let the Lord live his life in ignorance of my presence. But this Lord is unaware of his own powers, which makes for a most delicious opportunity."

"How so, my lord?"

Baalthelmass's hunger grew as It tried to imagine the possibilities. "In his ignorance he is vulnerable, helpless, defenseless, and might be overcome with ease. If I can control such a Lord, he'll be the most luscious prey I have consumed throughout my entire time on the Mortal Plane. And that's where you come in, my dear. You must summon a couple of emergents to a certain young man's apartment."

Belinda frowned uncertainly, as he knew she would. "Tertius caste, my lord. Such netherlife when manifest on the Mortal Plane will be most unreliable. They'll not be able to control themselves, will feed uncontrollably and draw the attention of mortal practitioners."

"Yes, dear Belinda, it is a bit of a gamble. But I can help you control them, though there is some risk they'll feed on the Lord himself, which would be a terrible waste. You'll do this for me, won't you, my dear?"

"Of course, my lord," she said happily.

"It should be an easy task," It said. "He's placed no Wards, is ignorant and completely unprotected."

Yes, It would have this Lord. It would feed on him, though not consume him completely. Better to bend him to Its will, enslave him, for with a Lord-of-the-Unliving under Its dominion, nothing and no one could stop It. Ever!

••••

Walter McGowan parked his car in the darkness between two streetlights more than a block away from Conklin's apartment. As so often happened in San Francisco, a layer of cold mist had come in off the ocean, blanketing the city in a damp, hazy vapor, sucking all the warmth out of a September night.

He scanned the street looking for the backup he'd called, glanced at his watch and mumbled, "Where is she?" He waited in his car for another ten minutes, but when he sensed the young man going into the early stages of his summons, he knew he had no choice but to go forward, alone if necessary.

He climbed out of the car, locked it and walked casually up the sidewalk. The mist that blanketed the city softened the shadows of the night, and while it wasn't a heavy fog, the glow of the streetlights gave the impression that the world ended only a short distance up the street. He was only a few doors away from Conklin's building when a voice out of the darkness stopped him in his tracks. "Valter," it said in a thick Russian accent.

He cringed and turned toward the voice as Vasily Karpov, flanked by two of his thugs, emerged from the shadow of a nearby alley. Karpov was McGowan's age, wore a coat and tie, a dark wool overcoat, and a cheap hat that looked like it belonged in some old private-eye movie. To either side of him stood Alexei and Vladimir, younger fellows dressed in cheap, black, heavy, wool business suits that looked like they'd started out as horse blankets. Both were large, physically-imposing men, Karpov's muscle and always close at hand. Vladimir on the left had high, Slavic cheekbones pitted with acne scars, and long, straight, greasy blond hair that hung lankly down to his shoulders. Alexei on the right had a square face, with bristly, dark hair and a heavy, black mustache. He reminded McGowan of a young Joseph Stalin, and had a reputation for being just as brutal.

McGowan asked, "What're you doing here, Vasily?" Both thugs tensed at the apparent lack of respect in McGowan's voice.

Karpov tilted his head to one side, smiled and said calmly, "Valter! I'm here for the same reason you are, to stop a rogue sorcerer, a dangerous undertaking for us both. The least you can do is accept my help graciously."

When it came to manipulating the arcane they both knew McGowan was stronger than Karpov, could probably take the Russian in a fair fight, though he wouldn't walk away from it unscathed. But while Alexei and Vladimir were both relatively weak practitioners, they were enough to tip the balance in Karpov's favor. "Vasily, when you help, someone usually gets killed."

Karpov's smile disappeared. "He's a rogue, summoning demons without the proper protections. If we don't kill him first, many innocents could die."

McGowan couldn't hide his anger. "Since when do you care about innocents? And we don't know what he is."

Both thugs took a step forward, which, together with Karpov, now enclosed McGowan in a semicircle. They made no effort to hide the threat in their stances. "Valter, Valter, Valter! Why risk ourselves for some stupid, untried amateur? He's a fool, dangerous, so we take no chances, kill him quickly and be done with it."

McGowan looked sharply at Alexei, the more sociopathic of the two, and gave him a hard angry look. Alexei didn't back away, but his smug posture disappeared and he leaned slightly away from McGowan, an unconscious reaction to the older man's superior arcane strength. McGowan turned slowly to Vladimir and gave him the same look. The ugly blond backed up a step, his right hand involuntarily lifting toward his coat. McGowan had no doubt he had a gun there, and narrowed his eyes in warning. Vladimir's hand stopped well short of its goal.

To Karpov, McGowan said, "If we have to kill him, then we'll kill him. But I won't condone murder until I know it's absolutely necessary."

Karpov's smile returned, but it was more of a challenge than a greeting between friends, and he was clearly ready to push this to the limit. He opened his mouth to say something, but a shadow stepped out of the darkness on McGowan's left, and from the shadow a woman's voice spoke in a thick Irish accent. "Well now, Vasily, I happen to agree with Walter."

The Russians stiffened and turned to look at the shadow that stood openly in the light of a streetlamp. Other than its slight stature, and the timbre of its voice, the shadow itself gave no hint as to its owner's nature.

McGowan couldn't hide his relief as he said, "Colleen!" His backup had just arrived and the odds had tipped heavily in his favor.

The shadow spoke again. "Vasily, please instruct your young men that should there be any uncalled-for violence, I will be most displeased."

Karpov's lips straightened into a thin line of displeasure, and he gave Colleen the smile of a man forced to chew on a lemon. "As you wish, Colleen."

"Good," she said. "Then we'll let Walter call the shots." It hadn't been a question, but she waited for Karpov to acknowledge the statement.

He grimaced, the smile turned into a scowl and he grumbled an unhappy, "Of course."

She said, "Then let's go."

4

Emergents

PAUL WAS CONTENT. Suzanna and Cloe were back, and the interviews were going well, and he was hoping to get a couple of offers next week. He sat at the dinner table, stomach full, watching his beautiful wife clean up the dishes while Cloe struggled over her homework in the living room. What more could a man want?

What more could a man want? And yet he knew full well what more he could want. He wanted Suzanna in his bed again. Not because he was horny, though he'd always loved the taste of her skin, the feel of her body pressed against his, and he certainly wouldn't mind drowning in the passion they'd always shared. But his thoughts weren't focused on a good roll-in-the-hay. He just wanted to hold her again, to have her lying beside him as he slept, to wake in the middle of the night and hear her soft, even breathing next to him, to wake in the morning and have her roll away from him, grumbling something unintelligible, frequently spiced with a bit of unconscious profanity about not wanting to get up—she'd never been a morning person. And he wanted Cloe to bounce on his knee again, or to have her charge into the bedroom to wake him and Suzanna up on a Saturday morning. He wanted to lift her high over his head, hear her squeal with delight as he spun her around. He wanted to go for a Saturday walk in Golden Gate Park with the two of them, have a little picnic lunch in the shade of a tree. He wanted so many things, but he knew the only way he could have them was to allow his hallucinations to grow so powerful and intense that he lost all contact with reality.

Normally he'd put that thought out of his mind, but tonight it kept coming back and he couldn't lay the thought aside. It was frustrating, because a part of him knew there was something else, a part of him buried so deep he could usually squash it back down into that place in his soul where he'd hidden it. But tonight it wouldn't stay squashed.

Suzanna turned and looked at him, and his heart climbed up into his throat with such longing. *I want it too, Paulie-boy,* she said. *We're not complete without it. But what if we find what we desire? Will it be wrong? Will we regret it? And can it really be that easy?*

Yes, Paul thought, *it could be that easy. She could be real again, not some figment of his fucked-up imagination. All he had to do was want it enough, wish for it enough, long for it enough. All he had to do—*

Cloe walked into the kitchen, her beautiful little face marred by fear. *Daddy, there's something in the living room.*

Without consciously considering it he stood, and his legs were trembling so much he had to lean on the table for a second. "What? What is it?"

I don't know. But something's wrong.

"Wait here, both of you," he said, and walked quickly into the living room.

Earlier he'd been opening and paying bills, and the checkbook, pen, letter-opener and an unorganized pile of envelopes where still scattered on the couch. Cloe had spread her homework on the coffee table in front of the couch, but other than that, the living room was empty, no sign of any trouble, no sign of an intruder. He breathed a sigh of relief, realizing he'd probably been the victim of a child's vivid imagination. But then he recalled she'd said there was *something*, not *someone*, in the living room. *Something's wrong,* she'd said, and he too could sense the wrongness of it.

Paulie-boy, what is it?

"Nothing," he called. "Just wait there." He scanned the room a second time, spotted his reflection in the mirror hanging on the wall above a little knick-knack table Suzanna had purchased. He was reminded of his dream. But he wasn't dreaming now, and a piece of framed, silvered glass just didn't induce that kind of fear in anything but a dream. Nevertheless, he looked at his reflection cautiously, noticed that the mirror appeared to be damaged, or perhaps just poorly made, because the glass distorted his image, made his face appear wavy and slightly misshapen. He crossed the room to look closely into the mirror, and as he watched, the face staring back at him began to distort further, a circular swirling as if someone had dropped a pebble into a mirror-smooth pond. It churned, began to twist into a spiral, as if his image was nothing but wet paint on a canvas with a child smearing it around.

The image in the mirror so engrossed Paul that when someone started pounding on the front door, it barely registered on his consciousness. It was not a polite knock but loud, incessant pounding, and yet to Paul it was a distant, remote sound that couldn't draw his attention away from the mirror. A man's voice came from the same distant place, shouting, "Let us in." The voice carried real desperation, almost hysteria. "Now, please."

Paul's image in the mirror distorted even further and took on an almost reptilian cast. His skin darkened to near black, his nose elongated into a flat snout with gaping nostrils, his ears morphed into tall, spiked, leathery things more on the front of his head than on the sides. The pupils in its eyes slowly elongated until they were slit horizontally like those of a goat, and they glowed an angry blood-red. The monster in the mirror looked at him greedily, and he sensed its hunger and hatred as if it welled up from his own soul, as if he was himself the monster in the mirror.

Suddenly a hand emerged from the depths of the mirror. It was the black, clawed thing from his dreams, with knobby joints and knuckles. And just like in his dream it reached forth and gripped his throat viciously, snapping him out of the stupor that had possessed him. He grabbed at the monster's wrist, praying that it was a dream, that he'd snap awake suddenly, lying in bed and bathed in sweat. But as he tried to pull the claws away from his throat there was no dislodging the vice-like grip.

The pounding on the door changed suddenly to a wall-shaking thud, as if someone large had thrown a shoulder against it.

The hand protruding from the mirror emerged farther, pushing Paul back a step and revealing a spindly arm with a web-like, leathery flap attaching it to a bony torso. The head emerged and it screeched at Paul with a sound like fingernails on chalkboard. With its other hand it gripped the frame of the mirror, thrashed about as if the glass were a viscous puddle of some thick fluid sucking at it and resisting its efforts to struggle free. And with blood pounding in his ears, terror clutching at his heart, Paul could do nothing as it shook him about like a child's doll.

Bit-by-bit a bat-like being out of hell emerged into the room and stood in the middle of the floor, holding Paul at arm's length. He struggled uselessly as it craned its neck and screamed out a cry of triumph and hunger. It looked at Paul with the hungry eyes of a starving predator and its blood-red goat-slitted pupils flared blindingly, a stream of ichorous drool dripping from its chin. It stepped forward with an ungainly shuffle, pushing Paul until the back of his legs hit the coffee table. He tumbled backwards, pulling the monster down on top of him, landed on the couch in a flurry of envelopes and bills and was almost impaled on the letter opener. A horrid smell of rotting meat washed over him as he shouted, "Suzanna, run."

The monster clamped down on his throat, digging its talons into his neck, cutting off his air and any possibility of shouting another warning. Behind it another monster emerged from the mirror, born of the same hell as the first. The monster atop Paul looked over its shoulder at its companion, turning its head about as no human could. "Get the necro," it growled in a snake-like hiss. Its companion nodded and darted into the kitchen with ungodly speed.

The monster turned back to Paul, and as it opened its mouth to reveal a bony ridge of razor sharp teeth, he thought of the letter opener still jabbing him in the back. Paul beat at the side of the monster's head with his left fist, searching behind him with his right hand. He wasn't a weak man, and the monster did nothing to defend itself, nothing to block his blows, nothing to avoid them, and yet they had no effect other than to momentarily snap its reptilian head from side to side. But Paul didn't care. He only cared about Suzanna and Cloe, and the monster that had run into the kitchen after them. Let this monster do what it would, he cared only to stop the monster in the kitchen from harming those he loved. He could sense it hunting them, stalking them. He could sense its hunger, ravenous, uncontrolled, a blinding desire to rip them limb from limb. And while the monster on top of him beat at him, tore at him, choked him senseless, he concentrated on the beast in the kitchen, focused on it, and wished for only one thing, prayed, hoped, demanded it be gone from the here and now. And then something went pop, like a cork pulled from a bottle of wine.

The monster atop him flinched, looked momentarily toward the kitchen, then turned back to Paul and they locked eyes.

It was as if he was a little child terrified of the dark in his bedroom, and suddenly one of his parents walked in and flicked on the lights. At that moment all fear and terror fled. He looked into the creature's eyes and felt it pulling on him, not pulling physically, but pulling on something through the contact between its clawed hand and his throat. It felt as if the creature were reaching deep into his heart, into his soul, pulling on the core of his being. And Paul wanted to give it everything it desired, for suddenly he loved and trusted it as he'd never loved anything before. But a small spark within him knew he must resist that *pull*.

As if his mind had split into two separate beings Paul yielded to the *pull* and embraced the desire he saw in the monster's eyes, while that spark within him found the letter opener and gripped its handle. But it and his right hand were now pinned beneath his back. He tried to look away from the monster's blood-red, goat-slitted eyes but couldn't. The monster continued to pull through the physical contact with his throat and he was beginning to see sparkling motes of unconsciousness as he threw everything into resisting that *pull*. The monster snarled, cried out and reared its head back.

Paul got the letter opener free, swung it out in a roundhouse arc just as the monster's claws tightened with crushing force on his throat. He punched the letter opener into the side of its head and buried it there.

The monster screamed, rolled off him in a snarling frenzy, its jaws snapping at empty air, hissing and spinning around like a maddened animal. Where the letter opener protruded from the side of its head the wound sputtered a greasy smoke as if the letter opener were a red-hot brand.

Paul staggered to his feet looking for another weapon, and then the door to his apartment exploded. The blast peppered Paul's left side with splinters and knocked him to the floor. It blew the monster across the room and slammed it against the wall in a shower of splinters where it slumped to the floor.

Paul's head reeled from the concussion of the explosion. He rolled onto his back, thinking he had to get to his feet no matter how much the room swayed. He got to his elbows but could go no further until the dizziness subsided. He was surprised to see the older fellow who'd knocked on his door last week stride purposefully across the room to the monster, a young version of Joseph Stalin a few steps behind him. The old fellow leaned over the monster, pulled a shiny, needle-shaped spike from his coat, plunged it into the monster's chest, and held it there as the monster struggled and kicked. The old guy began chanting something in a language Paul didn't recognize. Two more strangers, another old man and an ugly fellow with long, greasy, blond hair, rushed past the old fellow into the kitchen.

Joe Stalin looked up from whatever the old man was doing to the monster, looked at Paul and frowned angrily, then reached into his coat and pulled out a revolver the size of a howitzer. He crossed the room to Paul and stood over him, carefully aimed the muzzle of the cannon between Paul's eyes, grinned menacingly and slowly pulled the pistol's hammer back with his thumb.

Just as it clicked into place, in a flash, the mere blink of an eye, Suzanna and Cloe appeared in the doorway to the kitchen. Paul blinked again, and now Cloe straddled Joe Stalin's back, her arms wrapped around his throat as she pulled with all her might, her face twisted with anger and fear. A real child, even such a small one, should've had more effect on Joe Stalin, should've at least made him stagger. As it was all he did was hesitate, frown, and reach up with his left hand to touch his throat for just an instant, apparently completely unaware of the spectral child riding his back. But the instant ended in a blink and he lowered the gun back toward Paul's face.

Suzanna wrapped her hands around Joe's wrist, tugged at it and tried to pull the gun to one side. Again, a real grown woman should've had more effect. But Joe seemed no more aware of her than Cloe, though the gun did waver for a moment and shifted a few inches to one side just as he pulled the trigger.

The gun roared in Paul's face with a deafening explosion that sent Paul's senses reeling. He cringed, laid there for an instant with his ears ringing, blood pounding in his head, and it took him a second to realize his brains weren't splattered all over the room.

Joe Stalin lowered the gun again toward Paul's face, with Cloe still riding his back and Suzanna tugging on his wrist. He pulled the hammer back just as a middle-aged hippie-woman shot across the room and touched him with a lightning bolt of electricity. Joe staggered and Paul rolled to one side as the gun roared again, the muzzle flash only inches from his face. Paul tried to sit up, looked up at the hippie woman who stood over him in a dress that looked like she'd hung a bunch of scarves of all colors from her torso, covering her from neck to floor. She wore her bright red hair in a wild tangle, tussled and curly in that way of the classic redhead. In it were about a dozen, thin, braided strands into which had been woven small, silver trinkets.

The lightning bolt she'd hit Joe with had had considerable effect. He staggered about like a drunkard as she charged at him. The hippy struggled with him for a moment but he slapped her to the floor. He lifted the gun unsteadily, aimed it at Paul, the barrel waving about wildly as Joe continued to stagger and Suzanna continued to pull on his wrist. Paul rolled to one side as the cannon roared again. The bullet plowed into the floor where he'd been a moment ago, digging a furrow in the carpet and slapping his face and shoulders with an explosion of splinters. It was pure luck he didn't lose an eye.

Paul got to his feet and staggered toward the shattered front door of his apartment, looked over his shoulder just as he reached it. Joe Stalin still tottered drunkenly, but the ugly, blond fellow appeared in the entrance to the kitchen carrying another howitzer. He aimed it at Paul, but the hippie-woman hit him with one of those lightning bolts just as he fired and the shot took out part of the doorjamb only inches from Paul's head. Paul staggered out into the hall as Joe Stalin fired another shot, punching a hole through the apartment wall behind him.

Paul stumbled and half-rolled down the first flight of stairs, but a surge of adrenaline cleared his head and he managed to stagger down the next flight without falling. After that he took the stairs three at a time, was grateful he didn't break his neck before he slammed out the front door of his building and tumbled into the street.

5

Crazies Everywhere

MCGOWAN DIDN'T DARE turn away from the demon until he finished destroying it, knew Colleen could handle the Russians. He continued releasing the spell he'd locked into the silver spike, and wisps of smoke began swirling up from the monster's eyes and ears and mouth. It thrashed wildly, struggling, kicking, and screaming out an ungodly, high-pitched cry. McGowan refused to waver and held it pinned to the floor with the spike. And then suddenly the monster slumped back and lay motionless. McGowan didn't waver, held it pinned and continued the chant, relentlessly bringing the spell to its conclusion. Slowly the monster's skin grew translucent, the beast shrank, and then it dissipated completely in a cloud of smoke and ash that dissolved into the air of the room

McGowan stood and turned to find Colleen blocking the door to the hallway, Karpov facing her angrily, no sign of his two thugs. "Enough," McGowan shouted.

Karpov turned to face him.

"What did you think you were doing?" McGowan demanded. "We're going to have half the city down on us any minute."

Karpov opened his mouth to say something. A moment ago, with McGowan occupied by the emergent, he'd clearly been willing to take on Colleen alone. But now that McGowan was free to back her, the Russian apparently thought better of it. He raised his hands in a placating gesture, shrugged and said, "Valter, my two colleagues are young and inexperienced. Sometimes they act with a bit too much . . . enthusiasm. You will forgive them, of course."

McGowan wanted to strangle the Russian bastard. "Call them back, now."

Karpov frowned and shook his head. "They're doing what needs to be done."

McGowan took a step toward him. "Do you really want those two morons out there unsupervised? They'll shoot up half the city."

Karpov grimaced. "You do have a point, Valter." He pulled out a cell phone and dialed a number, waited for a few seconds then said something in Russian. He put the cell phone away and said, "They'll be here shortly."

Paul stumbled as he hit the street, fell to the asphalt in a tumble, tearing his shirt and pants, and badly scraping his hands, knees and elbows. He figured he had only seconds before Joe Stalin and his blond friend followed him and blew his brains out. At least a light mist had blanketed the street, which might help him hide.

"Come on, ye daft idiot," someone snarled in his ear in a thick Irish accent. "You've no time to be a lying here enjoying the scenery."

With his ears still ringing from the thunder of the gunshots Paul was surprised he could hear anything. He rolled over, struggled to his hands and knees and found himself nose to nose with a midget. The little fellow wore green leggings, a brown doublet over a purple shirt, with bright orange-red hair spilling out from a floppy, red-felt hat perched jauntily on his head. He was shorter than any midget Paul had ever seen, not even knee high. He sported large, mutton-chop whiskers, with a nose shaped like a ski jump that separated green eyes filled with disapproval.

He grabbed Paul's arm, and with surprising strength, pushed and cajoled him to his feet. "Come on, ye fool," he said as he turned and ran up the sidewalk. "This way, hurry."

Paul ran after the little fellow in an uneven, limping gait, gained a little distance but each step was an excruciating exercise in futility. As he hobbled down the sidewalk he ran a hand down his thigh, could feel large wooden splinters protruding from his jeans. "Stop," Paul cried after the midget. "I'm hurt. I can't run."

The midget dug in its heels, spun and raced back to Paul, took one look at his bloodied thigh and said, "Aye. Sure, I should've seen that."

The midget grabbed his hand, tugged him off the sidewalk into the shadows of some shrubs. "Lay down, ye daft fool, and be still."

Paul obeyed the little fellow. In his present condition, hiding and hoping for the best was his only chance. He and the midget laid down side-by-side and watched the front of his building as Joe and his ugly, blond friend spilled onto the street, guns in hand. The two thugs looked up and down the street, spoke hurriedly and gestured for a few seconds. Then the ugly blond started down the street away from Paul while Joe Stalin ran up the street toward him.

Paul knew his situation was hopeless. The shrubs weren't that large and the shadows weren't that deep, and the mist helped a little, but not enough. The midget apparently agreed with Paul's assessment. He said, "This just won't do. We'll have to go someplace else." He reached out and grabbed Paul's hand and said, "Come with me, young fella."

Paul wanted to protest, was about to say something about splinters in his leg and that he was in no shape to go anywhere. But before he could say anything the mist began to dissipate, and the night sky lightened toward a soft orange, as if the sun was rising prematurely. Little by little the horizon turned a dark pinkish-purple, a strange false dawn that was just plain wrong. He looked over his shoulder hoping to find a normal sun, hoping brush fires in the distant hills had laid down a cloud of smoke that filtered the sun's light into this strange off-colored dawn.

The midget hissed, "Hold still, ye daft fool."

The street in front of Paul's apartment had grown indistinct, had become almost transparent, as if an image of it had been overlaid onto the more solid image of a strange, rolling countryside, though the midget was still solid and well defined. "Where are we?" Paul whispered.

The midget smiled knowingly. "Well now, we're a little bit here, and a little bit there, and a little bit nowhere. And you should be still and quiet. Don't move and don't make a sound."

Joe Stalin trotted up the street, and like everything else he was almost transparent, defined more by his edges than his substance. He carried the howitzer openly and looked to right and left as he ran right past Paul's hiding place. He stopped at the corner, looked both ways and stood there for a moment of indecision.

Paul heard the refrains of some heavy-metal band, thought for a moment he might be hallucinating. He had splinters embedded in the side of his face, along his left arm and ribs, down his hip and leg, and they produced enough pain to make anyone hallucinate. But then Joe Stalin reached into his coat, pulled out a cell phone, and when he answered it, the heavy-metal tune ended. He spoke some hurried words in what sounded like Russian, stuffed the phone back into his coat and ran back to Paul's building.

••••

"What happened to the other emergent?" McGowan demanded. "I sensed two cross over."

Karpov gave him a smarmy smile. "We searched the apartment carefully. There was only the one. And you took care of it with admirable dispatch."

The shadow that was Colleen left the doorway, drifted over to the ashes that remained of the demon, squatted down and nudged at the scorched and blackened letter opener. "Cheap letter opener," she said. "But some silver plating, otherwise it would've had little effect on an emergent demon."

Alexei appeared in the destroyed doorway breathing heavily, Vladimir behind him. He grumbled in a thick Russian accent. "We should get out of here. The cops are on their way. We can hear the sirens."

Karpov turned to McGowan. "We will find this rogue, Valter. My men and I will find him and eliminate him." He and his thugs made a quick exit.

Colleen had arrived in a cab so she joined McGowan in his car. Neither of them said anything until they'd put several blocks behind them, then Colleen broke the silence. "You were right. There were two emergents."

"I know," he said. "But what happened to the second one?"

He'd meant it as a rhetorical question, but she answered anyway. "I think something pushed it back into the Netherworld."

"And that's another thing," McGowan continued. "How did two emergents cross over? Conklin's summons wasn't that strong, strong enough to attract a minor demon like that succubus, but for emergents to physically cross over—Conklin wasn't using that kind of power and he didn't even come close to a full summoning. This just doesn't add up."

"No," Colleen said, her voice almost a dreamy, absent-minded sigh. "It doesn't. And let's not forget they were undoubtedly Tertius caste, new emergents, and yet they exercised restraint, didn't feed blindly, didn't simply go on a killing spree. That young man should've been dead within seconds of their emergence, unless something else helped them, controlled them. And it clearly was not that young man."

McGowan looked at her sharply and was surprised to see she'd dropped her shadows. "You said *something*, not *someone*. You don't mean to imply a nether-being summoned them?"

She shook her head. "No. We all know that's not possible. But I sensed something else at work here, and I don't know what that something was."

"And let's not forget the succubus," he said, returning his attention to the street in front of his car. "Before the emergents showed up I sensed one, I'm certain of it."

He could hear her breathing as she considered his words for a long moment. "Yes, there was something. For a few seconds it was right there in the room with us. I'm almost certain it tried to protect the young man from those Russian thugs. But it wasn't a succubus. In fact, I don't think it was a demon of any kind."

"Then what was it?"

"I don't know," she said, "and that bothers me no end."

This whole situation bothered McGowan. "We have to find young Conklin. And fast."

"So you can kill him?" she asked, and he could hear the disapproval in her voice.

He'd known her too long to be anything but honest with her. "Maybe. I don't know. We can't allow him to summon demons without the proper protections. You know as well as I that one demon loose in this city could kill hundreds before we put it down. And if it was healthy, really healthy—unlike that wasted emergent I put down tonight—it could hide among us and feed off the population for years."

She spoke hesitantly. "I felt no summons, just yearning. The young man was filled with pain and sorrow, and a lot of love and a deep longing. But he performed no summons."

McGowan looked at her again, but she'd recalled her shadows so he looked back to the street ahead. When Colleen spoke again, her Irish accent had thickened considerably. "Old Wizard, do you think you could find it in your kind heart to offer an old woman a shot of good whiskey? Just a wee dram, purely for medicinal purposes, of course."

He looked at her with a glint in his eyes. "Your place or mine, sweetheart?"

She breathed a deep, exasperated sigh. "Well now, old man, my place is six thousand miles from here, so it'll have to be yours. But all I want from you is good whiskey and something to eat, and a good night's sleep . . . by myself, you old pervert."

"Sorry, my dear," he said. "I can offer you the whiskey and food, but no sleep tonight. Karpov is resourceful, so we have to get to Conklin before he does."

She nodded and asked, "Did you catch the background scent in the young man's apartment?"

"Ya, Sidhe. Faint, but there, almost like a Sidhe nest."

She continued nodding. "Yes, a Sidhe nest, vacated for some time now, but still a nest, and unquestionably Unseelie, Winter Court."

••••

After Joe Stalin ran back into Paul's building the night sky lost its dark pinkish-purple hue, the otherworldly feeling that had overlaid Paul's neighborhood dissipated and the street returned to normal, as if anything about this night could be normal. He and the midget picked themselves up and the midget led Paul up the street, staying in the shadows as much as possible. Paul moved slowly, limping and shuffling painfully. He felt guilty for abandoning Suzanna and Cloe, but he knew he was bug-fuck nuts, and they were just figments of his imagination. Come to think of it, the man-sized bat-thing that climbed out of his mirror had to be another hallucination. That meant his delusions were getting worse. And then there was the hippie woman throwing around lightning bolts. A police shrink would have a field day with him.

Paul managed to put three blocks between him and his building when a police car turned the corner two blocks up, sirens screaming and lights flashing. It came his way and he tried to flag it down, but it roared past him, continued down the street and came to a screeching stop in front of his apartment. Moments later two more squad cars joined it, all three parked at odd angles in front of the building, lights flashing and sirens now silent.

Paul considered turning back now that help was at hand, but if the cops were going to shoot it out with those thugs he didn't want to end up in the middle of that. Walking hurt like hell and he could barely stay on his feet so he couldn't go on. And as the sidewalk beneath his feet swayed like the deck of a ship he staggered to the steps leading up to someone's front door, sat down clumsily on the lowest step and buried his face in his hands.

"Come on, ye fool," the midget said. "You can't stay here."

The little fellow was right. Paul struggled to his feet and swayed drunkenly. "Lead the way."

The midget ran ahead.

"Young man," a deep male voice said. "Are you ill?"

Paul turned to find a tall stranger with unusually black skin standing next to him. "You've been hurt!" the man said, his voice filled with concern. "You're bleeding. What happened?"

"Crazy people," Paul said, unable to get the words out without slurring them. "Broke into my apartment and tried to kill me."

"My god!" the man said. "What's this neighborhood coming to? There's a fire station just a few blocks from here, and I know they have an ambulance and paramedics. Let's get you to some help."

He gripped Paul's arm on the uninjured side and the old fellow was surprisingly strong. Paul leaned on him heavily as they staggered down the street, the midget running well ahead of them. There was something vaguely familiar about the man. His coal-black skin plucked the chord of a memory hidden somewhere within Paul, but no matter how hard he tried he couldn't recall it.

They turned a corner and the fire station loomed halfway down the block. As they staggered toward it Paul said, "Thank you, Dayandalous," though he couldn't remember where he'd heard that name.

The man stopped in his tracks and looked at Paul carefully. "Very good, Paul," he said. "That you remember anything is a real testament to your possibilities."

Paul looked into the man's face, and the streetlight reflected blood-red from his vertically-slit eyes. "We shall meet again, Paul," the man said.

Paul squeezed his eyes shut, shook his head, and when he looked again the man was gone. He looked up the street, saw no sign of the fellow and decided he must've imagined the whole thing. Apparently, this was going to be one hell of a night for hallucinations.

He turned back toward the fire station and limped on, his left shoe making squishy noises, which seemed odd until he realized the shoe had filled with blood from the splinters in his leg.

As he approached the fire station the midget stepped into his path and stood blocking his way with his hands on his hips. "I'll have to leave you now, young fellow. Just remember your mundane friends can't be helping you in this. Oh, they can heal your wounds but they can't heal your soul."

Paul stepped around the little fellow, saying, "The last thing I need is riddles from some midget in a clown suit."

"Midget!" the little fellow shouted. Somehow he'd gotten in front of Paul, though Paul hadn't seen him move. He was just there, again with his hands on his hips. "Sure, I ain't no midget, you daft fool. And I'll have you know I prides meself on the cut of me attire, better than most. Few of the little people cuts a finer figure than Jim'Jiminie."

Paul shook his head, decided the little fellow was another hallucination, stepped around him again and walked up to the front door of the fire station.

6

No Time to Heal

KATHERINE MCGOWAN SAT up groggily in bed, thinking it was still too early for the alarm, realized it was her phone ringing insistently. She had a full roster of patients due in the morning, and that was on her mind as she lifted the phone, put it to her ear and grumbled, "McGowan here."

"Katherine," her father said. She didn't need him to say, "It's your father."

The clock showed a little past midnight, so she realized it must be something important. "Is something wrong? Are you hurt?"

"No! No! Well ya, something is wrong. But no, I'm not hurt. No one's hurt. Well, there's a young man I know, and I think he's hurt, but Colleen and I are just fine."

"Colleen's in town?"

"Ya, she came to help me with something. And I need your help."

If Colleen had come to town to help her father with something, it would be something arcane and very important. "What can I do?"

Her father spoke in a breathless rush. "A young friend of mine, name of Paul Conklin, we think he's been hurt, probably assaulted. He's probably going to wind up in an ER somewhere, either stagger into it on his own or riding in an ambulance. I'd like to know as soon as he shows up."

"I don't know that much about the city's ERs."

"But you're a shrink. You know people."

She'd tried for years to get him not to use the word *shrink*. But yes, as a psychiatrist, she did know people. She asked, "Where did this happen?"

"Far north end of Pacific Heights."

She wracked her brains to dredge up what little she knew about ER locations. "Up at that end of town I think California Pacific and Saint Francis Memorial are the only facilities with twenty-four hour ERs, but I'll have to confirm that. Let me make some calls. I can probably arrange to get a call if he checks into one of those facilities."

"If you hear anything, call me right away."

"I will, father."

Katherine was well known at both hospitals. But it still took several phone calls to locate a neurology resident she knew at California Pacific, and a surgery resident she knew at Saint Francis, both of whom had pulled a night shift. They promised to spread the word to their ER staffs, so she went back to bed.

••••

The windows on the second floor of the fire station were lit, so someone must be up. Next to the giant garage doors for the big trucks was a normal house-sized door. Paul leaned against it and pounded on it for a good two or three minutes, was still leaning against it when a large fellow opened it. Paul stumbled into his arms and collapsed.

"Carlyle, Baksh," the fellow shouted, "get down here. This guy's hurt."

The fellow laid Paul gently down on a concrete floor as two of his station mates rushed up carrying large kits. They pulled on surgical gloves as they knelt down over him. "What happened, buddy?" the big guy asked.

As one of the paramedics started cutting away his shirt with scissors he grunted out, "Big guys, with guns . . . and accents . . . in my apartment."

The other paramedic, who was busy attaching some sort of monitoring devices to Paul's chest, looked up at the big guy and said, "Fucking home invasion."

"Are you shot?"

Paul shook his head. "Not shot. Least I don't think so. Blew the door off its hinges. Splinters . . . in my leg . . . my side."

"Some in your face too. An inch higher and you'd' a lost the eye."

The big guy said, "Can't believe it, fucking home invaders using explosives to blow doors now."

"Not home invaders," Paul said. "Russians . . . wizards . . . giant bat things . . . a hippie with lightening."

A crowd of their station mates had gathered, and Paul caught several of them sharing sidelong looks and raised eyebrows. One of the paramedics grumbled, "Probably concussion," and Paul realized he'd better shut up.

They wouldn't listen to him after that, clearly figured he wasn't lucid due to a head injury. They trussed him up rather thoroughly, and with his head and neck in some sort of brace one of them said, "Ok, let's roll him, check for exit wounds."

They rolled him onto his side, prodded him a bit, and there was general agreement he hadn't been shot. They bundled him into an ambulance and Paul lay back as the lights of the city rushed past, the horn blaring, the ambulance jerking and swerving about.

At the ER someone asked, "Call said GSW?"

"Looks like maybe not," one of the paramedics said, "but you should check him anyway. And he's not lucid. Probably head trauma."

The ER staff poked and prodded at him, asked him to count fingers and other tests for lucidity. By the time the cops arrived they'd given him a sedative and the pain began to ebb.

"Ya," one of the cops said. "We got the call earlier. You should see his place. Looks like a navy seal team took it apart."

"He said something about Russians."

"Fucking Russian Mafia," the cop said. "Ass holes must be going into home invasions now."

The cop leaned into Paul's field of view. "Sorry, buddy, but we'll probably never find the bastards. But you are one lucky stiff. Those fuckers are stone-cold killers."

He was too stoned to really feel anything as they plucked all the splinters and stitched him up. A doctor told him he didn't have a concussion, but they still wanted to keep him overnight for observation. They finished bandaging him up, wheeled him through a maze of halls and up an elevator, then parked his bed in a large ward. He drifted off into a hazy, drug-induced slumber.

••••

Baalthelmass had learned much this night. As expected Its two minions had failed to devour this Lord. But It had learned this Lord was weak, even weaker than It had believed. He hadn't demonstrated any defensive powers, even against such weak underlings as the two Tertius caste, had instead fled into the night while his mortal companions disposed of the emergents. And, in fact, they'd only annihilated one with the usual methods, while something unknown had sent the other back to the Netherworld. It was that unknown that gave It pause.

Another test was called for. Another minion, but this time not the wasted, half-living, ravenous creatures with no experience on the Mortal Plane. No, this time It would send Its protégé, one much stronger than the others, one capable of casting a powerful glamour, of using caution and finesse, one perhaps even capable of devouring this Lord-of-the-Unliving, if it was resourceful. It would be a shame if Baalthelmass missed out on such a sumptuous feast, but if this Lord proved more resourceful than anticipated, better to let something else suffer annihilation, if it came to that.

••••

Katherine got the call around 4:00 AM. Paul Conklin had apparently been the victim of a home invasion, had suffered some nasty injuries but nothing life threatening. He'd been brought in by paramedics and was resting comfortably.

She called her father, but only got his voice mail so she left a message with the details. This young man was apparently quite important to her father, and she couldn't confirm that he'd gotten her message, so she decided to start the day early and check on the fellow herself. She took a quick shower, put on her makeup and a not-too-conservative Donna Karan business suit with the skirt cut just above the knees. She finished it off with some Prada four-inch heels; she knew she looked good in heels. She could check in on this Conklin fellow, probably run into her father at the hospital, get a bite to eat somewhere and be in her office long before her first appointment.

She loved driving the Jaguar. It was an extravagance, but she didn't care, and after she parked it in the reserved parking at the hospital, she patted it on the hood like a pet and said, "Don't miss me too much, darling."

The night receptionist greeted her with a friendly smile. "Dr. McGowan, you're up rather early. Or is it late for you?"

"Early," Katherine said. She didn't recognize the woman, couldn't remember her name. To locate Conklin she needed a teensy lie. "One of my patients was brought into the ER a little earlier, was checked in for the night, name of Paul Conklin."

The receptionist consulted her computer and said, "He's on the fourth floor. You'll have to ask the floor supervisor exactly where."

One of the nurses on the fourth floor recognized Katherine and she repeated the lie that he was one of her patients. Without asking, the nurse handed her his chart and led her to a ward with twelve beds. It was a long, rectangular room, with six beds lined up along the left wall and six along the right. Ten of the beds were unoccupied, while privacy curtains hid the remaining two, "He's in the last bed on the right," the nurse said, then marched back to her station.

••••

The night receptionist looked up from her book as the three men stepped into the lobby, an older fellow flanked by two younger, larger men, all wearing cheap, dark suits. The older fellow wore an outdated hat that would've been stylish in the fifties. The younger fellow on his left was an ugly blond with pock-marked cheeks, while the big fellow on his right had a bushy mustache that almost hid his square face. The younger men radiated a badass attitude like the thugs that hung out with her junkie nephew, and she took an immediate dislike to them.

The older fellow in the middle spoke in a thick accent of some kind. "We're looking for Paul Conklin. I believe he was brought into emergency earlier this evening."

She wasn't going to give these fellows anything. "Sorry. We don't release information to anyone but relatives. And you'll have to wait for visiting hours."

"But I am a relative," the old fellow said. "Here, my card."

He held out a business card. She reached out and took it, and as it touched her fingers they tingled slightly. She didn't really need to look at it, because of course he was a relative. Since she'd looked up Conklin's records for Dr. McGowan only ten minutes earlier, she didn't need to do so again. "Mr. Conklin's on the fourth floor. But you'll have to wait for visiting hours. Only medical staff allowed this time of night."

"But I am medical staff," the fellow said in his thick accent. "Look again at my card."

She didn't need to look at his card, which still tingled in her fingers. Of course he was medical staff. She pointed down the hall. "The elevator's that way, doctor."

"Thank you," he said kindly, reaching out and retrieving his card.

As they walked away he said to the two younger men, "See what you can do with a little finesse."

Some minutes later she wondered why she was just sitting there staring at her hands as if she was holding something. She must've zoned out, one of those senior moments they told her would happen as she got older.

••••

Katherine found Paul resting in a light, uneasy sleep. She'd assumed he was younger, but realized now that, like her, he was in his early thirties. His light brown hair was a tousled mess at the moment, and beneath the bandages on his left cheek she thought he might be quite attractive. And there was something familiar about him, some memory that pulled at her so strongly she couldn't brush it off as some vague recollection. She stared at him for quite a while, trying to resurrect the memory, and then it hit her: the shoe store! The Pradas! The ghost! A ghost that had clearly meant something to him and led him to her. And now she suspected it had done so quite purposefully.

Out of curiosity she decided to check his aura. Like most practitioners of the arcane she normally suppressed such vision, much like selective hearing at a loud cocktail party: the background voices might be louder than the person you were listening to, but it took almost no effort to tune them out. The same was true of the *sight*; it was always there but controlled and suppressed. Otherwise it would interfere with simple mundane tasks like driving a car.

She focused on it now and saw the fellow's aura blossom about him like the petals of a flower opening to the sun, filled with the indigo and violet of a strong practitioner of the arcane. But intertwined with his primary colors were streaks of black that moved and swirled within the other colors, and that frightened her a bit. The aura of a demon was wholly black, frequently with a halo of gray ash, and this was nothing like that. Nor did the black overlay his entire aura like that of someone truly evil; if that were the case the black would darken the other colors, and obscure them in some places. Instead, the dark streaks were tangled within the colors of his arcane abilities, woven throughout them like the intertwined strands of a thick rope, ever changing but always focused within them. No, he was no demon, and not evil, but she'd never before seen such black streaks, and that bothered her.

"You my doctor?"

His voice interrupted her thoughts. He'd spoken in a groggy, muddled croak, and she had to concentrate to close off the *sight*. Dim light from the hallway spilled through the open door at the far end of the ward, lighting the floor between the two rows of beds but leaving the beds in shadows. She'd pulled back the privacy curtain part way so she could see something of the fellow, and when she saw a faint glint she knew he'd opened his eyes. "No, I'm just checking on you for my father. He asked me to help find you. He's worried about you."

"Your father?" he asked, clearly unable to shake off the lethargy of the painkillers.

"Yes, I'm Katherine McGowan. I believe my father's a friend of yours."

That statement had the most startling effect on the fellow. His eyes shot open as if she'd just confessed to being a serial killer and at the same time given him a shot of adrenaline, and on the bed he scrambled away from her on his elbows as if her mere presence poisoned the air around him. That sometimes happened when a person returned to full consciousness from the haze induced by painkillers, especially if they were the victims of a violent attack.

Her cell phone started vibrating. She dug into her purse for a moment to find it. "Just a minute," she said to Paul. "I'll take this out in the hall."

As she walked the length of the ward she looked over her shoulder, and he still sat watching her with wide, terrified eyes. The display on the cell phone told her it was her father calling. Out in the hall she answered it. "Hi father, it's Katherine."

"Wanted to thank you for finding young Conklin. Colleen and I are just pulling into the parking lot now."

Katherine hadn't seen Colleen in quite some time, and was looking forward to a little reunion. "I'll come down and get you past the front desk."

"You're there?" he demanded, suddenly upset about something. "At the hospital?"

"Well . . . yes. I thought—"

"Get away from him, now. Get out of there. He's dangerous."

"What do you mean dangerous. He looks anything but dangerous. He's just—"

"He's a rogue. Move, now."

The young man didn't seem like a rogue, though Katherine had to admit she didn't know what a rogue looked like. "I'll meet you in reception," she hissed into her phone, then killed the call and started toward the elevators. She was half way there when the elevator doors opened and Vasily Karpov stepped out, flanked by two young men that made her think, *thug*. She and Karpov had never met so she thought he wouldn't recognize her. But she'd seen a few pictures of him and knew him by reputation—not a nice reputation—so she raised Paul's chart to hide her face, turned and pretended to study it as she walked away from the Russians. A few doors past the ward she ducked into a private room. Luckily it was unoccupied.

7

In It Together

TROGMORESSH'S MASTER, BAALTHELMASS, was being kind. To give It such a boon was a gift beyond imagining: a Lord-of-the-Unliving, weak, injured, ready for the kill. Trogmoressh was young compared to Baalthelmass, and had been summoned to the Mortal Plane by one of Its master's thralls less than a hundred years ago. Its master had immediately taken It on as a protégé. Without Baalthelmass's guidance during the first days of Its emergence, It might've succumbed to the early need, the initial hunger that dominated every thought of a new, Tertius emergent. But Its master had fed It carefully, and now It was ready for bigger things.

It looked at Itself in the mirror. Well, not at Its true self, but rather the glamour It projected for the mortal cattle: a beautiful, young woman. After a hundred years of feeding It had gained enough strength that It no longer needed to hide in some squalid ghetto. It could now conceal Its true nature while living in the middle of the feeding ground. Its wealth and power were growing, and It could even maintain the glamour with sufficient strength to fool some sorcerers, though only the weakest and only for a few moments. Another hundred years of feeding and building Its strength and It would walk among the mortal mages freely, as Baalthelmass did now.

Finding the Lord-of-the-Unliving was a fairly simple matter: take to the air, go to his apartment building, pick up the scent of his power and follow it, first to a fire station, then from there along a direct path to a hospital emergency room. Once there It stepped into the shadows across the street from the ER, adjusted Its glamour to that of an old woman, and It waited. Within minutes an ambulance pulled up and two paramedics, one male and one female, wheeled a patient into the ER. It needed to hear one of them speak, so It crossed the street and blended into a shadow near the ER entrance. Twenty minutes later the paramedics emerged from the ER, and as they replaced the equipment in the back of the ambulance they talked of getting a pizza for dinner. Then they climbed into the ambulance and drove away.

It adjusted Its glamour to that of the female paramedic, checked Its appearance carefully, then entered the ER.

"Back already, Jan?" one of the nurses called to It.

"Just need to pee," It said in the female's voice.

The nurse turned back to her work as It walked down the hall, chose the stairwell and stepped into it, adjusted Its glamour to that of a middle-aged woman in a dark, conservative skirt, a gray blouse and a white lab coat with a stethoscope around her neck. It shook out well-groomed, shoulder-length hair and examined Its image carefully for any flaws. It would have to check each floor for the scent of the Lord's power, but that wouldn't take long.

••••

Pain medication always prevented Paul from sleeping deeply. It killed the pain and he could doze a bit, but it was a light, restless sleep, almost awake, almost asleep, both and yet neither. And when someone approached his bed and stood beside it, the almost-awake part of him realized it and struggled back to a modicum of alertness. He opened his eyes groggily and saw a pretty, young woman standing there, shoulder length auburn hair, dressed in a business suit that looked expensive, nice smile, a red blouse cut just a bit low with a black, lacy something showing above it. She held his chart in one hand, but was staring at him in an almost trancelike way. And there was something familiar about her. "You my doctor?" he asked.

She shook herself as if she had to make an effort to focus on him. She said something about her father that didn't register. He grumbled a question at her and she said, "Yes. I'm Katherine McGowan. I believe my father's a friend of yours."

Katherine McGowan? McGowan? The name sounded familiar, and he had to think for a moment to place it: Walter McGowan, the old professor type who'd knocked on his door a week ago. Yes, now he remembered the fellow, the same fellow that showed up tonight in his apartment with Russian thugs with guns. *Their leader? His daughter? Shit!*

A flush of adrenaline cleared his head instantly. She said something about her cell phone, dug in her purse for a moment and retrieved it, then turned and headed for the hall, her high heels clicking loudly on the linoleum floor. She must be calling them so they could come and finish the job. He had to get out, get away and escape.

Paul slipped carefully out of bed on the side away from the door. His stitches pulled painfully as he crouched down in its shadow. He had a groggy recollection of the nurse telling him his clothes were on a shelf under the bed, but the shelf was empty.

"Looking for these, ye daft fool?"

He maintained his crouch behind the bed as he turned toward the voice, found another midget in a clown suit: different midget, though not so different clown suit. This midget looked to be the same size as the one from earlier in the evening. It wore similarly outlandish clothing in similarly outlandish colors, but this one's nose was an inverted ski jump, almost like a parrot's beak, and it stood there holding Paul's bundled clothes.

"He ain't too quick, Boo'Diddle."

Paul glanced over his shoulder, found the midget from the street near his apartment standing behind him. The other midget said, "It appears he ain't, Jim'Jiminie."

Paul hissed, "Give me my fucking clothes, god damn it. Those maniacs are coming after me."

The midget named Boo'Diddle handed Paul his clothing, spoke around Paul to the other midget, "Looks like he's finally catching on."

Paul peeked up over the bed; the pretty, young woman was gone. He crouched back down, started pulling on his blood-encrusted clothing, and realized the paramedics and ER staff had cut his shirt and pants to shreds. He had to tie pieces off to make it all work. He was thankful they hadn't cut his belt in two. Without that he wouldn't be able to keep the pants on. The midgets tried to assist, hindered him more than helped, but he finally managed it.

••••

McGowan marched into the hospital's reception with Colleen behind him. She'd put away her shadows since a shadow walking around on its own would raise a few eyebrows. Katherine would be down in a matter of seconds, and using her to get past the receptionist would be easier than spelling the woman. But as he approached her he sensed a faint hint of magic in the air.

"Good evening," the receptionist said in a dreamy, not-there voice that seemed badly uncharacteristic of this apparently formidable woman. He glanced at Colleen and she raised an eyebrow, confirming she too sensed something out of place.

The slightest touch was all he needed to confirm his suspicions. He leaned forward, held out his hand and smiled his most charming, handsome-older-gentleman smile. "I'm Walter McGowan, Katherine's father," he said, trying to make it sound more like an invitation for a date.

The woman blushed, smiled at him and took his hand. "Of course, pleased to meet you, Mr. McGowan."

The instant her hand touched his he could sense the residual of the spell. He turned to Colleen. "Shit! She's already been spelled."

Colleen said, "Karpov!"

••••

Paul remained crouched as he stepped out from behind his bed. Light from the hallway spilled through the open door of the ward and lit up the floor between the beds on either side, leaving the beds themselves in shadowed darkness. Paul felt exposed and vulnerable as he stepped into the light and tiptoed carefully up the length of the ward, the two midgets tiptoeing behind him. He passed one bed, then another, keeping his eyes on the open entrance to the ward. He couldn't see down the hallway to either side, so he was moving blind, and he'd almost reached the ward's entrance when he heard voices in the hall coming his way. He looked about desperately but there was no place to hide, so he ducked into the shadows behind the nearest bed. He didn't dare look up over the bed, but the smear of light on the floor of the ward suddenly filled with moving shadows. He heard a woman's voice say, "He's in the last bed on the right, doctor."

A man answered in a thick Russian accent, "Thank you. You can return to your station."

Paul's heart started hammering in his chest and felt like it was climbing up into his throat. He tried to crouch even lower and hold his breath as the shadows on the floor started walking down the ward. The three Russians appeared in silhouette only a few feet from him, first the old fellow, then the ugly blond and finally Joe Stalin, the two thugs screwing cylindrical silencers onto the end of semi-automatic pistols. If any of them glanced even a little to their left they'd see Paul easily and there'd be no escape. But Paul and the midgets had ducked into the shadows behind the first bed on the left, while the Russians were focused on his bed at the far end of the ward, so his luck held and they passed him by.

He heard the older man say, "We won't need the hardware. He's already unconscious, so a simple spell will make it look like the hospital was at fault. Much cleaner that way."

As they walked toward his bed all three of them had their backs turned his way, but that wouldn't last once they reached his bed, so he took his chance when they were half way down the ward. He knew the moment he stepped into the light from the door he'd alert the Russians with his own shadow, so he stayed in the shadows near the beds as he dashed on tiptoe toward the entrance. When he reached the wall at the end of the ward he looked back toward the Russians. They were still walking away from him, so he sprinted at a shallow angle through the door and out into the hall.

His shadow momentarily darkened the ward and he heard a single, startled exclamation from one of the Russians, but as he pressed his back to the wall outside he heard no running feet coming his way so he guessed they hadn't turned quickly enough to identify him. He had only seconds before they discovered his bed was empty, so he turned toward the elevators at the far end of the hall, only to freeze when he saw McGowan and the hippie woman talking to the nurse.

Jim'Jiminie snarled, "This way, hurry!"

Paul looked down at the midget, who hooked a thumb over his shoulder. "The stairway, you idiot."

The two midgets ran back the way they'd come, toward a red exit sign at the far end of the hall past the ward from which he'd just emerged. To follow Paul would have to pass in front of the ward, and he'd be exposed to the Russians again, but he had no choice so he ran after the midgets. As he passed the ward he glanced inside, saw the two young thugs angrily ripping the sheets off his bed, and the old Russian looking his way.

He kept running, heard shouts from the Russians in the ward, heard a shout from McGowan and the hippie-woman at the nurse's station, tried to ignore it all as he ran for the stairwell. And then a door just in front of him opened and Katherine McGowan stepped in his way, her eyes wide with surprise and a gasp escaping her lips. He plowed head-long into her and they both tumbled to the floor in a tangled sprawl, overturning a wheeled metal cart in the process, medical supplies clattering loudly across the floor. Paul only managed to get to his hands and knees when Joe Stalin stepped into the hall-way about fifty feet away. Paul instinctively rolled to one side just as Joe raised his gun and fired. The silenced gun popped like a muffled firecracker, and the bullet dug chunks of tile and concrete out of the floor next to Paul's hand, kicking up debris that stung his face and arms.

Paul desperately reversed direction, rolled the other way and took refuge behind the overturned metal cart. The Russian's gun popped repeatedly, more chips of mason-ry splattering all over the hall, the cart jerking as bullets slammed into it. He caught a glimpse of old-man McGowan and the hippie running toward the Russian, probably to help him finish Paul. The two midgets had opened the stairwell door and were shouting for Paul to join them. Paul scrambled to his feet while Katherine struggled to her hands and knees, her tight skirt split in a tear almost up to her waist. She looked at the midg-ets with undisguised awe, looked back and forth between them and Paul, then at the Russians. She reached into her purse just as Joe Stalin raised his gun and aimed it straight at her face.

A flood of thoughts poured through Paul's head. If she was working with them, why would Joe Stalin try to kill her, literally execute her with a bullet in the face at al-most point-blank range? The metal cart wasn't large, and Paul had adrenaline working for him. He lifted it, swung it in an arc and threw it at the Russian, realizing as he did so he didn't have the strength to throw it far enough. But as it bounced in the hall in front of Joe Stalin it startled him just as he pulled the trigger. The bullet slammed into the wall inches from Katherine's face just as she pulled something out of her purse, spit on it and threw it up the hall toward Joe. It landed in the middle of the hallway, made a sound like a cork popping from a Champaign bottle, and a shimmering, translucent veil of something filled the hall from wall to wall. Joe Stalin fired his gun three more times, but when the bullets hit the veil they came to a stop in midair, moved forward at a snail's pace for a second, passed through the veil then dropped to the floor of the hallway without any energy, bouncing on the linoleum with a faint plinking sound.

"Run," Katherine shouted, struggling to her feet.

Paul reached down and hooked a hand under her armpit, heard some part of her clothing tear as he hauled her to her feet and dragged her toward the midgets, but she hobbled in a horribly uneven gate. She hesitated for an instant and growled, "Broke a heel," kicked her shoes off and turned a really pissed-off look toward Paul. "Fucking Russians ruined my Pradas. I'll kill the bastards."

She looked back up the hall, and the shimmering veil appeared to be dissipating. "Run, run, run," she shouted. "The spell only lasts a few seconds."

Paul's feet got the message and she and he slammed through the stairway door together, the midgets barely a step in front of them. The midgets turned, put their shoulders into the door and slammed it shut. "We'll hold the door," they shouted in unison. The two of them leaned into the door, and Paul couldn't believe what he was seeing, a couple of little men that, between them, couldn't weigh a tenth of what Joe Stalin massed.

He shouted at Katherine, "They can't hold the fucking door."

She looked at him as if he was an idiot. "Of course they can," she shouted back. "You know the power of the little people." She grabbed his arm and started pulling him down the concrete stairs.

"The *little people*?" he demanded.

"Yes," she screamed, for some unknown reason clearly exasperated with him. "Leprechauns. You know how powerful they are."

"Leprechauns!" he shouted back. "Fucking leprechauns!"

She'd dragged him down a flight of stairs to the third-floor landing. "Yes. If they're on your side then you're no rogue wizard." She hesitated, closed her eyes and shook her head. "Damn! My shield spell just expired. Those Russian maniacs won't be far behind."

As if to punctuate her statement he heard a loud thud from the floor above, the sound of a large man throwing his shoulder against the door. "Run," both midgets shouted in unison.

"Spell!" Paul shouted as Katherine dragged him down to the second-floor landing. "Wizard! Leprechauns! You're fucking nuts." He yanked his arm out of her hands violently. "You're all fucking nuts. I'm not going anywhere with a nut-case like you."

Next to them the stairwell door on the second-floor landing opened without warning and a middle-aged, female doctor in a white lab coat stepped onto the landing. She gave Paul an odd, dreamy look and smiled at him longingly; as if they were lovers who'd just found each other after a long separation. "I've found you," she said, wonder and joy coloring every word. She reached out and touched his cheek, and in her touch he felt that strange *pull*, the same *pull* he'd experienced in his apartment when the monster had gripped his throat. More through reflex than anything else, he resisted that *pull* and she jerked her hand back as if she'd touched a hot flame. Her eyes filled with pain, like that of a lover scorned.

Paul's vision flickered as he looked at the doctor. She looked like a middle-aged doctor in a white lab coat, but then *blink*, and for the tiniest fraction of second he thought he saw something else. He was bleeding from a dozen small wounds and thought he might be close to passing out. But as he looked again at the doctor he saw nothing out of the ordinary.

Katherine demanded, "Who are you?"

"Oh, child!" the doctor said. She reached out and touched Katherine on the cheek in much the way she'd touched Paul, a loving caress more than anything else.

Katherine gasped and her eyes rolled back in her head as she swooned, then staggered into Paul.

Paul managed to catch her and kept her from falling. "What'd you do to her?" he demanded.

The doctor shuddered and let out a deep sigh, as if she'd just reached some sort of ecstatic high. "Nothing," she said dreamily. "She must be hurt. I can help her."

Joe Stalin! With the gun! Spraying bullets indiscriminately at them both. He'd heard of people being shot and not realizing it until they collapsed sometime later. Two floors above, one of the midgets—leprechauns—shouted, "We can't hold much longer."

"Follow me," the doctor said, giving Paul a look of pleasurable anticipation. *Blink*, there it was again, and then just as quickly gone again, just a doctor, trying to help them.

Katherine could barely stand, her eyes fluttering dazedly. "Vama . . ." she said mushily, her words slurring as if she was seriously drunk. She leaned heavily against Paul as they staggered together behind the doctor onto the second floor. But Katherine resisted, fought against him as if she didn't want to follow and said something that sounded like, "Va . . . pie . . . Ole . . . va . . . pie . . ."

The stairwell door closed behind them. Paul pressed Katherine against the wall, didn't dare let her drop to the floor because he knew that in his own weakened state he couldn't lift her again if he did.

She was covered with smeared blood, probably most of it Paul's, so he couldn't use obvious bleeding to locate a wound. He tried patting her down, looking for wounds. But he was no doctor and realized he was doing little more than feeling her up—a distant little piece of him thought he might enjoy that in a different time and place, as long as the feeling was mutual. He shrugged that off and snarled at the doctor, "Help us, god damn it."

The doctor grinned, a look of rapt pleasure on her face. She stepped toward them and reached out smiling dreamily, acting unlike any doctor Paul had ever encountered.

Blink; she'd been something else, something dark and frightening that he might recognize if the image lasted for more than an instant, or if he had the time to think about it carefully. But just as the spooky doctor was about to touch him, Katherine suddenly jerked on his arm with renewed energy. She'd regained some coherency as she dragged them both away from the doctor and the stairwell. "Issss a fucking vampire," she snarled. ". . . old vampire, strong."

8

One More Time

TROGMORESSH COULDN'T BELIEVE Its luck. The Lord-of-the-Unliving had come to It, and brought along a young witch, and together the two of them were a sumptuous feast beyond imagining. It had tried to feed on the Lord, but he'd shown surprising strength and resisted. It had fed on the witch a bit, a small mistake since any feeding produced a certain sluggish indolence for a short while. And too, the witch was now alerted to Its true nature, and was this moment dragging the Lord away from It. It would have to be more careful.

It watched the two of them struggle up the hallway of the second floor, followed leisurely and vowed to refrain from any further feeding until It could enjoy the entire banquet. And in any case, it was time to alter Its glamour.

••••

"There's something wrong here," Colleen hissed as she and McGowan ran down the hall toward the Russians.

The two young thugs were taking turns throwing their shoulders against the stairwell door as she and McGowan skidded to a stop next to Karpov. McGowan ignored her and started shouting at Karpov, and of course the Russian shouted back. The hospital, like many hospitals, had been built at the intersection of two ley lines. She pulled power, lots of it, fed it into her words as she threw *voice* at all of them. *Stop, now, I command it.*

The two thugs froze in place and blinked dazedly, while McGowan and Karpov, more powerful and less vulnerable, merely hesitated. Karpov shook off the effects of her *voice* and snarled, "Don't use those Druid tricks on me, woman."

The ley lines were still flooding her with power. She glared at him, took a step forward and let him see some of that power trickle out through her eyes. He took an involuntary step back as she said, "Something doesn't add up here. Didn't you see the little people?"

The two older wizards looked at her uncertainly. She added, "There were two of them helping the young man. The little people wouldn't be helping a rogue who traffics in demons."

McGowan and Karpov both tried to speak at the same time. She threw the *voice* at them again. *Silence.*

Karpov's lip curled up in a snarl, but he held his tongue. She said to him, "You made this mess so you clean it up. I've spelled a nurse and two orderlies on this floor, so no one's yet called the police. Clean it up and make sure they remember none of this. Walter and I'll try to find Katherine and the young man." Karpov started to say something but she cut him off. "And if he is a rogue, we'll help you kill him. But no more guns until we know why the little people are helping him. Agreed?"

Karpov hesitated.

"Wizard's oath," she growled, "or one of us dies here and now." With the ley lines feeding her power she knew she could take him, and he knew it too.

Karpov looked as if he'd just swallowed a mouth full of sour milk. He snarled, "Agreed."

••••

Karpov watched McGowan and Colleen run back toward the elevators. He turned to Alexei, swung as hard as he could and caught him in the side of the head with a round-house slap that probably hurt his hand more than the young fool's face. "You idiot," Karpov said in Russian.

Vladimir stepped back, clearly hoping his boss's anger would stay focused on Alexei.

Alexei lowered his eyes and said, "I'm sorry, Mr. Karpov. I didn't mean to shoot the place up, or to anger the Druid."

Karpov slapped him again and growled, "That wasn't for shooting the place up . . ." He slapped him again. ". . . or angering the Druid, you idiot." He slapped him again, and Alexei was smart enough not to protect himself. "That was for missing when you had the rogue in your sights." He slapped him again, and though it hurt his hand it yielded considerable satisfaction.

Karpov held out his hand. "I gave her my oath. No more guns."

Alexei looked at the open hand for a long moment, then, pouting like a recalcitrant child, he reluctantly placed his gun in Karpov's hand. "Good," Karpov said. "Now use your hands."

Alexei frowned.

He'd never been a thinker, so Karpov helped him out. "I gave my oath no more guns, but I didn't promise her you wouldn't kill him with your bare hands. While Vladimir and I clean up this mess, go find the rogue and finish this."

Alexei thought those words through carefully for a few seconds, then smiled happily, almost eagerly. He looked down at the trail of smeared blood leading into the stairwell. He'd have no trouble tracking Conklin.

••••

"Vampire!" Paul shouted. "What the fuck are you talking about? She's a god damn doctor."

They found another stairwell at the far end of the second floor hall, ducked into it and stumbled down the concrete stairs. Katherine stopped on the first floor landing and leaned heavily against the banister breathing rapidly, gulping for air as if she'd just run a mile. "That's no doctor. That's a vamp, an old one." She looked at him, looked in his eyes, and he made no attempt to hide his disbelief.

"You don't understand any of this, do you?" she asked.

Paul was bleeding from a dozen new wounds where chips of masonry, ripped up with considerable force by the bullets, had punched shallow holes in his face and arms. He was probably carrying a few bullet fragments also, and rolling on the floor of the hospital dodging bullets had torn out all his stitches and opened all the old wounds. He hurt, and he was scared, and there was no way to explain away all he'd seen in the past several hours. But he still wasn't going to buy into this bullshit about spells and vampires. "I'll tell you what I do understand," he growled. "I understand there's no such thing as vampires, and witches, and spells and leprechauns—ok, midgets in clown suits but no leprechauns. You people are just fucking nuts." Paul's own words reminded him of his visions, and that he too was fucking nuts.

Still struggling to catch her breath, she growled, "That vampire fed on me."

He demanded, "What happened to Count Dracula in a tuxedo?"

She shook her head. "That's for the movies. Real vampires don't suck blood, they suck life force. They suck the very essence out of their victims. They feed on their souls."

He shook his head, didn't want to hear any of this shit. But she grabbed him by both shoulders, pushed him against the wall, looked unflinchingly into his eyes and continued relentlessly. "Ok, time for *Vampire Basic 101*. A demon from the Netherworld, Secundus or Tertius caste—Primus caste don't need a human body—possesses a live mortal, feeds on its essence until there's only a faint spark left, leaves that spark untouched, which must be a forever living hell for its victim. Over time the demon's nature warps the body into a disgusting, human-sized bat thing. It's not any kind of vampire like you've ever heard of in stories. It's a demon from hell, but we call them vampires because they feed on humans—human souls actually."

It sounded too much like the monsters that climbed out of his mirror.

"Listen to me," she snapped angrily. "Our lives depend on this.

"Now if the vamp is stuck in the Netherworld and can't feed on mortals, it remains a wasted, bat-thing. But if it gets loose on the Mortal Plane—usually because some idiot sorcerer summons it without the proper protections—we call that a rogue—then it can feed on humans, and in doing so it gains power. Feed on enough humans on a regular basis and it gains enough power to cast a glamour and look like us, maybe live for centuries among us, feeding on us. But its real body is still that disgusting bat-thing. Never forget that. No matter what it looks like to your eyes, it's really that monster."

Paul tried to wrap his mind around such alien concepts. "And that doctor upstairs is one of these old vampires?"

The door in the stairwell on the floor above creaked open. "Shit," she said and grabbed him by the arm. "For some reason it's after you. Don't look in its eyes. Don't let it touch you."

He started to tell her it already had, wanted to tell her about the *pull* he'd felt, but before he could say anything she pulled on his arm painfully and dragged him out into a hallway on the first floor. Guiding him down the hallway she spoke as they limped down its length. "If you have to face it remember your one advantage: it can't just kill you then feed; you have to be alive while it consumes your soul."

Paul knew the two of them made an odd sight, her skirt and blouse torn badly, both smeared with blood, most of it Paul's, she weakened by the vampire feeding—he couldn't believe he was believing this crap—he weakened by blood loss and pain. He wondered if either of them could walk on their own, if the only way they managed to remain standing was by leaning heavily on each other, limping together through the halls of the hospital and leaving a trail of blood smeared on the floor behind them. The receptionist at the front desk looked at them fearfully as they staggered by, hurriedly picked up her phone and started punching in numbers.

They stumbled out into the dark of the wee hours of the morning. Her knees started trembling and he realized she was about to collapse, and in the odd position in which they supported each other, leaning heavily on each other, the only thing he could do was wrap his arms around her in a lover's embrace to hold her up as her knees gave way.

She smiled up at him. "I like you too, Mr. Conklin. But is this really the right time or place?"

He felt his face flush and she laughed. "You're blushing."

He eased her over to a concrete bench to one side of the hospital entrance and lowered her onto it carefully. She reached into her coat pocket, pulled out one of those little black, plastic car-alarm things, pressed a button on it and a car in the parking lot nearby flashed its lights and honked its horn. "My car," she groaned, almost pleading. "We have to get to my—"

Looking up at Paul her eyes suddenly widened and focused on something behind him. Thinking it must be the vampire, he pushed her over into the bushes behind the bench, trying to push her to safety. He spun to face the vampire, but a big meaty fist slammed into his cheek . . .

He didn't recall going down, didn't recall the act of falling, didn't recall the time it took to go from full upright to prone. One instant he was standing there as Joe Stalin's sledgehammer of a fist closed on his face, and the next instant he bounced painfully off the concrete bench and onto the sidewalk in front of it. Head spinning, cheek throbbing, ribs aching, he rolled over and saw Joe standing over him. The big Russian reached down, grabbed him by the tattered remnants of his shirt and lifted him like a child's doll.

A fist slammed into his ribs, another into his face and Paul went down again. Joe Stalin stood over him, drew his foot back to give him a good kick, but Katherine landed on his back screaming like a banshee, legs wrapped around his waist, one arm around his throat, the other swinging a rock the size of a baseball.

Paul crawled painfully to his feet as Joe spun around blindly, swiping ineffectually behind his own head trying to dislodge her, while she slammed the rock into his face and head. Paul waited until Joe's spinning brought him around one more time, then kicked him as hard as he could in the balls. Joe grunted, stopped spinning and bent forward into a crouch, Katherine still riding him like a cowboy on a rodeo bull. She raised the rock one more time and slammed it into the side of his head. He curled up and crumpled like a deflated balloon. Katherine rode him down and hit him one more time in the back of the head with the rock.

Her legs were tangled in Joe's so Paul helped her free them, then helped her struggle to her feet. The ground beneath Paul swayed and he staggered away from her drunkenly, staggered toward the concrete bench. He had to sit down before he fell down, but as he turned to do so he saw two identical Katherines standing over Joe Stalin, who lay between them groaning. One Katherine kicked Joe hard in the head and he stopped groaning, then the two Katherines looked at each other and their jaws dropped. Both Katherines wore the same torn and ripped suit, torn and ripped stockings, torn and ripped coat and blouse exposing a black lacy chemise, blood trickling from identical cuts and bruises on their faces, makeup smeared and hair in wild disarray, with bits of twig and bush tangled into it. It occurred to Paul that seeing double meant he had a serious concussion, but then he realized he wasn't seeing double Joe Stalin, or double anything else for that matter.

The two Katherines backed warily away from one another, one toward the hospital entrance, the other toward the bench and the bushes. Both turned to Paul and said in identical Katherine voices, "It's the vamp, throwing a glamour."

Blink; the image of the Katherine standing in front of the hospital entrance did that strange little flash of something not quite real. Behind her, Paul saw McGowan and the hippie-woman inside the hospital running their way.

The Katherine in the entrance took a step toward Paul and both Katherines said, "Let's get to my car." They both turned and pointed to the other and said, "Don't trust her, it's the vampire."

The Katherine in the entrance took another step toward Paul, reached out carefully toward him and said, "Trust me, Paul."

The Katherine near the bench cringed back and said, "Don't let it touch you."

Paul looked at the Katherine in the entrance; *blink*, and again *blink*, and again *blink*. And with her hand only inches from his cheek he had it, the image in the *blink*, the black, leathery bat-like thing.

At that moment Paul reached the limit of his patience, reached the end of any sanity or reason or forbearance he might possess. The world no longer made sense, was filled with strange and completely inexplicable creatures. He just wanted Suzanna and Cloe back. He just wanted everyone to leave him alone so he could understand how they had come back to him, or, if he was nuts, the certainty of which seemed more and more likely every day, he wanted them to leave him alone in his insanity so he could at least enjoy their return. It all finally boiled up in him, coalesced into his fist as he swung a wild, roundhouse punch. He put his shoulder behind it, put every bit of strength and frustration and anger he had into it, heard the real Katherine shout, "Nooo don't touch it," felt her hand grab his left wrist just as his right fist slammed into the vampire's cheek, heard a satisfying crunch as it connected, felt a not-so-satisfying pain in his fist that shot up his arm. A blinding flash exploded from his fist where it connected. A thunderous clap accompanied it, numbing his arm to the shoulder and lifting him off his feet. Reality shifted and slid along a sideways track, a strange sensation at the same time both sickening and thrilling. Then he landed face down in the dirt. It was warm dirt, uncomfortably so.

He could recall no dirt in the hospital entrance, just concrete sidewalk, the blacktop street, and across the street a paved parking lot. As he lost consciousness his last thought was that there was no reddish-brown dirt in front of the hospital; he shouldn't be lying on dry dirt . . .

••••

The explosion had shattered the glass in the front entrance of the hospital. McGowan struggled painfully to his feet, noticed Colleen sitting on the floor nearby, her back against the wall, her legs splayed out in front of her. She shook her head dazedly and mumbled, "What happened?"

McGowan helped her to her feet, trying to recall what he'd seen in the instant before the explosion. He and Colleen had been following Conklin's smeared trail of blood, had spotted him and Katherine just outside the entrance to the hospital and begun running toward them. Katherine had been standing with her back to the hospital facing Conklin, saying something to him. And then without warning Conklin had drawn his fist back, and McGowan realized he was about to punch Katherine, a heavy blow that could hurt her seriously. But an instant before his right fist slammed into her face another Katherine stepped into view and grabbed his left wrist, shouting something McGowan couldn't hear. And then Conklin's fist connected with the first Katherine, and a searing, white-hot light, accompanied by an explosion, erupted from the point of contact. That was all McGowan could remember. And now both Katherines and Conklin were gone.

Colleen leaned heavily on him for support as he said, "There were two Katherines."

"I know," she said breathlessly, sounding like someone who'd just sprinted a mile. "Had to be a vampire, old one, under glamour. But where did they go?"

McGowan thought he knew, but to say the words was a death sentence for his daughter. No, possibly not a death sentence, but death would be preferable to the alternative. "I think it dragged them into the Netherworld."

"Oh dear God!" Colleen said. "We have to get them back."

McGowan shook his head. "We may not be able to."

Something tugged at his pant leg. He looked down to find two leprechauns standing there. "We can help," one said excitedly.

"Ya," the other said with a big grin on its face. "Isn't this fun?"

••••

Baalthelmass stood in a glamour of deep shadow across the street from the hospital. The Lord had dragged the stupid Tertius and the young woman into the Netherworld, either a very cunning move, or a very stupid one. Baalthelmass would try to bring Trogmoressh back, but Its protégé might now be beyond hope. In any case, if the Lord made it back from the Netherworld still possessed of his soul, and that was by no means a given, then Baalthelmass would have to reevaluate Its entire approach to this Lord-of-the-Unliving, perhaps something less direct. Cloaked in Its shape and identity as a human mortal, It could draw on many resources. It could afford to be patient and careful.

9

Oh Hell!

PAUL SCRAMBLED TO his feet and stood there unsteadily, his right fist surrounded by a pale blue halo. A hot wind howled overhead in a dirty brown sky lit by a sun Paul had never before seen. The vampire, no longer draped in a glamour of human disguise, climbed awkwardly to its clawed feet a few paces from Paul, one leathery wing twisted at an odd angle. It faced him for a moment and hissed at him angrily, exposing a snouted mouth filled with razor-sharp teeth. His heart climbed up into his throat as he took an involuntary step back, instinctively putting more distance between him and that thing. But it turned away from him, turned almost casually as if he didn't matter, turned toward a dark form lying in the reddish-brown dirt at its feet. A slimy, ichorous drool dripped off its chin as it bent over the form, which Paul suddenly realized was Katherine lying on her back with her arms and legs sprawled at odd angles.

Blind panic tugged at him. His instincts told him to take to his heels and run, screaming hysterically like a madman. In his present state of mind he thought he could probably let out a good girlie scream as he ran, but he owed her. She'd come to his rescue in the hospital. She'd warned him this monster was a monster, even when it looked like a nice middle-aged female doctor, and she'd fought by his side in front of the hospital, fought this thing and fought homicidal Joe Stalin.

As the vampire bent down over Katherine's still form he charged, screaming hysterically, ran straight at the monstrous creature, trying to convert his fear into anger, trying to turn it into a hard and determined fury. He slammed into the vampire's back at full speed and hit it with a shoulder block.

Paul was not a small man, and he was in good shape, had been working out again, but he bounced off that thing like a small child running headlong into a concrete wall. Again, a blinding flash erupted from the point of contact with the monster, hammering Paul to the ground. But where Paul's momentum failed to have any effect, the flash made the monster stagger drunkenly and fall.

Paul tried to get to his feet, made it only to his hands and knees where a dizzy wash of power and strength prevented him from rising further. The vampire flapped about aimlessly on the ground paying no attention to Paul or Katherine. She still hadn't moved so Paul crawled toward her, and his movement drew the vampire's attention. It looked at Paul with blood-red goat-slitted eyes, then turned and loped away with an uneven gait. Paul reached Katherine on his hands and knees and collapsed in the dirt next to her.

••••

The Lord had fed on It. Twice! Trogmoressh hadn't fed on the Lord; the Lord had fed on It, badly weakening It and damaging one of its wings. No mortal should be able to do that, and It dare not approach him until It understood more. No, It would bide Its time, find a moment to feed on the young witch first and gain the strength It needed to battle the Lord.

••••

Paul lay next to Katherine in a stunned daze, his cheek resting on the reddish-brown dirt, warm dirt, uncomfortably so. He hurt everywhere, was bleeding in a dozen places. And yet, he felt an odd strength flowing through him, a strange, almost giddy sensation unlike anything he'd ever experienced. It was as if touching that vampire, demon-thing had energized him.

He struggled to his hands and knees and tried to take in his surroundings. A nearby building bore only the slightest resemblance to the hospital, though after careful consideration Paul decided it did appear to be the hospital. But it was a twisted, blasted, crumbling hulk, with only the vaguest outlines to hint at what it had once been. He looked again at the dirty brown sky with the hot wind howling overhead, blowing gusts filled with reddish-brown grit.

"Mr. Conklin, you mustn't dally."

Still on his hands and knees, Paul rolled to one side and sat down on the dirt, found a tall, handsome man with coal-black skin standing over him. "I just need a minute. Don't know what's going on."

"Don't take too long," the man said. "You and the young lady need to find hallowed ground, and quickly."

Paul nodded impatiently. "Ok, Dayandalous, ok. But why hallowed ground?"

Dayandalous squatted down to be more on a level with Paul's eyes. "Again, you remember. That you remember anything, even just my name, is most unusual."

Paul shook his head, trying to clear his thoughts. "And every time you leave I forget."

Dayandalous smiled pleasantly. "Yes, that's the way it must be. But don't forget how you got here? You'll need the memory of that if you hope to get back with your soul intact. And if I might offer a bit of advice . . ."

Paul looked into Dayandalous's eyes. The pupils were fiery red vertical slits, like those of a cat, not the horizontal slits of a goat-eyed demon. "I'll take any help I can get."

Dayandalous said, "Look not into the demon eye, mortal. Look *through* the demon eye."

Paul closed his eyes, lowered his head and ran a hand through his hair. His hand came away caked with the reddish-brown grit that permeated everything here. He was tired of riddles and supernatural bullshit. He opened his eyes, about to deliver an impatient retort, but the man had vanished. He scanned his surroundings quickly, opened his mouth to shout the man's name, but couldn't remember it. And then a moment later he couldn't remember why he thought he should be shouting someone's name.

Hallowed ground. He did remember that. And *you and the young lady.* He remembered that too. Katherine!

She was still lying on her back, head turned slightly to one side, arms and legs sprawled haphazardly, her dress torn in a dozen places, her hair frazzled and wild, a few twigs and clumps of dirt tangled in the strands. He knew he wasn't supposed to move an injured person until they could determine how badly she was hurt. But he was no doctor, and he couldn't tell if she was breathing so he dropped to his hands and knees and pressed his ear to her chest to see if he could hear a heartbeat. He was listening carefully, hoping desperately she was unhurt. Then suddenly she took a breath and spoke groggily, "Is that how you get your jollies, sneaking a look down my blouse for a boob shot?"

He suddenly realized that part of her blouse had been torn completely away and his face was pressed against an almost bare breast, and he could see into her blouse, could see most of the other breast quite clearly. He snapped his head up and said, "I uh . . . I wasn't . . . uh. I mean . . . I didn't."

She laughed quietly, waved his complaints aside impatiently. "I know you didn't, Conklin. But it's so easy to toy with your little mind. Help me up."

He helped her to a sitting position where she sat for a moment with her face buried in her hands. Then she leaned back, opened her eyes and took her first look around. And as she did so her eyes slowly widened and her face filled with horror. "Oh shit!" she said, scrambling to her feet. "Oh shit, oh shit, oh shit!"

Paul scrambled up beside her. "What's wrong?" He had to shout to be heard above the howl of the wind.

She turned on him and shouted. "We're in the Netherworld. We're in the Netherworld. How did we get in the fucking Netherworld?"

"Netherworld?" Paul pleaded. "What the hell is the Netherworld?"

"Exactly," she shouted. "It's hell, or at least what hell in most mythologies is loosely based on. Why did you bring us here?"

"I didn't bring us anywhere. I just hit that fucking vampire on the chin."

She looked around desperately. "We have to find hallowed ground."

"You mean like a church?"

"Ya, church, or graveyard, anything like that. You know this part of San Francisco better than me. Is there anything like that nearby?"

Paul couldn't believe what he was hearing. "But this isn't San Francisco. You just said that yourself."

"But it is," she said, grabbing him by both shoulders and shaking. "In a twisted, hellish sort of way, it is. The Mortal Plane and the Netherworld are connected in many places, so the reality of the Mortal Plane leaks into the Netherworld, producing counterparts everywhere. Look around."

He scanned the twisted and tormented cityscape about them. Something had blackened and burned all of the buildings, a few so badly little more than rubble remained, and there appeared to be the flickering reddish glow of massive fires on the horizon. The dry wind howled constantly, a scorching hot air laden with a noxious combination of sulfur and wood smoke that made it difficult to breathe. An almost continuous thunder rumbled in the background, constantly waxing and waning with a vibration he could feel through the ground at his feet. But this twisted and tormented city did bear a certain resemblance to the San Francisco he knew, so he tried to recall the local layout.

"I think there's an old church about three blocks from here," he said tentatively. "But I'm not sure. I'm not really religious, not a church goer."

She shrugged. "Most wizards aren't."

"I'm not a wizard."

"Sure," she said. "We'll talk about that later."

••••

Paul and Katherine moved carefully, but quickly, down the street. The structures on either side had once been the classic San Francisco nineteenth-century, wood-frame houses with three or four stories of bay windows. But then Paul wondered if anything in this hell had ever been whole, if perhaps everything here was created in a state of destruction. Their condition varied from abandoned, derelict hulks, to piles of mere rubble, and everything in between.

They crossed through an intersection and the street dropped down one of those steep San Francisco hills. They'd gone about a block when Katherine suddenly said, "Wait, stop."

"What is it?" Paul asked.

She pointed to the top of a pile of rubble that had once been a three-story Victorian. "I thought I saw that Tertius, but without the glamour. It's following us, and I think it was limping."

Paul quickly told her about his brief battle with the demon when he'd first awakened. When he finished she looked him over carefully, then stepped in close, intimately close. "That was very gallant of you, Mr. Conklin."

He suddenly became conscious of her torn blouse and the serious cleavage it exposed. She had small breasts, and she seemed to be teasing him with them. And he realized he was staring at them.

She said, "And you need to get your mind out of the gutter, Conklin, get it back on finding us some hallowed ground." She turned and started walking down the street.

He wanted to protest, tell her she was being unfair. She was the one who'd stepped in intimately close, had practically shoved her cleavage in his face. But all he could get out was, "Why hallowed ground?"

She looked over her shoulder impatiently. "Of course, hallowed ground. We're in the Netherworld."

He pleaded, "There's no *of course* for me. I don't know what the hell you're talking about."

She stopped and turned back to face him. "You really don't have a clue, do you?"

He lifted his hands in a prayer-like gesture. "Not the vaguest."

She turned around and continued marching down the street. He followed while she spoke. "Ok, crash course in demonology. I told you about the vampires, and how they're a human possessed and warped by a demon. There're three main demon castes: Primus, Secundus and Tertius. Beyond that there're non-caste demons like imps and succubuses and incubuses, kind of a fourth caste, the least powerful of them all. By the way, the one that attacked us in the hospital was clearly Tertius caste, maybe one or two hundred years on the Mortal Plane."

He interrupted her. "How do you know that?"

"If it'd been a Secundus, when it fed on me the effect would've been far more devastating. And a Secundus wouldn't feed on me on the spur of the moment, not like that. Besides being more powerful, Secundus demons are far more calculating and patient. A Secundus vamp would likely have tried to enthrall me first, take me to its nest and feed on me at its leisure.

"In any case, demons cannot, by themselves, cross between the Mortal Plane and the Netherworld. They have to be summoned by a mortal or Sidhe sorcerer."

"Sidhe?" he asked.

"Ya, you know, Faerie."

"No, I don't know any fairies." He couldn't hide his frustration and his words tumbled out in a rush. "Well, I do live in San Francisco, but that's not the kind of fairies you're talking about, is it?"

She'd been marching along like a storm trooper; again she stopped suddenly and turned back to him. "Who's been teaching you? Who're you apprenticed to, that they'd leave you so ignorant?"

He shook his head. "I don't know what you're talking about."

She frowned and opened her mouth to say something but the ground beneath their feet started to shake, threatening to drop them both on their butts. They were in the middle of the street with no tall buildings looming overhead, so they faced no danger of injury by falling debris. But Paul couldn't help thinking of an earthquake in an old low-budget movie, opening a giant crack in the ground and swallowing them both, then closing completely. He tried to ignore his own vivid imagination.

As suddenly as it started the shaking stopped, the wind died and utter silence descended on the city about them, an eerily complete stillness that felt wrong and out of place. Something in the distance cried out a high-pitched screech. Similar screeches quickly answered it, baleful, inhuman cries.

Katherine looked his way as she said, "This is scaring the shit out of me. We'd better run for that church."

Katherine had ditched her spike-heeled shoes in the hospital and was in her stocking feet, so the best they could manage was a jog. Paul led the way and the creatures—demons—cried out now in a chorus of excited screeches and howls. The sound they made had an oddly human timbre to it, disturbing and frightening at the same time. Paul could hear them advancing up the streets on either side, flanking them, moving much faster than he and Katherine could manage.

Up ahead something crawled out of an alley and he and Katherine slowed their pace. It appeared to be no more than a black smear oozing across the ground, a dark blot of nothing that broadcast hatred and loathing to assault his senses. He staggered under the attack, stumbled to his knees and vomited, thought of the stupid heroine in some cheap movie who fell for no reason just as the evil villain was chasing her, and you wanted to kick her for being so clumsy. Katherine too was on her hands and knees vomiting. He struggled to his feet and helped her to hers, felt as if he carried an enormous weight on his back. Supporting each other, they edged around the black smear, and Paul didn't need to be told they shouldn't let it touch them. They staggered on, and the nausea subsided as they got farther from it.

They'd lost precious moments eluding the black smear, could hear the cries and screams of whatever was chasing them all around them now, and knew the creatures had surrounded them. They could run, but there was no place to run, and it was clear they couldn't hide.

Something loped out into the street in front of them, a misshapen, distorted form of human being. It scrambled forward on its hands and knees as fast as any dog might move and stopped in the street about twenty feet from them. It stood on its hind legs, lifted its arms high and cried out in triumph from a human mouth warped by rows of needle-like teeth. It had the genitalia of both man and woman, though they were disgustingly swollen, and like the rest of the creature badly distorted.

Paul looked over his shoulder and saw that a half-dozen similar creatures had come to a stop in the middle of the street behind them. To both sides more of them yipped and shouted and jumped up and down on the rubble that remained of old houses. Paul moved slowly, reached down and lifted an old board that he could use as a club. It probably wouldn't do much good, but he wasn't going down without a fight.

Katherine fumbled in the pocket of her coat and said, "I'm going to clear us a path."

She lifted something out of her pocket, raised her closed fist to her mouth and spit into her palm. Whatever she had cupped in her hand began to glow with a harsh, blue light and spears of radiance escaped between her fingers. She turned toward the pack of creatures behind them, lifted her glowing hand high above her head and waved it like a sword. The intensity of it grew steadily and the creatures cringed and backed away.

She turned toward the lone creature standing in the street in front of them, probably their leader. She charged at it and screamed like a banshee. Paul charged after her, caught up with her and shouted, "Hope you know what you're doing."

The creature in front of them suddenly dropped to all fours and charged. But in that instant Katherine threw the glowing thing in her hand directly at it. When it hit the monster loping toward them it exploded with a thunderclap and enveloped the thing in a ball of incandescent fire, with swirls of electricity discharging at its edges. The concussion kicked Paul in the gut and slammed him to the ground.

Get up, he told himself. *Get up. Get up. Get up.*

Katherine helped him stagger to his feet and said something about, ". . . sorry . . . didn't have time to protect you . . ." but his ears were ringing too much to hear it all.

"What the hell was that?" he asked.

"A little spell I prepared in advance. I don't have many left so we'd better move."

Katherine's fireworks display had scared off the pack of distorted humans so they staggered on, leaning on each other heavily. When they got to the bottom of the hill he turned left, trying to recall the exact location of the church. His vague memories told him it should be in the middle of this block, but there was no church visible.

"Why are you stopping?" she demanded. "We can't stop now."

He pointed at a pile of rubble. "I thought the church was here, but clearly it's not."

Katherine slowly turned a complete circle, scanning the horizon. Paul wasn't sure what she was looking for, but then she stopped and pointed past his shoulder. "Look."

He turned and saw the crumbling remains of a steeple rising out of the rubble one block further on. "The steeple is symbolic," she said, "and symbols contain power. That'll be the last thing to fall."

The silence that descended earlier continued as they both started running, the only sounds that reached their ears the patter of her bare feet, the clop of his shoes, and their own struggling breaths. Using the steeple as a guide they made it to the end of the block and turned right, but as Paul rounded the corner two strides ahead of Katherine he heard a painfully familiar screech behind them.

He looked over his shoulder as he ran, saw Katherine behind him doing the same, the vampire-demon thing about a hundred feet behind her and loping toward them with an ungainly gait. Katherine stopped looking over her shoulder and shouted at him, "Ruuuuun!"

Paul did exactly the opposite. He slowed a bit to let her pass because, in her stocking feet, she was slower than him even though she was sprinting like a madwoman, obviously ignoring any pain she felt.

The church was still half a block away. Paul kept glancing over his shoulder as they ran, and they were gaining distance on the demon because it just wasn't made for running. And then it flapped its leathery wings, and within two strides took to the air, rose to a height of about ten feet and swooped down toward them. Paul looked ahead to the church, realized they weren't going to make it, recalled that he'd been able to have some sort of effect on the monster, so he swerved to the edge of the street and dug his heels in near a pile of rubble, came to a stop, bent down and picked up another club. He turned and stepped into the middle of the street to face the monster.

"What are you doing?" Katherine shouted.

He glanced over his shoulder to find she too had stopped. "We're not going to make it," he screamed, and turned back to the demon. He shouted over his shoulder, "Get to the church. I'll try to stop it."

It glided down toward him, it's wingspan a good fifteen feet. If it hit him on the fly, at the speed it was traveling his only hope was to try to hit it with the club just before impact. He watched it glide toward him, watched it coming and tried to gauge the timing of his swing. But when it was about twenty feet away it suddenly flared its wings upward, rose slightly, then settled almost gracefully about ten feet in front of him.

It looked at him quizzically, its head moving side-to-side.

Katherine stepped up to stand beside him holding her own club. "Don't look into its eyes. Remember that."

He looked at her. "We're screwed, aren't we?"

She didn't look at him as she answered, "Ya." But then she did look his way and said, "But it's wary of us, for some reason."

The demon took a step toward them. Paul raised his club like a batter in a baseball game waiting for the pitch. Katherine raised hers as the demon took another step. It seemed to grow more confident and took another.

Katherine hissed, "Back slowly toward the church."

They both took a step backward, and the demon took two forward, and another, and another. Then it raised its head high as if preparing to lunge for them. But it hesitated, froze without moving for several seconds, looking at something behind them. Then slowly, carefully, it dropped its head, scrunched it down low on its shoulders, leaned forward and lowered its snout to the ground. And it started whimpering, piteous sounds like those of a badly beaten dog. Then, cringing fearfully, it turned and literally began crawling away from them on its belly.

Paul glanced over his shoulder to see what had frightened it so, and standing behind them was Walter McGowan. He smiled.

Katherine turned to look and shouted happily, "Father! Thank god!" She started trotting toward him.

Paul hesitated. Earlier he'd thought McGowan had tried to kill him, and while Katherine had nothing to fear, Paul had to be more cautious. He wasn't going to just run up and wrap his arms around the old fellow, even if he was their salvation from hell. But as Katherine moved toward him Paul saw the old man's image *blink*, and for the tiniest fraction of a second it appeared something else stood there. It had been too short of an instant for him to recall the image, but he was certain it wasn't one of the bat-like vampire things. Then there it was again, *blink*.

Paul acted on impulse. Katherine was halfway to her father when Paul charged like a baseball player trying to steal home plate. He started from a standstill and it took agonizing seconds to build his speed, seconds during which he watched her closing the gap with her father, reaching out to him hopefully. Old man McGowan raised his hands to envelope her in a fatherly embrace, but Paul's instincts screamed that it would be a deadly embrace.

Paul hit her an instant before she stepped into the circle of the old man's arms. He hit her like a linebacker and she grunted as he wrapped his arms around her, spun to one side, dropped to the ground and used his momentum to whip her at an angle past her father. She tumbled head over heels off the sidewalk and onto the church steps. Paul skidded and rolled to a stop at McGowan's feet, hoping desperately the church steps were hallowed ground.

McGowan looked down at him kindly and asked, "Now why did you do that, young man?"

Blink.

Katherine groaned and rolled over. Blood trickled from a cut on her cheek as she shouted, "What did you do that for, you fucking idiot?"

Paul looked up at McGowan. *Blink.* "It's not your father," he said.

The being wearing McGowan's image stepped toward him, and Paul, lying on his back on the ground, scrambled away from him in a crab-crawl. McGowan's image stopped and looked down at Paul. He smiled a very unfriendly smile, his eyes blood-red and goat-slitted. "Since you deny me her . . ." he said, and his voice was no longer McGowan's. It rumbled like the earthquake that shook them earlier. ". . . then I'll have you."

Blink. The demon wore two images. *Blink.* It looked like the old man, but blurred over that image was something else. *Blink.* Paul tried to focus on that other image as he crawled backward and scrambled to his feet. The demon's mouth had lengthened into a bird's beak, and as Paul looked on its hair disappeared and a comb of feathers appeared on its head. Its legs twisted and warped and began to writhe, and in McGowan's place there now stood a chimera-like monster with the head of a rooster, the body of a man, and legs made of writhing serpents. A large squirming phallus hung between its legs with four testicles hanging beneath it, each the size of a grapefruit. The legs slithered and squirmed, bringing the monster closer. "Interesting!" it said, looking Paul over carefully. "I wonder who brought me such a delightful present."

Its goat-slitted eyes fascinated Paul and he studied them, mesmerized by the power he sensed in them. He could see dominance and supremacy there, and he felt an overwhelming need to embrace this monster, even as he realized his need was wholly unnatural. He also wanted to run away screaming hysterically, but couldn't lift his feet to run, couldn't turn, couldn't move.

"Don't listen to it, Paul," Katherine shouted. "That demon's at least Secundus caste. Don't listen to it. Don't make any deals. Don't agree to anything no matter how trivial it seems. And above all, don't look into its eyes."

But her warning had come too late. Paul could see deep into its eyes to the core of its power, a swirling maelstrom of hatred and loathing. It moved closer, and if the beak of its rooster head were capable of human expression, somehow it grinned and said, "Your plaything can't remain on hallowed ground forever. And I do have forever." The demon leaned toward him, sniffed at him like a hound. Its eyes narrowed uncertainly, it frowned and said, "And why do you stink of Dragon, mortal?"

This close Paul could see millennia in its chicken-headed, goat-slitted eyes, thousands of years of torment, untold numbers of souls heaped upon the fires of its hunger. It had always existed to torment and devour unwary souls. It had no beginning and it would have no end. Paul could see all that in those eyes, and he could see something else buried deep, deep inside them, a center of existence, a core of being, a name.

Paul said, "I know nothing of dragons, Abraxas."

The demon screamed and backed away, its serpent legs writhing frantically, the phallus between its legs swelling to unbelievable proportions, then shrinking and disappearing altogether. It turned its eyes away from him shattering the enthrallment, but Paul couldn't put the images and torment he'd seen out of his mind. He was too disoriented to move as he tried to comprehend the agony he'd witnessed.

Something hit him hard, wrapped arms around his shoulders and lunged, pushing him backward. He landed painfully on his back on the steps of the church with Katherine on top of him. Still disoriented and hurting everywhere he rolled over, rolled on top of her.

"Gee, Conklin," she said in his ear. "You sure have a one track mind. But nice girls don't do that on the first date. You'll just have to settle for lots of smooching and heavy petting."

••••

McGowan's house was one of those early twentieth-century wooden structures built on a steep hill in such a way that the entrance opened onto the second floor, with the first floor down the hill and at the back, a total of five floors in all. McGowan's workshop occupied the entire first floor and it had a workbench, shelves and chairs, though all were located along the walls, leaving the center of the room open and clear. McGowan had tiled the floor in marble, and installed a large circle of beaten silver permanently embedded in the marble. Outside the silver circle he'd also fashioned a silver pentagram, also embedded, its interior lines touching the circle. He'd beaten that silver and installed it with his own hands. Otherwise it wouldn't work for him, not as a circle of power to contain dangerous magics.

Colleen and the two leprechauns, Jim'Jiminie and Boo'Diddle, followed him down the stairs and into the workroom. She was one of the few people in the world he'd allow in here, and he'd made an exception for the leprechauns since they'd offered to help, relinquishing their traditional neutrality. "Walter, what're you planning?" she asked as he rummaged through a storage cabinet.

He brushed her concerns aside impatiently. "I'm going to try a summons, try to get Katherine back."

She grabbed his arm, forced him to turn and face her. "That'll be a major summoning, and it's well past dawn."

He shook her off angrily. "I don't care. We're talking about Katherine here, trapped in the Netherworld. Every moment she's trapped there could mean a fate worse than death."

Colleen spoke carefully, "And it won't do her any good if you perform a major summons without the proper preparations and release a demon onto the Mortal Plane, or get yourself sucked into the Netherworld."

"She's right, Old Wizard," Jim'Jiminie said.

Boo'Diddle added, "You know she is."

McGowan sat down at the workbench, his shoulders slumped and he buried his face in his hands.

Colleen paced back and forth across the workroom. "We should fast for twenty-four hours, perform the proper cleansing rituals in the evening and begin the summoning at midnight."

McGowan lifted his face from his hands. "But that'd mean we couldn't really start fasting until midnight tonight, and not begin the summoning until midnight tomorrow night."

Colleen continued to pace back and forth as she impatiently waved his objections aside. "I agree. That's too long. In any case, starting the ritual at midnight is more important than a full twenty-four hours of fasting. It's still early morning and we've barely had anything to eat, so I'm comfortable if we fast through the rest of the day. We'll start the cleansing rituals immediately after sunset, and the summoning at midnight tonight."

She stopped and turned to the old man. "Katherine's a smart girl, and a good witch. She'll seek hallowed ground. That should protect her at least that long. Do it this way and I'm with you all the way. Do it now without the proper timing and preparations and you're on your own."

He nodded, and when he spoke his voice was just a whisper. "We'll do it your way."

••••

"Your Majesty," Anogh said. The Summer Knight of the Winter Court stood before the Winter King, King Ag, arrayed in the hereditary armor of the Summer Court, layer after layer of lapis lazuli, silver and mother-of-pearl covering him from head to foot. And as always, for the last several hundred years, he felt it was blasphemy to even wear the Summer Armor anywhere in the Winter Court, unless, of course, he was coming to war against them. "Last night there was an incident on the Mortal Plane. An incident of some . . . significance."

Ag lay upon a couch covered in white silken sheets. Dressed in a white linen buskin over a white, silk, ruffled shirt, his long, coal-black locks drifted on a slight breeze that was anything but natural. At the Summer Knight's words the Winter King didn't move for several seconds, then he slowly raised his eyes to the Summer Knight. "Yes, Anogh, there was. Some sort of nether interaction any fool could sense. Even a fool such as you."

Even with his face hidden behind the mask of the great, horned helm of the Summer Armor, Anogh, the Summer Knight, knew the Winter King would know of any expression that crossed his face. And if Anogh did anything to produce even the faintest hint of doubt, the Winter King might question him. For the past six hundred years of his binding to the Winter Court Anogh had carried no secrets worth dying for, but now that the Morrigan had lifted some of the enchantment that had clouded his thoughts, that had changed. Anogh couldn't lie, so if Ag asked the right questions in just the right way, Anogh's only course would be to refuse. And that would give Ag the justification to take his life. It had been millennia since an immortal Sidhe of royal blood had lost his life, but there were ways.

So, displaying no emotion, he lowered himself to one knee and bowed deeply before King Ag. "Forgive me, Your Majesty. Of course you would sense it long before we who bow before you. I did not mean to imply—"

"Enough," the Winter King snarled, examining his fingernails as if considering a manicure. "You are forgiven. But of course I must think of some penance for you. And while I'm doing so, please assemble the Privy Council, and call the Winter Court to order. The incident was of sufficient significance to deserve further investigation." Ag flicked his wrist in an impatient gesture of dismissal.

"Your Majesty," Anogh said, backing carefully out of the royal presence while maintaining a deep bow.

Simuth, the Winter Night, waited outside the Winter King's chambers dressed in the finest of Faerie silks, with a slender, silver rapier at his side. Simuth leaned against the wall of the long corridor, picking casually at his fingernails with a small dagger, blocking the Summer Knight's path. "And so, my dear Anogh," he said. "What matter brings you into the presence of our dear King?"

"You must ask that question of His Majesty," Anogh said, bending his knee in the deep formal bow of the Winter Court. "I'm not at liberty to reveal the King's counsel."

Simuth rolled his eyes and gave Anogh a condescending tilt of his head. "Come now, my dear Anogh. We are brothers, are we not: if not by blood, then by circumstance and fortune? Or should I say misfortune? Surely, you wouldn't begrudge me the details of some trifling incident on the Mortal Plane?"

"Again, Your Highness, I'm not at liberty. But, apparently, you're already aware of the . . . incident."

Simuth stepped aside, giving Anogh room to pass. "Very well, brother knight."

Anogh curled his lips up in an unpleasant smile. "I'm not your brother, either by blood or association."

Simuth returned Anogh's smile with a malevolent grin. The Summer Knight stepped forward cautiously, turned just as he passed the Winter Knight to nod his head politely and back-step a few paces. More than being polite, it was an excuse to avoid turning his back on a viper with a blade in his hand. One must always be careful around Simuth, and not until well out of Simuth's reach did he turn and continue on.

Bound by law, custom and magic, Anogh could not betray the Winter Court to the Summer Court. But his first loyalty lay with the Summer Court, and he hoped dearly the Summer Queen too had sensed the *incident of some . . . significance* on the Mortal Plane.

••••

High Chancellor Cadilus knelt before Magreth, Summer Queen and mistress of the Seelie Court, his head bowed. "Rise," she said coldly.

Cadilus stood, grimaced as he looked into her eyes and saw the flames dancing there. She sent her voice brushing though his spirit like a hot, dry wind, "Have you learned what it was?"

"Not completely, my queen," Cadilus said. "But it did involve the Old Wizard, and some of his more powerful colleagues—the Druid for one, the horrible Russian for another. It also involved a young wizard of whom we had not, heretofore, been aware. And it involved the Old Wizard's daughter, and a demon, probably Tertius caste, that left its scent on the Mortal Plane."

She lifted an eyebrow. "A demon, manifest on the Mortal Plane! That will rouse all the mortal wizards and witches."

Cadilus inclined his head slightly to one side. "Our mages have been able to determine it's no longer on the Mortal Plane. Furthermore, neither is the Old Wizard's daughter."

She looked at him pointedly. "That is bad news indeed. Not that I care one whit for the young girl. I've never met her, don't know her in the slightest. But the old man is extremely powerful, dangerous when aroused, and he'll stop at nothing to protect his offspring."

She paused and considered her words carefully. "It would behoove us, dear Cadilus, to offer the old man our assistance, should he so desire."

"An excellent idea, Your Majesty. He won't accept, of course. But such a diplomatic overture would not be wasted. I'll see to it myself."

She smiled, though, again, there was no warmth in the Summer Queen's face, only the flames that lit her eyes and reflected her disdain. "Do so, dear Cadilus."

That was clear dismissal, but Cadilus hesitated. He wouldn't have done so were it not important.

"Is there something else?"

"Yes, Your Majesty. The young wizard's abode, it stank ever so faintly of the Unseelie Court."

"But that's to be expected," she said, clearly impatient and irritated that he'd bring such trivial matters before her. "They would investigate such an incident with no less fervor than we."

Cadilus shook his head. "It was not that kind of scent, Your Majesty. It had the permanence of Unseelie habitation."

"Are you telling me the young wizard was living with an Unseelie witch?"

Again Cadilus shook his head. "He was living alone, to the best of our knowledge. And the scent was old, long gone, perhaps from before he took up residence there. But it does bear further investigation."

"I trust you'll see to that as well?"

"Yes, Your Majesty." Cadilus bowed deeply and withdrew.

10

Temptation

PAUL AND KATHERINE staggered up the steps of the church supporting each other. They stumbled through the church's entrance, though all that remained of any doors were a few split pieces of blackened lumber that hung from twisted hinges. The church's roof had long ago collapsed, leaving a rubble-strewn interior with a large pile of twisted beams and broken roof tiles in the middle of the floor. With exhaustion weighing heavily on them both, they managed to find a couple of pews that were still intact, and brushed debris off them. Katherine pulled off her coat and rolled it up into a pillow, then lay down on a pew facing Paul.

"If you wake before me, don't leave the confines of the church. We're safe here, at least as safe as we can be in hell."

Paul didn't have a coat so he had no pillow, but when he lay down he fell into the near-death sleep that comes after too much adrenaline and fear. When he awoke some hours later he rubbed at his eyes groggily, learned that was not a wise move since it just ground the reddish-brown grit in deeper. He noticed Katherine no longer occupied the pew where she'd slept. His bladder was uncomfortably full; he assumed she'd probably awakened in the same condition and hunted down a place to relieve herself. He struggled to his feet, felt like an old man, and while every little movement reminded him of a cut or bruise or wound of some kind, he ignored the aches and walked carefully to the back of the church. He stepped through a hole in the wall there, relieved himself against the outside back wall of the church, tucked his tattered and cut-jeans back in place, and turned around to survey the back of their sanctuary.

The back yard of the church contained a small cemetery, and near the very back he saw Katherine standing at its edge with her back to him, probably taking stock of the surrounding buildings. He recalled she'd said cemeteries were also hallowed ground, so he walked down the back steps and threaded his way between old gravestones toward her. He was a dozen paces behind her when he called her name.

She jumped, turned toward him with wide, frightened eyes, saw it was him and put a hand on her chest. She took a deep breath and let it out slowly. "Oh," she gasped breathlessly. "It's you."

He felt like an idiot, stalking up behind her without warning. "I'm sorry. I didn't mean to startle you."

"That's ok," she said breathlessly. "I think we're both going to be jumpy as long as we're in this predicament."

She raised a hand to her torn blouse, modestly tried to rearrange the material to cover her breasts. Without the coat the tear exposed even more skin and she failed miserably. But in the process she'd accidentally drawn his attention to her half-exposed chest, unwillingly displaying far more cleavage than would be polite or fashionable in any venue. He tried not to stare, but for some reason he couldn't look away. And as he watched her chest rise and fall with each breath, he realized he was strongly attracted to her. Only a few paces separated them and he had a sudden fantasy of crossing that distance, of tearing her blouse open completely, cupping her breasts in his hands and licking the reddish-brown grit from her nipples. And he could see in her eyes she shared the attraction, that she wanted him to come to her and take her in his arms. They were alone, with no one to disturb them, and no one to stop them from enjoying each other's bodies.

He took one step, his eyes focused on her heaving chest, watched longingly as it rose and fell. Her breathing came now in deep, longing sighs, and with each breath her breasts grew, swelled and spilled more flesh out of her torn blouse. He took another step, feeling a need rise up in him that he hadn't felt in a long time. And now she reached up again to her torn blouse, but this time she opened it further, exposing her heaving breasts completely and inviting him to fulfill his desire, to yield to the need that blossomed within him, a demanding obsession he could no longer deny.

"Paul," she shouted from far behind him. "Don't. It's the demon."

Behind him! She was behind him. But she was standing in front of him. Her breasts had spilled out of her blouse, had grown to massive heavy globes with dark brown areolas. And it was that more than anything that made him hesitate, for the heavy, swollen breasts in front of him did not belong to Katherine. And in another place and time he could easily be attracted to Katherine, the real Katherine, not this rounded, voluptuous, porn-star queen of a Katherine standing in front of him.

He took a step back. The porn-star's pupils glowed red and she glared at him with goat-slitted eyes. He heard the real Katherine's footsteps as she approached behind him. She put a hand on his shoulder and spoke softly, "That's the demon."

He backed up another step and drew even with Katherine, turned his head to look at her carefully and glanced momentarily at the skin exposed by her blouse. Until the demon had drawn his attention to it, he hadn't realized he was attracted to her, that he found the extra skin exposed by her torn blouse sexually exciting, like a small boy catching a boob-shot when an attractive woman across the room bends over without realizing how much skin is exposed by her billowing blouse.

She blushed, so he took his eyes off her chest and raised them to meet hers, though he noticed her right hand lifted almost involuntarily to her torn blouse in a wasted effort to smooth the tear back in place. The hand gave up the effort and she lowered it to her side in a gesture that seemed almost defiant.

"I know it's the demon," he said, thinking she had nice eyes, brown eyes set in an oval face with a strong jaw. "But I thought you said it couldn't go in a graveyard."

She kept her eyes locked to his, clearly appraising him as he was appraising her. She tilted her head slightly to one side, a kind of apologetic shrug. "Sometimes they bury a suicide, or some other outcast, at the edge of a graveyard without religious ceremony and without sanctifying the ground. Another step or two and it would've had you."

"And can it read my thoughts?" he asked, thinking that was the only way it would have known to use her as bait.

She looked at the demon and Paul followed her gaze. No longer the porn-star queen, it now looked more like her. She looked at Paul, at the demon, then back at Paul, and he could see in her eyes she suddenly understood why her image had been such effective bait. She blushed again.

"How trite!" the demon said. It was odd to hear such a deep rumbling voice coming from a small woman. "Why don't the two of you just rip your clothes off right here and fuck your brains out? I might enjoy the show."

Paul turned his back on the demon and said, "Come on. Let's go inside."

Katherine took his arm and walked beside him back to the church. Inside they sat down on the pews they'd slept on. Katherine tore a small piece of cloth from her coat, dabbed a little spit on it and tried to clean the cut on her cheek. Paul yanked off his tattered shirt—he was wearing an equally sliced up T-shirt beneath it—handed it to her and said, "Here, use this. It's not too sweaty, and hell's a warm place anyway, definitely T-shirt weather."

While Katherine dabbed at her face he asked, "How did we get here? How do we get back?"

She looked at him and frowned. "Are you sure it wasn't you who dragged us here?"

He threw up his hands in frustration. "How could I? I don't know any of this sorcery mumbo-jumbo."

She mirrored his frustration. "Well it can't have been the Tertius caste that came here with us. I told you, demons can't effect a crossing like that one way or another. It has to be done by a mortal or a Sidhe with power, and always after a rather drawn out ceremony that involves a lot of ritual. And it wasn't me. Even if I tried, I'm not that strong a sorceress."

"So that leaves me?"

She shook her head. "That doesn't add up either. You clearly don't know how, and probably aren't that strong."

She seemed satisfied that, with the aid of Paul's shirt and some carefully applied saliva, she'd cleaned her face reasonably well. She rolled the shirt up and put it on the pew next to her. Paul didn't have the heart to tell her that her makeup was smeared all over her face. A bright red smudge of lipstick radiated out from the right corner of her mouth. Mascara from her left eye had run down her cheek, and her right eye now appeared almost devoid of makeup. The contrast between her two eyes gave her an odd, clownish, evil-eye sort of look.

Paul needed to know more about demons, if for no other reason than that his ignorance might get them killed, though here in hell there apparently were some fates worse than death. "When I was out in front of the church here, facing that big, bad hoodoo with the snake legs, you said don't look in its eyes, and don't make any deals. What's with that?"

She frowned and looked at him oddly. "Snake legs! What snake legs?"

"The demon," Paul said. "The one with the chicken head and snake legs. The one in front of the church yesterday."

Her eyes narrowed, and he thought he saw distrust there. "I don't know what you're talking about."

"You saw the demon, right?"

She spoke carefully. "Yes . . . I did."

"And it had a chicken head and snake legs?"

She shook her head. "No, it looked like my father."

Paul tried to describe the monster he'd faced and she listened carefully, then said, "Apparently, it was showing us each a different glamour. I don't know a lot about demons, but I suppose that's possible."

"And why not look in its eyes? Why no deals?"

She considered his question for a moment as if she wasn't sure where to begin, then said, "Primus and Secundus caste demons are patient and calculating. They'd rather gain control over you than merely devour your soul, and there're many ways to do that. If your eyes meet theirs directly, and you haven't prepared the proper spells to protect yourself, they can enthrall you, and then you'll happily do anything they want. In the early stages, if you break eye contact you break the enthrallment. But if they have you captive in some way so they can repeatedly enthrall you over a long period of time, then eventually they can maintain the control, even without eye contact. That's what they usually prefer to do with a mortal wizard or witch. They then have a powerful slave that can bring them other souls to devour, a thrall. And if their thrall is adept at sorcery, and they're resident on the Mortal Plane, they can use it to bring minor demons over from the Netherworld as servants and slaves. I still don't understand why the Secundus out front broke eye-contact with you."

She waited for him to enlighten her in some way, but Paul didn't recall being enthralled. He remembered everything up to the moment he'd looked into the demon's eyes, and after its control had shattered he had a hazy memory of lying on top of Katherine on the steps of the church. But it was not until she'd made her witty remark about first dates that he'd truly returned to conscious thought. And then, embarrassed, he'd scrambled off her clumsily. He even remembered a little bit about the moment of the shattering, but the time during which he'd been enthralled was all a blank. He told her that now, and finished by saying, "But I have a fleeting memory it had something to do with a name."

She closed her eyes, grimaced and shook her head. "Oh, I hope you didn't give it your name."

"No," he said. "No, not my name. Its name. Something to do with the demon's name."

Her head shot up and her eyes opened expectantly. "Did you get its name?"

He closed his eyes and tried to recall the moment. "No. No, I didn't . . . Well . . . maybe something that starts with an A . . . Ah . . . something . . . I just don't remember."

She waved a hand impatiently. "I don't see how you could've gotten its name, not without a lot of negotiation, and certainly not while you're enthralled. And not without something to offer it in return, something a lot more valuable than your name."

"So names are important?"

"Oh, very much so! If it possesses even a portion of your name, it has some control over you, and the more of your name it has, the more control it has."

He suddenly thought they might've betrayed each other, and he tried to recall every word they'd spoken here in hell. "But certainly it heard me call you Katherine, and you call me Paul."

"No, no, no," she said. "It doesn't do it any good to just know your name. It gains no power over you unless you agree to give it all or part of your name. It has to be part of some sort of bargain."

"Why would I do that?"

"As I said, they're patient and calculating. If it has something you want bad enough, then you might negotiate some sort of agreement to get that something, and it'll always seek to bind you in some way, probably with a portion of your name. And they're tricky; their agreements are fraught with loopholes and pitfalls that play in their favor. By the way, that may be the only way we can get out of this mess. If my father can't reach us, we may have to cut a deal with that Secundus out there to get back to the Mortal Plane."

"So I have to learn demon contract law?" he asked. "Do they give courses at Berkeley? Probably only graduate level, right?"

She ignored his sarcasm. "Learn it, Conklin, or get caught in a fate worse than death."

Paul leaned forward, put his elbows on his knees and his face in his hands. He tried to avoid rubbing at the grit in his eyes. "I can't believe I'm believing this crap." He opened his eyes and scanned the inside of the roofless church. The reddish brown dirt caked everything, including him and Katherine, a reddish brown world with a dirty brown sky, illuminated by dim, unclean light. "I sometimes think I'm really lying in a coma in some hospital somewhere dreaming a really bad dream. Or maybe I'm in a straightjacket in some nuthouse hallucinating my brains out."

"I don't know what to tell you, Paul. I guess the best advice I can offer is that if it feels real, then go with it. If you're hallucinating it won't hurt to do so, but if it's real and you ignore the dangers, you might end up very dead, or worse."

That was the crux of the matter. In this strange new reality he'd stumbled upon, there were quite a number of fates worse than death. "So if we can get this demon to agree to give us some of its name, we can get some control over it?"

She ran her fingers through her frazzled hair and scratched at her scalp. The grit clearly irritated her as much as him. "Actually, no. With demon names it's both easier and harder than that. It's easier, because if you can learn its name in any way, you gain control. It doesn't have to be part of an agreement. But it's harder, because a demon's true name is a highly kept secret. Names are one way in which we're quite different from them."

Paul thought of snake-legs, and bat-thing, and had an urge to snarl angrily that there were many ways in which they were different. But he swallowed his sarcasm and asked the final question. "So how do we get the hell out of hell?"

She shrugged, looked him in the eyes and said, "For the time being we wait and hope my father can do something. And if he can't, then we'll have to cut some sort of deal with that Secundus out there."

••••

Colleen followed McGowan and the two leprechauns down into his workshop, and when she stepped through the door he closed and locked it, sealing them in. He carried a small cage containing a live chicken, Colleen carried a small paper bag McGowan had handed her, and they all wore floor-length, white, linen robes and thick slippers knitted from heavy cotton thread. Beneath the robes they each wore white cotton trousers held up by a belt of hemp rope, and a white cotton tunic with no buttons or opening in the front, forcing each of them to don it by pulling it over their head. Everything they wore had been woven from plant fibers of some sort, nothing made of metal or plastic, nothing artificial, and nothing made from animal tissue. McGowan had commissioned several such outfits long ago from a seamstress who was also a minor practitioner of the arcane, though for the leprechauns he'd simply cut two robes short with a pair of scissors.

Earlier that morning each of them had personally hand-washed their own outfit using crude, unscented soap, then hung them to dry through the afternoon. In the early afternoon they'd rested and slept, then in late afternoon bathed with unscented soap, and were careful afterward to apply no perfumes, oils, deodorants or after-shave, nothing that might contaminate the cleansing of their bodies and clothing. In the early evening a priest, a friend of McGowan's and also a practitioner, came by and blessed the two humans, and anointed them with holy water. The leprechauns, having no souls, remained hidden while the priest was present. Then they'd spent the next several hours meditating and clearing their thoughts.

Colleen had dropped her shadows, and looked upon the coming ritual with some trepidation. "I'm frightened, old man. I don't like the black arts, and I must confess I've never participated in a major summons before. I'm not terribly knowledgeable in sorcery."

"Never?" he asked dubiously.

"No. I've avoided it. I've banished a few demons, but never summoned one."

Jim'Jiminie said, "It's going to be fun."

Boo'Diddle added, "Exactly."

McGowan strode across his workshop, put the chicken cage onto a workbench and turned to a tall storage cabinet. "As a rule I don't like trafficking in demons either. But circumstances occasionally force my hand. All you need to do in this is guard my back, actually my soul. I'll walk you through it."

McGowan lifted a small copper dish out of the storage cabinet. He also retrieved a knife and four wax candles, each about six inches long, and a large, flat cardboard box. He opened the box, and from it he pulled a mirror about three by two feet mounted in an ornate wooden frame. He handed the mirror to Colleen and she noticed it did a poor job of reflecting her image. "That's a dark mirror," he said. "Essentially a piece of glass painted black on the back side. We're going to use it to look into the darkness of the Netherworld."

McGowan placed the four candles at four of the five points of the silver pentagram embedded in the floor, saying, "The point without a candle is the principal point of the pentagram, where I'll be seated controlling the entire summons. When I light the candles I'll do so with my power, not matches or any other physical means. And I myself will be the fifth candle, completing the symmetry of the pentagram, and defining the principal point with my power."

McGowan then cut a few strands of his own hair and placed them in the copper dish. Colleen handed him the sack, and from it he withdrew two hairbrushes. That morning they'd returned to Paul's apartment and stolen a hairbrush, then they'd stopped at Katherine's home and stolen one of hers. He plucked a few hairs from each brush and dropped them into the copper dish, then placed the copper dish and the dark mirror in the center of the circle, arranging them so that when he sat down at the principal point of the pentagram, he could see his own faint reflection in the mirror, with the copper dish resting just in front of it. He sat down in front of the copper dish, lifted the knife in his left hand and cut into the flesh of his right hand. It was a shallow cut and he had to squeeze it to get the blood to drip into the dish. "The knife is made of cold iron" he said, "not steel. It's rather soft and doesn't hold an edge well, but it does the job."

Colleen watched closely and counted thirteen drops of blood, after which the old man used his left index finger to draw a small rune over the cut in his palm. After sketching it seven times it began to glow and the cut closed. He stood, crossed the room to the workbench and retrieved the chicken from its cage, then returned to the center of the hammered, silver circle. He knelt, held the squawking chicken by its throat in his left hand, and with the knife in his right he passed it over the chicken thirteen times, all the while whispering something arcane. Colleen felt the old man's power begin to coalesce as the chicken slowly ceased screeching and calmed, appearing to drift into a still slumber. Then he placed the chicken on the floor in front of the copper bowl and cut its throat, severing its head completely. Bright red blood spurted from the severed neck for several seconds, and when it ceased McGowan laid the chicken's body in the puddle of blood on the floor.

Colleen followed his gaze as he glanced at a clock on the wall: ten minutes before midnight. The clock was set to rotational time. It would hit the stroke of midnight only when the earth's rotation placed the sun exactly opposite their position on the planet's surface.

McGowan went to one of the four candles, paused before it, passed his hand over it seven times, again muttering something arcane, then lit the candle with a small fire spell. He repeated the procedure at each of the other three candles, taking care not to step inside the pentagram. Then he sat down on the floor at the principal point of the pentagram, facing the dark mirror. He instructed the leprechauns to sit to one side and Colleen to sit down behind him, adding, "If I appear to become unresponsive, or start acting strange in any way, banish the demon immediately, but don't open the circle. After that, if I don't return to normal, kill me."

He handed her the iron knife. "With cold iron, in my heart."

••••

"Dragon-stink," the demon called, "come out and talk. And bring your little witch."

Paul and Katherine cringed, hiding behind the half-crumbled wall of the church. They sat on the floor with their backs against the wall. "Why does it call you Dragon-stink?" she asked.

"I don't know," Paul said. He looked suspiciously at Katherine. "You're not going to tell me dragons are real too, are you?"

She hesitated for a moment, and inwardly Paul cringed. She grimaced as she said, "Not . . . exactly."

"What does *not exactly* mean?"

Katherine got her feet beneath her, rose in a crouch and peeked over the edge of the wall. "He's wearing the image of my father again."

Paul rose up beside her and looked over the wall, and for him the demon looked nothing like McGowan. "For me he's wearing that chicken-headed snake-legged image again. I hate that."

"Come on out, Dragon-stink. I have all eternity to wait for you."

Paul took hold of Katherine's arm, pulled her down and forced her to sit beside him. "Tell me about god damn dragons."

She shook her head and said, "There aren't any dragons."

"You don't sound too convinced, or too convincing."

"They don't really exist," she said, grimacing. "They're myths. That's all."

She finally looked at him directly. "There're Three Realms: the Netherworld, the Mortal Plane, and Faerie, sometimes referred to as the *three lives*."

"Faerie?" he asked. "You mentioned that once before. You mean like elves and goblins and leprechauns and all that kind of stuff?"

She shrugged. "You've already met a couple of leprechauns. They're drawn to you for some reason. But never trust them. They're tricky little people. And above all, never harm a leprechaun. To kill a leprechaun, in anything other than self-defense, is to bring a hundred years of bad luck. They're kind of like the Swiss; they try to stay neutral as much as possible. Even a murderous demon will hesitate before killing a leprechaun. It still bothers me those two are giving up their neutrality to be involved in this."

"Listen, I've seen a couple of midgets in clown suits. Why should I believe they're leprechauns?"

She shook her head and closed her eyes. "Don't be stubborn. It's either a strait-jacket in an asylum, or . . ." She opened her eyes and waved a hand casually at the dirty brown sky.

"You do have a point there."

She continued. "The little people are part of the non-aligned fey. They bear no hereditary allegiance to either of the ruling courts, Seelie and Unseelie, Summer and

Winter. Leprechauns, sprites, the black fey, pixies, they're all non-aligned, though one might choose to swear allegiance to Ag or Magreth for its own purposes."

"Ag or Magreth?"

Paul's head was spinning and she smiled rather sympathetically. "King of the Winter Court, and Queen of the Summer. It's a lot to take in, huh?"

"Ya . . . a lot."

"You mentioned goblins," she continued. "They're non-aligned. But pray to god you don't ever meet a goblin. As to elves, don't ever let a Sidhe Warrior hear you call him an elf. He'll probably gut you on the spot. The Sidhe rule Faerie, and it's quite rare to see one, rarer even to actually meet one. Most of us, even practitioners, live our entire lives without ever doing so. I personally have never seen one, at least not that I know of. But if you ever do meet one, remember you can't trust them. They won't lie to you, but they'll help you fool yourself."

"Dragons," he said. He was rather proud of the fact he managed to keep all sarcasm out of his voice. "We were talking about dragons, McGowan."

Apparently he let some scorn slip out because her eyes flashed angrily at him. "The Dragon Realm is the mythical fourth realm. Legend has it the Dragon Realm is the source of all magic, that Dragons are powerful beyond imagining, and without Dragons there is no magic. But it's purely mythical. No one's ever seen a Dragon, or spoken to a Dragon. No one's ever been to the Dragon Realm, and Dragons have never visited the other Realms. They're no more real than . . ."

"Dragon-stink, I'm waiting."

"No more real than snake-legged, chicken-headed demons?" he asked, and this time he made no effort to hide the sarcasm.

She took a deep breath and let out a long sigh. "We have to go out and talk with it, probably cut some sort of deal. We can't put it off any longer."

Paul stood and helped Katherine to her feet. Even though her skirt was torn and ripped, it was still too tight for her to move freely.

"Let's get this over with," he said.

11

To Hell and Back

MCGOWAN FED POWER into the circle and the pentagram, and as Colleen watched the old man's arcane strength accumulate she cringed inwardly like a child standing before an intense blaze that threatened to singe her hair. His power began to manifest in little motes swirling up and down his arms, and the hair on his head tufted and twirled in a breeze that didn't exist. Then she felt the old man complete the circle and close it, like a heavy plank door slamming shut. He then cast a fire spell to ignite a small flame in the palm of his hand so magical fire now burned at all five points of the pentagram. She watched him focus on the dark mirror, focus on his own faint but visible reflection there. "Darkness rules the night," he said, his voice a hoarse whisper. "Bring forth the night. Bring forth the darkness, and its minions."

He repeated that thirteen times, and with each repetition the mirror appeared to become more of a mirror, his reflection more visible and defined. After the thirteenth repetition the mirror reflected his image clearly, like a platter of quicksilver. But his image quickly began to distort, to twist and spiral away from his regular features. It coiled into an unrecognizable swirl, then suddenly stopped. It remained still and undefined for several seconds, then began swirling again in the opposite direction, and as it did so it took on form and recognizable substance. When the moment came, when the image reformed fully, she could sense the opening into the Netherworld, a painful scar on the Mortal Plane.

The image in the mirror was that of Katherine, a tiny replica of Katherine that fit nicely in the small mirror. The Katherine image stepped out of the mirror to stand in front of it, standing only about two feet tall. But then she began to expand and grow, and in a wink she stood her full height, though the Katherine standing in the middle of the pentagram had a massive chest with quivering breasts, an abundance of cleavage erupting from her blouse, a full, rounded figure, luscious hips with curves any exotic dancer would envy, and swollen red lips puckered into a pout. In every other way though, it was Katherine, in one of her expensive business suits, though the skirt was practically a micro-mini. "Hello, Old Wizard," she said in a deep rumbling voice that sent a shiver up Colleen's spine.

McGowan remained silent for a moment, then asked, "Do I know you?"

The demon ran its hands over its breasts, down its belly, stopped at its crotch and fingered itself offensively through the fabric of its skirt. "Am I not your daughter?"

McGowan shook his head. "You look nothing like my daughter."

The demon Katherine spread its hands, looked down at her chest. She pressed her hands up under her breasts, squeezing copious amounts of cleavage up from the blouse. "You don't like this, mortal. Well then, let's fix that." Her breasts slowly shrank to the proper size, her figure and lips thinned and the skirt lengthened until she truly did look like Katherine.

Colleen knew the demon couldn't read their minds, not while they remained outside the circle and it within. But somehow it knew Katherine's image and her relationship to the old man.

As if it could read her thoughts, the demon said, "I own your daughter's soul, wizard, and that of her lover. If you want them back, you'll have to pay dearly."

••••

Paul and Katherine limped carefully down the steps in front of the church, stopped well short of the sidewalk where the demon stood. Paul had agreed to let Katherine do all the talking since he was wholly out of his element. And he now knew not to meet the demon's eyes, so he focused on its beak when it spoke.

"Your father wants you back, little witch. But he told me I can keep Dragon-stink here." It nodded toward Paul.

Katherine hissed at Paul, "Don't believe anything it says. They're masters at lying. They'll put a tiny bit of truth into the lie to make you doubt everything."

Unfortunately, Paul's only experience with McGowan was that the older man had always been present with a bunch of Russian thugs and a demon that kept trying to kill him. It was all too possible the old man didn't give a damn about him, and might gladly sacrifice Paul to get his daughter back. But now was not the time to reveal his doubts to Katherine.

Katherine said, "My father would never give up a human soul to such as you."

The demon's laugh came out almost as a growl. "And what do you know of *such as me*, little witch?" The demon leaned close, its beak stopping right at the edge of the sidewalk. "You mortals are consumed by your needs and cravings. I merely offer you what you want, and strike a fair bargain in the process." It turned its attention to Paul, but still spoke to Katherine. "I should offer your companion his desire."

Katherine asked, "And what's that?"

The demon emitted a deep rumble in its throat and the chicken beak grinned. "He lusts after you with unbridled desire, can barely keep that cock of his in his pants."

Katherine looked at Paul, threw a hip in his direction. "Really," she said smiling, looking him up and down, stopping with her gaze on his crotch.

"That's not true," Paul said. "It's lying, making it all up."

She frowned and said, "Ah darn, I'm disappointed." She turned back to the demon. "I guess you are lying, demon." Then she looked back at Paul and winked. "Though hopefully it's not a complete lie."

Paul shook his head, looked at the demon and it happened again: *blink*. Katherine said something to the demon, but the momentary flash of vision had distracted Paul. It was the same sensation he'd had when they'd first encountered it wearing the image of McGowan. He'd seen something of its true nature then, and he suspected he might've seen even more of its nature when it enthralled him.

Blink. Something about the demon's name came back to him. He could remember none of it, but he thought a bluff might not hurt, so he said, "I know your name, demon."

The demon opened its beak and emitted a deep growl, and the ground beneath their feet shook as if in tempo to its grumbling. Clearly, it had some reason to believe Paul might have learned its name. "If you know my name then let it cross your lips."

Katherine must've understood he was bluffing and spoke quickly to help. "The name of a Secundus caste demon is not to be used lightly."

The demon threw its chicken-head back and roared with laughter. "Oh little witch, you know nothing." It leaned toward her, stopping just short of the boundary between sidewalk and church steps. Katherine staggered back a step as it said, "I'll take great pleasure in haunting your soul. You'll be mine for eternity, little witch. Mine."

Katherine's eyes widened and she looked at Paul. "I think I was wrong. I think this thing might be Primus caste."

Again the demon roared, and its image shifted rapidly from that of McGowan to Katherine to Paul. It ended with the snake-legged monster.

Paul said, "Even more reason to hold your name in trust."

The demon's serpent legs writhed and it turned its eyes on Katherine. "Your friend is a fool. He longs for a past that cannot again be."

The demon's image blurred, shifted, swirled and twisted, then coalesced into the form of Cloe, a perfect little Cloe without distortion or alteration. She had on her school uniform, her blond hair tied into two little pigtails on either side of her head. "Daddy," she said. "Where have you been? I've missed you."

He could hear the betrayal in her words. Somehow he'd failed to bring her back, failed to be there for her, failed at everything.

Cloe's image blurred and swirled, and a moment later Suzanna stood there, the real Suzanna wearing a light, cotton summer dress with a full sweeping skirt. He remembered that dress. She'd worn it the last time he'd seen her. "Paulie-boy," she said longingly. "I've missed you so much."

Paul felt tears running down his cheeks, tasted the saltiness of his own sorrow as one touched the corner of his mouth. His Suzanna had a small nose in a long, elegant face, eyes with a slight slant as if she had a tiny bit of Asian ancestry far in her past. He missed those eyes, and he looked into them now—

••••

Paul opened his eyes, laid there for a moment in the dark listening to Suzanna's slow, steady intake and outflow of breath. He rolled over in bed to face her.

It was the middle of a warm night, and they'd both kicked off the covers. She was lying on her side with her back to him. He had the strongest urge to wrap his arms around her, to hold her tightly as if he might never do so again. But he didn't want to wake her so he just traced the curve of her hip with his hand, making certain it was properly and indelibly committed to memory. He watched the slow, steady rise and fall of her shoulders as she took one breath, and then another, and he tried to commit that to memory as well. Lying with her back to him he couldn't see her face, but he knew that while sleeping she frequently scrunched it up into a little pout, and that too he tried to commit to memory.

He slipped out of bed quietly, wearing nothing but his boxer shorts, and crossed the room on tiptoe. He walked down the hall to Cloe's room, found her sleeping soundly and had the same urge to wrap her in his arms. But he didn't want to wake her either so he just stood there looking down on her for a few moments, and was content with that. In sleep, she pouted just like her mother, and he knew he must remember this, all of it, for eternity.

Out in the hall he met the tall black fellow with the coal black skin. The man wore an expensive dark suit that defined elegance. "Walk with me for a bit," the man said.

It never occurred to Paul to do otherwise. The man turned aside, and Paul, now fully dressed in a dark suit much like his companion's, accompanied the fellow down a pleasant path through a quiet garden. It was almost a jungle, dense, entwined foliage that choked the sunlight until nothing remained but shadow. They walked along a path of crushed, white stone, and they always seemed to be walking toward an impenetrable wall of vegetation just a few steps away. But as they approached it parted before them like the Red Sea parting before Moses. It wasn't as if the leaves and vines moved aside, but more as if, within a certain distance from Dayandalous, they just didn't exist.

"This is the first real test, Paul," Dayandalous said.

Paul asked, "I know. But how do I pass it?"

Dayandalous stopped, turned and looked at Paul carefully. "You must remember. I can only help you so much, and the rest is up to you."

"Remember?" Paul asked. "Sometimes I think I can remember it all, and sometimes nothing."

"But what comes first to mind, Paul?"

Paul looked into the man's eyes. They glowed red through vertical slits. "Katherine says I shouldn't look into a demon's eyes. And you told me that too. But you also told me I could look through its eyes."

Dayandalous smiled. "Exactly."

Paul frowned, "But I don't know how to do that."

Dayandalous shook his head patiently and spoke like a kindly teacher prompting a favorite pupil. "But you do, Paul. Look into your heart, look with the love you bear your wife and child, and you'll find it easy to defeat such evil. Look through the demon eye, child. Look through the demon eye."

••••

Looking out through two sets of eyes from two different perspectives, Paul had to fight a wave of vertigo. He was standing on the steps of the church next to Katherine looking at the hoodoo, and at the same time standing on the sidewalk in front of them, looking thorough the demon's eyes at him and Katherine, looking through a red haze of hatred and desire. "I have you now, mortal," the demon rumbled into his thoughts.

In that instant Paul felt a strange urge, a compulsion to go somewhere as if being called from a great distance. It was as if he stood in a slowly flowing river with the current tugging relentlessly at him. It had direction and force, and the more he resisted the more it pulled him toward some unknown destination. On the steps of the church Katherine reached over, tugged on his arm and whispered, "I think I sense my father's summons."

The compulsion grew to such an intensity it became a need he could not resist, or perhaps a need the demon could not resist. Reality shifted along a sideways track, a slippery, unclean pathway and *blink*, Paul was now in a third place as well as the other two. He stood in the middle of a silver circle inlaid in a marble floor, with the circle surrounded by a silver pentagram also inlaid in the floor. Enormous breasts weighed down his shoulders uncomfortably. He looked down at his own chest, at the wealth of quivering cleavage exposed there. He ran his hands over his breasts, down his belly, stopped at his crotch and was surprised to find that, beneath the material of his skirt, he was no longer a man, but now possessed the genitalia of a woman. Confused, he explored the strangeness of it for a moment, then looked up and saw McGowan seated on the floor in front of him, and the older hippie woman seated behind him. McGowan sat at one point of the pentagram with the hippie woman leaning forward and whispering something in his ear. They both wore white gowns of some sort, and McGowan held fire cupped in the palms of his hands.

To one side sat the two leprechauns, dressed just like the humans. Both of them smiled and beamed at Paul, one of them winked at him comically, and the other flashed him a thumbs up. Then they high-fived each other.

Paul's mouth opened through no volition of his own and he said in Katherine's voice, "Am I not your daughter?"

••••

Both leprechauns shouted in unison, "It's lying."

The demon glanced their way unhappily and its eyes flashed an angry red. Then it turned back to McGowan and changed its image to that of young Conklin. "The two lovers are with me at this very moment. I think I'll have the young man fuck her while I watch. I'll make him fuck her in every hole she's got. She has lots of holes to fuck. Then I'll fuck them all myself." To emphasize its point, the demon's image of Paul suddenly grew a large bulge in its pants. The bulge grew steadily until the front of its pants ripped open and a massive phallus tumbled out.

The leprechauns shouted, "You're disgusting."

Behind McGowan Colleen whispered. "It's just trying to goad you. Don't let it get to you."

McGowan was surprised he could keep his voice calm and even. "I don't believe you own their souls. You'll have to prove that to me."

The demon suddenly took on the image of McGowan, seated in one of his wingback chairs in his study, a glass of cognac on a small side table near at hand. It spoke in McGowan's voice. "Do not these images tell you the truth of my words, wizard? Could I have such knowledge of you and her and the young man if she wasn't already my thrall?"

McGowan had learned long ago one didn't enter into a debate with a demon. It would be a horrible mistake to allow it to set the agenda, to allow it to pick each point they might argue, and the order in which they argued them. "Yes," he said. "You could have such knowledge without her enthrallment. So prove she's enthralled."

The demon smiled with McGowan's lips, but its eyes still contained goat-slitted blood-red pupils. "As I said, they're with me now, as we speak. Ask them a question through me. Ask me any—"

The demon, in McGowan's form, suddenly closed its eyes and grimaced. It lifted its hands and cupped them over its ears as if trying to block out some noise, and it shouted, "Nooooooo! You are mine to command, mortal. You are mine. Mine! Mine! Mine!"

••••

Katherine watched the demon shift its image to that of a young child she didn't recognize. It said, "Daddy. Where have you been? I've missed you."

Paul's mouth opened stupidly, then the demon's image changed to that of a pretty young woman. "Paulie-boy," it said longingly, "I've missed you so much."

Paul cringed, and tears flowed freely down his cheeks. Clearly the child had been his daughter and this young woman probably his wife, for he looked upon her now with such longing and pain. And then he looked up, looked into the demon's eyes.

Katherine cried out, "No," and lunged for Paul. But she was too late. She stepped away from him as the look on his face turned to that of blank wonder.

But suddenly the demon, still wearing the shape of the young woman, grimaced, cupped its hands to its ears and shouted, "Nooooooo! You are mine to command, mortal. You are mine. Mine! Mine! Mine!"

Katherine looked at Paul, then at the demon, and Paul looked back at her with eyes that had turned hard and angry. Fully enthralled, he'd do anything the demon commanded, including dragging her with him off the church steps, off the protection of hallowed ground. Then he closed his eyes and stood very still for a moment, as if listening to a faraway voice. She took another step back, and then Paul opened his blood-red goat-slitted eyes and lunged for her.

••••

Standing on the steps of the church, standing on the sidewalk in front of it, standing in some dark room with McGowan and the hippie woman and the leprechauns, the images Paul saw from all three perspectives collided, clashed, formed a confusing collage of overlapping scenes. He tried desperately to sort them out, failed miserably and couldn't distinguish one image from the other.

"Obey me," the demon snarled into his thoughts.

He thought back at it, "Fuck you, asshole."

At that moment the two demons, the one standing on the sidewalk in front of the church, and that standing in the dark room with McGowan, both closed their eyes, cupped their hands over their ears and started shouting at him. Its words rang in his thoughts as if he was standing in the bell tower of a giant cathedral next to a massive bell.

With two sets of eyes closed, the Paul standing on the steps of the church looked at Katherine. She stepped away from him fearfully. As the demon's shouts continued to hammer into his skull, he closed his own eyes, and with the confusing kaleidoscope of images now shuttered, he could see his connection to the demon on the sidewalk, and its connection to the demon in the dark room with McGowan. And then he saw how to create a path directly between where he and Katherine stood on the church's steps, and the demon in the dark room, and from there he saw the path to the dark room itself, without the aid of the demon. It was that slippery sideways track in reality he'd sensed earlier.

He opened his eyes and saw a terrified Katherine cringing away from him on the church steps. He lunged for her and wrapped his arms around her as she screamed, "Nooooooo."

He closed his eyes.

Blink.

••••

The demon in the protective circle had gone mad. It thrashed about wildly, its image shifting crazily from Katherine to Paul to McGowan to a frightening chimera with serpent legs. It pounded on the shimmering veil of the protective circle. One instant it was McGowan doing the pounding, then Katherine, then Paul. Then suddenly it stopped, stood as still as a statue for just a moment. Then it screamed in Katherine's voice, "Nooooooo."

The room rang with an explosion that sounded like a massive cork the size of a freight train popping out of a Champaign bottle the size of a skyscraper. McGowan's ears popped, and behind him Colleen grunted painfully. The two leprechauns jumped to their feet and cheered like fans at a baseball game as young Conklin and Katherine appeared in midair in the circle about six feet above the floor. They were horizontal, in a lover's embrace, young Conklin's eyes squeezed tightly shut, Katherine's face twisted in terror as she screamed the single word "Nooooooo." It seemed as if they hovered in the air for a moment, but McGowan understood that in reality his own sense of time had frozen in an instant of utter surprise. And then the instant ended and the two young people plunged to the floor.

Young Conklin landed on his back, his head smacking into the marble floor. Katherine landed on top of him, their faces smashed together painfully, and blood sprayed from her nose. She groaned and laid there on top of him, the wild tangle of her hair cascading over both their faces. Then she rolled off him, groaned again and lifted a hand to her face.

"Quickly, Walter," Colleen shouted. "They're hurt. Break the circle."

"Wait," he growled, still holding the fire of magic in his palms. He saw no sign of the demon, but he dare not weaken the circle until he could be certain the monster had returned to the Netherworld. And yes, there in the dark mirror he saw his own reflection, his mortal image with blood-red goat-slitted eyes.

"The darkness no longer rules here, minion," he said, speaking the ancient formula. "Return to the darkness, now. I command it."

The demon's image disappeared and the mirror went dark. Satisfied, McGowan killed the flame in the palm of his hand, simultaneously extinguishing the flames in the four candles, and the shimmering veil of the circle vanished.

Colleen rushed past him to Katherine, while the leprechauns danced a jig as if it was all some big party. McGowan strode purposefully to young Conklin, who lay unmoving on his back. Katherine mumbled weakly, something about ". . . enthralled . . . demon eyes . . ." while Colleen said, "It's all right, child. You're back. You're safe now."

McGowan squatted down next to young Conklin and looked at him carefully, trying to see something more than just an ordinary young wizard. Yes, the fellow was a practitioner of the arcane, which, to one such as McGowan, was neither extraordinary nor unusual. And yet the old man didn't know what he'd just witnessed.

Colleen helped Katherine to her feet, helped her limp to the door and open it, but she paused and turned back to McGowan. "What just happened, old man?"

McGowan shook his head. "I don't know. But whatever it was . . . it reverberated throughout the Three Realms."

••••

"What just happened?" Magreth shouted as she marched into the room where her advisors and mages had gathered, her eyes lit with incandescent fire, the shadows of ancient Sidhe spirits darting about her in a display of maddened chaos.

Cadilus stepped forward. "We know very little, Your Majesty. We've been monitoring the Old Wizard's abode, so we know it took place there, but even our most powerful mages cannot penetrate his wards."

All of her advisors, including Cadilus, cringed as she strode across the room, stood with her back to them and stared out a window at the horizon of Faerie. "The old man cannot throw such powerful magics around without being held accountable."

Cadilus approached and stopped only a short pace behind her. "I think even he would agree with you on that, Your Majesty. I recommend we send a diplomatic mission, and politely demand an explanation."

"Yes," she said, turning to face him. He watched her struggle to calm herself. "He's always proven to be . . . reasonable."

For the first time she looked into his eyes. She frowned, leaned forward and whispered, "You know something."

He whispered back. "I don't know, but I suspect. There was a powerful summoning. I fear one of the Nine Princes tried to cross over to the Mortal Plane."

Now he had her full attention. "That hasn't happened for almost two thousand years."

He nodded. "Yes, and when it did those conquering Romans fell, were swept aside by an age of darkness that corrupted both Faerie and the Mortal Plane for five-hundred years. But I think the Old Wizard banished the demon in a most spectacular fashion."

Magreth leaned away from Cadilus and spoke in an offhand manner, as if thinking out loud. "That would mean the old man is even more powerful than we suspected."

••••

Ag shouted and screamed as he beat and kicked Anogh mercilessly. "You were there," Ag screamed. "How can you plead ignorance?"

Anogh lay on the floor and did not resist. To so much as curl up into a fetal position would be considered an act of defiance. Even when Ag stomped on his hand, crushing several bones, even then Anogh merely laid still and absorbed the pain. Simuth stood to one side, watching Ag's cruelty with a smile on his face, a look of envy Anogh recognized all too well, though Anogh could never be sure if Simuth envied Ag's place delivering the beating, or Anogh's place receiving it.

Oddly enough, Anogh was grateful for the beating. As long as Ag's temper ruled him, he'd ask the wrong questions, or ask no questions at all. Anogh could not lie to the ruler of the Unseelie Court, not outright. He could at best evade and dissemble, and while Ag could be a fool in so many ways, he was quite adept at unraveling the deceits of his courtiers. If he asked the right questions he might gain a hint of Anogh's subterfuge, and given even the tiniest of intimations, he'd gnaw at it like a dog worrying a bone, and eventually uncover the truth of the matter, a truth Anogh had only recently discovered, and one Ag must never know. At least not until certain preparations had been set in place.

Eventually Ag wound down, more through his own exhaustion than any sense of compassion. Compassion was not a word known in the Unseelie Court. Ag stepped away from Anogh and sat casually on his throne. "If the Old Wizard is that powerful," he said, still breathing heavily, "then perhaps we should see to his death."

Simuth stepped forward haughtily. "I would be most honored, Your Majesty, to accept such a commission."

Anogh shook his head and sat up, but couldn't stand. He was careful not to put any weight on the crushed fingers of his left hand. "May I speak, Your Majesty?"

Ag negligently gave him permission with an impatient wave of his hand.

"The Old Wizard will not be an easy target, especially if, as we now believe, he's even more powerful than we'd thought."

"You do have a point," Ag said petulantly.

"Have faith in me, Your Majesty," Simuth pleaded. "I'll lay the old man's head at your feet."

Anogh added, "And succeed or fail, to merely make the attempt will mean open war with all mortal practitioners."

"You're right," Ag snarled, though he clearly didn't like the taste of the truth. He turned to Simuth. "That was a stupid idea, you idiot."

No one bothered to correct the king, to point out that the idea had been his.

••••

Baalthelmass had sensed the Lord's return to the Mortal Plane, and Its hunger blossomed ten-fold. It had also sensed the momentary emergence of the Primus caste, and was pleased it had been banished. As Secundus caste, Baalthelmass did not want to live in the shadow of some cruel master. It wanted the role of cruel master for Itself.

That foolish Tertius had gotten itself banished back to the Netherworld, though even Baalthelmass did not understand how. However, the Tertius could still be useful, perhaps even worth the cost of summoning it back.

With no more than a thought It summoned the thrall Belinda, and in a matter of seconds the door opened and she stepped into Its study. As always she knelt before It and bowed her head, then waited for Baalthelmass to speak.

It looked at her carefully. She was a truly beautiful and desirable creature, at least in the eyes of mortals, a woman capable of arousing the most carnal needs in even a man of the cloth. But such physical desires were meaningless to Baalthelmass; the erotic needs of mortal flesh meant nothing to It, held no sway over Its desires.

"Belinda, my dear," It said, "I have a task for you. You must bring back that foolish and troublesome Tertius. And then I think I'll have you play a more direct role in this young Lord's seduction."

12

Elves?

MCGOWAN HELPED A badly dazed Paul up to one of the spare bedrooms, helped him out of his clothes and into bed, then spelled him into a deep sleep. He called a doctor, a friend and an arcane practitioner who understood the need for discretion.

The doctor prodded and poked, peeled back eyelids and did other doctor things. "He was conscious when you brought him up here?"

"Pretty groggy," McGowan said, "badly dazed. Nasty smack on the head when he hit the floor."

"Remove the sleep spell, please."

McGowan extinguished the spell and Paul responded immediately. "Wassa happens . . ." He tried to lift his head, blinked his eyes.

The doctor pressed Paul's shoulders back down to the bed. "I'm a doctor. You've had a bump on the head and I'm examining you, so hold still."

That calmed Paul a little. The doctor did more prodding and poking while asking Paul a continuous stream of questions. Paul answered each in a reasonably coherent fashion, though between answers he kept mumbling about snake-legged demons.

The doctor looked at McGowan. "It would be helpful if he slept now."

McGowan renewed the sleep spell and Paul lay back peacefully.

The doctor stitched up a few cuts and bandaged them while commenting, "Nasty concussion, though not life threatening. But it wouldn't hurt to have Colleen do some healing on that. She's better at that than me.

"Couple of nasty cuts, some serious bruising, but no broken bones. Fellow took quite a beating."

When the doctor finished McGowan escorted him to the front door, thanked him, then returned to the bedroom where Paul slept peacefully. From the small wastebasket near the bed he retrieved a bloody bandage and examined it carefully. With threads containing Paul's blood he could locate Paul almost anywhere, at least while the blood remained fresh; a spell like that could remain viable for three or four days.

And Katherine's bloody nose had dripped all over the floor of his workshop. He had the means at hand to keep a close eye on both of them. With that thought, he turned and headed for his workshop.

••••

McGowan was standing before the fireplace in his study when the knock on the door interrupted his thoughts. He'd been contemplating the flames in the hearth, trying to see in them some insight into young Conklin. He didn't turn from the flames as he said, "Come in, Sarah," knowing with his wizard's senses it was the woman he employed as an assistant, a witch of medium strength who would not look askance at his unusual lifestyle.

"There's a man at the front door, Mr. McGowan. He wishes to see you, and he offered his card."

McGowan turned toward Sarah. She was an attractive, older woman, though there'd never been anything between them but shared loyalty and mutual friendship. And trust; he trusted her implicitly. They met in the middle of the room, she held out the visitor's card, and said, "And he's clearly a Sidhe mage, Seelie Court, I'd say, and powerful."

McGowan took the card, knowing that since it was meant for him it would be blank to her eyes. For him it bore one, single word: *Cadilus*.

She added, "I didn't give him permission to cross your threshold."

Sarah was not strong in arcane powers, but McGowan had attuned the wards of his house to her so she could activate them even if he was absent. Even one so powerful as Cadilus wouldn't attempt to breach such defenses. "Please tell Colleen Cadilus has come, and ask her to wait for us here in my study. I'll see to this personally."

Sarah smiled and said, "I thought you might," then turned and left the room.

McGowan followed her out into the hall. She turned toward her office at the back of the house and he turned toward the front door. When he opened it, he found Cadilus waiting there casually, a sardonic half-smile on his face.

"Old Wizard," the Sidhe mage said politely. In front of mortals he always affected the appearance of a British diplomat: expensive, conservatively cut, dark, pinstripe suit, white shirt, dark tie. And though he hadn't opted for the Bowler hat, he did carry a silver-tipped walking stick. His dark hair had just the right hint of gray at the temples, and he spoke with a refined accent. The pointed ears were hidden by a glamour, but McGowan knew the aristocratic nose, cheeks and jaw line were as close to the reality of Cadilus as any mortal would ever see.

McGowan chose his words carefully. "Lord Cadilus, I'm honored. I'd invite you in . . ." he said, taking great care to insure there was no invitation in his words until the proper protections had been agreed to, ". . . but I must have your parole before doing so."

Cadilus smiled, though the smile contained no mirth or joy. "We've been friends for so long, Old Wizard, you know I have only your best interests at heart. You can rest assured I'll bring no harm to you."

McGowan shook his head sadly. "Your parole. Now. Plainly spoken, with none of the dissembling typical of Sidhe promises, or there'll be no conversation between us today."

Cadilus shrugged and sighed. "While I am your guest, I'll take no action against you, your family, friends, guests, acquaintances, colleagues or enemies. I'll leave nothing behind, not a hair, a fiber, a whim or a wish, nothing magical, nether, or mundane. I ask of you only audience. You have my parole, and that of my queen. But only while I'm your guest."

McGowan stepped to one side and gestured down the hallway. "Well then, old friend. Please join me in my study." He looked at Cadilus and smiled warmly. "I have some of that cognac you like so much."

Colleen was waiting for them in his study, but it was a different Colleen who stood before the fireplace looking into the flames as McGowan had looked earlier. She was turned away from them, and did not turn to face them as they entered. Her hair had been carefully arrayed atop her head, and she wore a dark-green gown of rich brocade. Embroidered into it were Druidic symbols that shifted with the shadows cast by the dancing flames of the fire. Like any woman she could take hours to prepare for such a meeting, and yet she'd managed to change her appearance to that of an elegant courtier in a matter of seconds. And McGowan knew full well it was no illusion or glamour.

Cadilus stopped in the middle of the room and hesitated. Only Colleen could do that to an immortal Sidhe mage. He spoke tentatively, "Lady Armaugh!"

She didn't react in any way for several seconds, then turned slowly to face him. "Lord Cadilus," she said coldly, like the noblest of queens addressing a common peasant. Somehow, in all her court elegance, she still projected a hint of the savagery of her Celtic ancestors.

Cadilus stepped forward with care, and dropped to one knee in front of her. She held out her hand and he kissed it gently, then he stood, and still holding her hand he said, "It's been some time since I've had the pleasure of your company, Your Ladyship."

Without moving a muscle her eyes glanced down disapprovingly at the hand he still held. He released it, and she said, "But you're not here for the pleasure of my company."

McGowan turned to the bar and poured three glasses of cognac. Colleen had known exactly how to put Cadilus off balance, or at least as off balance as an immortal

Sidhe mage could be. McGowan had long suspected she and Cadilus had once been lovers. It also appeared Cadilus had done something to poison the relationship, and still regretted his mistake.

McGowan handed them each a glass, got them seated in two high-back chairs, though he remained standing. Cadilus took a sip of the cognac and looked at McGowan. "It is excellent cognac, Old Wizard."

Colleen said, "Nor are you here to discuss the quality of the old man's cognac."

Cadilus nodded his acquiescence almost imperceptibly, then spoke slowly. "My queen wishes me to inquire after some arcane incidents that recently manifested on the Mortal Plane." He paused and looked carefully at Colleen, then at McGowan. "Incidents in which you played some role, Old Wizard. Are you trafficking in demons now?"

McGowan swirled the cognac in his glass. "And why would you ask that, Lord Cadilus?"

Cadilus ignored his question. "These incidents involved your daughter, and a young sorcerer of which we had previously been unaware. And someone in this house opened a portal to the Netherworld, a portal of the kind that might portend chaos and destruction in our realm as well as yours. Is this young mage a demon, or demon possessed? Need we concern ourselves that he might be a danger to us all? Need the Seelie Court act in this matter?"

••••

McGowan watched Cadilus stroll down the sidewalk away from his house, and as the probability of the Sidhe's existence on the Mortal Plane diminished, his image slowly grew translucent, then disappeared altogether. The old man and Colleen had verbally sparred with the Sidhe for more than an hour, attempting to gain as much information as possible, and yield only enough to keep the Sidhe Courts out of it.

Back in his study Colleen had returned to wearing her Druid garb. He asked her, "Do you think they'll stay out of it?"

"For the time being," she said. "But they're going to watch closely."

McGowan stepped up to the fireplace and looked into the flames again. "I didn't like that question about Conklin being a demon. It's natural for them to ask if he's demon possessed, but to ask if he's actually a demon. I don't like that."

"Neither do I," Colleen whispered. "Especially since it's a concern I share."

McGowan turned to her sharply. "Why do you say that?"

McGowan could see fear in her eyes as she spoke. "Because I'm not sure he's human. Because I don't know what he is. And he could be quite dangerous."

••••

Paul struggled to find consciousness. In a bleary state half way there he recalled a sequence of half-formed, disjointed memories of some doctor working on him. He recalled something about a "serious concussion," and some of the memories clearly belonged more to the land of delusion. Then there came a stretch of time in which he laid in bed, conscious, but with no volition to move, like sleeping in on a Sunday morning with the unfettered knowledge there were no demands on his time that day. And then, between one heartbeat and the next, he made that last leap to full consciousness.

It must've all been a dream. The story was just too fantastic to be real: demons and vampires and leprechauns, wizards and witches and sorcerers. He hoped Katherine McGowan was real, but he couldn't believe the rest of this crap. The answer was clear enough. He'd hallucinated his wife and daughter so much lately he'd gone over the edge, had completely lost touch with reality and was lying in that bed in that straight jacket in that nut house he and Katherine had talked about.

He was lying in a nice, comfortable bed, covered in soft, maroon sheets. He sat up slowly, though his abdominal muscles complained painfully, had been strained a bit in his exertions. He was alone in a large bedroom with the kind of furnishings and decor that were far beyond his meager means. Someone had carefully bandaged his ribs and stitched up several cuts in his arms and shoulders. He threw back the sheets and paused for a moment to inspect the bruises on his legs and more stitched-up cuts. A clock on a nearby table told him it was early evening, though he didn't know which evening.

He swung his legs off the bed and that hurt like hell. He sat there for a moment to catch his breath and let the pain subside, then climbed to his feet like a frail old man and was not surprised to learn his legs were still a bit unsteady. He wore nothing more than a lot of bandages. He spotted a pile of clothing folded neatly on a nearby chair, with a pair of his sneakers on the floor beneath it.

He shook out the shirt and pants. They weren't the clothes he'd been wearing, but they were his so someone had gone to his apartment to retrieve them. He found the clothes he'd been wearing in a wastebasket near the bed: cut to shreds by the paramedics, torn further by his misadventures, caked with blood and sweat and that dirty brown grit from hell. He dropped them back into the wastebasket.

He tried to dress quickly, which wasn't at all easy, and turned out to be a painful exercise that left him panting to catch his breath while the pain from a dozen injuries slowly receded. He found a small bathroom attached to the bedroom, was appalled at what he saw when he looked in the mirror. The left side of his face was badly swollen, had turned into one giant, yellowish-brown bruise. Cuts above his left eye, neck and cheek had been stitched, while several other cuts had been left to heal on their own. He carefully splashed water on his face and felt a little better.

He noticed his wallet and keys and a few coins sitting on a small writing desk against one wall. They hadn't been in his pants when he'd retrieved them from beneath the bed in the hospital, so someone had gone to the trouble of retrieving them for him. He tested the bedroom door, found it unlocked and opened it cautiously, then stepped into a short hallway with three more doors like the one through which he'd just come. One end of the hall opened onto a broad staircase, the kind of space usage found in only the most expensive places in the city. Feeling like an intruder, he limped his way carefully down the stairway to what appeared to be an entrance foyer. A large door inset with leaded glass panels clearly opened to the outside world.

In the other direction he heard someone talking calmly. His recent delusions had made him paranoid enough to want to know what he was involved in, so he limped and tiptoed quietly down the hall to the back of the house. He stopped just short of the end of the hall and hung back in the shadows there. He could see just a little bit of the room beyond, barely enough to know it was a kitchen.

"Thank you for staying with Katherine last night." That was McGowan's voice.

The hippie woman answered him. "She seems to be ok. A lot of cuts and scrapes and bruises, but nothing serious."

"And young Conklin?"

"The only thing of real concern was the concussion. But I healed that. We'll have to let the bruises and cuts and sprains heal naturally. How long are you going to keep him asleep?"

He heard McGowan sigh wearily. "I need to think. I'll remove the sleep spell after I've had a chance to think."

Neither of them spoke for several seconds, during which Paul heard what sounded like someone stirring a spoon in a glass or coffee cup or something. The hippie broke the silence by asking, "What're you going to do with him?"

The long silence during which McGowan didn't answer stretched out into an ominous statement of its own. When he finally said, "I don't know," Paul almost jumped, almost made some noise that would have alerted the two of them to his presence.

"He deserves a chance, old man. From what Katherine told me, he saved her life three or four times."

He snarled, "And she wouldn't have been in the Netherworld in the first place if it hadn't been for him, god damn it."

Paul heard her sigh. "Promise me you won't kill him."

"I can't promise that. Not if he's a rogue."

That was all Paul needed to hear. The old Paul would've walked into the kitchen and tried to reason with the man, especially since the old fellow, at least in appearance, seemed eminently reasonable. But that was the old Paul, the one who hadn't had the enlightening experience of looking down the business end of a howitzer as an ugly Russian thug that looked like Joe Stalin pulled the trigger. That was the Paul who hadn't been chased through the halls of a hospital by a vampire, the Paul who hadn't stood face-to-face with a hoodoo in hell, the Paul who hadn't just heard a distinguished look-ing gentleman casually discuss killing him. It was at that moment he decided to adopt a new philosophy for living: *better paranoid than dead.*

The new Paul tiptoed back up the hallway, slipped quietly out the front door and headed down the street. What he didn't hear was the end of the conversation.

"But then," McGowan continued, "the little people have taken his side so he can't be a rogue, probably isn't dangerous."

She added, "They wouldn't side with him if he was anything at all dangerous, not in a bad way."

McGowan capitulated easily. "Ok, I won't kill him. In fact, I'll protect him until I can find out what it is about him that's got the little people giving up their traditional neutrality. And then I'll try to teach him how to protect himself."

••••

Katherine limped down the busy San Francisco sidewalk, knowing she'd been foolish and vain to drive her own car. But she liked the Jaguar, especially since that dead-beat ex of hers never approved of the extravagance. When they were married she couldn't afford extravagances, mainly because he could, with her money. No, she should've been practical and taken a cab right to the front door of her father's house. She also shouldn't have worn the damn stiletto heels. But the Louis Vuittons looked good on her.

She was a block away from her father's place when she saw Paul emerge, skulk down the steps to the sidewalk, turn down the street and sneak away. Every nuance about him was furtive, and her father wouldn't have let him leave on his own, unpro-tected and unguarded. So he must've snuck out of the house, though she couldn't really blame him for being a bit paranoid. But still, her father was the one man he could count on, the one person who might help him get through this alive.

She was too far away to shout his name, and when she tried to run or speed up, the limp and the heels made it clear that wasn't going to happen. But he was limping too, so she followed him, hoping to catch up to him when he stopped at a streetlight.

••••

Hidden by a glamour that turned away any mortal eye, Anogh watched Paul leave the Old Wizard's home. He watched the old man's daughter watch Paul leave, then decide to follow him. He watched Simuth ignore them both, allowing Paul to stroll casually up the street without so much as a glance, Katherine about a block behind him. Then there was the Seelie mage watching Simuth and Paul and Katherine, a high mage, powerful and dangerous, obviously sent by Magreth to watch and observe. The Seelie mage followed Katherine.

Ag had ordered Simuth to watch the Old Wizard's home. So Simuth, in his arrogance, was focused on the powerful old man, and not the least bit concerned with this young fellow or the old man's daughter, both of whom appeared to be minor practitioners. The Seelie mage seemed focused on this Paul Conklin. Anogh hesitated for only a moment of indecision, then turned and followed close on Katherine's heels as she followed Paul.

Though he might want to, Anogh could not assist the Seelie mage. The tenants of his oath to the Winter Court prohibited that quite clearly. But without specific instructions from Ag, those same tenants did not obligate him to openly oppose the Summer Court. So Anogh followed the mage as he followed Katherine, as she followed Paul.

••••

The events of the last few days had taught Paul to be wary. But he had to try hard not to skulk suspiciously down the street. He was so paranoid at this point he feared that if he looked too wary or fearful, combined with his bandaged, battered and bruised face, he'd attract the attention of every cop in town. And that, he knew, was just more paranoia.

He wanted to get to the east bay, so he turned down Nob Hill on Powell Street, headed for the Powell Street BART Station. But he needed cash, because cash couldn't be traced, and he didn't know how powerful his enemies were. So he stopped at an ATM and withdrew a fist full. He knew not to turn and start counting a bundle of twenties walking down the street, counted it carefully in the shadow of the ATM, then shoved it into his wallet and turned to continue down the street.

"Paul."

He stopped at the sound of his name, stopped because he recognized Katherine's voice. He turned around, watched her limp down the street toward him, looking incredible in a dark pinstripe suit. She'd chosen a man's style of suit, pants, white shirt and tie. But this was no man's suit, cut to emphasize her figure, and the pants ended in stiletto heels that looked to be expensive. He decided it wouldn't be politic to mention the practicality of stiletto heels combined with a limp.

"You snuck out of my father's house, didn't you?" She didn't seem as angry as she sounded.

"Of course I did. He wants to kill me."

She grimaced and shook her head. "No. Absolutely not. He wants to help you."

"Then why did he say he wants to kill me?"

Her eyes narrowed suspiciously. "He said that? I don't believe it."

"Believe it, sister." She was irritating him so he played the stiletto heel card. "With all the bruising you took, don't you think the heels are a bit impractical?"

Her eyes flashed angrily, so he added, "Though I do have to admit you look pretty good in them."

Her eyes remained angry, but her lips curled up into a smile. He was about to tell her the story of the conversation he'd overheard between McGowan and the old hippie, but over her shoulder he caught a glimpse of a rather tall man who stood staring directly at him and seemed oddly out of place, one of those passing glances that didn't register on conscious thought until a moment after it was over. It made Paul hesitate and look back toward the fellow. But as his eyes settled on the spot where he knew the man was standing, his gaze slipped to one side and his attention was drawn to a young woman nearby. Now that was odd.

He tried again, swung his eyes back toward the man, but they shifted past him to an older couple struggling up Nob Hill. It was like trying to take hold of something greased and slippery. Paul tried twice more to look at the fellow, and each time he found it impossible to do so, found his gaze sliding unerringly away from the tall figure. But always, he was left with the impression the man stood there staring directly at him.

Katherine had been saying something about how he could trust her father, and he cut her off abruptly. "There's something weird going on here."

He had to give her credit. She shifted gears instantly. Her eyes narrowed, she hesitated for a moment, then asked, "What?"

Paul purposefully looked away from the tall guy, closed his eyes and tried to reconstruct what he thought he'd seen. "There's this tall guy standing about fifty feet behind you up the street. Distinguished looking, handsome, fortyish, stands a head taller than everyone around him. He's wearing a dark business suit that seems a little out of place here. And he's carrying a walking stick as if he's stepped out of Savile Row in London. All he needs now is a bowler hat to complete the image."

Paul concentrated on the image in his mind's eye. The distance was too great for him to be certain, but . . . "And I think he has fucking pointed ears."

Only a few days ago he would've shrugged the incident off, chalked it up to inattention, or his imagination, or any of a hundred things real people dealt with every day. But not today, not the new Paul. He'd learned the hard way not to shrug off anything strange, unusual or out-of-place.

Her eyes narrowed suspiciously, but she didn't dismiss him out-of-hand. "Try to look at him again. Try to focus hard on him."

Paul slid his eyes toward the fellow and tried, and his gaze slid off him as if he wasn't there. "I can't. I know he's there, but when I try to look directly at him I find myself looking at something nearby."

Katherine leaned toward Paul, put her arms around his neck, leaned forward so her lips were close to his ear. "Pretend we're lovers," she whispered.

He thought he might like pretending that, so he put his hands around her waist and pulled her close, knew full well he was using the subterfuge as an excuse to do so. She didn't resist, but she didn't really respond either. She continued in a whisper, "This is scary. You're describing a Sidhe, probably a high mage. He's using a glamour that turns your eyes away, a compulsion that forces you to look at something nearby, but never him. And you say he's looking straight at you."

He leaned back a bit so they were face-to-face, their lips a fraction of an inch apart, and he looked into her eyes. "Staring at me like no normal person, like some crazy stalker."

She moved a little closer so that, as she spoke, her lips were brushing lightly against his. "He can get away with that since no one can see past the glamour. And the fact that you can . . ."

Her eyes widened, she started and pulled away from him. "Shit! Don't try to look directly at him. If he realizes you can see through his glamour it might piss him off. He might even kill you. We have to get out of here."

He regretted that their little moment of intimacy had ended so abruptly. "I'm headed for the BART station." He took her by the arm and turned down Powell. She walked beside him, both of them limping.

When he glanced over his shoulder and confirmed that Pointy Ears was following them, she said, "Don't be too obvious."

When they got to Post Street he leaned toward her as if he was kissing her on the neck and hissed, "Crowds in Union Square. Let's try to lose him there." They cut diagonally through the Square.

There were quite a few people taking advantage of a warm summer evening, listening to street musicians, kids gawking at the guy painted head-to-foot in silver and pretending to be a statue. Paul purposefully sought out thick clusters of people through which he and Katherine edged their way carefully. And as he did so he looked repeatedly over his shoulder. He didn't see the tall man again, but several times someone in the crowd appeared to be jostled aside almost rudely. And more than once the victim stopped and turned indignantly to confront the jerk who'd shoved them, but there was never anyone there, never a culprit upon which to blame such rudeness. But Paul had learned if he allowed his gaze to slide past the disruption, he was left with the unmistakable impression of the tall man in the dark suit. And now he was certain the fellow had pointed ears.

He took Katherine's hand and leaned toward her. "The fucker definitely has pointy ears," he whispered, "and he's definitely following us. Let's head for the Montgomery Street BART Station."

At the far corner of Union Square they turned down Geary Street. He'd learned he could keep track of the fellow following them by never trying to look directly at him. Instead he'd look at something nearby, then let his gaze drift past where he thought the fellow might be, which left a strange, ghostlike impression.

After a couple of blocks they turned east on Market Street, conscious of the wraithlike being following them.

••••

Anogh's excitement grew as he followed the Seelie mage and Paul and Katherine. The mage had cast a powerful spell that made one's eyes turn away from him, even more powerful because of its subtlety. And yet the young man had seen through the glamour, a feat few mortals could achieve, which led Anogh to the conclusion Paul was a wizard of unusual talent. Perhaps not powerful in the sense of wielding arcane magics, but certainly unusually strong in his ability to see through the magics of others.

Anogh followed them down Powell Street, then through Union Square, watched as Paul grew steadily more aware of the pursuit behind him, watched as the Seelie mage arrogantly shoved mortal's aside to keep up with them. This could be a most interesting confrontation. Then they turned down Market Street.

Market Street! A Boundary!

Anogh felt almost weary as he watched the mage follow the two mortals onto the busy thoroughfare. An old boundary, a street that had existed for more than a hundred years, a main route that separated two old sections of the city. The poor fellow was making it rather easy for the mage, choosing a path down a Boundary where the separation between the Three Realms was thin and tenuous. While the Sidhe might pass freely from one Realm to another, it was difficult, sometimes near impossible, to bring a mortal across without the use of an old boundary. And Paul had now made it easy for the mage following him.

How could such a wizard be so stupid?

••••

Paul glanced over his shoulder at the apparition following them. As the sun slipped toward the horizon the sky in the west was turning a deep-purple, the kind of sunset that didn't happen in San Francisco, more like something one might see farther up the coast on a summer night in Seattle. The crowds were thinning as he and Katherine hurried down the street. And farther down Market Paul spotted some sort of street entertainer wearing medieval garb and leading a donkey pulling a two wheeled cart piled with thatch, or hay, or something like that. The guy was going to get arrested. San Francisco didn't let anyone lead a live donkey down the street.

Katherine tugged on his arm, pulled him to a stop and forced him to face her. "This is all wrong, Paul. Something's really wrong here."

As dusk settled over the city the buildings around them had turned tenuous and indistinct, and between buildings he caught glimpses of a green and verdant, rolling countryside. "This is more of your weird shit, isn't it?"

She put her hands on her hips and frowned angrily. "It's not *my* weird shit. In the short time I've know you I've had more weird shit happen to me than in the rest of my life."

Paul glanced back up Market, saw no sign of Pointy Ears. "Well we still gotta worry about your elf friend." He grabbed her elbow, turned and continued east down Market.

At Montgomery Street they stepped off the curb, though they had to skip over a lot of dirt in the gutter. They crossed the street against the light, though, oddly enough, there was no traffic, and he almost slipped in a large stretch of grass in the middle of the street. They both danced around a small shrub, and he wondered for a moment what grass and a shrub were doing in the middle of the street. Katherine stopped and looked at the shrub. "This is not good, Paul."

"You just figured that out?" he said. "Maybe some delivery truck from some nursery accidentally dropped part of its load, didn't bother to stop and clean up the mess."

She turned and continued across the street, grumbled over her shoulder, "You don't believe that crap any more than I do."

He followed close on her heels, dared not slow down, really didn't want to find out what would happen if Pointy Ears caught up with them. But reality shifted, twisted out of control down a strange spiral track, and when they got to the other side of Montgomery there was no curb, just a muddy track and deep grass.

Katherine stopped abruptly and Paul almost ran into her. The sky in the east had taken on the same deep-purple hue as the western horizon where the sun had set. From one heartbeat to the next the street had emptied of all traffic and people, and Paul and Katherine now stood alone on the muddy corner of Market and Montgomery. The buildings around them had grown almost translucent, were now really just shadows of what they'd once been.

Katherine whispered, "We're in deep shit."

"Yuh think?"

Paul turned around and looked back up Market, which wasn't Market anymore. It was just a long dirt road in the middle of a green countryside. And Paul could see Pointy Ears clearly now, alone, no crowds in Union Square, no Union Square for that matter, just Pointy Ears marching toward them purposefully.

Paul turned full circle. San Francisco was just plain gone. The entire sky had taken on that deep-purple hue, and he and Katherine now stood on a dirt road in the middle of a vast moor. The dirt road snaked into the distance, passing near a stone hut with a thatched roof, where the fellow with the donkey and cart had stopped. The road led to some sort of large medieval structure on the far horizon. It was too distant to make out details, but it appeared to be a castle.

Paul turned back to Pointy Ears, and as the man strode up to them, Paul stepped in front of Katherine protectively. The fellow stopped a few paces away and smiled, and in the fading light Paul noticed the pupils of his eyes were vertically slit like those of a cat.

Reality blinked and Paul felt a strange shift in his guts; and now the fellow wore armor brightly enameled in a myriad of colors, with a dangerous looking sword strapped to his side, his face partially hidden behind a masked helm, his cat-eyes peering through narrow slits, his mouth and chin visible below an ornate nose-guard.

Paul took a step back and bumped into Katherine. "Who are you? What do you want?"

The fellow's smile turned into an unfriendly grin. "I have what I want."

"And what's that?" Paul demanded, thankful the fellow hadn't drawn that sword.

"You, mortal," the man said, and his grin turned absolutely cheesy. "Welcome to Faerie."

••••

Standing on Market Street, Anogh watched the mage use the Boundary to manipulate the probability of Paul's existence on the Mortal Plane, watched Katherine sucked into the vortex the mage had created about Paul, watched the two of them slowly grow more indistinct and intangible as they hurried down Market Street. And then reality shifted and they no longer existed in the here and now of San Francisco.

"What say ya, Boo?"

Anogh turned toward the sound of the voice. Boo'Diddle stood leaning against the pole of a streetlight, while Jim'Jiminie sat atop a post office box cleaning his fingernails with the tip of a small dagger. Boo'Diddle said, "Tis a sad day, Jimmie me boy. Sad indeed when a fine Sidhe warrior such as this boy-oh . . ." He indicated Anogh with a nod of his head. ". . . stands idly by and allows such injustice to be perpetrated on a poor mortal."

"Injustice?" Anogh asked. "The young man is a wizard and the young woman a witch. They should've known better, but instead were easily—almost foolishly—trapped by a mage. Where's the injustice in that? And why should I intervene?"

Jim'Jiminie finished working on one of his fingernails and examined it carefully as he said, "You'll not want the wrath of the old man when he learns of the abduction of his daughter."

"No one abducted the daughter. She was merely in the way."

The leprechaun looked at Anogh and grinned. "Do you really think he'll see it that way?"

The leprechaun was not incorrect in that. "You do have a valid point there, little man."

Jim'Jiminie cocked his head. "And don't forget the young wizard is yet unaware of his own powers."

Now that was something Anogh had not known. And it explained the fellow's ignorance.

A large black crow fluttered out of the sky and landed on the streetlight above. The triple goddess often appeared in the form of a crow, and Anogh eyed it warily. At the moment he didn't sense the presence of the Morrigan, but then he couldn't sense her if she didn't want him to. And she certainly was in play in this, had awakened after centuries of silence and taken interest in this Paul Conklin fellow.

Boo'Diddle looked up at the crow and grinned. "And the Morrigan will frown upon anyone who prevents him from realizing his full potential."

Anogh approached the little man and demanded, "And what's the Morrigan's interest in this?"

The little man shrugged. "The old hag has not chosen to enlighten me humble self."

The little fellow pointed a gnarled finger at Anogh. "But take care, knight. Ignore her summons at your own peril. Ignore her summons at the peril of all Faerie."

The crow squawked angrily, leapt from the top of the streetlight and dove straight for Anogh. He ducked, wary of its talons, but at the last instant it unfurled its wings and pulled out of the dive just above his head, shrieking as it gained altitude. With its wings hammering at the air it screeched and cawed, and as it dwindled in the distance its cries sounded like the insane, diabolical laughter of a madwoman.

Jim'Jiminie waggled his dagger in Anogh's direction. "The old hag has made her wishes known, knight."

"And you," Anogh demanded, looking from one little man to the other. "Why such interest from the non-aligned fey? What game are you playing?"

The two leprechauns looked at each other, grinned, then disappeared.

••••

When Colleen found Paul's bed empty she used the arcane voice to call McGowan. *Walter, the young man is gone.*

She heard McGowan coming up the stairway, taking the steps two at a time. When he burst into the room he stopped just inside the door and snarled. "He broke my sleep spell."

"Maybe he's just immune to it."

McGowan shook his head. "He broke my locator spells too."

"But how do you break a sleep spell when you're not conscious to break it."

McGowan reached into his coat pocket and retrieved a couple of fetishes. "Nothing about this young man adds up."

As he studied the charms carefully she asked, "What have you got there?"

"Used some blood-soaked threads from his bandages to make it easy to locate him." He took one fetish in each hand and separated them, looked carefully from one to the other. "Made one for Katherine too. They're both not far away."

He turned and strode out of the room, saying over his shoulder, "Let's go."

Colleen followed him down the stairs and out onto the street. The old man moved quickly and she had trouble keeping up with him. "Slow down," she shouted.

He stopped, turned and waited for her to catch up, though he vibrated with impatience. "There's something wrong about that young man. And if Katherine's anywhere near him, she might be in danger."

Colleen walked by his side as he marched down the street. When he turned onto Powell and headed down Nob Hill, she sensed something else of the arcane, something in play she couldn't quite identify. A few blocks above Union Square McGowan stopped at an ATM, sniffed around it like a hound on the scent. "They met here, then continued on together."

When he turned to follow she snarled, "Wait."

He stopped and turned to face her, frowning.

She stepped a few paces away from him to lessen the scent of his arcane influence. Trying to understand the undercurrent she sensed, she turned around slowly, and then she had it. "I sense a Summer Court mage in this—two of them actually—though one of them reeks of the Winter Court."

At that moment McGowan started, lifted the two fetishes and looked at them carefully. "They're gone. Both of them. They're no longer on the Mortal Plane."

"The Netherworld again."

He shook his head. "I don't know. We'll have to follow their trail. Maybe we can find out."

She walked with him down Powell, then diagonally across Union Square, then down Geary and onto Market. "Faerie," she said as they hit Market. She could feel the influence of the fey in her bones.

"Yes," he said as he stopped on the corner of Montgomery. "Seelie Court. Magreth is going to answer for this."

13

Down the Drain

STANDING BEHIND PAUL, Katherine kept her eyes on the Sidhe mage as he said, "Welcome to Faerie, mortal. And you brought a friend. How quaint!"

Katherine leaned forward and whispered in Paul's ear. "Let me handle this."

He turned his head slightly. "Do you know what you're doing?"

"Probably more than you."

Paul agreed with a shrug. "You got a point there."

He stepped aside, let her step forward to stand beside him, though she had to walk on her toes to keep the stiletto heels from sinking into the dirt road. Eric would've insisted on the macho thing, would've demanded she be the weak and submissive woman so he could handle the tough stuff, had always relegated her to that second-class citizenship, and she liked the way Paul didn't do that.

"No names," she whispered. "Not until we know more."

She'd never before met a Sidhe, but her father had trained her carefully and she knew not to look into its eyes until she'd had time to prepare the proper protections. "Who are you? And why have you brought us here, to Faerie?"

He gave her a patronizing smile. "I am Cadilus, High Chancellor to the Seelie Court. And I didn't bring you here." He nodded toward Paul. "I brought him, and you stumbled into the vortex of his possibilities. Rather foolishly, I might add."

"Then why did you bring him?"

The mage looked at her and his eyes narrowed. "He is a curiosity. He is more than he seems . . . and less."

He looked her over carefully, assessing her. "And I begin to think you are more than you seem. But enough of this. Her Majesty grows impatient."

He waved a hand in a wide gesture, and both Paul and Katherine took an involuntary step back. Katherine forgot about the heels and she stumbled as one of them sank into the road. Paul caught her by the elbow and she leaned on him. "Conklin," she said angrily as she bent down to remove the shoes. "You are shoe-hell personified."

"What?" Paul pleaded, frustration dripping from every word. "What'd I do?"

She pointed the heel of one of her shoes at him like a wand. "That little shoot-em-up in the hospital cost me a beautiful pair of Pradas. This better not cost me these Louis Vuittons."

"Silence," Cadilus shouted.

The magic in his words struck her like a whip, and that infuriated her.

••••

At the mage's shout Paul was struck dumb, couldn't have uttered a word if he'd wanted to, knew it was some sort of magic thing he was powerless to resist. But Katherine was apparently unaffected by whatever the mage had done. Her eyes flashed with anger, she turned and marched up to the mage in her stocking feet, waving one of her stiletto heels at him like a sword, the air about her crackling with some sort of power. The mage stepped back warily, almost fearfully, as she snarled, "Don't you dare attempt to command me. My father trained me well, and your *voice* has little effect."

A woman's voice, regal and haughty, said calmly, "And who is your father, child?"

In a heartbeat they'd gone from standing on a dirt road in the middle of a vast moor, to standing in the middle of an immense hall built of pale yellow stone. Tapestries covered the walls, depicting images of knights hunting unicorns, and flaming sconces lit the room with flickering light and dancing shadows. It was all very medieval.

Paul and Katherine both turned toward the woman's voice. They were now standing beneath a dais upon which rested a massive throne made of what appeared to be hundreds of bleached-white human skulls. Or maybe they were Sidhe skulls; Paul wouldn't know the difference. But the throne was as nothing compared to the woman seated upon it.

Her stark white hair had been piled atop her head in an elaborate coif decorated with gems and silver trinkets. She wore a gown that shimmered with a rainbow of colors and changed constantly with the dancing shadows. The skin of her face was pale white, stretched over an oval face with high cheek bones. She had a small, delicate mouth, with lips the color of dark, reddish-brown blood. Had it not been for her eyes, she'd have been the most beautiful woman Paul had ever seen. But her almond shaped eyes were filled with fire, angry flames that burned into his soul when she cast her gaze upon him.

Behind him, Paul heard Katherine say, "Your Majesty," and any anger or challenge had left her voice completely.

He turned toward Katherine, who was now gowned in something from an eighteenth century European court. She curtsied, did a better job of it than any courtesan might.

"Rise," the queen said.

Paul prayed this wasn't going to turn into an *Alice in Wonderland* thing with a mad queen shouting insane commands at them. He looked down at his clothing, really didn't want to find he was wearing a doublet and hose from the eighteenth century, took some comfort in the fact he was still wearing his jeans and sneakers.

"Why is he not attired properly?" the mad queen demanded.

The mage responded with, "I know not, Your Majesty. Perhaps he resists."

She turned her fiery eyes upon Paul. "You insult me by coming before me dressed as a common huckster."

Paul knew he was totally out of his element. He wanted to say something like, *Fuck you, bitch*, but he suspected that wouldn't go well. No, think of some movie, some period piece, and try to mimic the courtiers. "I didn't come before you, Your Majesty. I was taken against my will, and brought before you without my knowledge or permission. If you dislike my attire, or you find it insulting in some way, perhaps you should look to this . . ." He turned toward the mage. ". . . this Cadilus fellow."

The mad queen looked from Paul to Cadilus to Katherine, then back to Paul. If she'd had real eyeballs, instead of just pits of fire, the gaze she turned upon him would have been angry and hard. But it was just fucking fiery. "You mock me, mortal?"

Something dark and really scary suddenly emerged in the hall, and Paul knew he was on the edge of oblivion with this mad queen. He bowed from the waist, did his best imitation of an eighteenth century courtier in a movie, held the bow and said, "No, Your Majesty. I merely, humbly, speak the truth. And I pray you judge me on that." He held the bow and waited.

The dark something that had invaded the room suddenly disappeared, though a hint of it remained hovering in the background, like a dangerous beast brought to heel at the foot of its master. "You may rise, mortal mage."

Paul straightened slowly, though some instinct told him to keep his eyes downcast.

The queen lifted a hand, waggled a finger at Katherine and said, "Come forward, girl."

Katherine advanced with the soft hiss of swirling petticoats, stopped at the base of the dais, bowed her head and said, "Your Majesty."

"There is the matter of your father, my dear."

"Yes, Your Majesty."

The queen leaned forward, her brow furrowed, and if flaming eyes could be said to narrow, hers did. "His name? Though I begin to suspect I know the answer."

"Your Majesty, in Faerie he's known as the Old Wizard."

The queen leaned back on the throne and nodded. "As I thought."

She lifted her gaze to Cadilus. "You should have been more careful, High Chancellor. This does complicate matters."

••••

One moment Paul stood before the mad queen, and in the next heartbeat he stood in a box of a room with walls, floor and ceiling all made from the same pale, yellow stone. There was an elaborate writing desk and chair that must've come out of some expensive antique shop somewhere, a soft bed against one wall, but no doors or windows. The old Paul would've spent some time wondering how he could get into a room with no way in or out, but the new Paul had come to accept these things.

He explored the room carefully, which didn't take long, because it was just a box. Walls, floor, ceiling, desk, chair, bed; really just a prison cell. At least it wasn't some dark dungeon.

There was nothing he could do so he laid down on the bed and tried to sleep. He lay there for quite some time, but sleep eluded him. He did need to piss, wasn't sure what he was going to do about that, sat up, wondering if there might be a chamber pot beneath the bed. But now there was a door in one wall, a door he knew full well hadn't been there before.

He approached it warily, tested the knob and it opened easily. Beyond it he found a modern bathroom not unlike that in his apartment. He used the toilet, and as he was washing his hands his stomach growled. He hadn't eaten anything since before going to hell and back, and now that he thought about it he was famished.

When he returned to the main room he found a tray of food had appeared on the desk. It was Suzanna's famous pot roast. Suzanna! And Cloe! He sat down on the bed, buried his face in his hands and cried like a baby.

Suzanna sat down beside him, threw a comforting arm over his shoulders. *Don't worry, Paul. It'll be all right.*

Yes, daddy, Cloe said, standing in front of him and tugging at his sleeve. *Everything's gonna be all right.*

••••

Paul found, through simple experimentation, that merely wanting something made it appear. He took a hot shower, needed to change the bandages on his cuts, found supplies of gauze, bandages and medication waiting for him in a cabinet that had suddenly appeared in the bathroom. There hadn't been a razor and shaving cream before, but when he wanted them they appeared. And he could make things go away as well, like the dirty dishes from his meal. Just a thought, with desire behind it, that's all it took. A clock on the wall to keep time, a dresser with changes of clothing and underwear, a book to read. Little by little he furnished the room, turned it into a comfortable bed-room. He even desired, and received, a separate room furnished more like a study where he could sit and read one of his books.

These spooky fairy people must have a direct conduit right into his brain, knew every thought, whim or desire, were willing to give him almost anything he wanted, anything but an exit. He tried for a way out, a door, a window, anything. He wished for it, desired it, did everything but shout out a demand. Nothing. No, these pointy-eared people had definite limits on what they'd allow.

He thought about desiring the presence of the mad queen so he could ask her some questions, decided even if he could make her appear, that really wasn't a good idea. And then he thought about desiring Katherine's presence, and blink, she appeared right in front of him, now wearing her modern business suit and standing in her stock-ing feet, still holding her stiletto heels dangling from one hand.

She started, said, "Paul!"

Her eyes blinked rapidly, she turned about slowly and took in her surroundings, turned full circle until she came back to him. "Where are we?"

"My prison cell."

She looked about the room again. "Doesn't look too much like a prison."

He explained about the room, how everything appeared or disappeared with merely a thought, everything but a way out.

She frowned. "How long have you been here?"

He wasn't sure his watch, or the clock on the wall, were keeping accurate time. "I'd guess about a full day. I read a book for a couple of hours, ate a couple of meals, got a good night's sleep. Why? Where've you been?"

They were standing in the study, and with a dazed look on her face she turned and walked into the bedroom. He followed her there, watched her look around, open a drawer in the dresser, peer at its contents for a moment, then close it. She walked to the bathroom, stopped in the doorway and glanced around quickly, turned back and started across the bedroom.

He followed her as she walked into the study, looked around again, then turned and faced him. "Only a few moments ago I was standing in the throne room next to you listening to Magreth tell Cadilus I was a complication."

"That's crazy."

The dazed look disappeared, was replaced by determination. "No, this is Faerie. I've never been here before but my father told me time doesn't operate the same here. Said it isn't linear, whatever that means."

She looked at him and he could tell her thoughts were racing. She walked up to him, still dangling the stiletto heels from one finger. "So, whatever you want, you just desire it . . . and it appears?"

"Ya, basically."

She moved in closer, traced a finger along his chin and cocked her head coquettishly. "Do you think you could desire some Pradas? Maybe some Fendis too, and some Christian Louboutin's." Her eyes brightened and she continued almost breathlessly. "And the matching purses. And some Vera Wang dresses. And some pant suits. I still have to hide the bruises on my legs . . ."

She suddenly hesitated, frowned, looked at Paul side-long and grimaced, continued in a more subdued tone, "I kind of lost it there . . . for a moment, didn't I?"

Paul raised an eyebrow at her. "Yuh think?"

She gritted her teeth and pleaded, "Maybe just the shoes?"

••••

"Your Majesty," Cadilus said carefully, cautiously. "I believe we may have made a mistake."

Magreth turned emerald green eyes upon him. "How so?"

"Indulge me, Your Majesty, if you will." Cadilus opened a portal into Paul's *apartment*. Magreth turned to step through it, but he stepped in front of her. "Please, allow me to precede you, as a matter of safety."

"Safety! You feel the need to protect me. No one can harm me in my own realm."

"How true, Your Majesty. And yet, there have been . . . unusual occurrences surrounding this young mortal mage. I would counsel . . . caution, until we know more."

She said nothing and stepped aside.

Cadilus turned and stepped through the portal into Paul's study. Paul and Katherine stood facing each other, frozen in time like two statues, he with a wry frown upon his face, she with her shoes dangling from her fingers. Cadilus looked about, turned to the portal. "It appears to be safe, Your Majesty."

Magreth stepped through the portal, looked about the room for a moment, then walked past him and into the other room, the bedroom. He followed her. She scanned the room carefully, stepped briefly into the bathroom, then returned and walked back into the study to look upon the two mortals standing motionless.

"I see nothing unusual here," Magreth announced, "other than that you seem to have been somewhat generous with your accommodations."

"But I have not, Your Majesty." Cadilus strolled about the room, indicating various pieces of furniture and other accoutrements. "I placed him alone in a bare stone cell with a small cot, and a chamber pot beneath it."

She spun about, looked more carefully at the contents of the room, and the flames appeared in her eyes. "Then how came this?"

"The young mage conjured it all."

Her voice hardened as she demanded, "Conjured?"

"Yes, Your Majesty. With merely a thought. A thought here, a thought there, conjured it all with such ease one might think he was Sidhe. I didn't anticipate this so I didn't really resist him. He hasn't been able to penetrate the bounds of our circle, though he's tried repeatedly. But inside the circle, it appears he can conjure almost anything."

"And the girl, how did she get here? He didn't conjure her."

"No, he transported her here, with no more than a whim. We constructed the circle so we might enter or leave, which allowed him to pull her into it, though he can't send her out. It's as if he's more powerful here than on the Mortal Plane."

"Impossible."

"Yes, Your Majesty. I concur. He is mortal, so here in Faerie he must be less powerful. But that means on the Mortal Plane his power must rival that of the Old Wizard."

Magreth walked carefully around the two young mortals, looked at each in turn, looked carefully. After completing a full circle she said, "It's almost as if they're lovers."

She hesitated and looked closely at the young girl. "She is a lovely creature. See to it no harm comes to her. The Old Wizard's wrath would be . . . dangerous. We'll return her to him as a favor."

She stepped back, looked at the young fellow from a distance, as if he was a wild animal and she dare not get too close. "But as to the young man . . . let's not take any chances. Kill him and be done with it."

Cadilus bowed deeply. "As you wish, Your Majesty."

••••

This once, McGowan had chosen to not wear wizard's robes in the Seelie Court. Magreth would have to receive him in modern mortal attire, sport coat, tie and slacks, not the long flowing robes that made him look like something out of a Tolkien novel. His casual street attire would irritate her, and that was just fine with McGowan.

Two Seelie warriors in ceremonial armor swung back the great double doors of the throne room as he approached, and beyond them he saw dozens of courtiers huddled in small groups. When he stepped across the threshold, one of the warriors announced, "A mortal wizard, Your Majesty," and the buzz of dozens of inconsequential conversations died abruptly. Announcing him that way had been an open insult. He paused for dramatic effect, focused on Magreth who sat upon her throne at the far end of the room.

She'd been speaking to Cadilus, with her head turned to one side. But now she took an infinitely long moment to turn her gaze slowly toward McGowan, looking upon him with those intense, green eyes. Had he been following protocol he would've waited for her to invite him to approach. Instead, he immediately began marching toward her, and the green of her eyes turned to flame. Had he been following protocol he would've stopped a goodly distance from her. Instead, he marched right up to the base of the dais. Had he been following protocol he would've bowed deeply. Instead he stood there, facing her angrily.

All present felt her power rising as her anger grew, so the old man summoned his power and let them feel a taste of it. At that moment he did bow, but only a slight nod of the head, as one equal to another. "Your Majesty."

The flames in her eyes blossomed, and her anger became a palpable presence. "Old Wizard," she said, conceding to him his title.

He allowed a tight smile to touch his lips. "We haven't spoken in quite some time. Shall we stand here, snarling at each other like two hissing cats?"

She stared at him silently with her flaming eyes. Then slowly the flames disappeared and once again she looked upon him with those beautiful green eyes. Almost human eyes, if one could ignore the cat-like vertically slit pupils. "I do owe you a daughter, don't I?"

"Yes, Your Majesty. It would save us both a great deal of trouble if you returned her unharmed."

She eyed him carefully. "And what of the young wizard?"

"Return him as well."

"Return," she said. "That word implies you had possession of him, and wish that possession reinstated. But you did not. He was on his own. Do you have some claim on him? Is he of your blood?"

"No, not of my blood." McGowan considered lying, claiming Paul was his apprentice. But Magreth would sense the lie, or at least suspect it, and that could endanger his ability to get Katherine back. "He's a friend of my daughter's, and therefore a friend of mine. And my mortal colleagues and I will not take it kindly if you abduct our mortal friends. The Mortal Plane is not your playground."

She gave him an unkind grin. "Your daughter will be returned. But the young wizard . . . we'll have to consider that further."

••••

Katherine leaned in close to Paul, a mischievous glint in her eyes, her lips a fraction of an inch from his. "Give you a kiss for a pair of Fendis."

"What are Fendis?" he asked.

"They're a girl's best friend." Her lips touched his, brushed them lightly, barely made contact, wouldn't have passed muster as a love scene in some movie. But while it almost didn't qualify as a kiss, it was still very sensual.

She leaned back a few inches, scrunched her nose up and said, "Oh, this just won't do."

She hit him with a curl-your-toes, grand-slam, hit-it-out-of-the-ballpark kiss that backed him up a step. She put her arms around his neck and stayed with him. He put his arms around her waist and pulled her close, and as their tongues danced she pressed her body against his. When she leaned back and their lips parted she didn't pull out of his embrace, was breathing as heavily as him.

"Whoa!" he said. "Whatever Fendis are that was worth a whole store full of 'em."

She gave him a Cheshire-cat grin. "Shoes. They're shoes, and you say the nicest things."

"What do I get for a pair of those Kristine Labootins?"

She laughed, shook her head sadly. "Actually, Mr. Conklin, my kisses are not for sale. You got that one simply because I wanted it myself. And you'll get this one for the same reason."

She started to close the few inches between them, but a familiar voice said, "It's sad, Boo. Both of them have their minds in the gutter."

Paul and Katherine jumped away from each other like little kids who'd been caught smooching behind the garage.

Jim'Jiminie sat on top of the dresser Paul had wished into existence, while Boo'Diddle sat on the desk.

"Children, children, children," Jim'Jiminie said sadly, shaking his head. "Can't you be behavin' yerselves? Especially when the young man's life is at stake."

Katherine turned on him. "What do you mean, his life is at stake?"

Boo'Diddle answered her, which forced her to turn about to face him. "Right this moment your father's making arrangements for your release, lass."

Jim'Jiminie continued, and Katherine spun back to face him. "But the lad here, he has them scared. So they're going to kill him."

"Kill me," Paul said. He stepped back so he could look at both little men at the same time. Katherine stepped back to stand at his side. "Why would they want to kill me?"

Boo'Diddle said, "You escaped from the Netherworld."

Jim'Jiminie said, "And you did it with all the finesse of a thunderclap on a clear, cloudless day. So we're here to save you, me and Boo."

They both jumped off their perches and headed for the bedroom door. "Follow us."

Paul and Katherine followed them through the bedroom and into the bathroom. Paul demanded, "I didn't do anything. It was old man McGowan got us out of the Netherworld."

Boo'Diddle marched up to the bathtub, pulled the shower curtain aside, said, "They don't know what you are, don't understand you, and the Courts fear what they don't understand."

He turned back to Paul and Katherine. "They have you locked in a circle."

Katherine said, "We can't break a Sidhe circle."

Paul demanded, "What's a circle?"

"A circle of power," Katherine said. "It can both contain and protect. And it's impossible to break."

Jim'Jiminie said, "Not if it has a hole in it, lass." He pointed at the bathtub drain. "They didn't think of that. We'll leave that way."

Paul didn't try to keep the sarcasm out of his voice. "You mean I'm going to squeeze myself through the fucking bathtub drain?"

Neither leprechaun caught the sarcasm. They frowned and said in unison, "Of course."

Paul looked at Katherine. "They're serious?"

Her eyes widened and she said, "This is Faerie. I guess they are."

"Come on, lad," Jim'Jiminie said, tugging on Paul's hand. The two little men climbed into the bathtub.

Paul reluctantly joined them there. Katherine started to join them as well, but Boo'Diddle held up a hand. "Sorry, lass. You won't be coming with us. Your father's made arrangements for you."

Katherine shook her head angrily. "If Paul's life is in danger, then I'm staying with him."

"No, lass," Boo'Diddle said. "We'll get him back. Your father'll get you back. And then you and he have to start the lad's training."

The two leprechauns made Paul stand over the drain. Boo stood behind him, Jimmie in front, and they wrapped their arms around his ankles. "Hold on, lad," one of them said, "It's gonna be a fun ride."

Paul looked at Katherine, couldn't hide his apprehension. She said, "It'll be ok. Just trust them."

The room started to spin, very slowly like the second-hand on a clock. But then Paul realized it wasn't the room, but he and the two little men who were spinning. They picked up speed slowly, each revolution just a bit faster than the last, and for a moment Paul wondered if he might puke, which would make a real mess while spinning like this. Faster and faster they spun, each revolution picking up more speed until the walls of the bathroom blurred into a dizzy streak of colors. Then the leprechauns shouted,

"Weeeeeee," and suddenly there was nothing beneath his feet. Paul and the little men plummeted downward, he flashed past the bathtub drain into darkness, and when he looked up the last thing he saw was a round circle of light above him dwindling farther and farther away.

14

On A Whirlwind

FUCKING PURPLE GRASS and pink sky, Paul thought. Not basically green grass with a few purple hints, and not a blue sky shading a bit toward pink, but bright purple and vivid pink.

"Hurry, mortal," a nearby flower said.

Oh ya, and fucking talking flowers!

The flower tilted its bright yellow bloom to one side angrily. "You watch your language, young man."

Paul lurched after the two leprechauns. Somewhere along the way he'd surrendered his sanity card, decided at this point he was just bug-fuck nuts. As he trudged along he kept thinking of Katherine's kiss, though thinking about it made him feel guilty since Suzanna and Cloe were trudging along beside him.

Don't worry about it, Paulie-boy. I'm the past. And anyway, I like her.

Yes, daddy, she seems real nice. If mommy wasn't my mommy, I'd like to have her as a mommy.

For two little men with such short legs the leprechauns kept up a grueling pace. Paul shouted ahead, "Where're we going? And why the hurry? We're out of that fairy castle."

Jim'Jiminie looked over his shoulder. "If we're within the bounds of the Seelie Court when they discover you've escaped, they'll scoop you up in seconds. And Magreth gave orders you're to be killed."

Paul felt a sudden spurt of renewed energy, quickened his pace and caught up with the two little fellows. "So where're we headed?"

Boo'Diddle answered breathlessly. "When we cross into the territories of the non-aligned fey, you'll be safe."

"Now, Boo," Jim'Jiminie said, "I wouldn't go that far. Some of the non-aligned might want him dead too."

"But not all," Boo said. "So maybe he won't be completely safe, but surely safer. And then there's Katie'O'girl."

"Aye, Boo, you got a point there. I'd wager even Magreth would think twice before risking the wrath of our sweet, dear Katie."

Paul didn't even want to think what kind of monster this Katie'O'girl thing was, not if she could put fear in the mad, white queen.

••••

Katherine watched Paul and the two leprechauns swept up on a swirling tornado of magic, watched as they stretched and spun, and were pulled down through the drain of the bathtub like something from a Saturday morning children's cartoon. This must be hard for Paul. It had only been a few days since the Russians had shot up his apartment, and in that time he'd been attacked by demons, dragged into the Netherworld, faced down a real doozy of a demon there, been kidnapped into Faerie and forced to stand before Magreth, which was a scary thought for any mortal.

Katherine turned away from the bathtub and wandered back into the bedroom. She decided to explore the place further, was about to do so when the wall opposite her began to fade. She felt reality shift for a moment, and then her father and Cadilus stepped into the room out of nowhere.

Her father smiled and said, "Katherine." He crossed the room and wrapped her in his arms, and she felt his power probing at her. She knew he had to be certain she wasn't some illusion or glamour, some sort of avatar dreamed up by the fey. It would be just like the Sidhe to try to pawn off a chimera instead of the real Katherine.

She whispered in her father's ear. "Rather dramatic entrance, eh?"

He released her and stepped back. "I'm just a guest here, a passenger, as it were. I've secured your release."

She knew she had to stall, buy Paul and the leprechauns as much time as she could before Cadilus found out he'd escaped. "What about Paul?"

Her father frowned unhappily. "I wasn't able to secure his release."

"Well then I'm not leaving without him." She looked at Cadilus. "Not while Magreth has ordered his death."

McGowan stiffened, then turned slowly to Cadilus. "His death? You didn't tell me about that. Isn't that a bit extreme?"

Cadilus shrugged. "Her Majesty does as Her Majesty pleases."

Cadilus looked toward the study. "Where is the young man?" He took a step toward the door, but paused. "I don't sense him here. That's not possible."

He looked at Katherine, looked through her with his cat eyes, and she knew he could sense the lie implicit in her demeanor. He blinked out of existence.

Her father asked, a bit of wonder in his voice. "Paul escaped from a Sidhe circle?"

She smiled at him. "He had a little help."

"How much farther?" Paul asked.

"Exactly the distance from here to there," Jim'Jiminie said. "No further, no less."

He'd been trying to get them to give him a distance, a length, some measure of how much farther they needed to trudge through this alien landscape. But the fey didn't seem to think in such absolute terms, and he was beginning to think when it came to time or distance, there were no absolutes in Faerie. He was pondering that, trudging along, when he sensed that dark presence again, the same ferocious rage he'd sensed in the throne room. It crawled up his spine an instant before the horizon began to churn and boil with angry black clouds. Jim'Jiminie and Boo'Diddle both stopped and looked at each other. "Owe!" they said in unison. "Magreth's wrath is upon us."

Jim'Jiminie said, "Now we have no choice."

Boo'Diddle agreed. "Aye, I'm afraid you've the right of it."

Paul demanded, "What?"

They ignored him. "It won't be nice. Not with the Seelie Court resisting us."

"No, it won't."

"The lad'll pay hell."

"Yes, he will."

Paul pleaded with them, "What're you two talking about?"

They turned toward him, wrapped their arms around his ankles the way they'd done to flush him down the bathtub drain, and said in unison, "This."

The wind started blowing, picking up leaves and twigs and bits of dirt and sand. It stung Paul's eyes, and the three of them began to spin again like the tornado in the bathtub. Paul steeled himself to be flushed down something, but instead they lifted, rose high above the ground spinning wildly.

They were the center of a tornado that began picking up things far larger than a few leaves and bits of dirt and sand. A small rock bashed Paul in the side of the head. A tree limb slammed into his ribs with crushing force. He knew they were travelling rapidly across the countryside, leaving a trail of destruction behind them in a nauseating spiral of destruction, the spinning ground far beneath them. And then he was falling, like in a falling-nightmare, but there was no waking up from this, no sudden gasp in the night to awake with the comforting thought it was only a dream.

He thudded into the muddy turf on his stomach, rolled over and vomited all over his clothing. He gagged a couple more times, then laid there as the spinning and nausea receded, which allowed him to give his full attention to his other aches and bruises.

He sat up slowly, a trickle of blood running into his right eye, half blinding him.

"Ye daft fools," a little female voice said. "You could've killed the poor mortal."

A little female version of the two leprechauns stood over him, or rather, in front of him. He was sitting in the mud, and he was still taller than her. She wore a bright green dress, with a white apron and a deep red shawl. Her grayish hair was tied back in a bun, and her ample bosom jiggled as she unleashed her anger, "The Morrigan would've been sore displeased if you'd killed the fool."

The two little men winced. "But Katie—"

"Don't you *But Katie* me. You've—"

She was interrupted by the call of a hunting horn, and she turned to look toward the horizon.

Paul climbed slowly to his feet, made a half-hearted effort to wipe the vomit and mud off his clothes. They stood on the banks of a small river, and arrayed on the other side was a troop of Sidhe warriors in brightly colored armor, all mounted atop magnificent chargers, with Magreth in their midst in pure white armor on a pure white steed. And even from that distance Paul could see the flames in her eyes.

One of the warriors raised a bow in which he'd knocked a black arrow, and Paul had no doubt the fellow was aiming at him. What does one do when an immortal Sidhe warrior aims an arrow at you? Run? Hide? Paul suspected there would be some magic involved that meant there would be no hiding from that arrow.

Jim'Jiminie hit him low and Boo'Diddle high. He went down in a tangle of little limbs. As he struggled to get up Katie'O'girl hit him upside the head with her hand, a little teeny hand that sent his senses spinning. "Stay down, ye fool."

"Ok," he said, thinking the little people must know a thing or two. "Ok."

She turned toward the hunt on the other side of the river, stood defiantly between Paul and them with her hands on her hips. Apparently, they'd have to kill her to get to Paul, and he was reminded of Katherine's words about a hundred years of bad luck.

No one moved for several seconds, then, without warning, Magreth, in her white armor on her white charger, simply disappeared. Then one-by-one the entire Sidhe host vanished.

Katie'O'girl turned on Paul. "You're a sorry excuse for a wizard. But we'll get you back."

••••

Paul awoke about four feet above the floor of his living room. How he got there he really couldn't say. But he had an infinitesimal instant to realize he was four feet above the floor of his living room, prone, in midair, with nothing to support him. And then gravity kicked in.

He hit the floor with a thud that hurt like hell. He groaned and rolled over, curled up into a fetal position on his side, laid there for a moment catching his breath.

He was in his apartment. He had to believe everyone who was looking for him would look first in his apartment, so he knew he didn't have time to lay there and nurse his wounds.

Getting to his feet was a struggle. He felt like an old man climbing a steep hill, but he managed. He was covered in mud and bruises and blood, had left a bloody, muddy smear on his living room carpet.

He stumbled into the bathroom, stripped off his clothes, found he still had his wallet and cash and keys. Such things probably meant little to elves and fairies, so they hadn't bothered to take them.

He left his clothes in a pile on the floor, turned on the water in the shower. He probably had a short window of time before they came here looking for him, so he just rinsed the mud and blood off, then toweled off quickly. The towel was a bloody mess when he dropped it on the floor.

He limped into his bedroom, put on fresh clothes and crammed a baseball cap on his head. He grabbed a duffle bag and frantically stuffed clothing, toiletries and his small notebook computer into it, was out on the street less than ten minutes after landing on his apartment floor. He walked rapidly, looking over his shoulder continuously. It was really the first time he'd been on his own since the bat-shaped nasties and the Russians and McGowan had invaded his apartment.

He considered going to the police, but then he thought about the story he'd have to tell, knew full well after he blabbered about wizards and witches and demons and leprechauns, if they didn't lock him up, they'd certainly write him off as a nut-case and take no action. He zigzagged randomly through the streets for several minutes, didn't see any signs of pursuit, didn't see any invisible elves pushing people aside behind him.

He didn't know if McGowan could trace him through his credit cards and ATM withdrawals—the man certainly had resources—so he decided to do as much as he could with cash. If he hit ATMs that weren't near where he was hiding, or hit one just before leaving the area, they could look all they wanted and he wouldn't be nearby. So he took a paranoid, zigzag path to the nearest ATM, withdrew more cash, paused for a moment at a newspaper stand and noted the date on the paper. He was surprised to learn it had been just a little more than seventy-two hours since McGowan and his Russian thugs had busted into his apartment. He headed for a nearby BART station and caught the train for the east bay.

At the Castro Valley BART station he caught a cab to his parents place. Actually, it had been his place since his mother had died three years ago, but he never could think of it that way. And right now it was an excellent, if temporary, sanctuary. McGowan was clearly a wealthy man, had considerable resources, but it would take him time to connect Paul to his parents old home. Paul figured he had at least a couple of days, and he needed that time to think, to regroup.

He'd kept his parents old car, a twelve year old Chevy, kept it in the garage at their house. Several times a year he and Suzanna and Cloe would come out, take the car up to Tahoe or down to Carmel or over to Yellowstone for a long weekend or a nice vacation.

He climbed into it, drove to a nearby grocery store, bought a cheap bottle of red wine, stopped at a pizza place and carried out a pizza. But he didn't need the pizza. Suzanna showed up and cooked dinner for him, and she and Cloe kept him company while he ate.

••••

Paul needed some means of defending himself. If the police happened to be on the scene when some bug-eyed hoodoo came out of the shadows, maybe they could help. But after thinking it through carefully he knew he'd probably be long dead before they got there, so he couldn't depend on them.

Paul's father had raised him hunting and fishing, so a gun wasn't something that frightened him, unless it was aimed at him, something that had never actually happened until recently. But guns weren't themselves inherently frightening. And while Paul hadn't owned or used a gun in years, and hadn't felt the need to have one around, a lot had changed in the last few days.

California had a ten-day waiting period on the purchase of any firearm, but it wasn't hard to get a couple handguns on short notice. Paul did his homework and drove across the border into Nevada, though on the way there he stopped at a branch of his bank and withdrew $3,000.

In the state of Nevada only Clark County, which encompassed Las Vegas, required handguns to be registered. So he headed up toward Tahoe and found a small gun shop in suburban Reno. It was a seedy little place, and with a few hints and a fifty-dollar bill, while the shop's owner did look at Paul's driver's license, he didn't make note of the fact the name and address Paul wrote on the shop's forms was nothing close to that on his license. And he only pretended to run a background check on Paul.

Paul had done his homework on the internet and bought a nine-millimeter Sig Sauer P226 for what the shop's owner called a *home piece*. He also bought a smaller P250-Compact for a *carry piece*, plus a thousand rounds of cheap full-metal-jacket practice ammunition. Real stopping ammunition would be a different matter.

He stayed in a cheap motel. It had a small dinette and Suzanna showed up and cooked dinner for him. He returned to his parent's house the next morning, decided to stay there only one more night. They had to be looking for him, and with their resources it wouldn't do to press his luck.

••••

Paul had thought long and hard about real killing ammunition. Katherine had told him silver burned a demon's flesh like a hot poker. But he couldn't afford ammunition with slugs made entirely out of silver. He was hoping to find a gunsmith that could make sliver-plated lead slugs for him on special order. And that meant he'd have to order it from a gunsmith in the bay area, because he'd have to return later to pick it up.

He started in Oakland, went to every gun shop he could find, then worked his way down the east bay toward San Jose. He stayed away from large, well organized shops, focused on small, seedy little places, of which there were plenty. In each he carefully identified the owner, then asked him if he knew of a gunsmith that could make custom ammunition, for a price. He got a lot of strange looks, but got one or two names and phone numbers. He called the numbers, spoke to the smiths, and when he told them he wanted silver-jacketed hollow-points, he got a wide range of varying reactions. One fellow answered him with silence for several seconds, then hung up the phone without a word. Another said, "I don't do crazy shit for nut-cases." The third name on his list said, "Don't ever call me again, ass hole."

He'd worked his way all the way down the east bay, had covered San Jose and started working his way up the peninsula, always staying in cheap motels, never in the same place two nights in a row. He was religious about not leaving any credit card or ATM tracks until just before leaving an area, and then he withdrew enough cash to last him for quite a while.

It was late afternoon of the third day of his search when he parked his car on the street in front of a shop with a sign that read, *South-bay Guns and Ammo*. Like so many of the other places he'd tried, outside it looked small and seamy. It was just as seedy on the inside, a long row of glass display cases running down the right side with handguns displayed under glass, and racks of rifles on the right wall behind the cases. Along the left wall were racks of ammunition, clothing, holsters, cleaning kits, all sorts of paraphernalia.

A fellow who looked to be in his mid-sixties, sat on a stool behind the counter at the back, wiping his hands on a cloth. He had shoulder length gray-blond hair pulled back into a ponytail, three or four days of stubbly beard growth, and wore an old army fatigue jacket with an NRA cap on the top of his head. He looked up as Paul walked through the door. "What can I do for you?"

"I need some custom ammo," Paul told him, "and I was wondering if you could recommend a smith who could make it for me."

The man continued to wipe his hands on the oily cloth as he looked Paul up and down carefully. "I'm a smith," he said. "What kind of ammo you looking for?"

This was the point where Paul would get the strange looks and unhappy reaction. "Silver jacketed hollow-points."

The man's eyes narrowed and he didn't stop wiping his hands. Paul felt a little tickle at the back of his spine, as if the man were looking through him. Then the man nodded and asked, "Why silver jacketed?"

Paul shrugged. "I have some special kinds of varmints that're real hard to kill. Silver helps. It kind of . . . poisons them, burns 'em, you might say."

The man nodded slowly, cautiously, his head moving up and down several times, his eyes evaluating Paul carefully. "I know just what kind of varmints you're talking about."

He turned, walked toward the back of the shop and called over his shoulder at Paul, "Come back here with me." Then he shouted, "Shirl. I got business in back. Watch the front."

Paul followed the man. A plump female in a faded moo-moo, about the same age as the fellow, but with frizzy, unkempt hair, passed them going the other way.

The back room appeared to be a combination gunsmith workshop and storage room. The fellow bent down and retrieved a large box from a shelf against one wall. He dropped it on a workbench and it thudded heavily. "I got lots of experience with the kind of varmints you're talking about. Had some trouble with them myself, upon occasion. But full silver jacket is expensive, and silver's soft, with a low melting point, so the slugs can deform in flight. I make a lead hollow-point with a dusting of silver and iron powder mixed in, and then a copper jacket to keep it from deforming at high velocity. Keeps the cost down and it's just as effective. Inside the varmint the slug deforms and splits the copper jacket, exposing the varmint to the silver and iron. If you need shotgun ammo I also make double-ought buckshot with the same formula."

Paul asked, "Why the iron powder, sir?"

The man grinned and winked. "No *sirs* around here fella. Name's Clark Devoe." He stuck out his hand and Paul shook it. He continued, "And the iron's for them other varmints. Fuckin' fey can't be hurt by lead, and the silver only hurts 'em a bit, but cold iron brings 'em real grief. The silver's mostly for the nether nasties. Hurts 'em bad, sometimes'll even stop 'em cold."

••••

When the private line in McGowan's study rang, only a select group of people had that number so he always answered it. He picked up the handset and said, "McGowan here."

"Mr. McGowan. It's Clark Devoe."

"It's good to hear from you Clark," McGowan said cordially. "What can I do for you?"

"Something kind of funny happened in my shop today. Young fellow come in. Nice looking kid, handsome, clearly a practitioner, though he looked like he'd been in a nasty fight recently and got the worst of it. Limped a bit. He bought a couple thousand rounds of my special nine millimeter. Wouldn't have thought twice about it because, like I say, he's definitely a practitioner. But after he left I got to thinking, and he didn't know shit about the right kind of ammo. Didn't know shit about hurtin' fey. So I thought I should let you know."

McGowan carefully described Paul Conklin, including the location of a deep gash on his forehead that had been stitched shut only a few days ago.

"Ya," Devoe said. "That's him to a tee. Did I do wrong, Mr. McGowan?"

"No, Clark," McGowan said. "You didn't do wrong. In fact, the young fellow is in some trouble, though not of his own making, and I'm glad to see he's taking this seriously now. Our trigger-happy Russian friends think he's a rogue, but the little people are on his side so Colleen and I believe they're wrong."

"Karpov?"

"Exactly."

"Fucking Russian bastards."

"Exactly."

"And you say the little people are involved?"

"Two of them gave up their traditional neutrality to protect him."

"Holy shit!" Devoe said. "I ain't never heard of that before. Anything I can do to help?"

"Not right at the moment, Clark. But if you ever come across the young man, and he needs help, and you can assist him, I'd take it as a personal favor if you did so."

"Certainly, Mr. McGowan. Be happy to."

"And Clark, I'd appreciate it if you didn't mention this to anyone else."

"Sure 'nough, Mr. McGowan."

••••

Paul spent a couple of afternoons at a gun range in the Livermore valley practicing with both Sigs. None of it was new to him so it didn't take long to go through a thousand practice rounds. And by the time he was done he knew both weapons well. He wasn't going to be demonstrating any fancy marksmanship, but at twenty-five feet he could put five rounds in a target the size of a man's chest in just over two seconds.

He'd purchased a lightweight windbreaker specifically designed to conceal a shoulder holster—he'd been surprised to learn there were whole lines of apparel designed to conceal weapons. He didn't have a concealed carry permit, had learned it was virtually impossible to get one in California, so the gun weighing heavily under his armpit was highly illegal. The fifteen round clips he carried were also illegal in California, but he justified the danger of arrest with a variation on his new motto: better illegal than dead.

He didn't need the car any more so he stashed it at his parents place, then caught BART back into the city. It was time to find Katherine.

Paul's biggest problem now was he needed advice and information on this magic stuff, and he didn't know where to turn. The Russians wanted to kill him, and so did the old man and the hippie woman. The little midgets—leprechauns, he reminded himself—were apparently on his side, but how did one go about contacting leprechauns? That left Katherine. She was the only—practitioner, they apparently called themselves—that wasn't trying to kill him on sight. But how to find her?

She was a doctor of some sort. He knew that much. So he tried the yellow pages: nothing.

Next he tried calling hospitals: the one where she and he had fought it out with the Russians and the demons, and a couple more in the area. He was repeatedly told, "I'm sorry, we don't give out information over the phone." But finally, speaking to a receptionist, she responded with, "Oh! Dr. McGowan. You mean the child psychiatrist." He got the phone number of her office, but they wouldn't give out the address.

If Katherine answered the phone, he'd simply tell her the truth. But if she had a receptionist he didn't want to give out his real name, because, for all he knew, Katherine might not take the call. So before calling the number, he carefully considered various scenarios for how it might go.

"This is Dr. Katherine McGowan's office. How can I help you?" Katherine's receptionist sounded like a nice, middle-aged woman.

"Hello," Paul said. "My name's Tim Armstrong." Paul had decided any simple name would do. "I'd like to see if I can arrange for an appointment with Dr. McGowan, for my son."

"And the reason for the appointment, Mr. Armstrong?"

"Well . . . I'm not sure how to explain this. You see, Jack's been pretty normal, up to a few months ago." Paul reached back into his own memories, remembering how his parents had reacted to some of the strange things he'd occasionally glimpsed as a child. "He's eight, you know. And he's . . . well . . ."

"Mr. Armstrong. Eight year old boys experience all sorts of difficulties growing up, some serious and some not. I assure you, Dr. McGowan has seen and heard it all."

Thinking of the hoodoo in hell he and Katherine had faced, Paul was tempted to say something like, *You bet your ass she has*, but instead he said, "Well . . . Jack's started seeing things, things that aren't there. And his mom and I are really worried."

"I believe Dr. McGowan has handled similar cases, Mr. Armstrong. Though, I should add, I myself am not privy to her patients' confidential information. I assume you were referred by a colleague of Dr. McGowan's."

"Ya, one of the doctors at California Pacific. I don't know his name. My wife got the referral, and she's out of town on a little family emergency. Why don't we make an appointment for an initial consultation, and we'll bring that information with us when we come."

He pressed for an appointment sooner rather than later and played up the distraught parent angle rather heavily. She let him fill in for a cancellation and made the appointment for two days hence, then gave him the address of Katherine's office. He had no intention of keeping the appointment, thinking of his new motto: better paranoid than dead.

He bought a wig at a costume shop, shook it around a bit to tousle it. He wasn't about to attempt to become a master of disguise, but anyone looking for him would likely overlook some hippie fellow with unkempt, shoulder-length hair.

The next afternoon he found one of those fancy coffee-internet places across the street from Katherine's office. He bought some coffee and parked his butt at a small, inside, window table where he could keep an eye on Katherine's building. A little after six that evening, she and a middle-aged woman—whom Paul assumed to be her receptionist—emerged from the front of the building. They stopped on the sidewalk and chatted for a moment, then the receptionist turned and walked one way while Katherine walked the other.

It wasn't hard to keep up with Katherine. She wore a cream-colored dress that was really just a giant sweater. It hugged her figure tightly and ended just above her knees, with dark-brown, opaque stockings that completely covered her legs, and long, spike-heeled boots. The spike heels prevented her from walking too fast, and he tried not to pay too much attention to her very nice figure as he stayed about a half block behind her. He followed her to a parking garage that advertised: *No daily parking, monthly and yearly permits only.* She got in the elevator and he lost her there.

••••

Wearing the glamour of a middle-aged businessman, Anogh watched the Old Wizard's daughter emerge from her office building, chat for a moment with another woman, then turn and walk up the street. He might not have noticed the young man with the shoulder length hair had the fellow not walked right past him on the sidewalk. Mortal practitioners of such strength were quite rare, maybe no more than a few dozen in all of North America, and to run across one so near the Old Wizard's daughter stretched the bounds of coincidence no end. Anogh had known he could count on the connection between the two young mortals.

At the parking garage he had to decide which to follow. But he already knew where the young lady lived and worked, and he had no idea where the young man had chosen to hide, so the decision was an easy one. He followed the young fellow back to a cheap motel in the Mission District.

15

A Friend

PAUL COULDN'T JUST loiter inside Katherine's parking garage, or out front for that matter. So the next day he donned his wig, strapped on the shoulder holster with the Sig, loaded some extra clips into slots in the shoulder holster, donned the windbreaker, and a few minutes before six sat down at a bus stop across the street from the garage. Sure enough, fifteen minutes later he saw Katherine walking up the street, carrying a folded magazine, her attention focused on some article within. Today she wore an expensive looking pants suit, gray, and again the high heels. Yesterday he'd been focused on following her and hadn't noticed she walked with a slight limp. Obviously, neither of them had escaped last week's mess without injury.

He did a little mental calculation to pick the right moment, then stood, jay-walked across the street and walked into the garage entrance, got there about ten feet behind her. She stopped at the elevator, pressed the up button and only gave him a cursory glance when he stopped next to her. When the elevator arrived she stepped in and to the right, turned her back to the wall and pressed the button for the fourth floor. He followed her in, stepped to the left and put his back to the wall facing her.

He suddenly doubted everything he was doing. She'd been an ally in so many ways, but she was the daughter of a man trying to kill him. He stood there paralyzed with indecision.

She gave him another cursory glance, but returned her attention to the magazine. A second later she looked at him again and frowned, and this time she didn't look away. She stared at him intently and her eyebrows narrowed. Then her eyes widened with incredulity, she said, "Conklin?" and started laughing, emitting deep throated hoots while she pressed a hand against her chest and gasped for air. "You look ridiculous," she said as the elevator doors opened on the fourth floor.

He marched up to her indignantly, closed the distance between them to a hand's breadth. "Until you and your friends came along, nobody ever tried to kill me. And your father still wants to. So forgive me if I choose paranoia over death." The elevator doors started to close and he blocked them with an arm.

"That's not true," she said. "He's trying to help you."

They both stepped out of the elevator sidestepping and still facing each other. He lowered his voice. "As far as I'm concerned, among all you magic people, you're the only one who hasn't tried to kill me. That's why I'm here. I need help with this crap, and you're the only one I can trust."

She considered that for a moment, then tossed her head toward her car. "Ok. Get in my car. We'll go to my place."

He followed her to her car, a rather expensive looking Jaguar. She got in behind the wheel and he climbed into the passenger seat. She fumbled in her purse for a moment and came up with a cell phone.

He grabbed her wrist. "Who're you calling?"

"My father. He's been looking all over for you."

"Of course he has. He wants to kill me."

"Let me call him and I'll prove that's not true."

He shook his head adamantly. "No. No one knows where I am until I know I can trust them. If you don't like that then I'm out'a here. I'll disappear on my own."

She looked at his hand holding her wrist and her eyes narrowed unhappily, clearly demanding he let go, so he did. "I mean it," he added.

She nodded. "All right, as long as you're with me I won't let anyone know where you are without your permission. Girl scouts honor. But I do have an idea. I might be able to prove to you my father's not trying to kill you."

••••

Mikhail watched the Jaguar pull out of the garage, right on time like every weekday evening. Except this time the young woman had a passenger, a man with shoulder length hair. He hadn't paid particular attention to the fellow that walked into the garage only a few feet behind the young woman. After all, the fellow had come from a different direction and was probably just another patron of the garage. And he hadn't gotten a good look at the fellow's face, just his backside and the shoulder-length hair. And, because of the glare from the car's windows, he hadn't gotten a good look at the passenger's face as the car sped past. But he was almost certain it was the same fellow who'd followed her into the garage.

He pulled out his cell phone and dialed Karpov's number. "Da," a heavy voice answered. Alexei. The man was a stupid bear, though stupid bears could be quite dangerous, could maul you rather badly.

"I have important information for Mr. Karpov," Mikhail said in Russian.

"You can tell me."

Stupid bear, dangerous bear. "Mr. Karpov instructed me to talk to him personally if I had news of the young man. I don't want Mr. Karpov to be unhappy with me. Do you want him unhappy with you?"

There was a long moment of silence then the bear growled, a low rumbling from deep in his throat. Again, silence for several seconds, then Karpov said, "Mikhail, what is it?"

"I think I just saw the young man leave with the Old Wizard's daughter, a passenger in her car."

"You think?"

This was a dangerous moment. If he didn't say this properly, Karpov might assume he'd been negligent, and other men had lost their lives for less. Mikhail told him about the young man with long hair that followed her into the garage.

"Describe him," Karpov demanded.

"Thirtyish, six feet, two hundred pounds, trim waist, looks like he's in good shape I'm certain it was the same fellow in her car. But he had long hair, shoulder-length, nothing like the man you described."

"Any fool can buy a wig. It's him. Get your car and go to her place, don't let him leave until I get there. If he tries to leave, stop him, but don't kill him. Not yet."

"Yes, Mr. Karpov."

"And Mikhail . . . you did good."

"Thank you, Mr. Karpov."

••••

Belinda was an excellent sorceress, and Baalthelmass was quite pleased with her. It took considerable power to retrieve Trogmoressh from the Netherworld, but she was up to the effort. Of course, since the Tertius had spent more than a week in the Netherworld it had lost all its power, but more importantly it had lost all control. It could no longer maintain a glamour, and a ravenous need to feed ruled it completely. It would've gone on a killing spree as soon as she released it from her circle, devoured her and perhaps a half-dozen more souls before gaining any self-control. But by then it would be too late. The local mortal sorcerers would be alerted to its presence, would band together and hunt it down, and they'd do more than merely banish it, they'd destroy it, annihilate it completely.

But when Belinda released her circle the outcome was different because Baalthelmass was there to subdue the Tertius. Belinda had acquired, and Baalthelmass had enthralled, a half-dozen mortals for Trogmoressh's initial feeding. Baalthelmass locked them in a cellar with the Tertius and released their enthrallment so they could experience the feeding without its sedative effects. And the screams as the Tertius devoured their souls awakened Baalthelmass's own hungers, but It suppressed Its desires, keeping the greater prize in mind. It had taken a full day, but the Tertius was now ready to maintain a glamour, and to hunt.

"You've tasted the young witch before," Baalthelmass said. "At the hospital."

Trogmoressh had chosen to adopt the image of the young Lord-of-the-Unliving.

Baalthelmass made the Tertius meet Its eyes. "You may taste her again, but only a little. Only enough to weaken her, enough to subdue her, to enthrall her and bring her back to me. If you lose control and consume her, or you fail in this task in any other way, I'll feed you back to the Netherlife myself."

The Tertius bowed its head. "I'll not fail you, master."

With a light touch Baalthelmass imparted to the Tertius the knowledge of the location of the young witch's home. "Go. Night approaches, so you may hunt without hindrance."

When the Tertius had gone It turned to the sorceress. "You've done well, my dear Belinda." It reached out and touched her cheek. She quivered, threw her head back and gasped. Trembling in the throes of ecstasy, she so completely lost control she slowly sank to her hands and knees rather than fall to the floor, then laid down. For several seconds she laid there grunting and panting as waves of pleasure washed through her, and when it finally ended she laid there struggling for breath.

Baalthelmass said, "A little reward for you, my dear. But when you've recovered enough, I want you to bring the young Lord to me. Use whatever resources you have. By all means use your body, if you so choose, for certainly the mortals find you attractive enough, and that is one of your best assets. Use your body and take enjoyment of it, but bring him to me. Bring him back whole and only a little damaged and your reward will be ecstasy beyond imagining. Fail and I'll feed you to the Tertius."

••••

Clearly, money ran in the McGowan family. Katherine owned one of the larger places in the Sunset district south of Golden Gate Park. It was one of those three-story fifties homes, with half the bottom floor taken up by the luxury of an enclosed garage. From the outside, even in the dark, Paul could tell the place had been extensively renovated. And the inside looked like it had been gutted, then completely rebuilt and redecorated.

Katherine marched across the living room, threw the magazine and her purse casually on a large couch, then turned and pulled off her coat as she disappeared through a doorway that must be the master bedroom. "Make yourself at home," she shouted at him from the bedroom. "There's beer and wine in the fridge, or make a pot of coffee if that's your preference. I'll take white wine. Pour me a glass while I change into some-thing more casual."

Paul found some white wine in the refrigerator and glasses in the cupboard. He poured two glasses, but hesitated to pull off his windbreaker. At the prospect of letting Katherine see the gun and the shoulder holster, he suddenly had doubts about his new motto, began to wonder if perhaps he was overreacting.

"What're you thinking about?"

He jumped at the sound of Katherine's voice. He'd been standing at the kitchen counter staring at the wine in one of the glasses, and hadn't heard a sound as she'd walked right up to him.

"Relax," she said. She reached out, and before he realized what she intended she grabbed the zipper on the front of his windbreaker and tugged, pulling it down. "Get rid of the coat," she said as she pulled it open. But she suddenly froze with her mouth open, and slowly her eyes widened. "Is that a gun?"

He turned away from her, pulling the coat out of her hands, and carried his glass of wine into the living room. She followed him, saying, "Don't you think you're overreact-ing? I mean a gun! Really! Or did you always carry a gun?"

He pulled off the windbreaker and the wig, tossed them on the couch next to her purse. "No, I didn't carry a gun before all this. And maybe I am overreacting. I don't know." He popped a buckle on the shoulder holster and dropped the whole rig on the couch with his windbreaker.

She'd changed into a long-sleeve, white cotton blouse and shorts, and he noticed the black and blue and yellow splotching of the bruises on her legs. "I see you picked up a few bruises too."

She looked down at her legs. "Ya, isn't that atrocious? I'm covered with them." She slid one of the sleeves of her blouse up, exposing a forearm also covered with bruises. "It's going to be long sleeves for a while, and pant suits, or fully opaque stockings. And I like tight skirts. I look good in them."

A piece of him agreed with her on that point and he almost said so. But he thought of Suzanna and guilt silenced him. So to get his mind off that line of thought he asked, "So what's this idea you've got? How're you going to prove your father's not trying to kill me?"

She gave him a secretive smile. "Simple. We'll just call him and ask."

••••

Trogmoressh dropped Its glamour, unfurled Its wings and took to the skies. The knowledge Its master had provided concerning the location of the young witch's abode confused It a bit. But since It had tasted her once already, all It needed to do was get close, then It could find her by the scent of her magic. Tonight It would feast on her. It would find her alone and feed slowly, a banquet of power like nothing It had ever tasted.

No! It must remember It was only allowed to taste a bit of the young witch's soul. It must not consume her, for then It would face the wrath of Its master, Its very cruel master.

••••

"I'll admit, Katherine, if he'd turned out to be a rogue, and I couldn't get him to stop summoning demons voluntarily, I probably would've had to kill him." McGowan's voice, coming from the speaker in the phone in Katherine's home office, seemed sincere.

Katherine's plan was simple. She called her father from her home office, put him on the speakerphone, and didn't reveal Paul's presence while she asked him a few simple questions. They'd agreed in advance Paul would make the decision. If he gave her a thumbs-up, she could reveal his presence. But thumbs-down meant she was to finish the conversation in a normal fashion without mention of Paul.

Katherine had opened up with, "Father, I need to know what went on that night in Paul Conklin's apartment."

McGowan had, in turn, activated his own speakerphone so Colleen could join the conversation at that end. Paul guessed Colleen was the older hippie, and intended to confirm that at the end of the conversation. McGowan and Colleen described their confrontation with the Russians in front of Paul's apartment building, and their description of the incident in Paul's apartment fit the events, as he knew them. Paul had seen Colleen blast Joe Stalin with some sort of lightning an instant before he pulled the trigger on his howitzer, and had to admit if she hadn't, it would've ended there with his brains splattered all over his apartment.

McGowan asked, "Why all the questions?"

Katherine raised her eyebrows at Paul, clearly asking if she could reveal his presence. He wasn't ready for that, and he didn't want her to end the conversation, so he just shook his head. She lied admirably. "Paul called me, at my office, and we had a long chat on the phone."

McGowan demanded, "Where is he?"

"I don't know. But he thinks you're trying to kill him."

"Damn! More damn, and double damn! What gave him that idea?"

"Weeellll," Katherine said, her voice dripping sarcasm. "Could it be that every time you show up it's with the Russian mafia in tow, and they do very unfriendly things like shoot guns at the poor fellow?"

"Damn!"

"And then there's the conversation you and Colleen had in your kitchen just as Paul was sneaking out of your house, the one in which you told her you couldn't promise you wouldn't kill him."

"Damn! Damn, damn, damn! He overheard that, huh?"

"Katherine, dear." That was the hippie. "Paul must not have heard the end of the conversation. Your father acknowledged the little people wouldn't abdicate their traditional neutrality for a rogue. And he finished by promising he'd try to help young Mr. Conklin."

McGowan said, "Something doesn't add up here."

Katherine demanded, "Like what?"

"Well, to start with, two emergents crossed over that night, but we only found one in his apartment. And I thought he was summoning a succubus, but Colleen says there was no summoning, and it wasn't a succubus. And the little people relinquishing their neutrality, that's unheard of. And that Tertius couldn't have pulled you and him into the Netherworld, so who, or better, what did? And that Secundus caste was no Secundus caste. I think the two of you ran into a Primus caste."

"Why do you say that?"

They could hear Colleen and McGowan quietly arguing in the background for several seconds, then McGowan said, "We're not in complete agreement on everything, but Colleen and I do agree something happened during our summons, something that reverberated throughout the Three Realms, which is the reason the Sidhe got involved. Colleen thinks it was your cross-over and the banishment of the demon. But you told me you thought the demon had enthralled Conklin. I know you changed your mind later because Conklin certainly couldn't break a Primus caste enthrallment. But I think he somehow did. I think that's what reverberated so loudly throughout the Realms."

Katherine frowned and tilted her head slightly to one side in thought, her eyes narrowing sharply. "I'd forgotten all about this, but that demon kept calling Paul *Dragon-stink*."

Colleen and McGowan uttered the same question simultaneously, "What? Dragon-stink?" They said it in a way Paul didn't like, and this conversation was raising more questions than it was answering, so Paul raised his hand and gave Katherine a thumbs-down.

She frowned at him and shook her head. He raised his lips in a silent snarl that said, *You promised. We had a deal.*

She rolled her eyes unhappily, then silently mouthed, *Ok.*

She said, "It called him Dragon-stink, repeatedly, and I have no idea what that means. Listen, I have a date, and I'm already late. Why don't we continue this tomorrow?"

There was a little more back and forth before the conversation ended, but the moment Katherine hit the button that killed the line, she turned to Paul and asked, "Aren't you satisfied? I think it's pretty clear my father's not trying to kill you."

"I'll give you that," he said.

"Then why make me end the conversation the way you did?"

Paul didn't know how to explain it to her. These were all people she'd grown up with, people she could trust implicitly. "I want less attention, not more. I want this all to blow over so I can go back to my ordinary old life."

She shook her head sadly. "That's not going to happen."

"Ya, I know," he said. "I'd better get going."

He walked out of her office. She followed him, saying, "You need to face reality. Just like in the Netherworld you can't pretend you're in some psyche ward somewhere wearing a straitjacket."

In the living room he retrieved his windbreaker and shoulder holster, held the holster up in front of her and said, "I'd say this is facing some pretty serious reality."

She rolled her eyes and said, "I do think the gun's going a little overboard. Colleen and my father and I can protect you without that."

As he turned toward the front door she stepped in front of him and held up her hands to stop him. "Don't go. You can crash on my couch. At least my place is warded. They're not the most powerful wards, but they'll give you some protection, so my place is the best chance you'll have to get a decent night's sleep."

He hesitated and she said, "I've even got a couple of unused tooth brushes, still in the wrapping from the store. Wait here."

She disappeared into her bedroom, reappeared a moment later and tossed him a new toothbrush and some toothpaste. She pointed across the room. "The bathroom's down the hall on the left."

Paul stepped into the bathroom, closed the door and looked at his image in the mirror. "What a fucking mess," he said. He'd harbored a small hope this could all blow over. After he and Katherine had literally been rescued from hell, and, as Katherine had explained to him, the Tertius that had come after them was now stuck in hell and powerless to return, he'd hoped things would cool down. But the Netherworld thing had drawn the interest of these elves—Sidhe, they called them—and after his escape from Faerie he didn't think for a second they'd walk away from this. And then there were the Russians, who struck him as a bunch of pretty tenacious bastards. And from the conversation they'd just had it was clear McGowan's interest was on the upswing, and he was now taking an even greater interest in Paul. He was going to help Paul. But Paul didn't want help. He just wanted them to leave him alone so he could go back to Suzanna and Cloe.

Paul brushed his teeth and splashed some water on his face. In the living room he found a blanket and a pillow lying on the couch. Katherine shouted at him from somewhere in her bedroom. "I've set up the coffee, so if you get up before me just turn the pot on. And help yourself to cereal or toast or whatever."

He pulled off his shoes, spread the blanket on the couch, crawled beneath it and laid there for a while, thinking if circumstances had been different, he might not have ended up sleeping on the couch tonight.

••••

As McGowan hit the switch on the phone, killing the connection, Colleen said, "She's lying, you know?"

"What do you mean?" McGowan asked. "You mean Conklin didn't call her, and she made all that up?"

Colleen shook her head. "You're such a man, old man."

"You mean she does know where he is?"

"Don't be daft. Of course she knows where he is. But that's not exactly what I meant."

McGowan threw his hands up and rolled his eyes. "Well then what did you mean?"

Colleen continued to shake her head sadly. "She knows where he is because he was standing there right next to her listening to our conversation."

"He was? That's impossible."

"Didn't you notice the little pauses here and there? They were short, and few, but they were whispering or making silent signs at each other."

"Why would she lie to me like that, my own daughter?"

Colleen couldn't suppress a laugh. "She and the young man have been through a lot together, in a very short period of time, saved each other's lives a couple of times. At this point I should think they trust each other considerably. And I don't doubt he did need to hear from your own lips you're not trying to kill him. And I think they're attracted to each other."

McGowan stood. "That shit better stay away from my daughter. He's too dangerous, at least until we get this cleared up. I'm going over there right now."

"And I'll go with you, just to keep you from acting too much like a father."

"What do you mean by that?"

She stood and headed for the door, shaking her head sadly.

••••

Katherine tiptoed into her small workshop—she liked to think of it as her little witch's den. While Paul had been in the bathroom she'd pocketed his hippie wig, and she sat down now at a small workbench to examine it carefully. As she suspected she had no trouble finding a few of his hairs stuck to the inside of the wig. She retrieved them carefully, then plucked a few of her own.

She took one of her hairs and one of his, and carefully entwined them into a single strand. She repeated the process to create a second woven strand and laid the two of them out in front of her. She'd also retrieved his wine glass when he wasn't looking, and very carefully she took each strand and ran it along the lip of the wine glass. Even the most fastidious person would leave a little saliva on the rim of a glass.

She positioned both strands horizontally in front of her, one above the other, then began carefully tracing a rune over the two of them. The symbol she'd chosen was the horizontal figure-eight sign for infinity, and she traced two such symbols with the tip of her finger, one over the other, one over each of the two strands of woven hair. But she was careful to intertwine the loops of the two sigils as she traced them, careful to intertwine them like the limbs of two lovers embracing. She traced the rune seven times, feeding power carefully into the strands until they glowed with a faint, ethereal light.

She lifted one of the glowing strands, wove it loosely into her own hair, then with her tongue placed a little saliva on the tip of her finger. When she touched the saliva to the strand woven in her hair it flared brilliantly for a second, then faded away. She didn't have to look to know the strand itself had disappeared.

She took the second strand of woven hair, tiptoed out of her workshop into her bedroom, out of her bedroom into the living room. Paul had crashed into a deep sleep and lay on the couch breathing heavily. Poor fellow must be utterly exhausted.

She knelt down beside him and carefully laid the remaining strand on his head among his own hairs. Then again she touched a finger to her tongue to retrieve a bit of saliva, then touched the saliva to the woven strand in his hair. Like hers it flared brilliantly, then died and was gone.

It was a variation on an old attraction spell, but with a few important differences. Saliva and hair from both of them, mixed and applied to both of them with the proper runes and a leavening of power. It was the strongest locator spell she could devise, much stronger than merely having a piece of him like a strand of hair. By mixing pieces of her with pieces of him, only the strongest of wards could prevent her from locating him.

Katherine was too keyed up to go right to bed, so she stood and walked to the French doors at the back of her house, opened one slightly and slipped out onto her deck. It was an elevated deck about ten feet above her back yard, and quite large. She crossed it and leaned on the rail. Her house was high enough that she had a nice view of the Pacific in the distance, but in the dark all she could see were lights from the half-mile of houses between her and Ocean Beach.

She liked Paul and sympathized with his frustration, though his stubbornness exasperated her no end. She tried to imagine how off-kilter he must be after having all this stuff dumped on him without warning. Until now he'd led a life without the need to look over his shoulder for the next Russian thug trying to kill him.

She heard a noise behind her, turned and saw Paul standing on the deck in front of the French doors. The light she'd left on in the living room behind him turned him into a dark silhouette. She must've awakened him with her spell. He walked slowly toward her, stopped in front of her just close enough to be a little intimate, stood there silently and she thought he might kiss her, and remembering the kiss they shared in Faerie she decided she wanted him to. So she looked up at him and met his blood-red goat-slitted eyes—

16

No Place Safe

PARKING IN THE Sunset district was almost impossible. Many houses there didn't have a garage, so most residents parked on the street. Mikhail found a parking place two blocks from the young woman's house and killed the engine. He slipped the Glock out of its holster and checked the rounds in his magazine. Like any practitioner, he used special ammunition.

He returned the Glock to its holster and checked the street carefully. It was a quiet residential neighborhood, the kind where the residents were quick to call the police if they saw a suspicious looking fellow loitering about.

He stepped out of the car, locked it and strolled casually up the sidewalk.

••••

Paul awoke with a start, had a vague recollection of some dream, but that didn't account for the uneasiness he felt. He sat up and scanned the empty living room, spotted some French doors at the back of the house, one of which was ajar, and realized they must lead out onto a deck or patio of some sort. He could just see enough through the glass of the French doors to know someone was standing on the deck there, realized it must be Katherine. He swung his legs off the couch and put on his shoes.

Against his own better judgment he knew he had to trust McGowan, let Katherine call her father and tell him Paul was with her. He really had no choice.

He stood and walked over to the French doors. From this angle he could see through the door's glass panes, could see a faint image of Katherine out on the deck. But with no lights on the deck, the single light in the living room cast a harsh glare on the window and it was nearly impossible to make out any details.

She wasn't leaning on the rail but had turned sideways. She stood there silently, her wine glass held in both hands looking up slightly, and he realized someone was out there with her. A man stood facing her, both looking into each other's eyes like lovers, and Paul's first thought was she had a boyfriend who'd come by while Paul was sleeping. They stared at each other so intimately Paul thought he should grab his coat and gun and just slip quietly away. But he should at least say good-bye, make some excuse and exit politely. He took a couple steps toward the French doors.

Katherine was medium height, and the man standing facing her was three or four inches taller than her, about Paul's height. In fact the man looked a bit like Paul, and for a moment he thought it must be his own reflection in the windows of the French door. But if it was his reflection it should've been face-on, not standing sideways facing Katherine, which seemed odd. Paul leaned forward, so close to the glass pane his breath fogged it slightly, and he realized the man looked exactly like him, a perfect doppelganger. It took him one heartbeat to put it all together, another to realize Katherine's life was in danger, another to realize he had to act now.

Paul spun, scrambled around the couch to the coffee table where he'd left the Sig in the shoulder holster. He fumbled at the gun in the dim light and had trouble getting it out of the holster. It was one thing to calmly pull off rounds at a firing range, quite another to get the fucking gun out of the holster when Katherine's life was on the line.

He pulled the gun free, dropped the holster onto the couch, pulled the slide and jacked a round into the chamber, then hurdled the couch and ran across the living room to the French doors. He considered kicking the one that was ajar wide open like some hotshot cop in the movies, but realized he needed to get closer or risk shooting Katherine as well. So he calmly shouldered the door open and took two long strides across the deck. Both Katherine and the demon were so locked in the enthrallment neither realized he was there. He dropped into a crouch, held the gun in a text-book two-handed grip, and from only a few feet away, aiming directly at the vampire's head, he pulled off five rounds in rapid succession.

His ears shut down at the thundering blasts from the weapon, but he saw the impact of the first round even through the blinding muzzle flash. It slammed into the side of the vampire's head, rocked it violently to one side and opened a cratered exit-wound that spewed fragments of bone and muscle. Amazingly, the vampire only staggered away from him, turned enough to take the second round just underneath its left eye, which rocked its head back and its chin up. The third bullet plowed into the underside of its chin and the top of its head exploded. The fourth bullet hit it in the throat and the fifth in the chest. It stopped with its back against the deck rail facing him, its head a smoking ruin.

"Paul!" Katherine screamed, coming out of the stupor of the enthrallment.

The vampire's glamour had disappeared, and one of those bat monsters stood before him. It slowly unfurled its wings and took a step toward him. At the firing range he'd practiced firing five rounds in rapid succession, pause, five more rounds, pause, five more and the clip was empty. So he pumped five more rounds into the vampire's chest, each bullet hammering it backward a step until again it backed into the deck rail. Paul lifted a foot, kicked it in the chest and it tumbled backward over the rail.

Paul stepped up to the rail, looked over it into Katherine's back yard, a big mistake. Before Paul could react one clawed hand grabbed the rail, and the other clamped viciously around his throat. The vampire started climbing back up on the deck, using Paul's throat and the deck rail for purchase. But Paul felt something else tugging at him, a blind ravenous hunger, a need to rend and murder and devour, and it pulled at him through the creature's claw where it touched his throat.

He could feel his life leaking out through that contact and his knees weakened, he almost collapsed over the rail and he realized it was feeding on him. He could sense the flow of energy, or life force or whatever it was, as it bled out through his throat and into the monster's hand, all in response to the *pull* it exerted on his soul. A sense of lethargy threatened to overcome him, and he couldn't resist as it pulled him forward so that he leaned heavily over the edge of the deck rail.

Suzanna's ghost dropped out of nowhere and landed on the demon's back. Apparently her ghost had much more effect on a demon's body than that of good old Joe Stalin. She wrapped her arms around its throat and pulled, forcing it to arch its back. And then Katherine hit it with a deck chair—a distant part of Paul wondered in amazement that a woman her size could swing such a chair high over her head with such force. The chair slammed into the creature's ruined head and the drain on Paul's soul suddenly stopped. It was like tasting two glasses of wine and comparing them one to the other in rapid succession, one with his life flowing outward and diminishing, one with no flow at all, and he thought he saw how to make it flow the other way. So he pulled with all his strength and miraculously it reversed. He felt a surge of power and strength and energy, and realized he was feeding on the demon's power.

With his left hand he grabbed the wrist of the claw wrapped about his throat, then he shoved the muzzle of the gun down into the smoking crater at the top of its head. He tore the monster's claw away from his throat and pulled off five more rounds. The slugs made a sickening, wet, splatting sound and the vampire, with Suzanna riding its back, toppled backward into the bushes below.

With the last round expended the slide on the Sig locked back, and Paul realized that in his amateurish haste he'd left the shoulder holster and the spare clips on the couch. He shouted at Katherine, "Spare ammo, on the couch."

Her eyes widened, and in an instant they both turned and scrambled through the open French door.

•••

Mikhail was careful to move discretely, though it was important to look casual, not like some thief sneaking about the neighborhood. That was the kind of thoughtlessness that resulted in a call to the police, the kind of stupid mistake Alexei or Vladimir might make. He needed to find a place where he could observe but be unobserved, so he slipped into a shadow to one side of the young woman's front porch. His orders were clear: wait for Karpov and intervene only if the man tried to leave.

Mikhail wasn't a strong wizard, otherwise he'd be more than just one of Karpov's shooters, but he was a trained practitioner. And he had enough capability to know when something unpleasant had arrived, something not of the Mortal Plane, and since he'd heard the other incidents involving this man also involved demons, he could guess what. He pulled the Glock and was creeping cautiously up the steps of the woman's front porch when the first shots rang out.

••••

"Out the front door," Katherine shouted. She scrambled around the couch while Paul jumped over it, dug his heals in, turned and grabbed the shoulder holster, turned again and ran after Katherine to the front door. When she yanked it open, standing side-by-side they found themselves facing a man with a gun aimed at them and they froze.

Katherine shouted at the man, "You don't understand."

The fellow was tall but quite thin, and he spoke in thickly accented English. "No, you don't understand."

Paul started to say, "But there's a—" But before he could finish the man's eyes suddenly widened and focused on something far behind them.

Hoping the man was smart enough to realize he and Katherine were not the real danger, Paul threw an arm around Katherine's shoulders and dropped to the floor, dragging her down with him. He turned just as the demon hit the French doors. It shredded them with a swipe of its claws, but as it lunged through them bolts of lightning erupted around it with a thunderous clap and the monster staggered.

"My wards," Katherine shouted.

The man in the doorway crouched and fired his weapon over them, short single bursts, each carefully timed. Beneath the muzzle flash Paul fumbled with the shoulder holster, retrieved one of his spare clips, ejected the empty and slammed the new one into place. He hit the release, the slide slammed forward, and staying on one knee he took aim.

The monster had made it half way across the living room before the newcomer had stopped it by emptying a clip into it. It lay on its side, and with one of its legs dangling by torn bits of cartilage it had trouble getting up. "Shoot away one of its wings," the fellow with the accent said as he changed clips. "Then it can't fly or run."

Paul took aim, fired several shots into its shoulder, which stilled that wing enough for him to empty the rest of the clip and pulp the entire shoulder joint. The Russian followed up by emptying another clip into the creature's other wing. The vampire lay on the floor and thrashed about weakly, its head a smoking ruin, its chest cratered by more than thirty hollow-points, one leg nearly severed, both wings splintered and shredded, and still it tried to rise, each wound hissing and emitting a dark, greasy smoke. Paul remembered the silver in the special ammunition and its effect on demons.

He looked at Katherine, "And this is one of the weaker ones, a Tertius?"

She nodded numbly. "That's why I was so afraid of the Secundus."

"Put the fucking gun down." Someone pressed the muzzle of a heavy gun against the back of Paul's head, and he easily recalled the thick Russian accent: Joe Stalin. "Do you want me to kill him, boss?"

Paul had emptied his clip and the slide on the Sig had locked back. But even if he'd had a full clip he didn't stand a chance with a gun pressed to the back of his head.

The older Russian slipped past them and headed for the struggling vampire, saying, "No. Just hold him while I take care of this."

Paul dropped the gun to the floor and watched in fascination as the older Russian pulled some sort of silver spike from his coat. He approached the struggling vampire carefully, stopped just out of its reach and drew some sort of symbol in the air with his fingertip. He repeated the symbol several times and it started to glow, and as it did the vampire calmed and grew quiescent. The older Russian bent down and plunged the spike into the bullet-ridden ruin of the vampire's chest. The vampire screamed, a sharp, piercing cry, but the Russian held the spike in place with his left hand while he mumbled something and drew another symbol over the spike with his right index finger. He repeated it several times, and as the symbol started to glow the vampire became still again, grew translucent and glowed with an eerie light for a few seconds, then dissipated into a cloud of fine ash.

The older Russian stood, turned to Paul and Katherine. "I'm Vasily Karpov." He nodded to Joe Stalin. "Let me introduce Alexei." He nodded to the Slav with the high cheekbones and greasy, blond hair. "That's Vladimir," then to the tall thin fellow, "and that's Mikhail."

He smiled at Paul unpleasantly. "And you, Mr. Conklin," he said it more like meester, rather than mister, "are coming with me."

He strode past them out the door, calling over his shoulder, "And bring the woman too."

They tied Paul's hands and feet, then wadded up some sort of dishrag from Katherine's kitchen, stuffed it in his mouth and tied it in place quickly. The last thing he saw was a black canvas bag as they pulled it over his head.

••••

Belinda had spent more than an hour crafting the shadow spell, and on a dark night like this it was extremely effective. She'd used Katherine McGowan's address to find her home, had parked two blocks away and stood now in her special shadows across the street. From the lights in the windows it was clear she'd arrived sometime after the young woman had returned home. If the young man wasn't with the McGowan woman, then she'd wasted a few hours and she'd have to resort to other means to find him. But if he'd accompanied her, she'd save days of hunting.

She watched the tall, thin Russian arrive, watched him take up a position to one side of the young woman's front porch. He was good, this Russian, stayed in a shadow and didn't move, didn't succumb to the temptation to light a cigarette and give his position away by the flare of the match, or the glow of the burning tobacco.

She saw the Russian start at the sound of the first gunshots, watched him climb the steps of the front porch as more shots sounded. And when someone yanked the front door open she saw him silhouetted in it by the light from the room beyond. Then he fired his weapon and the muzzle flash spilled past him, lighting up the street. Another car pulled up and double-parked in the street as more shots sounded from within. She recognized Karpov and his thugs as they sprinted up the front steps of the house.

There were no more shots and she sensed Karpov's flow of power as he disposed of the stupid Tertius. Then she watched the Russians bring two prisoners out, both bound and with dark sacks of some sort over their heads, one clearly a woman, the other clearly a man. She'd found her prey.

She hurried back to her car, had it started and idling before the Russians pulled away from the house. She activated a spell that hid her car from anything but the most thorough examination, and pulled out into the street to follow them.

••••

McGowan spotted the flashing police cruisers from several blocks up the street, and as he and Colleen got closer to Katherine's house he could see uniformed officers walking in and out of her open front door. There were four squad cars and an SFPD van parked at odd angles in the street in front of her house, their flashing red, white and blue lights illuminating the night of a normally quiet neighborhood. A few of Katherine's neighbors were huddled in a group on the sidewalk beyond the police tape.

McGowan stopped his car in the middle of the street next to one of the squad cars. As he climbed out of the car a uniformed policewoman approached, saying, "I'm sorry, you'll have to move on. This is a crime scene—"

McGowan interrupted her, shouting and pointing, "That's my daughter's house."

She held up a hand, glanced over her shoulder and shouted, "Frank, I got a relative here. Get Lasky, or one of the other detectives."

Sergeant Lasky, SFPD, wouldn't give any particulars until he'd seen identification and thoroughly questioned McGowan and Colleen. McGowan told him he'd had a phone conversation with Katherine earlier, and Lasky said, "Must've happened just after that."

"Exactly what happened?" McGowan demanded angrily.

Lasky shrugged. "Looks like a home invasion. Bad news is your daughter's gone, maybe kidnapped, maybe not. And there were apparently a lot of gunshots; you can smell the burned powder. Good news is there's no blood, so I doubt your daughter's hurt, at least not yet."

They wanted McGowan to walk through the place to see if anything was missing, and just inside the front door the demon scent hit him like a hammer. Two crime scene technicians, on their knees in the middle of the living room, were carefully examining a scattering of small gray lumps in the middle of a dusting of whitish ash. "What's that?" McGowan demanded, knowing full well the answer.

Lasky frowned. "Weirdest thing. It's a bunch of handgun slugs, must be twenty or thirty of them, deformed like we'd find in someone's body, but these're just lying in a pile in the middle of the floor with a bunch of ash around them."

McGowan confirmed that, as far as he could tell, nothing was missing from Katherine's home. They kept McGowan and Colleen there for another hour, took formal statements and let them go.

In the car Colleen said, "You caught the demon scent?"

"Ya," McGowan said as he started the car and accelerated up the street. "I'm guessing Tertius caste. Someone shot it up pretty bad, and then someone put it down with a very powerful spell. And when I think of that spell I just can't stop thinking about those fucking Russians. I know the scent of that old man's magic, and that means they've got my daughter."

17

To Feed

THEY STUFFED PAUL and Katherine in the trunk of a car, plastic zip-ties binding their hands and feet, their hands behind their backs. Paul had landed in the trunk on his back in a rather uncomfortable position, jammed between a lot of junk there. They'd tossed Katherine on top of him, facing him, the junk preventing both of them from moving about and finding a more comfortable position.

Paul could feel Katherine's breasts pressed against his chest, and under other circumstances he might've enjoyed the close proximity of a beautiful woman. But trussed up, with black canvas bags tied over their heads, gags stuffed in their mouths, and guilty thoughts of Suzanna filling his head—

Paul had realized rather quickly he couldn't dislodge the gag, though he tried. But he could hear and feel Katherine moving desperately, and when she spoke he realized she'd had some success with the gag, though her words were garbled so he knew her success was only partial. "Pauw, can wou ge woofe?"

His vocabulary was rather limited. "Huh uh."

"Amyfing?"

"Huh uh."

"Fuffer-fuckurs!"

Paul closed his eyes and tried to get comfortable. The car beneath them swayed a little, hit a bump now and then, but the driver drove cautiously. There was nothing he or Katherine could do until the Russians decided to retrieve them from the trunk. But in their forced intimacy, fully in contact from chin to knees, every bump or turn jostled him and Katherine together, like two horny teenagers engrossed in some heavy petting in a car. Paul tried to keep a tight rein on his imagination, but when he attempted to think about something else his thoughts always returned to Katherine and the kiss they'd shared in Faerie, and he started to get an erection.

Katherine had apparently had more success spitting out the gag because her words were less garbled. "Gee, Conklin, should I be flattered." She laughed and the erection disappeared.

The Russians lifted them out of the trunk almost kindly. They cut the zip-ties binding his ankles so he could walk, and with someone supporting him on both sides they hustled him along. He had no sense of direction or place, but eventually they forced him to sit on some sort of chair. They cut the zip-ties binding his wrists, attached both wrists and ankles to the chair with new zip-ties, then yanked off the black canvas hood.

It was clear the Russians didn't have much imagination. They'd tied him to a chair in the middle of a room underneath a light hanging directly overhead. The light lit up a circle of empty floor about him, beyond which he could see nothing but darkness. It reminded him of every cliché in every gangster movie he'd ever seen.

Joe Stalin stepped out of the darkness, untied the gag and pulled the wad of cloth out of Paul's mouth. The Russian grinned unpleasantly, and from down in his throat a deep rumble emerged, like the quiet growl of a large bear happily anticipating a meal. Behind Joe, Karpov stepped into the light with the ugly blond at his side. They approached Paul and Joe Stalin stepped to one side.

"Mr. Conklin," Karpov said. Again he said meester, not mister. "You are a curiosity to me, to many of us." He glanced to one side at Joe Stalin and said, "Well, not to Alexei here." He patted Joe on the cheek. "Alexei don't have much imagination." All three of them chuckled as if at some inside joke. "When Alexei here sees something doesn't add up . . ." Karpov looked at Paul pointedly. ". . . he just removes it from the equation. Then he don't have to be curious about it."

Paul asked, "Where's Katherine?"

There was a sudden struggle behind him and to one side, and he heard Katherine's muffled grunts. They'd obviously tied her to another chair and replaced her gag.

The ugly blond leaned down close enough that Paul could smell onions on his breath. His accent was even thicker than Joe Stalin's. "Mr. Karpov asks questions. You answer." He looked up at Karpov. "Ve can make him talk, boss."

Paul had a wild, hysterical thought. The blonde's accent reminded him of an old cartoon show in which the antagonists were a couple of comic, Russian spies. Paul couldn't stop thinking of the ugly blond as *Boris*, and any minute now he expected a sultry, female Russian spy to step out of the darkness, speak in a heavily clichéd accent, and say something like, "Come Boris, let's go beat crap out of moose and squirrel." A little hysterical laugh escaped Paul's lips. Boris didn't like that.

"Mr. Karpov," Paul said, trying to be as polite as possible. "I'll tell you anything you want to know, but I don't think I know anything you want to know. This is all new to me."

Joe Stalin growled, "You're lying." He lifted a fist the size of a sledgehammer, but Karpov put a hand on his elbow and stopped him.

"Don't damage him. Don't break anything. Not yet."

Joe Stalin looked at his fist, then opened his hand to expose a large flat palm. He swung it out in a wide arc and slapped Paul with his open palm. Paul heard the impact like a remote, distant thing happening to someone else, his head rocked to one side and he almost lost consciousness. The slap felt as if someone had hit him in the face with a frying pan. His cheek burned and smoldered, and he heard Katherine struggling and trying to shout through her gag. Another frying-pan of a hand hit the other side of his face and he did lose consciousness for a moment. But while he drifted in another place his thoughts focused on Joe Stalin's hand and where it had made contact with his face. The contact had been like the contact between the demon's clawed hand and his throat. And he thought there might be a conduit there, a channel through which he could draw power. But then he realized what he was contemplating and he recoiled mentally. He'd be feeding on another human being. He'd be no better than that monster he'd faced earlier.

The room drifted back into focus and he looked up at Joe Stalin, the floor spinning and tilting sickeningly. Helplessly he watched Joe raise his big bearish paw for another hit, but Karpov raised a hand, stopping him. In the background Katherine was struggling frantically, and Karpov said, "Let's hear what the little witch has to say."

A couple of his thugs carried her chair, with her still tied into it, into the circle of light and put her down a few feet from Paul. She glared at Karpov with smoldering hard eyes as one of them removed her gag and pulled a large wad of cloth out of her mouth. "You idiot," she shouted. "He had a serous concussion only a week ago. Beating him like that could cause hemorrhaging in his brain and he could die on you. I know. I'm a doctor."

Boris marched over to her and raised a hand to hit her. Karpov yelled, "Stop." Boris froze and Karpov added, "Don't harm the old man's daughter. He's a colleague after all, a powerful one, a dangerous one, so out of professional courtesy you'll not touch the young lady."

Karpov turned on her. "And you will speak to me with the respect I am due."

She said angrily, "I'm telling the truth. If you want to kill him, just put a gun to his head and blow his brains out. Because beating him up will kill him just as fast."

Paul wanted to disagree with her on that, wanted to tell them he'd prefer to take his chances with the beating rather than having his brains blown out all over the room. The bullet-in-the-head thing seemed awfully final, awfully quick, but sarcasm wasn't going to buy him anything here so he kept his mouth shut.

Without taking his eyes off Katherine, Karpov held out a hand palm up. "Alexei your gun."

Joe Stalin pulled out his howitzer and put it in Karpov's hand. Karpov very slowly and dramatically pulled back the hammer on the big revolver, allowed them all to hear its cocking mechanism click into place. Then he lowered the gun and put the muzzle against the side of Paul's head, his eyes still fixed on Katherine. "Then you tell me what happened last week. And the minute I think you're lying, I will blow his brains out."

Katherine considered Karpov carefully, then spoke slowly and gave them a heavily edited version of their sojourn in the Netherworld and their adventures in Faerie, all completely true, but not complete. She left out the thing about the demon calling Paul *Dragon-stink*. She left out the fact that Paul had been enthralled by a Secundus caste demon, and possibly broken that enthrallment. She gave them the impression her father had penetrated the barriers between the Mortal Plane and the Netherworld, and given them a portal through which to return. And of course, since neither she nor Paul was anything close to as powerful as her father, neither of them knew how he'd accomplished such things. That was for really powerful wizards and sorcerers like her father and Karpov.

She told them about their abduction by Cadilus, their audience before Magreth, Paul's cell, and how the leprechauns had helped Paul escape. And when she finished, Karpov raised the gun and lowered the hammer carefully. He walked to Katherine, handing Joe Stalin his gun on the way, leaned down to her and said, "You told me the truth, but not all of it. But that's ok for now. I'll get the rest of it eventually."

A cell phone rang. Karpov reached into his coat, pulled out his, put it to his ear and said, "Karpov." He stepped into the darkness that lined the edge of the room and Paul heard him talking, though too quietly to make out any words. Then he stepped back into the light, putting his cell phone away.

To Katherine he said, "Your father wants you back, and I can't really keep you so he can have you. We've arranged a meeting."

He turned and strode toward the darkness, saying, "Alexei, stay with the man, and soften him up a bit. I still have some questions, and I want him in a talkative mood when I return. The rest of you bring the woman and come with me."

••••

"Well?" Colleen asked as McGowan hung up the phone. They were in his office, he seated behind his desk, she seated in one of the wingback chairs in front of it. McGowan looked tired, and Colleen felt for him.

He leaned back in the chair behind his desk and rubbed his eyes. "He's got her, couldn't deny it once I told him I sensed his magic at her house, says he rescued her from a demon attack."

"From what we saw at her house, that's probably true."

"Ya," McGowan said angrily. "But he denies any knowledge of young Conklin, says he only has Katherine."

"Perhaps I was wrong. Perhaps the young man wasn't there. Or perhaps he escaped separately."

McGowan shook his head. "That old Russian bastard's a lying shit. Conklin was there and he's got him."

McGowan picked up the phone again, dialed a number, listened for a few seconds then said, "Clark, it's Walter McGowan. I apologize for the late hour and the lack of notice, but I need your help, right away, tonight."

McGowan listened for a few seconds, then said, "It's the Russians. They've got Katherine and I need backup."

Again McGowan was silent while he listened. "Great! I really appreciate it, Clark."

He hung up the phone and retrieved a notepad from a drawer in his desk, wrote something on it, tore off a sheet, leaned forward and handed it to Colleen. She glanced at it and saw an address written there. McGowan continued. "I've agreed to meet Karpov to pick up Katherine, but you don't need to be there."

He nodded at the piece of paper he'd handed her. "That's the address of Karpov's little hideout. I'd like you to go there and retrieve Conklin. If Karpov stays in character he'll bring a lot of muscle to deliver Katherine; it's an image thing for him, a big show of strength in front of a rival wizard of similar power. He'll probably only leave a few thugs to guard Conklin, the kind strong on muscle, weak in brains and arcane power. Nothing you can't handle on your own, though if I'm wrong and there's any real talent present use your own judgment about whether or not to abandon Conklin."

Colleen shook her head. "I won't abandon the young man."

"Damn it, Colleen!" McGowan snarled, leaning toward her. "Don't get all motherly on me. Conklin's not worth you getting hurt."

She smiled at him dismissively, knowing that would irritate him. "I'm no inexperienced child, Walter. And there's too much concerning young Mr. Conklin that doesn't add up to leave his fate in the hands of a bunch of hoodlums." She nodded toward the phone. "And I'm glad you're not going to meet Karpov and his army on your own. Who's the backup you called?"

McGowan looked like he wanted to argue with her, then gave up the thought. "Friend of mine named Clark Devoe."

"Will just the two of you be enough?"

McGowan grinned unpleasantly. "I trust Clark implicitly. And even the younger Russians, the ones filled with piss and vinegar, even they're afraid of him."

"He must be quite scary."

"Not if you're his friend."

••••

They'd left Paul alone, though for how long he couldn't guess. He struggled at the plastic zip-ties binding his hands and feet to the chair, was trying to crane his neck downward hoping to get his teeth on one of them and bite through it. He'd twisted into an oddly contorted position, but his teeth were still a good six inches from the zip-tie. Then a sledgehammer slammed into his ribs without warning, pain shot through his chest and Paul threw his head back and cried out. His eyes filled with tears and he gasped for breath as Joe Stalin back-stepped away from him, massaging his right fist with his left hand. Joe spoke in his thick accent. "Don't be stupid, shit head."

Joe began pacing back and forth, his eyes locked on Paul. Every few seconds he'd grumble something inaudible, though it sounded less like human words and more like the growl of an angry bear. As he growled and paced, Joe's eyes narrowed intently, clearly trying to think something through, something probably beyond his limited mental capabilities. "Mr. Karpov says I can't hit you in the head," Joe said as he paced. "Said we can't take a chance the witch was telling the truth. He doesn't want you dead . . . yet."

Joe abruptly stopped the pacing, turned and crossed the distance between them, plowed his fist into Paul's solar plexus. Paul gasped and couldn't breathe for the longest time as his diaphragm contracted in a series of spasms. Joe stood over him smiling and enjoying the show. "But I don't have to hit you in the head, do I?"

It only took a couple more blows for Joe to send Paul to a pain-wracked place halfway to unconsciousness. But then the blows stopped, and slowly Paul's awareness crawled back from that place and returned to the chair in which he was tied in the little circle of light. Joe stood over him. "I want Mr. Karpov to be happy with me, so tell me what you're going to tell him when he gets back."

Paul struggled to speak. "I don't have anything to tell you. I don't know anything."

Joe stared at him with his narrow little eyes for the longest moment. "Let's try something new, and we'll see if you hold to that story."

Joe turned on his heel and stepped out of the circle of light into the darkness. Paul heard the click of a light switch, and the room filled with the harsh glare of fluorescent lights hanging overhead. A kitchenette consisting of a sink and cupboards and a kitchen counter lined one wall. Several cafeteria tables and chairs were folded up and leaning against the far wall, and the only feature on the wall between the kitchenette and the folded tables was a lone door.

Joe grabbed the back of Paul's chair, leaned it over onto its two hind legs with Paul still bound to it, and dragged him across the floor to the kitchenette. Joe opened a cupboard, pulled out a length of electrical extension cord and plugged it into an outlet on the countertop. He rummaged around inside the cupboard, swore some sort of Russian oath, then retrieved an old electric food processor. He plugged the food processor into the end of the extension cord and carefully placed it on the floor beside Paul's chair. It was filthy, encrusted with some sort of dried, brown stain, its blades pitted with specs of rust and more of the brown stain. Joe smiled at Paul and said, "I wish the others were here. We like to bet on how many joints it takes to get a man to talk. Never seen anyone go past the second joint."

Paul's stomach climbed up into his throat and he almost vomited at the thought of the mutilation Joe had in mind for him. "I told you I don't know anything," he pleaded. "Ask me anything. I'll tell you everything I know."

Joe Stalin shook his head sadly. "But you said you don't know anything. Let's see how much you don't know after the first joint."

Joe hit the switch on the food processor; the blades inside it wound up to speed with an irritating whine and he let it race for a few seconds, clearly enjoying the sound.

••••

Belinda stood in a shadow outside the cheap tenement where Karpov kept his headquarters. She watched Karpov and his thugs drag the young woman out, her hands and feet still bound. They tossed her into the back seat of a car, and two thugs climbed in on either side of her. Karpov climbed into another car with more of his thugs and the two cars sped away.

She hadn't seen the young man. That meant he was still inside, and she was quite certain only a few of Karpov's thugs remained to guard him, all relatively weak practitioners.

She decided to wait for a bit. Following the flurry of activity surrounding Karpov's exit, his thugs would be alert and attentive, but give them a little time and the boredom of waiting would set in. And she knew the effect she had on men, especially bored young men with too much testosterone and not enough brains. This should be fairly easy.

She waited a good thirty minutes and was just about to drop her shadow spell and cross the street openly, when she sensed something approaching from up the street so she hesitated. It had triggered one of her spells, a passive charm meant to alert her to the presence of anyone capable of wielding arcane forces, passive and so almost impossible to detect. But the capabilities of whoever was approaching were at the limit of her ability to sense, so he was either quite weak, or so powerful he could mask his arcane abilities from her rather considerable powers.

Not *he*, she thought when the woman came into view. She'd heard of the Druid and had no qualms admitting the older woman outclassed her completely, so now was not the time to act. She held her shadows and watched silently as the Druid spelled the front door and entered the building without incident.

••••

Joe Stalin rummaged in a countertop drawer, retrieved a pair of wire cutters, leaned down and gripped the zip-tie holding Paul's right wrist. They were shoulder-to-shoulder, Paul seated with Joe bent over his right arm and reaching down to his wrist. Paul struggled frantically, tried to shake and jerk his hand back and forth, anything to delay this maniac.

"Hold still," Joe growled, and elbowed Paul in the chest. While Paul gasped for air Joe reached down and cut the zip-tie binding his right hand, and suddenly Paul had an opening. With Joe bent over beside him he raised his right fist and punched upward as hard as he could and connected with Joe's larynx. Joe dropped the wire cutters and stumbled backward, overcome by a fit of uncontrollable gagging and coughing. Paul stretched his right hand toward the wire cutters on the floor, but couldn't reach them. He rocked the chair from side to side, trying to tumble it toward the cutters, but Joe's paw slammed into the side of his head and he almost lost consciousness.

The room tilted sickeningly as Joe leaned down in front of him almost nose to nose. Joe had to shout to be heard above the whine of the food processor. "You going to pay for that, mother fucker."

Paul head-butted him, caught him square in the nose with his forehead, heard something crunch and got the satisfaction of seeing Joe stagger backward with his hands covering his nose, blood streaming freely between his fingers. Joe pulled his hands away from his face, looked at the blood on his hands and roared.

Paul still had only his right hand free, so Joe wisely stepped to Paul's left to get behind him. Paul swung his right hand wildly, hoping to catch Joe in the balls, but Joe caught his wrist easily and bent his arm painfully behind his back. Joe leaned in close to Paul's ear, blood dripping freely onto Paul's shoulder. "Now we see how smart you are, fuck head."

Even if he'd been untied and unfettered Paul would've been no match for Joe's brute strength. Joe slowly brought Paul's wrist around to the food processor on the floor beside him, and while Paul was no weakling, his resistance only managed to turn the struggle into a slow dance toward the inevitable, Joe holding his wrist with both hands as Paul jerked it side to side and back and forth, anything to make it difficult for Joe to shove his hand into the whirring blades of the food processor.

They ended up with Paul sitting up in the chair leaning to his left away from the food processor, his right arm extended straight down only a hand's breadth above the whining blades, Joe bent over beside him with both his hands gripped like a vise around Paul's wrist. It became a silent tug of war that Paul was slowly losing.

He tried not to think about the excruciating pain that awaited him, could think only of Joe's hands gripping his wrist, and the odd connection he felt where Joe's skin contacted his. He sensed the potential for Joe's animal strength, sensed the bearish life-force within the man, and with his shoulder close to popping out of its socket, he recalled how, when the demon in the hospital had fed on Katherine, she'd been seriously weakened. He didn't think he could suck energy or life or whatever it was out of Joe like the demon had sucked out of Katherine, but he thought he might weaken Joe in the same way, to extinguish a bit of what made Joe alive, and with that thought he mentally touched the core of Joe's soul.

Joe groaned, swooned, and his hands slipped off Paul's wrist, and with his own weight leaning so heavily downward, his own left hand plunged into the screaming blades of the food processor. The timbre of the machine's whine dropped an octave; it sputtered erratically and sprayed blood all over Joe and Paul and the room. Joe screamed hysterically and rolled away from the machine, weakly clutching his maimed left hand, blood spurting from a severed vein there.

The wire cutters were still out of reach on Paul's left, so while Joe lay on the floor moaning weakly, Paul rocked his chair side to side. With each rock the chair leaned a little farther to one side, then the other, though Paul had to be careful to fall toward the cutters, not away from them. Joe rolled onto his back and struggled to climb to his feet just as the chair balanced precariously on its two right legs and hung there for an eternity. But as it rocked back toward the left Paul shifted all his weight into it and the chair went over.

Paul's shoulder slammed into the concrete floor, but he ignored the pain and reached over his head. His fingertips barely touched the cutters, and he scrabbled at them as Joe made it to his hands and knees. With his fingertips flicking at them, the wire cutters moved a fraction of an inch toward him, and he had them. He cut the zip-ties on his ankles and left hand, rolled away from the chair and struggled to his feet.

Joe couldn't seem to get any further than his hands and knees, so Paul kicked him in the ribs and he collapsed, lay on his side and curled into a fetal position next to the whining food processor, groaning weakly. Paul unplugged the food processor and the extension cord. Joe was too weak to resist as Paul used a length of the cord as a tourniquet to stop the blood spurting from Joe's hand. He didn't deserve Paul's help, but he was too weak to help himself and Paul couldn't just leave him there to bleed to death.

Paul worked quickly, knowing there must be more of Karpov's thugs nearby, counting on the fact they'd expect to hear screams coming from this room and wouldn't know the difference between Joe's and Paul's.

"Fucking demon," Joe said weakly as Paul finished and stood. "You fed on me. You're a fucking demon."

Paul spotted his shoulder holster on the countertop. The Sig was empty, so he slid one of his spare clips into it and ratcheted the slide. He couldn't wear the holster on the street because he didn't have his coat to conceal it, so he wrapped it in a dishtowel he found on the countertop nearby. He arranged the dishtowel carefully so he could easily pull or replace the Sig in the holster without the need to unwrap it, then hugged the bundle tightly under his left armpit.

He killed the lights in the room, then opened the door slowly. It let out into a large, dimly lit space with bulky crates stacked haphazardly, a warehouse of some kind. With the Sig in his right hand Paul slipped out of the room and into the shadows behind a stack of crates.

He heard someone approaching, though whoever it was moved cautiously, darting from one shadow to the next. So he crouched down low and held his breath. Whoever it was passed Paul's hiding place and a moment later he heard the door to the room open slowly, then close again. He moved quietly to another stack of crates, hoping he'd chosen the right direction and was headed for the front of the warehouse.

He found an exit there, though nearby two of Karpov's men were seated at an old folding table, their heads slumped to the table and their eyes closed, a deck of cards piled on the table between them. He kept the gun pointed in their direction as he crept past them, but neither moved in the slightest. He opened the door a crack and scanned the street. It was empty so he stepped out onto the sidewalk, decocked the Sig and shoved it into the holster hidden in the dishtowel. He moved quickly up the street.

••••

Colleen had no trouble spelling the two guards just inside the entrance to Karpov's tenement. After all they were just hired help, neither of them a practitioner. But just as their heads slumped to the table something happened at the back of the warehouse that triggered one of her protection spells, though it didn't flare fully to life but remained quiescent and ready. At the same moment a horrible scream, muffled by the intervening walls, broke the silence. It had felt almost like a demon attack, but not really, for if it had been a demon attack her protection spell would've come fully to life.

She stepped into a nearby shadow and waited for whatever might come next. In all her years she hadn't felt anything like that, and she didn't want to go stumbling blindly into some unknown danger. She waited that way for a couple of minutes, but since the place remained eerily quiet, she moved cautiously toward the back of the warehouse. She found a lone door built into the wall there, and as she was about to open it she thought she sensed someone else moving in the dark of the warehouse behind her. But the instant passed quickly, though she decided to keep an eye on her back-trail. She opened the door carefully.

The room was dark, though she could hear someone groaning piteously within. She pulled a fire spell long enough to find the light switch, and flicked on a bank of fluorescent lights hanging overhead.

The young Russian with the square face was lying on his side on the floor next so some sort of kitchen appliance. Blood had spattered all over him and in a wide circle about him. Blood also covered his chin and it appeared his nose had been broken. He was clutching a bloody hand to his chest, and around his arm someone had tied a length of electrical cord as a tourniquet. His hand appeared to be badly mutilated, and Colleen actually felt a little pity for the sociopath.

She squatted down next to him and asked, "What happened?"

He opened his eyes, and it took several seconds for him to focus on her. "Your friend's a fucking demon," he said weakly. "He fed on me. Fucker fed on me. Fucking demon."

That strange sensation she'd felt earlier, the arcane flow that had partially triggered her protection spell, it could have been a demon feeding. But Colleen couldn't escape the fact that it should've triggered the spell fully.

The young Russian groaned and spit blood on the floor. "He's a fucking demon. Conklin's a fucking demon."

••••

Belinda watched the Druid enter the warehouse, then sensed what she thought was a feeding. For a moment she thought her master might've decided to intervene personally, but then she realized it hadn't felt exactly like a demon feeding, and on retrospect she couldn't identify exactly what it had been.

About ten minutes later she saw the young man step out onto the sidewalk, a gun in his right hand, a bundle tucked under his left armpit. He scanned the street cautiously, then tucked the gun into the bundle and walked down the street hurriedly. There was no sign of the Druid so she followed him.

18

False Rescue

DEVOE PICKED UP McGowan at his home and drove them to the meeting with Karpov. The Russian owned a long-term parking lot near San Francisco International, a large open stretch of tarmac that, at this time of night, was all but deserted.

Devoe pulled up to the entrance of the parking lot, where a middle-aged fellow sat in a kiosk reading a newspaper. He glanced away from his newspaper, stared at them for several seconds, then spoke with some sort of accent that wasn't Russian. "You don't need a ticket." He nodded over his shoulder. "Far southeast corner."

Devoe pulled the sedan forward carefully, turned south down a long row of parked cars, kept his speed down to about five miles per hour. About half way down the row of parking spaces the cars began to thin out, and by the time they reached the end of the row there were no cars around them, just open tarmac. About a hundred yards in the distance a car's lights flashed repeatedly.

They crossed the distance slowly, Devoe keeping the car's speed down all the way. He stopped the car about twenty paces from two black sedans parked alone near a chain-link fence topped by razor wire.

"Wait here," McGowan said. "Keep the headlights on my back and if I scratch my cheek then please join me."

McGowan climbed out of Devoe's car, closed the door and started forward at an easy walk. He stopped half way to the two black sedans and waited patiently.

The headlights on both sedans suddenly flared to life with a blinding glare. McGowan couldn't see past them, but he heard more than one car door open and close. Then Karpov walked forward, flanked by three of his goons. Vladimir was there, and it bothered McGowan that Alexei was absent.

"Valter," Karpov said. "It's always good to see you."

Karpov liked playing his games when he had the upper hand, but McGowan wasn't going to play along. He was careful to speak softly. "Where's my daughter?"

"She's completely unharmed, Valter. And I'm sure we can come to some accom-modation. I'm sure there—"

McGowan used the wizard's voice. He spoke in a faint whisper, but to everyone there it was almost a shout. "No accommodation. You have my daughter, and you have no right to hold her."

Karpov spread his hands. "Valter, Valter, Valter! You . . ."

McGowan stopped listening and reached up casually to scratch his cheek. A second later he heard a car door behind him slam shut. That was followed by calm measured footsteps as Devoe crossed the distance between them and Karpov's voice slowly dwindled to a stop. Devoe stopped beside McGowan, and while he wasn't armed in any obvious way, he wore a windbreaker that could conceal anything. A couple of Karpov's thugs shifted nervously from one foot to the other, and Vladimir started to reach into his coat.

Karpov reached up and put a hand on the ugly blonde's wrist, stopping him cold. The older man snarled something angrily in Russian, and Vladimir lowered an empty hand to his side.

McGowan spoke carefully. "Clark and I are not here to play games. I want my daughter, now."

Karpov stared at him for a long moment, then slowly raised a hand into the beam of the headlights above his head and gestured forward with a few fingers, though his eyes never left McGowan's. McGowan heard a car door open and close, and he heard Katherine snarl, "Get your hands off me, you pig."

When she stepped up beside Karpov, one of his thugs was holding both her arms tightly behind her back. McGowan waited. Again he and Karpov stared at each other for several seconds. Then Karpov said something in Russian to the thug and he released Katherine. She yanked her arms away from him and marched toward McGowan. As she did so Devoe stepped several paces to the side to insure a clean line of fire past her.

When Katherine reached McGowan she snarled, "They've got Paul. And they've already beat him up and they're probably going to kill him."

McGowan looked past her at Karpov. "So, Vasily, you lied to me about the young man."

Karpov grinned. "You've got your daughter, old man. Be content with that."

McGowan nodded and said, "Fair enough."

"No," Katherine shouted. "We can't abandon Paul like that."

McGowan gripped her upper arm, gripped it hard enough to cause pain and started marching her toward Devoe's car. She protested loudly, but he had to keep up the ruse. "Conklin's not worth it. We're going home and he'll have to take care of himself."

She spit and cursed and snarled all the way to the car, continued snarling as he shoved her into the passenger seat and climbed into the driver's seat next to her. He'd drive, leaving Devoe free to cover their backside as they drove away.

When the doors of the sedan were closed, when he'd turned the car about and hit the accelerator, only then did he shout, "God damn it, where the hell do you think Colleen is?"

That shut her up, and for the first time, she glanced around and took a head count. Then her eyes brightened. "Of course, you sent Colleen to rescue him."

She lurched across the seat and wrapped her arms around him. She jogged his arm and the car swerved wildly. He barely missed taking out the kiosk at the parking lot's entrance as she gave him a big kiss on the cheek. "Father, I'll never doubt you again, you sneaky son-of-a-bitch."

••••

Paul jogged for six blocks in a diagonal zigzag pattern along streets all but deserted. He didn't want to be anywhere near the warehouse when Karpov returned. Any time a car's headlights lit up the street he halted and stepped into the shadows of an alley or doorway. Better paranoid than dead.

A large jet passed overhead flying low and accelerating hard for takeoff. That meant he was somewhere north of the airport, probably in South San Francisco. He still had his wallet and some cash so he could hail a cab, if he could find one, which was unlikely in this neighborhood at this time of night. He decided to head for the South San Francisco BART station instead, and started jogging north.

••••

Belinda found it easy to follow the young man. When he ran she couldn't keep up and he opened the distance between them. But he stopped to hide from every car that came down the street, whereas she had her spells to keep her hidden. So each time he hid she caught up with him easily. And as she followed him she began formulating a plan.

He was clearly attracted to the Old Wizard's daughter. The girl was certainly beautiful, and it was human nature to be attracted to someone who saved your life. And there was no doubt he wanted guidance from someone experienced in the arcane arts. And now he'd been cut off from all that, so she decided to give him another beautiful woman who saved his life, another powerful witch who could share his danger, someone to guide him, to help him navigate this strange, new, frightening world into which he'd been thrust. It might take a spell or two, but amazingly enough he was completely unprotected, no wards, no spells, not even a rudimentary awareness of such. She had a nice little spell that would draw his attention to her, though not in an overt or obvious fashion, but it would provide the emotional attraction she'd need. As to physical attraction, she could provide that without resorting to witchcraft.

She had another spell to disarm any native skepticism he might harbor for a stranger who approached him. She'd also prepared a powerful illusion that would provide the excuse for them to meet, and for her to be his rescuer. And finally there was the obsession spell that would create in him a need for her, and bring him to her bed willingly, almost desperately. It was a subtle spell that would build on the initial attraction of the other spells. Not too much at first, but it would grow and eventually ensnare him so deeply he'd willingly surrender to her, and then to her master when the time came.

••••

At that time of night there weren't that many people waiting for a train in the South San Francisco BART Station. Other than Paul there was a bum, a couple of kids with an overabundance of piercings that couldn't keep their hands off each other, and an older, gray-haired woman. If Karpov returned to his warehouse, made an educated guess and sent his goons to check out nearby BART stations, there'd be no hiding from them. Paul's paranoia shifted into overdrive as he waited for the train; he was watching everyone suspiciously, even the old woman, constantly scanning every entrance or approach to the train platform. But even if he'd been half asleep he couldn't have missed the goddess that came down the escalator.

She had dark olive skin, almond shaped brown eyes and full red lips set in an oval face with high cheekbones. She'd fashioned her black hair in a tightly curled style of wild disarray that cascaded down past her shoulders. Medium height, she wore a classic tan-colored trench coat, unbuttoned and open in the front because the night air held no chill. Beneath the trench coat she wore a dress that might be dark blue silk, or some other material with a shimmery quality to it. The dress was cut just above her knees, and her long legs ended in black, medium-height high heels. She showed a little cleavage like most young woman, and there wasn't a man in the world who wouldn't appreciate her physical charms. Certainly she was beautiful, but there was nothing overtly unusual about her appearance, nothing to draw a man's attention in so compelling a fashion. And that made her even more attractive, sensual rather than sexual, for had she looked like some stripper or porn queen, it would've cheapened the effect.

Even the boy with the piercings had stopped molesting his girlfriend to stare at the new arrival. His girlfriend turned to see what had drawn his attention, stared for a few seconds at the goddess, then shoved him away angrily.

The goddess stepped off the escalator, stepped to the same side of the platform as Paul and waited patiently for the train. From South San Francisco there was only one train going into the city. When it arrived she got into the same car as Paul, and sat down a few seats from him in one of the seats facing the rear of the train, facing Paul. She pulled out a magazine and began reading.

Paul had decided to hide out for a few days at his parent's place in Castro Valley. He'd spent so little time there it was probably still safe, and he had most of his special ammunition stashed there, though he'd have to change trains somewhere in the city.

The train would get into the downtown area in a little less than half an hour. Paul's seat had him facing forward toward the goddess, and he was careful not to stare. She looked up once from her magazine and their eyes met. She gave him a shy little smile and returned her attention to the magazine.

A few minutes later she looked up again, and again their eyes met. If she'd given him another shy little smile it would've been a bit of innocent flirtation. And while a hint of smile did cross her lips, it quickly turned into a frown, cancelling any flirtatiousness in the look she gave him. She glanced about the car almost suspiciously, as if to reassure herself there was no danger present, then she lowered her eyes back to her magazine. It had been the oddest look. Something had bothered her, though apparently not something about Paul, but rather something nearby.

Before they got into the city she glanced up three more times, and each time her frown deepened as she looked about the car. It began to bother Paul so he scanned the car quickly, but other than the two of them it was empty. And then he realized he'd become overly paranoid, and he was acting like an idiot. So he turned and focused on his reflection in the window.

The tunnel through which the train sped was dark, with an occasional dim light at random intervals. Paul got a vague impression of pipes and conduit racing past behind his reflection, but it was hard to focus on anything but his own image. And while, in one short week, so much else had changed, the fellow he saw reflected in the window looked to be the same man he'd seen in the mirror every day, though he did look like he'd been in a nasty fight, and lost. Then his image shifted and Suzanna appeared in the window. She shook her head and said, *Be careful, Paul. She's dangerous.*

The only woman in his life right now besides Suzanna was Katherine. Did she mean Katherine? Katherine wasn't dangerous. Well, yes, she was quite dangerous, if she wasn't on your side. She was a witch, and he'd seen her do a couple of scary things. But dangerous, in a way that would lead Suzanna to warn him about her?

He looked into Suzanna's eyes, and was about to ask her if she meant Katherine, when her face began to twist and swirl. He'd seen it before in his apartment when his own image in the mirror had morphed into the bat-like monster. But this time it happened so fast it caught him totally unprepared. The black snout, goat-slitted eyes and pointed, leathery ears formed in an instant. Paul jerked back from the window, but wasn't fast enough to evade the clawed hand that reached out from the window and gripped his throat.

As the monster struggled to claw its way out of the window Paul desperately searched the seat behind him with his hands, trying to find the bundled towel in which he'd hidden his gun. And then suddenly a small, delicate, olive-skinned hand, with fingernails painted dark blue, gripped the monster's wrist.

A female voice shouted, "Be gone, servant of the nether life. I banish you back to the darkness." And where her hand gripped the monster's wrist, a thunderclap of an explosion erupted, knocking Paul on his ass into the aisle between seats. It had felt not too different from one of Joe Stalin's open-handed slaps. Paul knew he needed to get up, to run, but all he could do was sit there while his head spun crazily.

"Are you ok? I'm sorry. There was no time to protect you."

Paul looked into the face of the goddess from the subway platform. "It's gone," she said. "I banished it. You're safe now, but we need to get off this train."

She helped him struggle to his feet as the train pulled into a station. He had the presence of mind to grab the bundle with his gun as she dragged him onto a busy and crowded station platform. She stopped and turned to him as people rushed past them to get on the train. "Why did it manifest here? You didn't summon it. I would've sensed that."

Standing there, staring at her, with their lives dependent upon clear, unfettered thinking, all he could think of was that she was one of the most exotic creatures he'd ever looked upon. The trench coat had spilled open, and like a schoolboy he stole a glance at her breasts, and an inviting bit of cleavage there. Her dress was made of a thin fabric that hugged her figure closely, almost as if she was standing there naked before him. He could see the shape of her breasts clearly, her nipples protruding visibly through the material. They were medium sized breasts that stood up like those on a young teenage girl, and Paul imagined caressing them, running his tongue up and down her—

It took a conscious effort to tear his eyes away from her breasts.

She looked into his eyes and frowned with concern. "You're still stunned, aren't you? I'm sorry. There was no time to protect you from the side effects of my spell. We have to get out of here."

She took his hand, led him toward the exit, and he followed without question. After all, she'd rescued him from one of those monsters.

They emerged from the Powell Street Station into a busy San Francisco night, with a line of tourists trailing more than a block up Powel Street in the hope of taking a ride on the famous trolley. Still holding his hand tightly she hailed a cab on Market Street. She let go of his hand as she climbed into the cab. He hesitated, standing beside the open cab door, wondering if it was really wise to go with this stranger to some unknown location. He leaned in, and as she turned to face him, *blink* . . .

He'd seen something in her face, though he wasn't sure what. As doubts began to leak into his thoughts he asked her, "Where're we going?"

She said, "To my apartment. It's warded. You'll be safe there."

"But I don't really know you," he said, his apprehension growing.

"I saved your life, and I can protect you." She sounded almost hurt at the thought he might not trust her, and as she spoke she reached out and touched his cheek.

It was almost a caress, and where her fingers touched his face he felt a slight tingle. He felt guilty at the hurt in her voice as he considered her words carefully. She had saved his life, rescued him from one of those bat-thing monsters. She took his hand, touched it to her own cheek. "You can trust me," she whispered.

Yes, he could trust her.

He climbed into the cab beside her and his doubts fluttered away like butterflies lost in the night.

••••

When Katherine and her father returned to his house, Colleen was seated in a wingback chair in his study. And when Katherine saw that Paul was absent she hoped he was in the bathroom, or getting a drink, or resting, or something. She wanted to hear anything but that Colleen had failed to rescue him. "Where's Paul?" she demanded.

Colleen shook her head and Katherine's heart lurched. "I missed him," Colleen said. "But the good news is he'd already escaped on his own."

"Damn!" McGowan swore as he poured whiskey into three glasses. "He's in too much danger to be out on his own." He handed each of them a glass and sat down behind his desk. "What happened? Tell me about it."

Colleen took a sip of whiskey, then said, "As you predicted, Vasily took most of his hoodlums with him to your rendezvous. With the exception of Alexei, there were no practitioners present, just thugs. And Alexei was in no shape to do anything but whimper piteously."

Colleen described spelling the guards at the door, then skulking through the warehouse to the room in the back. She described the room in detail, along with the blood-encrusted food processor. "I think Alexei intended to torture Paul, but got a taste of his own medicine instead."

Katherine's anger grew with every word. "Those fucking Russians are maniacs."

McGowan added, "Dangerous maniacs." He looked at Colleen pointedly and frowned. "You're leaving something out."

She looked down into her drink, swirled it a bit and refused to meet his eyes.

He persisted. "I've known you long enough to recognize when you're holding something back."

Colleen took another sip of whiskey; her hand was shaking, the whiskey in the glass trembling ever so slightly, and Katherine could see she was stalling for time. Clearly, her father was right, but McGowan's phone started ringing, rescuing her from having to answer. It was his private line, so with a quick apology to the two women he answered it.

He listened for a second then said, "What can I do for you, Vasily?"

McGowan cringed, pulled the handset a few inches away from his ear, and even Katherine, standing on the other side of the small room, could hear the faint sounds of the Russian's angry shouts.

McGowan shouted into the handset, "Calm down, damn it, and speak so I can understand you. I don't speak Russian."

The sounds of the angry Russian disappeared; McGowan pressed the handset to his ear and listened intently. After a few seconds he said, "I don't believe it."

Again McGowan was silent for several seconds, then said, "I still don't believe it."

He listened further for quite some time, then said good-bye and hung up. He closed his eyes, put his face in his hands and rubbed at his temples tiredly. "Karpov says Conklin fed on Alexei, fed like a demon."

Katherine couldn't believe her ears. "That's insane," she shouted. "Those Russians are just pissed off, and looking for some excuse."

McGowan spoke tiredly, "Karpov may be a sociopath, and a brutal, homicidal thug, but he's a powerful practitioner and he knows his stuff. He says he left Alexei alone with Paul, with Paul tied in a chair, that Paul miraculously escaped and Alexei is exhibiting all the symptoms of a demon feeding. And Alexei says it was young Conklin who fed on him. Karpov's a lying shit, but he's not lying about that. It may not be true, but he certainly believes it is."

Katherine wanted to be calm about this and lower her voice, but the fact that her father might believe this garbage angered her no end. "Maybe something fed on Alexei, but it couldn't have been Paul." She looked to Colleen for support. "What about you? Do you believe any of this crap?"

Colleen hesitated, and that she would do so frightened Katherine no end. "I'm sorry, child," Colleen said. "Just after I first entered the warehouse I sensed something akin to a demon-feeding, and it triggered certain protective spells I'd prepared to warn me of such an occurrence." She looked at McGowan. "But it didn't trigger them fully, old man. And if a demon had fed, it would have."

McGowan stared into his drink and swirled it about for a long moment. "We're going to have to move more carefully with Conklin. If he's a demon, or perhaps just possessed by one, then he'll be a serious danger to us all. We need to confine him to protect ourselves, and to do that we need to find him. Any thoughts on that?"

Colleen said something, but Katherine had turned her attention inward. The locator spell she'd concocted from their saliva and hair was less than twenty-four hours old, was still strongly active and would remain so for at least another week before it weakened and dissipated. She could find Paul with only a little effort. And while her father meant well, he didn't know Paul the way she did, really didn't understand him at all, might choose to kill him in a misguided effort to protect everyone else.

No, she'd find Paul on her own, and help him learn to protect himself. That was the only possible course of action.

19

Obsession

BELINDA HELD TIGHTLY to the young man's hand. She'd learned quickly his arcane abilities were stronger than most, and he apparently had some natural resistance to many of her spells. But that resistance faded quickly when her flesh touched his.

In front of her apartment building she let go of him briefly to pay the cabbie. She was relieved to see her control faded more slowly this time, that holding his hand for the entire ride had apparently had some small cumulative effect. She was careful to get out of the cab first, so she was waiting for him as he stepped out. She took his hand immediately and led him up the steps at the front of her building.

She saw her control begin to slip slightly as she searched for the keys in her purse. But she found them, and quickly grasped his hand as she unlocked the front door. She didn't let go of him as they made their way up to her second floor walkup.

Once inside her apartment, inside her wards, she relaxed a bit. She'd lived here for several years, lived here when not living in her master's mansion, and the place was imprinted with her power. In here she didn't need to maintain physical contact with him at all times.

"You're safe here," she told him as she got him seated at the small table in her kitchen. "I'll make some tea, herbal tea. It'll help calm you, help you sleep."

"Am I really safe?" he asked.

She almost felt sorry for him. His face was drawn, his eyes haunted like prey in the den of a large predator. "Yes," she said as she put a kettle of water on the stove. "I've built these wards up over a period of years. And I've specifically warded each mirror. Nothing can manifest within these walls unless I allow it."

He raised his own hands and looked at them doubtfully. He was spattered with blood, and he had bruises on his face and a deep gash on his forehead that had been stitched up.

She sat down opposite him, took his hands in hers. "The blood?" she asked. "Are you hurt?"

He closed his eyes and shook his head. "No," he said. "Well, some bruises and cuts and scrapes, but the worst is more than a week old and starting to heal."

"The blood," she asked again. "Whose?"

He shrugged. "This Russian bastard, looks a lot like Joe Stalin."

He launched into his story, and as he spoke she knew the spells she'd cast upon him added an element of confusion to his thoughts, more so because he was such a strong practitioner. A mundane mortal, or a weaker practitioner, might not question his own senses, would probably accept the illusions and glamour she wrapped about him without a second thought. But with the strength this young man possessed, had he created proper wards he would've been immune to her manipulations, would've detected them and known her for what she was. Instead, he sat here wholly unwarded, and with such arcane strength at work there was a piece of him, buried quiet deeply, that knew something was wrong and it confused him. So until she had full control, she'd have to be on the lookout for any signs of resistance.

She leaned forward carefully, purposefully giving him a better view down her dress. She smiled warmly at him and said, "My name's Belinda."

He smiled back, and she could see he was warming to her. "Paul," he said. "Paul Conklin."

It was imperative she move quickly to make him hers. Physical contact was the key, and she was good at physical contact with handsome young men, oh so very good.

••••

Paul told Belinda an edited version of recent events. He told her about the Russians and McGowan and Colleen shooting up his apartment, and how they and the demon had hunted him down at the hospital. She was most interested to know what, or who, had drawn him and Katherine into the Netherworld, but he couldn't help her there. He didn't tell her about the chimera-like appearance of the big hoodoo demon, nor that it kept calling him *Dragon-stink*. That fact had bothered Katherine's father no end, and some instinct warned him to be cautious with that information. Nor did he tell her he'd looked into its eyes and somehow escaped. He pleaded ignorance, honestly so, about how he and Katherine had returned from the Netherworld. He told her of the abduction to Faerie, though he was vague about his escape, didn't mention the little people, and she didn't ask. He told her about the demon that trashed Katherine's home, and how the Russians had captured them both. And he gave her a slightly fictitious version of how he'd escaped from good old Joe Stalin. He wasn't about to admit to anyone he'd fed on a demon, then fed on that Russian bastard. He really didn't feel guilty about either.

He edited the entire story quite carefully, not because he didn't trust this beautiful, exotic witch. In fact he found he trusted her more and more as time went by. No, it wasn't that he didn't trust her, but more that he'd learned a considerable amount of caution in recent days.

"You've actually been to the Netherworld," she said with a touch of awe in her voice. "What's it like? Not that I ever want to go there."

He described the chaotic and hellish world that seemed to be a counterpoint to their own existence. "It's like the city, but not like it, like a destroyed or corrupted version of the city."

A wave of exhaustion washed over him and a wide-open yawn forced its way up out of his throat. She stood, walked around the table and put a hand on his shoulder. He could smell her perfume as she said, "You're tired. Can't blame you after the week you've had. It's time for bed."

He almost hoped that was an invitation as she turned and walked away, and he watched the sway of her hips as she crossed the living room. With the trench coat hung in a closet, the dress, while it covered her completely from shoulders to just above her knees, clung to her so intimately it still left the impression she was almost completely naked.

She disappeared into her bedroom, returned a moment later with some blankets and a pillow, and dropped them on the couch in the living room. "You can take the couch," she said. "You'll be safe here tonight. Believe me. I know how to protect you."

She turned toward her bedroom, called over her shoulder, "I'll see you in the morning."

Again he watched the sway of her hips as she disappeared into the bedroom, watched her go longingly, regretfully.

••••

Paul didn't really sleep. He lay awake for quite some time and couldn't get Belinda out of his mind. He tried to think of something else but it took a decidedly conscious effort to do so, and each time he started to drift toward sleep, as he relaxed and the conscious effort waned, thoughts of her returned to him and he found himself picturing her hips, her breasts, her eyes and her lips . . . then he'd snap back to full wakefulness, and try again to focus on something else.

When he did finally drift off to sleep she haunted his dreams. She wore a diaphanous gown of some sort that hid everything while tempting him with the ever-present hope he might see more. She drifted in and out of the shadows around him, and every time he reached for her she wasn't there. He finally awoke with a demanding erection.

He didn't understand what was happening to him. He'd never been so completely obsessive like this, not even in high school when he was trying to get laid for the first time.

He sat up, walked into the kitchen and looked at the clock on the stove. It had been less than an hour since he'd first lain down on the couch. As he returned to the couch he noticed Belinda hadn't closed her bedroom door, and a faint glow emanated from her bedroom as if she still had a small lamp on. He sat down on the couch again, couldn't stop thinking of the open bedroom door. She hadn't invited him to her bed, but she hadn't exactly pushed him away either. Several times that evening she'd caressed his cheek almost like a lover, and each time he'd felt a slight tingle as if there was some unusual attraction between them. He wondered now if she felt drawn to him as he felt drawn to her. He closed his eyes and buried his face in his hands, wanted to go to her, to touch her, to learn the taste of her lips, the taste of her skin, the taste of her entire body.

He lowered his hands from his face and opened his eyes. Somehow, without realizing it, he'd crossed the room and now stood in the doorway to her bedroom. A small bedside lamp cast a wan light over the bed where Belinda lay propped up by a wall of pillows, dressed in the diaphanous thing from his dreams. She wore shadows like other people wore clothing, and though the lamp didn't flicker the shadows appeared to dance about her.

He saw a faint glint in her eyes, realized they were open and looking at him. He crossed the room carefully, trying to think of what to say, ready to turn and leave at the slightest hint he wasn't welcome. But instead she raised her arms and opened them to him, and she spoke in a throaty whisper. "I've been waiting for you, Paul. I think this was meant to be."

He leaned down over her, lowered himself into her arms and their lips met. She tasted like a dark, exotic fruit, and he could feel her breasts pressed against his chest. He lowered his head, kissed her nipples and she cried out passionately.

They rolled over so she was now on top of him, both of them tangled in the sheets. The black cascade of her tightly curled hair enveloped him and they kissed again, their tongues darting back and forth. He hadn't made love to a woman since Suzanna had died, and for a moment he felt a pang of guilt that he'd betray Suzanna with this gorgeous creature. But as Belinda pressed her body against his, any thoughts of Suzanna and any guilt he might feel drifted away in a dark cloud of passion and desire.

••••

The obsession spell had worked magnificently. Paul had come to her and didn't even realize he had no choice in the matter. Physical contact was what Belinda needed to

truly enspell him, touch to touch, skin to skin, flesh to flesh. With their bodies entwined and driven by an uncontrollable desire spawned by her spells, this would be
physical contact to an extreme, and with her body she'd eventually enslave him.

She rolled over on top of him, opened her legs and gave into him completely, and
as he entered her a wave of passion flooded through her. She gasped, a purely sponta-
neous cry that escaped from her lips without any volition on her part. So she decided to
forget her manipulations this night and enjoy the moment, to drown in the pleasures of
this man's body. There would be plenty of time later to peel open his soul, layer by layer. She'd unlock the chains to his spirit one piece at a time, then truss him up and present him to her master, a gift bound by the strings of her witchcraft.

••••

After her rescue from the Russians, Katherine spent the night at her father's place, aus-
piciously because the demon had trashed her home and it was temporarily unlivable.
But she had an ulterior motive she didn't reveal to her father or Colleen: she knew Paul
had returned to the city and wasn't far away.

The matched locator charms she'd spelled into her hair and his, the little trinkets
concocted from their mixed saliva and hair, gave her a sense of direction and distance
to Paul. But she needed privacy and time and concentration to activate them and bring
them to full strength. And she certainly wasn't going to reveal to her father and Colleen
that she'd created a way to locate Paul, not if they were going to use it to hunt him
down and kill him. So, not until she left her father's study that night, could she properly
trigger the charms.

From her father she knew Karpov's warehouse was south of the city, so Paul had
started out there. But by the time she was alone in her old bedroom in her father's
house, shortly after midnight, and could properly activate the charms, she thought she
might have a good idea of Paul's general location. She couldn't take a map and point to
his position—it wasn't that accurate of a sense—but she knew he was back in the city
and not far from her, something she dare not reveal to her father and Colleen. He'd
escaped from the Russians, was safe for the time being, so she decided to bide her time,
get a good night's sleep and find him in the morning, though the charms were so strong
at this point that even while sleeping she was conscious of him as if he was in her
dreams. And then about two in the morning she slammed awake as he disappeared
from her senses altogether.

The charms themselves were linked by arcane forces, so even if he was dead that
shouldn't happen. If someone removed the charm by shaving his head, that could account for the complete loss of contact. But with a charm that was melded into his hair
the way she'd done, they'd have to completely shave his head. And while there were

plenty of Russian thugs out trying to kill him, they certainly wouldn't know she'd spelled such a charm into his hair—not even he knew that—so she didn't think any of them would stop to shave his head first. No, the only thing she could think of was that he must've entered the strongly warded home of a powerful practitioner. Such wards would easily block the oh-so-tenuous connection between the two charms.

At least she could take some comfort from the fact the link wouldn't trigger such wards, wouldn't warn their master of the charm's existence. The charms were wholly passive, so they were completely undetectable unless one knew to look for them, and knew exactly what to look for.

So where was Paul?

She'd slept poorly that first night at her father's place, awakened repeatedly and sat up in bed, tried to will the charms to relink, to give her some inkling of his whereabouts. But she'd come up with nothing. She'd even had moments where she'd begun to wonder if he'd been killed, had to think it through logically to convince herself he probably wasn't dead. She could only hope that that conclusion wasn't wishful thinking. If her father didn't have doubts about Paul's humanity, didn't think Paul was possibly a demon, wasn't ready to kill him because of that, she'd consult him. She'd describe the charms and how she'd made them, and let him reassure her that Paul wasn't dead. That's what fathers were for. They reassured you when you were terrified. And that was the first time Katherine realized she was terrified for this nice guy that had come into her life. She put that thought out of her mind.

So where was Paul?

She'd awakened that first morning after a fitful sleep. She knew he'd returned to the city, had been south of her when he'd dropped off her charm radar, and not too far south. She thought he might be somewhere South of Market, or SoMa as it was known by some, a district that surrounded the San Francisco side of the Oakland Bay Bridge.

She called her receptionist and cancelled her appointments for the rest of the week, then took a cab down to SoMa and wandered the streets, hoping to catch some inkling of Paul no matter how tenuous. And after an entire day without success she returned to her father's house.

She'd done that now for three straight days. And as dusk began to blanket the city she stood on a street corner, kicked the curb with an expensive pair of Gucci's and swore a string of epithets that would've made a dockworker blush.

Why did she feel so protective of this fellow? He was just some guy; granted, a nice guy, and a nice looking guy. And she'd saved his life a couple of times, pulled his ass out of some serious shit. He's the one who should be grateful to her, should be asking her out on a date or something.

Oh shit! she thought. *I'm one step away from twirling my hair and passing notes in class.*

She caught a cab and went back to her father's house.

••••

"Well now, I think me boy-oh's been enjoying himself, Boo."

"I do say, Jimmie me boy, I'd be enjoying meself too."

Paul opened his eyes carefully. He was lying face down on someone's bed, obviously not his own.

"Aye, but I think she's more than you could handle, Boo."

"Oh, Jimmie, you've got the right of that. And I wager she's a bit more than our boy-oh here can handle too."

Paul tried to roll over, but his legs were badly tangled in dark green sheets. He kicked the sheets off, sat on the edge of the bed and tried to collect his thoughts.

"But he's sure having a good time trying to handle her, ain't he, Boo?"

"Aye, Jimmie, to hear her say it, 'Oooh Paul! Oooh Paul! Oooh Paul!' The young fellow must be a right big horse between the legs."

Paul scanned the room, looking for the two leprechauns. He spotted Boo'Diddle seated atop a highboy dresser, while Jim'Jiminie stood casually on a windowsill picking at his fingernails with a small dagger. Paul growled, "Would you two kindly shut up and give me a chance to think?"

"Well now," Jim'Jiminie said. "It depends on what you'll be thinking with, the head on top of your shoulders, or the one on the end of your dick."

Boo added, "I think the one on the end of his dick is all thought out."

The sunlight slanting through the windows of the apartment told him it was mid-morning on a sunny day. Paul stood, realized he was as sore as an athlete who'd just competed in a strenuous event, though, in fact, Belinda was a rather strenuous event.

Belinda! She must've left the apartment for something. When would she return? He needed her, needed her beside him, needed to taste her, needed—

"Stop that."

One of the leprechauns landed on his shoulders, the other hit him in the back of the knees and he folded up, hit the floor hard on his shoulder. "What the hell are you two doing?" he shouted. He rolled over and struggled back to his feet.

Both leprechauns stood in front of him, facing him with their hands on their hips, a couple of angry little men. Paul shooed them aside and headed for the bathroom. He turned on the shower, let the water heat up for a few brief moments, then climbed in. He soaped down and rinsed off quickly, then let the hot water cascade over the back of his shoulders. He closed his eyes and tried to think. He let the water relax him, let it drive away his concerns and fears, though he shouldn't have any concerns or fears because Belinda would soon return. He closed his eyes and imagined her naked body beneath him in the sheets—

"None of that," one of the leprechauns said. The water turned suddenly icy and he screamed, danced for a moment like a madman under the frigid shower before he managed to turn it off.

"What the fuck!" he shouted. He climbed out of the shower swearing, faced the two little men. "Which one of you did that?"

Each one of them pointed at the other and said, "He did." Paul shook his head angrily, grabbed a towel and dried off quickly.

Back in the bedroom the leprechauns had piled his clothes on the bed. He couldn't remember wearing any clothes for some days now.

"Get dressed, yee mortal fool. Now."

He didn't remember dressing, didn't remember opening the door of the apartment. He did remember stepping across the threshold. It was like forcing his way through some sort of resistant membrane. It took a conscious effort to push through it, and when he emerged on the other side in the hall outside her apartment, his mind cleared a bit. It was the first time in days he could put two coherent thoughts together one after the other, thoughts that didn't involve Belinda.

"That's much better," Boo'Diddle said. Then the leprechauns each took one of his hands and led him down the stairs.

As they stepped through the front door of the building he met Belinda on the steps. "Paul!" she said, clearly surprised he was standing there. "What are you doing out here?"

Blink. There it was again, an image of Belinda superimposed over the Belinda standing before him. It was still Belinda he'd seen, but an older Belinda, still attractive, but with graying hair and dark circles of age under her eyes.

"My two friends," he said just as she reached out and took his hand in hers.

"What friends?" she asked.

Confused by her question, he looked around carefully. Other than a few passersby on the sidewalk, she and he were alone on the front porch of the building. "I don't know," he answered, then looked in her eyes. Beautiful eyes. Beautiful lips. He leaned down and kissed those lips, reached up and caressed one of her breasts.

20

The Search

KATHERINE HAD ALMOST given up hope. She knew Paul was somewhere South of Market, was absolutely certain of that, was also certain he must be hidden within someone's wards. The matched charms she'd made were powerful, and the link between them would be difficult to mask even for one as powerful as her father. Distance could do it, if Paul had left the city and was now several hundred miles away. But she would've sensed him in transit. Temporary wards, the kind one might use while travelling, just couldn't mask his location completely. No, she knew her spells and witchcraft, and to mask the link between the charms she and Paul shared required extremely strong wards, house wards prepared by a potent practitioner, built up and sustained over a long period of time. Several years, at least.

Once she'd been able to sneak away from her father and Colleen, knowing she'd be doing a lot of walking she'd donned jeans, blouse, sneakers and a windbreaker, and hit the streets. Jeans and sneakers weren't her style, but the jeans were DKNYs, and she'd found some Prada sneakers, so that made it acceptable. And for three days now she'd been walking the streets of SoMa, had literally walked every street in the district, and some of those surrounding it.

Time would also break the link between the charms as the power within them slowly but inevitably dissipated. Each day that passed with Paul hidden away meant the link between them had grown that much weaker. And that's what she feared most now. She was running out of time.

She stopped in a coffee shop to get a bite for lunch. She waited in line for about ten minutes, then ordered espresso and a small sandwich. She paid the barista, then stepped aside to wait for her espresso, and it was while the machine hissed and steamed that the link between the charms snapped back into place. Paul had emerged from his hiding place, and she sensed he was near, maybe only a few blocks away.

She spun on her heels and ran out of the store, while behind her the barista shouted, "Wait! Your espresso!"

She stopped on the sidewalk and closed her eyes, covered her ears with her hands and tried to block out the noisy city street. Sensing his location wasn't like looking at some icon marked *Paul* on the GPS navigation system in her car. At best it was a vague sensation of direction and distance, though direction was easier than distance. He was somewhere to her right. She opened her eyes, turned and ran down the street.

At the street corner she stopped and repeated the process, closing her eyes and covering her ears. In that way she zigzagged her way for three blocks, could sense him now quite close as she jogged down the sidewalk, breathing heavily. And then the link disappeared again, blinked out as if someone had thrown a switch and turned it off like the lights in a room.

She stumbled to a halt in the middle of the block, knowing she'd been close but not sure how close. Her frustration almost drove her to tears as she growled, "God damn it!"

An older man walking nearby glanced her way and hesitated, then took a wide berth around her.

••••

Simuth, the Winter Knight, had followed the young woman each day, all day, as she wandered the streets of the city. He suspected she was searching for the young wizard, about which they knew almost nothing. It bothered Ag that he'd never before heard of this young man, this young wizard who'd created such a stir in the Realms, this Paul Conklin. But they knew the Old Wizard's daughter and the young man were somehow connected, so Simuth had played a hunch.

When she emerged from the coffee shop at a run, he was standing not five feet from her as she stopped on the sidewalk to close her eyes and cover her ears. When she ran down the street at a jog he pulled a glamour so none of these mortal fools could see him. It wasn't invisibility, just a spell that turned their eyes away from him, and in that way he followed her easily until she stopped abruptly in the middle of a city block and swore an angry oath. Whatever trail she'd been following had ended abruptly without success.

She was actually quite attractive, and he thought it might be fun to bed her. He considered casting a spell of confusion over her. It would addle her wits and he could take her someplace, perhaps even back to Faerie, where he'd make her pleasure him. But the thought of some compliant, mortal whore complacently satisfying his wishes didn't really excite him. He preferred his women to fight back a bit, and she would be a fighter; he could see that in her. As he fantasized what he might do to her while she resisted him, he grew quite excited. Yes, he'd spell her here so she couldn't make a scene on this busy street, take her back to Faerie, remove the spell, then rape her at his leisure while she fought back.

She stood on the street with her back to him, so he pulled power, began concentrating it for the spell as he walked toward her. But a heavy hand settled on his shoulder and spun him about. He almost threw the spell at the intruder, but he hesitated as he sensed strong magic surrounding them, mortal magic. He looked carefully before acting, looked into Walter McGowan's eyes, an angry father's eyes, a very powerful angry father on his home turf.

Simuth allowed the power he'd pulled to dissipate slowly, lowered his hand and smiled at the old man. "Old Wizard," he said, employing his best court etiquette. "It's always a pleasure to meet you, even if by chance."

McGowan growled like an angry predator, "I wish I could say the same."

Simuth frowned and touched a hand delicately to his own breast. "You wound me. Have I given offense in some way?"

McGowan leaned close to him, and he could see the power in the old man's eyes, a frightening amount of power. "We both know it's not by chance. I've been watching you follow my daughter. And I watched you pull power as you approached her. And I do believe you did not have her best interests at heart."

Simuth smiled again. "You misjudge me. Surely you could not think I meant the young lady harm."

McGowan's eyes burned into Simuth as he said, "I compel you under *wizard's oath* to deliver a *wizard's message* to King Ag. Tell Ag what you were about to do. And tell him I caught you before you did it. And tell him he's now indebted to me."

Simuth cringed as fear crawled from his stomach up into his chest. He dare not fail to deliver such a message, and he knew what the result would be.

••••

Jim'Jiminie and Boo'Diddle watched Simuth turn away from the Old Wizard, fear and apprehension written plainly on the Sidhe's handsome face. Simuth walked up the street wrapped in his glamour, and with each step his presence on the Mortal Plane grew less certain. That was the way of the Realms, and of crossing between them. To exist in one and not the others one must manipulate the probability of one's existence in a particular place and time. And as Simuth marched up the street the probability that he existed on the Mortal Plane diminished, and that allowed the possibility of his existence in Faerie. With each step he reduced the certainty of his existence in the here and now, and his image in the present grew less substantial, until finally he was just a wraith of sparkling pixie dust that floated away on a casual breeze.

Mortals had a difficult time comprehending the probabilities of existence, seemed unable to process the concept that to get from here to there, one only needed to accept the intermediate stage in which the probability of your existence in any one realm was not wholly defined, not absolute. For that reason Mortals always needed a boundary to cross between the Realms, whereas most fey could step between them with casual indifference.

Both leprechauns watched McGowan watch Simuth cross out of the Mortal Plane. The Old Wizard wore the glamour of an old woman, though the leprechauns could easily see through that, could see the angry scowl on his face. When the Sidhe was fully gone the old man turned back to his daughter, but did not approach her. He stood some distance away and watched her, and, if he remained true to form, he'd change his glamour shortly so his daughter would not grow suspicious.

"What are you two reprobates doing here?"

Boo'Diddle started, and Jim'Jiminie, who'd been leaning casually against the tire of a car—a tire larger than him—pushed away from the tire and turned to face Colleen. They both bowed like elegant courtiers, and in unison they said, "Me Lady Armaugh. As always, such a pleasure."

Colleen stood over the two of them wrapped in her shadows, though the two leprechauns could easily see through them. "'Tis not the pleasure of my company you're seeking here. I know that full well."

A young woman walked between them intent on some destination, oblivious to the presence of the three of them. Boo'Diddle had to step lively to keep from being trampled.

"What brings you here?" Colleen demanded. "Why this sudden interest in the old man's daughter?"

Boo'Diddle said, "And why would you be thinkin' we have some interest in the young lady?"

"Sure," Jim'Jiminie added, "she's a right pretty lass. But perhaps it's you we're interested in, or the old man, or the Winter Knight." Jim'Jiminie decided to have some fun. He glanced across the street where he could see Anogh standing in a glamour of his own. He nodded that way, drawing Colleen's attention to the Sidhe warrior. "Or perhaps it's the Summer Knight that draws our interest."

Colleen's eyes widened.

Jim'Jiminie turned and looked up the street past McGowan and his daughter to where a tall, stick-thin man stood waiting on the corner. "Or perhaps it's the unpleasant Russians."

He turned back to Colleen. "Or perhaps we just enjoy watching foolish mortal games." At Colleen's frown he continued. "Be ready. He'll need her help, and the two of them'll need yours."

At that moment he decided he probably didn't exist so much on the Mortal Plane anymore.

••••

After her head-long flight from the coffee shop, madly following the vague sensation of direction provided by the charms; and after it had been so abruptly severed, Katherine was more certain than ever that the strong wards of a powerful practitioner's home were masking Paul's presence. But there were dozens of homes and apartment buildings here; even more if she included a one-block radius around her. He could be in any of them, and without the connection between the charms, or some other hint as to his location, finding him would be impossible.

She walked up and down the street desperately hoping the connection would return. And storming through the streets of SoMa, her frustration growing as each hour passed with no sign of Paul, she began to form a plan on how to locate him. Eventually she gave up any hope he'd reappear on her charm radar, decided to implement her plan and caught a cab back to her parking garage. She drove the Jag home, always keeping a bit of her focused on the charms in case her connection to Paul returned.

Her home was still a mess from the demon attack. She'd called in a contractor but he was still working on the repairs, though this late there was no one about. She headed straight for her workshop, a room in which she allowed no one. She knew the young Latino girls employed by the cleaning service that came in once a week were curious about it, since it was the one room they were instructed not to clean. But she kept it locked, with the door heavily spelled.

She spent half the night preparing an arsenal of spells and charms. When she did locate Paul—and she never doubted she would eventually—she might need to break into a powerful practitioner's home, and she wasn't foolish enough to go in unprepared.

When the spells were ready she packed a small overnight bag with a toothbrush, makeup and a change of clothes, then drove back to SoMa and found a cheap motel not far from where she knew Paul was being held captive—she didn't recall when she'd concluded he was being held captive, but deep inside she knew he wouldn't hide from her. She found a parking garage nearby for the Jag, checked into the motel, laid down on the bed in her clothes, and drifted off into a restless sleep.

••••

Belinda lay in bed next to Paul and watched his chest rise and fall as he slept soundly. Their lovemaking the night before had been intense, though at this stage it was more like raping a young boy than *lovemaking*. For her it satisfied her need for pleasure, while for him it fulfilled the powerful pull of the obsession, attraction and passion spells she'd cast upon him. She'd added the attraction and passion spells recently because, while the obsession spell seemed to be working nicely, it hadn't had as intense an effect on the young man as she'd expected. She was stronger than most witches, and her spells were quite powerful, and there was something almost elemental, almost magical, about her body and the way she could use it to control men. But for the first time in her life that, and the obsession spell, had not been enough. Something she couldn't quite identify was missing, and it had thwarted her every effort to control him. She'd achieved control, significant control after a fashion, but not the complete, absolute and unyielding control she had learned to rely on in similar situations.

Her master grew more impatient each day, and she sensed Its growing eagerness like a hungry, brooding presence hovering over her. She'd counseled her master to move slowly, to allow her the time she needed to fully enslave the young wizard. Certainly he was nicely under her power, and each day she had with him, especially each night, her control grew stronger. She'd established a fabric of control woven through the young man's aura, but for some reason it remained fragile and imperfect, still a bit tenuous, and she feared that once beyond the wards of her apartment, any outside influence might easily disrupt his growing dependence upon her. But she knew her master well, and Its patience was now exhausted. It wanted to speak with her; she knew that as only a thrall would know such things.

She eased out of bed, knowing Paul would sleep and dream of only her until she released him from the sleep spell she'd cast. Standing up completely naked, she admired herself in the mirror for a moment, admired the beautiful, young, voluptuous body that was one of her greatest assets.

She threw on a robe, walked out of her bedroom, down the hall and into the apartment's other bedroom, which she used as a combination study and workroom. She picked up the phone there and called her master, and It answered the call before the phone rang the first time. "I sensed you wanted to speak with me," she said.

"Ah, my dear Belinda. You're a treasure beyond value. Is the young Lord ready?"

She chose her words carefully. "There's something missing here, something I can't name. It might be best if we waited a few more days."

Her master answered her with a long, painful silence. Finally, It asked, "Have you failed me?"

A knot of fear formed in the pit of her stomach. "No, master," she pleaded. "It's just progressing more slowly than I anticipated."

"Perhaps you're enjoying him too much," It said. "That would be so like you, my dear Belinda. You do love the pleasures of that magnificent body of yours, though I'll never understand what mortal men see in your curves."

"No," she pleaded. "It's not that. I mean, I am enjoying him, but there's something missing."

"You do have him under your control, don't you?"

"Yes, master, of course I do. It's just that the—" She shivered as her master's anger washed through her, like a splash of icy water on a winter day.

"I'll send a car for you," It said. "Have him ready this afternoon."

••••

"You fool," Ag shouted, spittle flying from his mouth.

Simuth, on his hands and knees before Ag in his private study, blood dripping from his nose where Ag had struck him, cringed and tried to retreat, crawling like a dog. That enraged Ag even further; he crossed the distance between them in an instant and stomped on one of Simuth's hands. Anogh heard the bones snap as the Winter Knight cried out and curled into a fetal position on the floor. Ag gave full vent to his rage and kicked and punched at the helpless fool.

Anogh glanced at the other courtiers standing there watching Ag's cruelty. Many looked on with excitement or pleasure in their eyes. Cruelty was a hallmark of the Unseelie Court, bred into its denizens for millennia, and they all shared in a certain reverie whenever malice and brutality were manifest. Anogh wanted to look away. But to do so would draw Ag's attention, and after six hundred years attending the Winter Court, Anogh had learned Ag's attention was never a good thing. Simuth was immortal, and he'd survive and eventually heal from any wound, no matter how grievous.

"Follow her," Ag shouted. "Yes, an excellent idea. Abduct her and rape her! Fine, as long as you don't bring down the wrath of the Old Wizard. But to be caught, and in so doing obligate this Court, obligate me, to the old man—"

Ag kicked Simuth in the ribs several more times. Then he abruptly stopped, and spun toward Anogh. "Summer Knight," he snarled.

Anogh stepped forward immediately and dropped to one knee. "Your Majesty."

"Following her is a good idea." He glanced down at Simuth and gave him another kick, more as an afterthought. "But this fool can't keep his priorities straight."

He looked back to Anogh. "You follow her, keep a close eye on her. She'll lead us to this young wizard. I have no doubt of that."

Anogh said, "As you wish, Your Majesty."

He didn't mention he'd been following her for his own reasons. Now he could follow her openly, would no longer need to keep his activities hidden from Ag and the Unseelie Court.

••••

Paul sat up in bed. Dim, gray light leaking through the window told him it was a cloudy San Francisco day. His thoughts seemed unusually clear, and he wondered at that, because he was a clear-thinking type of person, and he shouldn't be so surprised to find himself thinking clearly. He stood, completely naked, climbed into his underwear, found his pants and pulled them on.

The apartment seemed unusually silent, deathly so, no sounds of Belinda moving about the place, no street sounds from outside. He stepped up to the window, pulled the curtain aside and looked down onto the street. It was a busy San Francisco boulevard, but frozen in time, pedestrians motionless in mid stride, cars still and silent in the middle of the street, with an odd sense of speed that had been arrested somehow. A young man in a business suit had just tossed a fast-food wrapper toward a city trash receptacle, and the wrapper hung motionless in midair, waiting for time to march forward again.

Confused, Paul wandered into the bathroom, found Belinda there dressed in a terrycloth robe. She'd clearly just finished her bath, now stood before the mirror over the sink in the midst of running a brush through a wet tangle of her magnificent mane of black hair. Like the pedestrians on the street she stood frozen in time.

A faint noise in the living room startled him, the only noise in a world gone deathly still. He walked down the hall and peered cautiously around the corner into the living room. Dayandalous sat in a comfortable chair there.

"God damn it," Paul said as he dropped all caution and stepped into the living room. "What're you doing here?"

Dayandalous smiled, exposing brilliant white teeth in his coal-black face, and his vertically slit eyes flashed blood red. "You young people!" he said sadly, shaking his head. "No sense of propriety. You should say something like, 'Hello Dayandalous, what a pleasure to see you again.' And then we'd have a little small talk, and slowly ease into the purpose of my visit."

Paul approached the seated Dayandalous and stood angrily over him. "It's all a game with you. Riddles and hints and puzzles and conundrums, and I'm tired of it."

Dayandalous sighed deeply. "I can understand that, Paul." His eyes narrowed and he turned serious. "But I'm rather disappointed in you. I thought you were taking control there, for a while. Purchasing the gun, while crude, was nevertheless effective. It showed you were becoming proactive instead of reactive. But now you've slipped into this cocoon of unthinking reaction, going where you're told to go, doing what you're told to do."

"I don't know what you're talking about."

"You will," Dayandalous said. "And if you hope to survive, you need to take control."

"Paul."

Paul turned at the sound of Belinda calling his name. She walked into the living room still wearing the terrycloth robe, and as she approached him he could think of only one thing. He reached out, opening the robe, exposing her naked, incredible body. "Who were you talking to?" she asked as he cupped her breasts in his hands and leaned down to kiss them.

"Not now," she said, taking his hands in hers and lifting them off her breasts. "You need to shower and get dressed. My father's sending a car for us. Who were you talking too?"

Paul turned back to the chair. For some reason he thought there should be someone sitting there, but it was empty. He said, "I must've just been thinking out loud."

21

The Trail

KATHERINE HAD AWAKENED early in the cheap motel, though her sleep had been shallow and fitful since she'd kept a piece of her always focused on the charms. The bathroom was clean, though the place smelled of cheap disinfectant. She showered quickly, combed her hair back into a ponytail—which was so not like her—carefully applied her makeup—there wasn't a demon in hell that could make her go out on the street without makeup—then pulled on a baseball cap—also not her style. Someone was going to pay big-time for this.

She checked out of the motel, found a nearby diner and ate a rather hearty breakfast, which wasn't good for her figure. Yes, she thought as she returned to the street, someone was going to pay dearly.

Her plan was simple. Yesterday Paul had stepped outside of whatever wards or spells were hiding him. Yesterday was close enough in time, and Paul was a strong enough practitioner, that he must've left some trace she could identify. She'd still had one of his hairs stored away in her workshop, and she'd used it to construct a charm she hoped would ring an alarm if she crossed his path, though it had to be recent, good if within the last day, better if within half a day.

She'd carefully mapped out a one block radius around Paul's suspected location, then started door-to-door. At private homes she knew the wards of a practitioner would be placed at all entrances, so if Paul had emerged from such wards there would be a trace of him on the front stoop. She simply walked up the steps to each front door, stood there for a moment and fed power into the charm.

Apartment buildings were a different matter. A practitioner would place wards at any possible entrances to the apartment—doors, windows, mirrors and such—but not at the front entrance of the building. But there was no time for her to walk up and down every hallway on every floor of every building. She hoped that yesterday Paul had at least made it to the front entrance. Sometimes she got in by ringing one of the bells and mumbling unintelligibly into a speaker, and sometimes she just spelled the lock on the front entrance, then checked out the foyer or lobby for any trace of Paul.

It was tedious work, and by late afternoon she'd illegally entered dozens of apartment buildings and stood on the front stoop of as many private homes. Her biggest fear was she wasn't certain the new spell would actually work, wasn't certain it would allow her to sense some residual trace of Paul. She'd only know it worked when it did. And if it didn't, she might've already crossed his path a dozen times and not known it. She stood on the sidewalk in the middle of a long city block and surveyed her surroundings. She wasn't even close to half-way done.

"She's tryin' her best, ain't she Jim'Jiminie."

At the sound of the Irish brogue Katherine spun and spotted the two leprechauns. They were both leaning casually on opposite sides of a light pole.

She marched up to them angrily, her patience at an end. "Can you help?" she demanded.

One of the little fellows looked at the other and said, "Can we help her, Boo?"

He shrugged and answered. "Not if she asks in that tone of voice."

"Aye, Boo, you have the right of it there."

"Ok," Katherine said, struggling to be polite. "Please help. Pretty please."

Jim'Jiminie considered her for a moment, then turned to his companion. "That's much better, ain't it, Boo?"

Boo'Diddle nodded carefully. "Aye, 'tis better, Jimmie-boy. But you know we're not supposed to be helpin' her."

Jim'Jiminie considered that with a grave look on his face. "Aye, Boo, you got the right of that too." He rubbed his chin contemplatively and tugged at his red beard. "But it occurs to me if we were to be just walkin' casually down the street, and this rude lass here was to be following us, and we didn't know she was following us, and we happened to be walking in the right direction—well now, that would just be coincidence wouldn't it, Boo?"

Both leprechauns stepped away from the light pole. "Jimmie, tell me more how this coincidence might work." And with that they turned their backs on Katherine and strolled casually, slowly down the sidewalk.

It was the *slowly* part that was infuriating. Katherine wanted to rant at them to hurry up. She wanted to shout crude epithets at them and kick them in the ass. But she knew full well she dare not. The little men would move at their own pace, for their own strange and unknown reasons.

They'd walked to the end of the block and just turned the corner when the charms kicked in. Without warning Paul had emerged from whatever wards or spells had hidden him. The leprechauns continued strolling casually as Katherine stepped to the curb and looked up the street. It was a busy San Francisco weekday, the sidewalks filled with people and the street with cars both parked and moving, as well as pedestrians illegally crossing in the middle of the street. Up the street she saw a black limousine double-parked, other cars stopping momentarily, then swinging around and past it, but there was nothing unusual in that.

Leprechauns were sneaky little people, always operating to their own agenda, so there was always a chance they'd chosen to lead her away from Paul. She turned and looked the other direction, tried to focus for just an instant on every face on the sidewalk. Then she remembered the connection between the charms, closed her eyes and focused on that.

The little men had led her true. She opened her eyes, looked back up the street just in time to see the limousine pull away from the curb.

She could sense Paul moving, coming toward her. She tried to look into every face on the sidewalk, every pedestrian in the street. She stepped between two parked cars, stood right at the edge of the flow of traffic and tried to look through the windows of every car that sped by. When the limousine passed her, its windows black and impenetrable, the sensation of Paul coming toward her changed to that of him moving away, and then she knew.

Her car! She had to get to her car.

••••

"It's Katherine," Paul said, pointing out through the window of the limo. "She must've come for me."

Belinda's control had begun to slip the instant they stepped past the wards of her apartment. So she'd held Paul's hand tightly, never let go of it, pulled power continuously and fed the spells in which she'd entangled him. And then they'd passed the McGowan bitch, and it all started to unravel. She could see reason returning to Paul's gaze.

Physical contact, hand to hand, skin to skin; physical contact strengthened the spells, as much physical contact as possible. She opened her blouse, lifted her bra and pressed the palms of his hands against her breasts. At the same time she opened his shirt and rubbed his chest, then slid a hand into his pants and began stroking him.

She tore the buttons off his shirt to open it completely, tore the buttons off her blouse to open it. She lifted her skirt, pushed one if his hands down inside her underwear, tried to ignore the pleasure that climbed up her stomach as he began stroking her. It took several seconds to get his pants down, and to get her pantyhose down, but as she expanded the physical contact between them she felt her control returning, and with that comforting thought she finally allowed herself to enjoy this. Physical contact, skin to skin, flesh to flesh, body to body.

A little piece of her realized the limo driver was getting one hell of a show in his rear-view-mirror.

••••

"Mr. Karpov, this is Mikhail." Mikhail spoke carefully into his cell phone as he followed the young woman up the street.

"What is it, Mikhail?"

"The young woman, she seems to be on the move."

"What do you mean, on the move? Has she led you to the demon-wizard?"

"No, Mr. Karpov. But suddenly she started running up the street. She seems frightened, frantic. I think she's headed to her car."

"You can follow her, yes?"

"Yes. I parked my car near hers. But I think she may be going to the demon-wizard."

Mikhail waited as he heard Karpov shouting orders in the background. Then Karpov came back on the line. "Stay close to her. And keep this line open. Give us directions so we can join you."

••••

Katherine wanted to shout at the attendant in the parking garage as he took his sweet time computing her bill. It was a little over twenty dollars, so she handed him two twenties and shouted at him, "Keep the fucking change and raise the gate. Now. This is an emergency."

His eyes widened, and he didn't say anything as he hit the switch that raised the gate.

Katherine hit the accelerator, slammed on the brakes as a young girl walked in front of her on the sidewalk at the garage entrance. The young girl paused and angrily flipped her off. Katherine blared the car's horn at her and hit the accelerator. The girl had no choice but to skip out of the way as Katherine shot past her.

She sensed Paul somewhere north of her. She struggled with traffic near the Moscone Center, was forced to wait through one interminable light after another, finally pulled onto Market Street heading southwest. She turned north on Van Nuys, basically the main street running north through the city. She intended to drive up Van Nuys until she spotted the limo, or sensed Paul to one side or the other. The afternoon rush hour had started and everything on the street moved slowly now, an odd sort of blessing since the limo couldn't outpace her.

Paul was still north of her and slightly west, getting more west all the time, so she concluded they must've turned that way. She pushed the limits on every traffic light on Van Nuys, ran a couple just as they turned from yellow to red, prayed that some SFPD cruiser didn't pull her over and ticket her. When she got to Lombard Street Paul was due west of her, so she turned west on Lombard. He was now directly ahead of her somewhere, though she couldn't see the limo, and she didn't know if she was closing the gap or not.

••••

Clark Devoe had a special cell phone and only special people had the number. When it rang he answered it immediately.

"Clark, this is Walter McGowan."

"Hello, Mr. McGowan, what can I do for you?"

"I'm sorry to impose on you at the last minute like this, Clark, but I have an emergency."

"Not a problem, Mr. McGowan. What do you need?"

"I need your help, Clark. Could you get in your car and head north into the city? Stay in touch, and as you get closer I'll know more about where we're all going."

"I'll do it right away, Mr. McGowan."

"And Clark, be sure to come prepared for trouble."

"Of course, Mr. McGowan. I'm always ready for trouble."

••••

Lombard fed into Doyle Drive, the traffic bumper-to-bumper and moving at a snail's pace. As he waited in the traffic that fed onto the Golden Gate Bridge, Mikhail hit the speed dial on his cell phone.

Karpov answered. "What is it?"

"I'm on Doyle feeding onto the Golden Gate. She's going north across the bridge. But the traffic is shit here, Mr. Karpov."

"Just stay close to her, Mikhail. We're on our way."

"Yes, Mr. Karpov."

••••

Sitting in the traffic, Colleen asked, "You put a tracer on your daughter?"

McGowan looked her way and grinned. "Of course I did. I'm her father. That's what fathers do."

"What kind of spell did you use? By now the blood is too old."

McGowan's grin broadened until it was absolutely cheesy. He held up a cell phone. "No spell," he said, clearly proud of himself. "I bought a GPS cell phone, with parental controls. I bought a set of them. Isn't this technology great? You can use a cell phone to track where your kids are."

Colleen knew the answer, but she needed to ask anyway. "You gave her one of those cell phones?"

McGowan winked at her. "Well I didn't exactly give it to her. I tossed it in the back seat of her car. I also tossed one in the back seat of that fucking Russian's car, the one that's following her. I can track him as well."

Colleen grinned back at him. "For once, old man, I'm glad you're a sneaky bastard."

••••

Once the traffic opened up on the Golden Gate Bridge, Katherine caught a glimpse of the black limousine about a quarter mile ahead of her. The traffic was too thick for her to catch up to it, but with the charms giving her a good, solid sense of Paul's location, she didn't need to. On Highway 101 north of the bridge the traffic opened up some. The limo driver seemed in no hurry and Katherine managed to catch up to them a bit. Her biggest fear was she might not see the limo exit from 101, that she'd only recognize her mistake when she passed them by and realized Paul was behind her. She'd have to continue on to the next exit, then backtrack, and by that time they could have him hidden behind the wards of any of hundreds of homes in the area. But the limo driver was careful to obey the law and he signaled well before exiting on Tiburon Boulevard, so her luck held. One had to have plenty of money to live in Sausalito, but Tiburon was home to a lot of old money.

Tiburon Boulevard wound back and forth as it led southeast onto the peninsula, and the rush hour traffic kept her from catching up to them. Twilight was settling over the roadway and the black limo was always just a momentary glimpse in the distance before disappearing around the next turn. And then suddenly Paul was behind her. They'd turned off onto a side street and she'd missed it.

Traffic going the other way was light so she hit the Jag's breaks and spun a quick U-turn. The cars behind her skidded and honked their horns, and someone shouted at her.

Going the other way now she used her sense of Paul to guide her and pulled onto a side street with no traffic. She gunned the Jag and sped recklessly down a winding road past expensive homes and mansions, turned a corner and spotted the limo just inside the entrance of a gated community, pulling rapidly away.

She spun the Jaguar's wheel, turned in front of an oncoming car, careened past it and screeched to a halt in front of the gate next to the guard station. A young woman in the uniform of a security guard leaned out of the guard station, a wary look on her face. "Is there some problem?" she asked as Katherine lowered the Jag's window.

"Not at all," Katherine said politely, keeping one eye on the limo as it disappeared over a small rise. "I have an invitation," she said as she reached into her pocket and pulled out a handful of charms. She selected one, leaned down so the guard couldn't see what she did and spit on it. She held it out the window toward the guard.

The guard frowned suspiciously and reached out cautiously, but the moment their fingers touched Katherine released the spell. The guard blinked her eyes rapidly and shook her head. She'd feel a strong sense of confusion and a need to believe anything Katherine told her.

Katherine said, "You've seen my invitation and everything's all right, isn't it?"

"Yes, it is," the guard said blearily, shaking her head and blinking her eyes rapidly.

"Then please open the gate and let me through."

The guard complied and Katherine sped after the limo, driving almost recklessly through the streets of the exclusive community. A tall stucco wall bordered the road on the left, and as she passed a large wrought iron gate a hint of movement caught her eye and her sense of Paul pulled her that way. She stomped on the Jag's brakes and skidded to a stop in a cloud of dust and scattering gravel. She threw the Jag into reverse and backed up to the gate.

It was just closing, moving silently on some motorized mechanism. And in the distance she spotted the limo pulling into a garage at the end of a driveway about four-hundred feet long, a five-car garage part of a rather large mansion. She watched the garage door close, concealing the limo from view. She waited for her sense of Paul to disappear as he entered the wards of a powerful practitioner, but oddly enough that didn't happen. She waited there for a good minute, the Jag's engine idling softly, and when nothing further happened, she pulled the Jag forward about a hundred feet and turned off the road into the dark shadows of a large tree.

Still sensing Paul's direction and distance, she climbed out of the Jag and locked it. It bothered her that the mansion wasn't properly warded, that the link between the locator charms hadn't been broken when Paul entered the place. She could sense him moving about inside as the dark shadows of a moonless night descended quickly, and she wished she didn't have to do this alone.

22

Into the Demon's Lair

PAUL FELT NO desire to resist Belinda as she led him down a dark hallway clutching his hand almost desperately. Back in the limo his thoughts had been completely consumed by the pleasures of her body. It seemed that when they made love his ability to think rationally abandoned him. His mind generated random snippets of thought, punctuated by his desire for Belinda. He'd have a thought of something else, something not-Belinda, something he should be aware of, something he should do, perhaps something he should worry about. And then the taste of her skin would distract him and he'd think of only her for a moment, and the not-Belinda thought would disappear. And then he'd have another not-Belinda thought, and he was certain if he could just put the not-Belinda thoughts together in a stream it would mean something much more. But the Belinda thoughts always interrupted the not-Belinda thoughts, and he could never put two of them together at one time, though he had to admit the Belinda thoughts were pretty good thoughts to have.

She pulled him into a dimly lit room that contained a large desk, with leather bound books lining the walls and a warm fire crackling in a hearth. She'd obviously brought him into a gentleman's elegantly furnished study.

The gentleman in question stood from behind the desk as they entered the room. He was tall, handsome, wearing an elegant dark suit, elegant dark hair with an elegant touch of gray at the temples. His mere presence made the room seem even more elegant.

He stepped out from behind the desk and crossed the room, saying, "Belinda, my love."

"Father," she said as he hugged her warmly, and she seemed overwhelmed with joy to be in his presence.

They separated, and the gentleman turned to Paul. "And this must be the young man you told me about." He spoke with a refined accent, not British refined, but as if America had its own aristocracy, and its own aristocratic accent.

"Paul," Belinda said. "I'd like you to meet my father, Cassius." When Belinda looked at her father it was as if Paul wasn't even in the room.

"Sir," Paul said, extending his hand.

The man grasped Paul's hand warmly in both of his. "Belinda told me you've been having trouble with demons."

Blink.

Paul had seen something overlaying Cassius's image, but it wasn't one of the bat-things like the demons. And in the same *blink* he'd seen that image of an older Belinda overlaying the image of the Belinda standing in front of him.

"I don't know what to do, sir," Paul said as Cassius continued to hold his hand. For an instant he thought he felt that *pull* where the flesh of his hand met that of Cassius, the *pull* he'd felt when the demon had touched him. But Cassius was Belinda's father, not some demon, and at the thought of Belinda Paul looked her way, couldn't take his eyes off her.

Suddenly an immense sense of weakness and lassitude overcame him. He struggled to keep from collapsing to the floor. Cassius stepped in closer, slipped an arm around Paul's shoulders and supported him. Belinda supported him on the other side and they walked him carefully toward a chair. "Don't worry, Paul," Cassius said. "When you don't know what you're doing demons can be quite dangerous. But when you do, they're no more than a minor inconvenience. I can help you, son."

They lowered him into the chair as his head swirled and he felt sick to his stomach. Cassius said, "Don't worry, Paul. I can help you."

Cassius leaned over his desk and touched something there, then spoke into some sort of intercom. Paul heard him say the name Joachim, then a few moments later the limo driver arrived. Cassius gave the fellow some hurried instructions, then Joachim helped Paul upstairs to a bedroom, all but carried him there.

••••

"Ah!" Baalthelmass cried. "The taste of him was wonderful. I only sampled him, but it was enough. He's like nothing I've tasted in centuries—no, millennia."

Belinda watched the demon lord pace back and forth across Its study. Then It turned toward her. "You have done well, my dear. You'll have great joy of your reward. Go to his bed. Keep him enthralled. I want him pliable, so I can consume him slowly."

Her master was in no mood to hear of complications, so she dare not tell It now of the young man's resistance, of the unaccountable strength he showed regarding her spells. She'd go to his bed, strengthen the spells that entangled him, and later there would come a time when she could help her master see the danger in the young wizard.

••••

Katherine needed to find a way over the wall onto the grounds of the mansion. About seven feet high, the wall was plain, unadorned stucco, probably with a brick and mortar structure beneath it, and no purchase for climbing. She tried to jump up and get some sort of hold, managed to get her arms on top of the wall with her head just above it. But there was nothing to grip and she didn't have the upper body strength to simply hoist her own weight over the wall.

From a distance she considered the wrought-iron gate. She might spell the mechanism and get it to open, but there must be some sort of security system to warn those in the mansion.

She turned away from the gate and started down the length of the wall, hoping to find some way to climb it. Traffic on the road was light, and as night settled over the peninsula, when the occasional car approached its headlights gave her plenty of warning, and for each she stopped momentarily and hide behind a bush. She didn't need the local police asking her why she was stalking about some wealthy person's estate.

About two hundred feet from the gate she found an oak tree about six feet outside the wall. There weren't any limbs close to the ground, nothing so convenient as to simply allow her to climb the tree and drop down on the other side of the wall. But there was one, stout limb growing from the main trunk about eight feet off the ground and extending out over the wall.

She crouched, leapt up and caught the limb on the first try, then, hanging by her hands, she edged slowly along the limb toward the wall. The limb was quite solid and thick, but it still bowed under her weight, and when she got to the wall her breasts just cleared the top of it. Still hanging from the limb she swung her legs side-to-side, like a gymnast on the high bar. The limb swayed with her, but she finally managed to throw her hips and legs up, and her butt smacked painfully on the top of the wall. With her butt on the wall, and still hanging by her hands from the limb with her torso suspended precariously over an eight-foot drop to the ground, she edged her hands along the limb until she could let go and remain on the wall. In the process she'd scraped her knees and elbows, torn her jeans and coat, and lost the baseball cap.

She sat there for a moment and sorted through her charms. She imagined snarling attack dogs patrolling the grounds, a pack of them bringing her down and ripping her throat out, but she put that thought away as being just a bit overly dramatic. This wasn't some spy movie, but she'd still feel better with something to protect her. She selected an aversion spell. It should work on animals as well as people, make them always want to look away, to look at and take interest in something else. She activated it with a touch of saliva, stuffed it back in her pocket, then eased over the edge of the wall and dropped down into the compound.

••••

The knock on the door didn't wake Belinda. She'd only just gotten in bed with Paul, and after their escapades in the back of the limo she was sated, so she'd spelled him into sleep.

She rolled out of bed, crossed the room and opened the door. Joachim stood there. She was barely dressed, her nipples protruding through the translucent fabric of her nightgown. He'd never tried to hide his desire for her, his pure, unbridled lust. And she'd always taken pleasure in the way she could control him with it, especially since she'd never allowed him to satisfy his desire. He looked her up and down and his eyes paused for a long moment on her breasts. Then he looked past her toward Paul, and nodded. She answered his unasked question. "He's asleep. And he won't wake until I want him to. What is it?"

Joachim's voice came out in a throaty grumble. "The master says there's an intruder on the grounds. He wants you downstairs, now. And bring the young wizard so we can keep an eye on him."

His eyes returned to her breasts as she said, "I'll dress and be there in a moment."

••••

Mikhail gave Vladimir explicit directions to the walled estate, then stuffed his cell phone into his pocket. The young woman had parked her car in the shadows at the side of the road about three hundred yards away, though now that night had descended it was no longer visible in the darkness.

The old man appeared in front of him as if by magic, and quite possibly it was by magic. The shadow standing next to him had to be the old hippie woman. Mikhail knew a few spells, but against either one of them he was completely out of his league.

"Good evening, Mikhail," McGowan said. His voice was not kind.

Mikhail took one step back, though he knew nothing would help him if the old man wanted a fight. "Good evening, Mr. McGowan."

McGowan stepped forward aggressively. Mikhail wanted to take another step away from this dangerous, old wizard, but his feet were suddenly immovable as if rooted to the ground. McGowan leaned in close so their noses were almost touching. When he spoke his voice had the timbre of a large predator. "Tell Vasily my daughter's in there. And if any harm comes to her as a result of any action he or any of you take, there'll be open war between us. Tell Vasily that."

The Old Wizard and the hippie disappeared just as quickly and silently as they'd appeared.

••••

The grounds of the estate covered several acres, most in a fairly pristine state. In case she needed some sort of defense beyond the aversion spell, Katherine kept a sleeping spell cupped in the palm of her hand as she worked her way through well-spaced red-woods, then through a stand of eucalyptus, always moving toward the lights of the house. It was one of those old-money mansions, with steep and complex rooflines, well-tended grounds close in to the house itself. So far, no snarling, attack dogs.

She paused at the edge of a stone patio, stayed hidden in the shadows of a wall of shrubs that surrounded it. Light spilled out through a set of French doors that opened onto the patio. She waited and watched for quite a while, but she saw no movement within, so she stepped out from behind the shrubs and crossed the patio silently, taking care to stay out of the light from the French doors.

She edged up to the doors carefully from one side and peered through the glass in-to the room. It was empty. She could easily spell the lock on the doors, and she was about to do just that when she heard footsteps approaching from behind her. She froze as a man and a woman walked casually onto the patio. The aversion spell would only work as long as she remained still.

The man stood well over six-feet tall, wore a chauffeur's cap and carried a metal water bucket. The woman wore an overcoat that covered her completely from shoul-ders to mid-calf, but something about her radiated a raw sensuousness that Katherine even envied a little. She exuded a fundamental, visceral, primal sexuality, something almost elemental in its nature. As she and the man approached the French doors, a cascade of tightly curled, black hair hid her face. "You can't see her?" the woman asked.

The man turned to look at the woman, which had him looking almost directly at Katherine. "No," he said. "Nothing." His eyes glanced past the woman toward Kathe-rine momentarily, then he looked away under the influence of the aversion spell.

"She's a reasonably strong witch," the woman said. "Not strong enough to fool me, but clearly strong enough to fool you."

Just as Katherine realized they were talking about her, the woman stepped back from the French doors and said, "And that's easily fixed." In the same motion she turned toward Katherine, threw her hand out and something that sparkled and shim-mered on the air fluttered about Katherine's shoulders.

Katherine tensed, activated the sleeping spell just as the man threw the contents of the bucket at her. A torrent of water hit her in the face and made her stagger backward, soaking her completely just as she threw the spell. But the spell fizzled like a wet fire-cracker as its energy dissipated into the earth and the trees and bushes about them. The man and woman both staggered, but they didn't swoon and drop to the ground in a deep sleep as they should have. And then Katherine tasted the salt in the water and realized the bucket had been filled with seawater. She'd been soaked from head to foot with saltwater, grounding her magic and shorting her spells.

Katherine spun on her heels, hopped a shrub like an Olympic hurdler and ran. She felt the force of some sort of spell slam into her. She stumbled and missed a step, but the spell sizzled and dissipated and she ran on. The saltwater dimmed her own powers, but since she'd been completely soaked it also limited the effects of spells they might throw against her. She heard the woman swear, "God damn it, get her."

Katherine dodged into the stand of eucalyptus. She heard the man grunt as he hurtled the shrub behind her. He was a big man, must outweigh her by a hundred pounds and none of it fat. And with legs much longer than hers she probably couldn't outrun him either. But she wasn't going to give up without one hell of a fight.

She wasn't counting on the tall, distinguished, older man that appeared directly in front of her without warning. She ran headlong into him, and like something as solid as an oak tree he didn't stagger, move, or even twitch as she bounced off him. She landed hard on the ground, wrenching her shoulder badly in the process.

She tried to struggle to her feet while the distinguished older man stood over her shaking his head sadly. He didn't move, didn't try to help or hinder her. She made it to one knee, and then the chauffeur hit her like a charging linebacker, slammed her into the ground and landed on top of her with his full weight, knocking the wind out of her. She struggled futilely until he backhanded her, sent her to edge of consciousness. In a semiconscious haze she was barely aware of what he was doing as he rolled her over onto her stomach, pinned her arms behind her back, then hoisted her to her feet, picked her up as if she weighted nothing. He held her upright as the older man looked her over carefully.

"Hmmm!" he said. "What do we have here?"

Katherine could barely hold herself upright as the sexpot witch appeared, and for the first time she got a good look at the woman. She realized there was something truly unnatural about her beauty.

The woman grinned and said, "It appears we have a little witch."

The older man reached down and took Katherine's hand. He lifted it to his lips like a nineteenth century gentleman and said, "A tasty little witch."

Then he kissed her hand like a courtier in some period drama, and as he fed Katherine understood his true nature: demon . . .

••••

Karpov arrived, as always, accompanied by Vladimir and Alexei. A heavy swath of bandages obscured Alexei's left hand. Mikhail had heard rumors this new wizard had gotten the best of him, but knew better than to ask questions. The stupid, dangerous bear had his pride, and only a fool ventured there.

"Well?" Karpov demanded impatiently as he climbed out of the car.

"The young woman went over the wall about a half hour ago," Mikhail said nervously, afraid to add the rest but knowing he had to. "I've heard nothing from the estate grounds, but the Old Wizard is somewhere around. He gave me a message for you, said if we did anything that caused harm to come to his daughter, it would be open war between you."

Karpov snarled and his eyes narrowed angrily. Men had died when he got that look. Mikhail added nervously, "I'm sorry, Mr. Karpov. There was nothing I could do."

Karpov's face softened and he smiled. "That's ok, Mikhail. At least you got the brains to know you were outclassed. That's why I like you. You got brains. Now Alexei here . . ."

Karpov turned to the big, dumb bear, reached up and knocked on the side of his head like he was knocking on a heavy wooden door. "Alexei here, he got no brains."

"Ya," Alexei growled, grinning stupidly. "I got no brains."

Karpov laughed. "Ya, he got no brains." Karpov knocked on the bear's broad chest. "But he got muscle. He got muscle here . . ." He continued knocking on the bear's chest, then reached up and knocked again on the side of his head. "And he got muscle here too. That's why I like him."

Alexei reached up and knocked on the side of his own head. "Ya, I got muscle here."

They all got a good laugh at that, though that ended when Karpov demanded, "Where's McGowan?"

Mikhail didn't want to admit he didn't know. But he was rescued by the old man who said, "I'm right here." Then the old guy did that trick of appearing out of nowhere.

Karpov grinned unpleasantly and said, "So we are going to do this again, eh, Valter?"

McGowan shook his head sadly, and it bothered Mikhail that he did so with such confidence. The old man said, "I brought a couple of friends." He looked over his shoulder and called, "Clark."

The old man's *weapon* stepped out of the shadows and Mikhail involuntarily tensed, though he was happy to see Vladimir and Alexei also tensed. Even idiots like those two knew better than to take the old man's *weapon* for granted.

"We're going to set some rules," McGowan said. "The first one being, you start shooting at the wrong people, Clark starts shooting at you. And we all know you don't want Clark shooting at you."

Karpov shrugged. "Valter. We are all friends here. Of course your daughter's off limits."

McGowan added, "And the young man."

Alexei erupted. "No!" he shouted and reached toward the old man angrily. But a shadow flitted between them, and a soundless, silent flash dropped the bear on his ass in the middle of the dark road.

The shadow said in a female voice with an Irish accent, "Control your children, Vasily."

Mikhail had never seen his boss capitulate to a woman, but he did now. "My apologies, Colleen."

Alexei struggled half way to his feet, but Karpov kicked him hard and he went down again. Karpov looked at Mikhail. "Like I said, Mikhail, no brains."

Karpov turned back to McGowan. "The young man's a demon, or possessed by one. He dies."

The Old Wizard sighed wearily. With his *weapon* at hand, there was no question he had them outgunned. And with the druid, he also had them out-spelled. "Vasily," he said calmly, one senior wizard to another. "I've had the young man in my home. He's no demon, and I don't think he's possessed by one—"

"You don't think," Karpov snarled, interrupting him in a way none of the younger men dared, "but you don't know."

The two old wizards stared at each other for a moment, and McGowan broke the silence. "No, I don't know. But I do know something doesn't add up here. And I want the young man alive. We still take him, but we take him alive."

That statement hung in the air for a long moment, until Karpov said, "Ok, Valter. We take him alive . . . if we can. If we can't . . . then we take him dead. But we take him, and we will protect your daughter."

McGowan closed his eyes for several long seconds, and when he opened them Mikhail saw the death of the young man there. "Ok, my daughter comes first. But we try to take the young man alive."

Karpov shrugged that off happily. "Agreed!"

They stared at each other for several seconds, like two cats waiting to see which one struck first. Then the Old Wizard did that thing, and he and his *weapon* and the druid were just, simply gone. No exit required.

Karpov waited for a few seconds, then reached down to the bear, who'd wisely remained seated on the ground while the big predators held their little pissing contest. He helped Alexei to his feet, then twirled his finger in the air, his sign they were all to gather close. Karpov looked at Vladimir and Alexei and said, "You don't shoot the young man. You get your hands on him you can hurt him all you want, but you don't shoot him."

The bear growled. Karpov gave him a look that meant he could die right here and now if he wanted to disagree, and the bear lowered his eyes. Karpov said, "On the other hand . . ." and his eyes slowly drifted to Mikhail, ". . . Mikhail here can use his special talents on the young man. You did bring your special talent, didn't you, Mikhail?"

Mikhail nodded and smiled, reached under his windbreaker and pulled the twelve-inch knife he always carried. They all grinned in return. Even Vladimir and Alexei would think twice before taking him on when he had his blade.

••••

"What did you learn?" McGowan asked as they walked away from the Russians.

"Not much," Colleen said. "Big estate, walled on three sides, the bay, private beach and boat docks on the fourth. No guards patrolling the grounds, no wards I can detect, though I may need to get closer to confirm that. Seems like the house of an ordinary citizen, a rather wealthy and mundane citizen, but still, just that."

She stopped walking in the street, which forced McGowan and Devoe to also stop, and to turn and face her. She dropped her shadows so they could look into her face. "But there's something I'm missing here," she said. "And it bothers me no end."

23

The Simple Way

KATHERINE DRIFTED BACK to consciousness slowly.

"... just his girlfriend ..."

"... strong witch ..."

"... neutralized ... salt water ..."

"... alone ... no other intruders ..."

She found it difficult to shake off the weakness and lethargy that had overcome her. Her limbs felt heavy and unresponsive, and her mind refused to form a cohesive train of thought, all typical symptoms of a demon feeding.

Demon! That thought brought a rush of adrenaline and fear. Her eyes snapped open and she jumped to her feet, only to be overcome by a wave of dizziness. The big chauffeur put his hand against her chest and shoved, and she fell back into the chair. She rose again, and contemptuously, almost casually, the big man shoved her again, and she landed on her ass in the chair.

The sexpot witch snarled, "Keep her still."

"Yes, Joachim," the older man said calmly. "Please keep the young lady in her seat."

Katherine would almost feel better if her hands and feet were tied and bound securely. That would indicate they had some concern she might be of danger to them. Instead, with casual indifference, they'd seated her in a wingback chair in a large room with books lining the walls and expensive furnishings, her clothing soaking wet, the taste of seawater still on her lips. They must have dosed her with another bucket or two while she was out.

She tried to summon power, and it gathered inside her, but muted and weak, like trying to hold sand cupped in the palm of only one hand. The sexpot called contemptuously, "Don't waste your time, bitch."

Katherine tried to calm her breathing and take in her surroundings. The chauffeur stood a few feet away, ready to slap her back down into the chair. Two metal buckets sat on the floor next to her chair, each obviously filled with more seawater. They intended to keep her heavily dosed, and weak and helpless in the arcane. The older man sat behind a large, ornate desk, the young woman standing before him. "No, master," she said. "I checked the grounds carefully. She came alone."

There was another wingback chair near the desk facing it, its back toward Katherine. She could just see the top of the head of someone seated in it. The color and length of the hair led her to believe it was a man, possibly Paul. He was completely still and silent.

Katherine looked again at the older man. She hadn't sensed the nether life within him, even before they'd dosed her with seawater. The demon must be Secundus caste, very old and very powerful. No wonder there were no dogs patrolling the grounds. Dogs would go insane at the presence of a demon—it might be powerful enough to conceal its nature from a practitioner, but never from the sixth sense of a dog. And of course, no powerful wards in the house or grounds. The wards of a home were anathema to a demon.

"Go ahead, my dear," the demon said to the sexpot. "They're so much more appealing when they're angry and frustrated and frightened. Play your little games."

The sexpot turned to the man seated in the wingback chair. Katherine felt the flow of magic as she released a spell. She saw the man shake his head and turn to look up at the woman. "Come, my darling," the sexpot said.

Paul rose from the chair and shook his head groggily. He reached out and took the sexpot in his arms and kissed her. Katherine felt a wave of jealousy wash through her, though she had no right to be jealous if Paul wanted to fuck some slut.

The kiss ended and the woman pushed him away almost forcefully. "Later, my darling," she said. "Right now we have a guest; I believe a friend of yours."

She turned him toward Katherine and, holding his hand, led him across the room like a puppy. On instinct Katherine opened her *sight*, and almost vomited at the condition of his aura. There must've been a dozen spells wrapped and tangled into it, powerful binding spells all. She guessed at least one had to be an obsession spell. She could see its black-magic nature twisting and turning in his aura, binding it like the coils of a large python wrapped around its prey, squeezing and crushing the life out of it. Such horrific spells, in such strength and quantity, could permanently damage a person, and those who practiced them were no better than murderers and rapists. Practitioners kept themselves carefully guarded with personal wards against such spells, but Paul's ignorance made him no better than a helpless infant.

And yet, Paul should be completely dysfunctional at this stage. Just one or two of those spells should've rendered him helpless and docile. Why did the sexpot witch need so many, and of such strength?

"Katherine," Paul said wonderingly. He tried to pull away from the sexpot, tried to reach out to Katherine, but the sexpot pulled him toward her forcefully and put his hand inside her blouse. With her own hands she made him feel her up, and slowly he grew docile again.

During the brief interaction Katherine had seen his aura shift. The python constricting it had weakened for an instant, and only strengthened when the slut had shoved his hand in her blouse. Katherine realized Paul was resisting the slut's magic, resisting it so well the sexpot needed a whole raft of such spells, and she also needed physical contact to maintain them, the more physical contact the better.

Katherine closed off her *sight*. She was helpless for the moment, so she'd have to bide her time.

Still holding Paul's hand the sexpot stopped in front of Katherine's chair. Katherine felt her pulling power, a lot of it, and Katherine realized this witch was stronger than her. With a dramatic wave of her free hand the witch released the power in a spell that enveloped Katherine, and even with the muting effects of the saltwater, Katherine felt an overwhelming compulsion to stand. She fought it, but slowly, struggling against the coercion of the spell, shaking with the effort to resist it, she climbed to her feet and stood facing the witch and Paul.

The chauffeur stepped toward her, thinking she'd stood on her own, but the sexpot waved him off with her free hand. "I can handle this, Joachim," she said, a contemptuous sneer on her lips.

Katherine tried to speak, but the witch waved a finger and her throat tightened up. She looked at Paul, their eyes met and he frowned, looked carefully from Katherine to the sexpot, then back to Katherine.

"How poignant!" the sexpot said contemptuously. "Perhaps I should make the two of you fuck in front of us all, give us a good show."

Rage boiled up in Katherine and she tried again to pull power, managed to coalesce little more than what a beginner might achieve.

The sexpot laughed and took one more step forward, still holding onto Paul. "Go ahead," she said to Katherine. "Let's see what you've got. Go ahead, show me your petty magic. I'll even stop hindering you, let you throw your pitiful skills at me without constraint."

Suddenly the control and compulsion spell dissipated and Katherine could move freely again. But she knew full well that, even if not weakened by the saltwater, this witch was stronger than her. The chauffeur stepped back, clearly wary of being too close to two powerful witches throwing spells at each other, and Katherine realized there might be another way. She said calmly, "I have a special spell for you."

"Oh really," the slut said. "And what would that be, little witch?"

Katherine grinned and said, "Oh, it's a very special spell. It's called a nose-buster." Then she put all her strength behind her arm and punched the slut in the nose.

Katherine had taken a brief interest in the martial arts in high school, mainly because a boy she was interested in was into that stuff. But she'd quickly learned it meant broken fingernails and bruises—not her style—so she gave it up after a few months of lessons, gave up on the boy too. But she'd learned a thing or two from those lessons: she knew how to throw a punch. She hit the slut with a full-blown knuckle-buster, not some limp-wristed girlie slap, but a hard, right punch with her shoulder behind it. It hurt like hell when she connected, but she got the satisfaction of feeling the crunch as she broke the slut's nose.

The slut went down hard, right onto her back, even bounced once when she hit the floor. And still holding onto Paul, she dragged him down with her. Katherine danced about shaking her right hand shouting, "Owe fuck owe fuck owe!" as the chauffeur, probably still discounting her, instinctively lunged toward the slut to help her. Katherine ignored the pain in her hand, turned toward the two metal buckets, picked one up and tossed its contents all over Paul and the slut. The chauffeur recovered and spun toward her. She swung the metal bucket at him, but he blocked it with a forearm and backhanded her.

••••

McGowan and Colleen approached a lighted window carefully. Colleen said, "I don't like splitting up. We can't trust those Russians."

The old man looked at her and shrugged. "Clark's with them. And trust me, he can handle 'em."

Colleen didn't know this Clark Devoe fellow, didn't have the same faith in the man as McGowan. They'd detected the security connections to the front gate, spelled those first so no one in the mansion would be notified when the gate opened, then spelled the gate itself and opened it. They'd left it open. They'd also detected, and neutralized, perimeter spells placed to alert a practitioner to the presence of an intruder. It bothered her that so strong a practitioner would place perimeter spells on the estate, but no wards. And this close to the house she could now sense there were no house wards at all.

She felt like some stalker as she peered into the lighted window while McGowan kept watch on the grounds behind her. The room was empty, and she was about to spell the lock when she suddenly sensed a strong and powerful demon-feeding. A moment later an anguished scream shattered the silence of the night. That was followed by the thunderous clap of one of those large guns the Russians carried.

She and McGowan both turned and sprinted toward the sounds.

••••

Paul knelt over Belinda, and for the first time in days his thoughts cleared. For some reason he was soaked, and he could taste seawater. Belinda lay on the floor groaning piteously, blood pouring from her smashed nose, and as he looked at her all his memories of her came flooding back. He no longer felt the intense desire for her that had clouded his thoughts, never really had felt it, and he understood now it was some sort of magic thing, that she'd used him and manipulated him.

Suzanna knelt down in front of him, Cloe standing beside her. *Come, Paul, we have to run.*

Yes, daddy. We have to run.

Paul scanned the room quickly as Cassius stood up behind his desk and snarled, "Tie her up this time."

Joachim stood over Katherine, who was lying on her back groaning and trying weakly to climb back to her feet. The chauffeur drew a leg back to kick her in the ribs. Paul shouted, "No," and lunged toward him.

Paul had never seen anything move so quickly. In a single blink Cassius went from standing behind his desk, to standing in front of Paul. Paul's momentum slammed him into the man, and he bounced off the fellow with no effect. Cassius reached out and wrapped both his hands around Paul's throat, and lifted him off his feet like a child's doll. Suzanna and Cloe beat at the man ineffectively as Paul felt that strange *pull* where Cassius's hands touched his throat.

Blink.

Paul couldn't understand why Cassius wanted to harm him. The man had appeared to be a friend, someone who wanted to help. But the *pull* was there, and Paul felt something flowing out of him into Cassius, and with it came a growing sense of weakness and lethargy. He reached up and gripped Cassius's wrists, wanted to ask him why he'd turned against him.

Blink.

For an instant the man's eyes turned goat-slitted and blood-red, and Paul realized he was facing a demon. Remembering Katherine's warnings, he looked away from its eyes and concentrated on blocking the *pull*. He'd done that before, thought he should be able to do it now, but the flow continued unabated. Paul sensed a growing chasm opening before him and knew he couldn't resist that *pull*, knew nothing could resist it.

Behind Cassius the two leprechauns appeared and danced around Joachim like two sparrows tormenting a large crow, trying to keep it away from their nest, in this case trying to keep him away from Katherine. Paul's eyes drifted to the French doors at the far end of the room, and as the flow of the *pull* emptied him of all will to resist, he thought he saw Joe Stalin's ugly, square face peering through the windows there, Vladimir with his greasy blond hair standing next to him.

The thunder and flash of Joe Stalin's howitzer shattered the glass of the French doors. Something thumped into Cassius's head and erupted out the other side carrying a splatter of bone and brains. With half his head blown away the demon staggered but didn't fall, though the flow of the *pull* stopped for an instant. With Paul still dangling from its hands the monster spun about and threw a look of rage at the Russian's spilling through the French doors.

Paul pulled on the flow, pulled hard with every ounce of strength he could muster in his spirit, and the *pull* reversed. Something slammed into Paul, a searing gush of pain and agony, with centuries-old memories of suffering and sorrow. Paul would've cried out, but with the demon's hands clamped about his throat he could barely breathe. Then the lethargy that had overcome him dissipated suddenly, and turned into a sense of power and strength.

The demon did cry out and shook Paul like a limp rag. Paul sensed it trying to restore the flow of the *pull*, to stop Paul from feeding on it. But Paul kept his grip on the demon's wrists as they thrashed about the room, and he continued to force the flow of the *pull* out of the demon, flooding him with some sort of power and strength.

Blink.

Paul saw something akin to the bat-thing, but different . . .

Blink.

. . . with writhing snakes for arms . . .

Blink.

. . . and reptilian scales covering its face and torso . . .

Blink.

. . . maggots crawling among the razor sharp teeth of its mouth and into the nostrils at the end of its snout . . .

The demon screamed and threw Paul across the room. Paul bounced off the wall several feet above the floor, then bounced off the floor. He should've broken several bones, but instead he felt strength and power flooding through him, and he could now see the true nature of the demon, a winged reptilian horror from hell.

Bullets thudded into the demon's torso as it picked Paul up off the floor and slammed him into the ornate desk, shattering the heavy wooden piece like part of a breakable Hollywood set. It should've killed Paul, should've broken his back and every bone in his body. Instead he just felt the power within him diminish with each blow from the demon.

The demon turned away from him, did that thing where it crossed the room in a blink. The leprechauns fled out of its way as it reached down, lifted Katherine by her waist as if she weighed nothing, then turned toward the shattered French doors.

As the demon moved with blinding speed Paul ran after it, thinking his attempt to keep up with demon-bred speed would be futile. But somehow Paul crossed the room in the same blink and slammed into the demon just as it got to the shattered French doors. This time he hurt the monster, and he and the demon and Katherine sprawled out onto the patio.

Paul staggered to his feet, realized the incredible strength and speed he'd gained by reversing the flow of the demon's *pull* had now left him. His shoulder ached from the force of the collision. He understood then that using whatever had flowed into him had consumed it, used it up like fuel for a fire. But the same must be true of the demon, because it no longer maintained the glamour of a distinguished older gentleman.

Jim'Jiminie pulled on Paul's arm while Boo'Diddle helped Katherine. "Run," they both screamed.

Joe Stalin stepped out onto the patio, raised his howitzer and aimed it at Paul. Suzanna and Cloe climbed all over him, unsuccessfully trying to deflect his aim as Clark Devoe stepped out behind him. Paul had one instant to wonder what the hell the gun-shop owner was doing here, then Devoe swatted Joe in the back of the head with butt of a sawed-off shotgun. Joe went down like a bag of rocks.

Not far away Paul saw Katherine's father and the hippie woman running toward them; more crazies coming to join the let's-kill-Paul party.

"Run!" the leprechauns screamed again.

24

Rule the Unliving

"COME ON, YE daft fool," one of the midgets growled.

As Katherine staggered to her feet, Paul looked back at the demon. Its image flickered back and forth between the distinguished older gentlemen and the bat-thing with snake arms and maggot lips. Katherine saw the same horror and she looked at Paul, her eyes wide with terror. She screamed, "My car," then she turned and sprinted for the gate.

Paul ran after her, limping badly, his right ankle sending sharp splinters of pain up his leg, the two leprechauns on his heels urging, "Faster! Faster!"

The run to the gate was a couple hundred feet, and Paul had slowed to an unsteady stagger by the time he got there, the leprechauns literally pushing him along. Miraculously, the gate was open. He stumbled out into the street but stopped abruptly as a tall, skinny Russian stepped into the street about ten feet away. The guy reached behind his back and pulled a blade the length of Paul's arm, then crouched into a fighting stance and advanced cautiously.

Paul back stepped slowly and the Russian advanced into the middle of the road. Paul glanced right and left, looking for some sort of a weapon, because without something this fellow was going to slice him to pieces. Then a pair of headlights about fifty feet away lit up Paul and the Russian, both standing in the middle of the road. The car roared to life, its wheels spun, spitting gravel as the car fishtailed and came their way. Paul back stepped to get out of its way, and the Russian dove into the bushes on the other side of the road as the car skidded to a stop in front of Paul. The passenger door slammed open, and Paul saw Katherine seated behind the wheel, an almost demonic look on her face as she screamed, "Get in."

Paul leaned forward, but the leprechauns hit him from behind, launching him head first into the car. He landed with his knees in the passenger seat, the shift lever jammed painfully in his gut, and his face in Katherine's crotch. "Not now, Conklin," she shouted. "We can do that later."

The leprechauns crawled into the back seat as he pulled his face out of her crotch. She looked at him, smiled, slammed the gearshift into drive, punched the accelerator and the tires squealed again as she spun a doughnut, straightened the car and rocketed down the street.

"Weeeeeee!" the midgets in the back seat shouted.

Paul glanced back toward the mansion. McGowan and the hippie and the Russians stood on the patio, and they all looked on helplessly as a black silhouette spread large wings, flapped twice, then climbed into the air.

"Aw shit!" Paul said.

••••

It boiled with rage. The Lord-of-the-Unliving had fed on It, actually consumed a portion of Its accumulated power when It tried to feed on him. For the first time in centuries It now struggled to maintain a decent glamour, so It decided not to bother.

It climbed to Its feet, glanced at the beings standing nearby: some lesser wizards, two powerful old wizards and a powerful Druid. For a moment It considered feeding on them, but together they were a dangerous combination. No, the Lord-of-the-Unliving was weakened and still ignorant of his true powers, and the witch accompanying him was also weakened, so they'd be easier prey.

It was time to end this. It could sense the Lord in the distance, would have no difficulty following him. It spread Its wings, always a pleasurable experience, and took to the air with ease.

••••

Colleen watched the demon rise into the air.

One of the young Russians said in a thick accent, "What the fuck was that?"

"That was a demon," she said. "An old one, probably Secundus caste. And it's after young Conklin."

Karpov said, "Then we go too."

"Ya," McGowan said. "But don't let the two thralls get away. Bring them too."

••••

"We're in deep shit," Paul shouted as the car careened around a corner, tires squealing in a black cloud of rubbery smoke.

"I know," Katherine shouted back, struggling with the steering wheel. "My father thinks you're a demon, or demon possessed, and I'll bet Karpov does too. That's why they're trying to kill you. And until I can convince them otherwise, we have to keep you away from them as much as that demon."

"That's gonna be a problem," he shouted. "That vamp took to the air."

Her head snapped around and she grimaced at him. "What?"

"It's flying," he shouted. "Yuh know, with wings."

Both midgets pointed through the windshield and screamed, "Look out."

Katherine looked forward, spun the steering wheel and swerved to one side, barely missing a young man in a crosswalk. The car spun out of control, swung about and skidded backward down the street in a cloud of smoke from screaming tires, amazingly missing the cars parked on either side as it slid to a stop. Paul caught a brief glimpse of the pedestrian running away up the sidewalk.

In the silence Katherine said, "Shit! Shit! Shit! Thank god I didn't hit him!"

The bat-vamp landed with a crushing thud on the hood of the car just outside the windshield, crumpling the hood like a potato chip. It screamed an ear splitting shriek. Katherine rammed the gearshift in reverse and slammed her foot on the gas pedal. The car shot backward, spilling the monster off the hood into the street. Paul watched it recede as Katherine kept the pedal jammed to the floor, stopping only when the back of the jaguar slammed into a parked car. The car's antitheft system started flashing its lights and honking its horn.

Far up the street the monster climbed awkwardly to its feet, glared at them with blood-red eyes that penetrated into Paul's soul. He sensed its hatred and malevolence and hunger on some level foreign to any past experience, and he knew it sensed him in return.

The monster started toward them, running on ungainly, clawed talons, slowly picking up speed. With the back of the jaguar smashed against a parked car they had only one hope, so Paul grabbed the gearshift, jerked it from reverse to drive, shouted at Katherine, "Ram the fucker."

It took her a second to understand him, then she jabbed the gas pedal to the floor and the Jaguar shot forward, the engine roaring, tires screeching and spitting gravel. The car and the monster both picked up speed rapidly. With her hands clamped on the steering wheel in a death grip, her knuckles turning white, Katherine screamed, "Oh shit, oh shit, oh shit," the midgets shouted, "Yahooooooo!" and Paul yelled, "Oh fuuccckkk!"

The front end of the car crumpled as it slammed into the vamp, the airbags fired with a series of staccato pops and the car careened to the left, slid diagonally into a parked car. In all the confusion Paul had forgotten to put on his seatbelt, but the airbag had saved him, though he had no conscious recollection of it opening. One moment they were speeding up the street playing chicken with a nightmare from hell, the next he was sitting there stunned and watching the airbag deflate. Paul guessed the dazed look on Katherine's face mirrored his own.

The door next to Paul suddenly shot open with the shriek of ripping, tearing metal. The monster tore it away completely, tossed it aside, grabbed Paul by the throat with a reptilian hand and dragged him out into the street. Its hunger had grown into an almost palpable fog that engulfed him completely, sucking at him with ravenous need. It screamed its maggot-breath in his face, tossed him contemptuously into the air. He landed on his shoulder on the hood of a parked car, a hammer blow of pain slamming through him, bounced off it and landed on the sidewalk on the other side.

Paul struggled wearily to his hands and knees, got to his feet just as the monster crawled over the top of the car, watched in fascination as its claws ripped through the metal of the car's hood like soft cheese. It stood up on top of the car, loomed over him, spread its leathery wings and cried out triumphantly as it lunged at him. He tried to leap to one side but it hit him like a freight train, pinning him to the ground with talons as long as his fingers.

It opened a mouth full of razor-sharp teeth and maggots, and screeched at the heavens, then lowered its head toward him. Katherine had told him not to look into its eyes, but too late its blood-red goat-slitted eyes became the center of his universe. They glowed with hunger and need, and in them he found a wasteland of death and despair, a landscape without hope or joy, and he recalled Dayandalous's words, *Look not into the demon eye, mortal. Look through the demon eye.*

••••

Katherine watched in horror as the vampire dragged Paul out of the car. "Come on," one of the leprechauns shouted, "Let's go watch the fun." They scrambled out of the car like children going to a carnival.

Her own door was pinned against a parked car so she crawled across the center console and out through the hole where the passenger door had been. She tumbled out onto the street just as her father's car skidded to a stop, with the Russian's two sedans screeching to a stop behind it. Her father and Colleen and the Russians all spilled out onto the street.

"This way," the leprechauns shouted as they ran across the street and disappeared behind a row of parked cars.

Katherine rushed after them, Colleen and her father and the Russians just behind her. They found Paul on his back, the vampire crouched on top of him, the two of them looking into each other's eyes like lovers, which meant Paul had succumbed to the vampire's hypnotic gaze and it was consuming his soul. She turned back to Colleen and her father. "We have to do something."

"No," the leprechauns shouted, stepping in front of her, blocking her path.

Karpov snarled, "Kill them both."

One of the leprechauns stepped in front of him. It was incongruous to see a little man barely knee high in a face-off with four full-grown mortals. "You'll not interfere in this, wizard." The little man looked at McGowan. "Nor you, old man. This is his battle."

Colleen gripped Katherine's arm, spoke with wonder in her voice, "Look, child."

••••

Paul looked deep into the demon's eyes, then looked through the demon's eyes and found a spark of life in that blasted landscape, a tormented soul chained by centuries of misery and hopelessness. He recalled Katherine's words, that the vampire . . . *possesses a live mortal, feeds on its essence until there remains only a faint spark of life, leaves that spark of life untouched, which must be a forever living hell for its victim.*

Paul could sense the torment in that soul, could feel it in his own soul, knew at some level it had died long ago and wanted to move on to wherever souls went when this life came to an end. For a moment he wondered if it was the same for Suzanna and Cloe, if they wanted to move on and something was keeping them from doing so. But that thought struck a sharp pain in his heart, and he put it aside. He had to deal with this soul, this spark of life the demon had trapped and tormented for centuries. And he knew he could free it, free that spark, and end its torment and captivity. And, with just a simple touch from his own soul, he did so.

••••

Katherine looked again at Paul and the vampire. The two of them remained in a frozen tableau of what seemed like joyous communion. Both Paul and the vampire started to glow with a grayish, ethereal haze that grew brighter with each second. The glow grew slowly in intensity until it lit up the entire street, but then the vampire's glow reached a peak and started to diminish, while Paul's continued to grow. Paul's glow brightened and the vampire's continued to wane until it was almost extinguished. And then Katherine felt a soul depart the Mortal Plane.

She gasped, thinking Paul had died. But in that moment the vampire's glow disappeared completely and it collapsed in a cloud of ash that settled down in a slow sprinkle over Paul.

Paul laid there glowing like some angel in a Hollywood movie, and both leprechauns spoke in unison, "Necromancer!"

••••

Paul's hands were glowing, and when he looked more closely he realized his arms too were glowing, and his chest and his stomach and legs and feet. Apparently he was glowing all over.

Every muscle, every bone, every part of him hurt. He explored his face with one hand, confirmed what he already knew, that his left cheek and the left side of his lips were badly swollen. It took an enormous effort just to sit up. Some sort of powdery ash fluttered off him as he did so. It caked his hair, encrusted the blood on his face, on his arms and legs. He crawled the few feet to a nearby parked car, propped his back against it, sat with his butt on the sidewalk, his legs sprawled out in front of him, closed his eyes and tried to rest in the silence that descended. He decided that if there was more craziness to come then let it, because he didn't have the heart to fight any more of this madness.

He heard footsteps on the sidewalk, opened his eyes to find the old man, the hippie, the Russians, Katherine and the two midgets standing over him. The humans looked at him with eyes wide, and something approaching wonder and awe on their faces.

Boo'Diddle turned to Jim'Jiminie and said, "You were right. You won." He held out a pouch.

Jim'Jiminie took the pouch, held it near his ear and shook it. Paul heard the sound of coins clinking as the little man said, "We both won," and they high-fived each other.

Paul closed his eyes again and wished for Suzanna and Cloe. He sensed Suzanna sit down on the sidewalk next to him on his left, Cloe on his right.

Tough night, eh, Paulie-boy?

He thought he might've broken several ribs, certainly torn some ligaments in his shoulder, probably his hip and ankle too. But while the physical pain was demanding and intense, it was the hurt in his soul that wounded most.

Why're you sad, daddy?

Paul opened his eyes and looked at Cloe. His swollen lips didn't work so well and his words came out in a mushy drawl. "Don't worry, munchkin. I'll be ok."

Katherine lowered herself to one knee in front of him, moving carefully like an old woman. "The demon's gone," she said. "You killed it. Well, since it was already dead, I guess you annihilated it."

Amazing, he thought, said, "And I don't even know how I did it."

Katherine looked at Cloe carefully, frowned, then looked at Suzanna. Her gaze returned to Paul and she said, "And now you need to let *them* go."

She could see them! And if she saw them that meant they were real. And if they were real then they weren't dead. He reached out and she put her hand in his. "You see them too?" he asked.

She grimaced with pain, and he knew that, like him, it wasn't physical pain that bothered her most at this moment. She shook her head. "No, I don't see them. But I sense them."

All his hopes crashed and compressed into a tiny black hole hidden somewhere deep in his heart. "Then they're not real, are they?" he asked, trying not to cry like a baby.

McGowan stepped forward, said, "It's not that they're—"

The hippie woman kicked him and said, "Shut up, old man. She's handling it just fine without you."

The Russians looked on warily.

Katherine said, "Paul, look at me."

She cupped his hand in both of hers as he looked into her eyes. It was the first time he'd really looked at her. Her hair was a frightening mess, her eyes bloodshot, blood trickling from a cut on her cheek, and he could only thank whatever gods existed she'd been there to help him through this night. "Who were they?" she asked.

"Suzanna and Cloe, my wife and daughter. They were killed, but then they came back."

She swallowed hard and said, "They're real, Paul. But they're not what you think."

He'd known she was going to say something like that. "Demons, huh?" he asked.

She shook her head sadly. "No, not demons. They're shades of your wife and daughter, summoned by you, a little piece of them you've brought back."

He didn't want to believe it. "Shades? You mean ghosts?"

Still speaking carefully she said, "You're a necromancer, Paul. It was visible in your aura when I first saw you, but at the time I didn't understand what it meant, not until our little friends here told us. You have power over the dead, like no wizard or witch can hope to have. That's extremely rare."

"Rare," he growled, all the fear and frustration of the last few weeks boiling to the surface. "I suppose wizards and witches and vampires and old hippies that throw lightning bolts and . . ." He almost said, *midgets in clown suits.* ". . . and . . . and leprechauns . . . aren't rare?"

She gripped his hand tighter. "They're rare, but not as rare as you might think, though most mundane people no longer believe in such things. But there hasn't been a necromancer on the Mortal Plane for . . ." She looked over her shoulder at her father for the answer.

The old man shrugged and said, "Twelve . . . maybe thirteen hundred years."

He could feel her compassion. It radiated out from her. "You have power over the dead, and by just wishing for your wife and daughter so hard you're not letting them go. You're keeping them from moving on to whatever comes next. You're holding them here, and it's not right. Let them go. Please, Paul, let them go."

Like the vampire and its victim, he thought. *I'm no better than that fucking demon.*

He closed his eyes, could sense Suzanna and Cloe sitting beside him. When Suzanna spoke, her voice sounded tired and weary. *She's right, Paulie-boy. It's time. I miss you so much, but I need you to let us go.*

Hard anger welled up in his gut and he growled, "I can't. I miss you too much." He was damn well not going to lose his Suzanna and Cloe again.

She's right, daddy. We have to go.

No! he shouted silently. *No, no, no, no, no!* But he knew he had to let them go, just like the soul the vampire held captive. He had to let them go.

Good-bye, daddy.

"Good-bye, munchkin."

And they were gone . . .

He looked up, met Katherine's eyes, and she said, "You did the right thing, Conklin. The right thing."

••••

The hippie woman helped Katherine help Paul to his feet. "Let's get you both back to Walter's house," she said. "You're both a mess, and that's something I can help with."

Joe Stalin stepped in their way. "He fed on me," he growled. "He's a fucking demon. He dies, here and now." He still held the howitzer in one hand, though it hung limply at his side, the barrel pointed at the ground. But Paul knew it would only take him an instant to raise it and blow a very big hole in Paul Conklin, necromancer-at-large.

McGowan intervened and stepped between them. "He's no demon. He's a necromancer. The little people confirmed that, and that explains a lot."

Joe Stalin growled, clearly torn between his need to kill Paul and his fear of confronting McGowan. Karpov reached out and gripped the wrist of the hand holding the gun, making it clear Joe wasn't to raise it. "Okay, Valter. He's not a demon. But there have to be rules. He doesn't feed. He doesn't—"

Colleen interrupted him. "What he did is not demon feeding. I'm not sure what it is, but it's not . . ."

They all started speaking at once, arguing over the rules for Paul's continued existence. He thought of Suzanna and Cloe and Katherine, and Boris and Joe Stalin trying to kill him, and a rage born of fear and frustration boiled up inside him. When he could no longer contain his anger he shouted at the top of his lungs, "You want rules?"

That silenced them, and they all stepped away from him, their faces marked with fear. Even the two powerful old men hesitated. "I'll give you rules," he shouted, and marched up to Joe Stalin, stopped when he could stand face-to-face with the man who'd repeatedly tried to kill him. "You try to kill me, I'll use any tool at my disposal to stop you, and I'll kill you first. Those are my fucking rules."

Amazingly enough, Joe just stood there trembling, then lowered his eyes and found the pavement very interesting. Paul turned to Karpov and shouted, "And if you don't like them rules then let's settle it right now."

Even Karpov seemed frightened.

He heard Katherine approach him quietly from behind. She whispered in his ear, "Paul, you're pulling a scary amount of power, a big, nasty whole shit-load of it. You could hurt a lot of people right now if you don't let it dissipate."

He turned to her and looked in her eyes, and the anger left him. "I don't know how," he said.

She nodded carefully and smiled. She was an absolute mess and she was still gorgeous. "That's better," she said. "It's dissipating as your anger dissipates. Just relax and it'll be gone soon."

Colleen approached them and stood next to Katherine. "Well now. I think we all understand Paul's rules. And I for one am perfectly happy with them. And as I said, we need to get you back to Walter's house, bandage up those wounds, then a good meal and a hot bath."

McGowan hooked a thumb over his shoulder. "Take my car. I'll stay here, and me and my Russian friends'll clean this mess up. Otherwise the police are going to be asking a lot of questions we don't want to answer."

"Why your car?" Katherine asked. Then her eyes widened and she gasped, looked at the smoking ruin of her car. "My Jag!" she cried. "My beautiful Jag!" She rushed over to it, brushed her hand over a twisted fender like petting a favorite animal. "My poor beautiful Jag!"

She whined about the Jaguar all the way to McGowan's car. As Paul was about to climb in the back seat he noticed the tall skinny Russian standing next to one of the two dark sedans. It was the fellow who'd tried to introduce him to a rather large knife. There were two occupants in the back seat of the sedan. Paul hesitated, took a moment to do a little head count, and suddenly realized who they must be: Belinda and Joachim.

Paul felt nothing for Belinda, understood now his desire for her had been wholly artificial, but nevertheless he needed to see her. He started toward the sedan slowly and the Russian tensed. Colleen caught up to him half way there and said, "Paul, what're you doing?"

"I have to see her."

Colleen held out an arm and stopped him about ten feet from the Russian. "Wait here."

Paul waited while she approached the Russian and spoke to him hurriedly. They argued for a moment, then the fellow shrugged and stepped aside. Colleen turned and said, "He now understands the situation, so it's safe."

As Paul approached he could see Belinda huddled in the back seat of the sedan, her head resting against the window as if sleeping. Joachim sat on the other side of the seat, his head resting on the other window. Not wanting to startle Belinda Paul opened the door slowly, but she started anyway, and he couldn't believe his eyes as he looked at the Belinda that looked back at him. Her nose was badly swollen and blood encrusted her upper lip, mouth and jaw. But he'd seen Katherine punch her so that didn't surprise him. The Belinda that looked up at him through the open door was gray and withered. The skin of her face bore a fine patina of wrinkles, with deep bluish circles under her eyes, and her hair hung limply about her shoulders, no longer shiny and exotic, but streaked with gray. She appeared to be in her eighties.

She smiled at him. "Paul," she said in a crackly, old voice. "It was fun while it lasted."

Paul looked at Colleen. "What happened to her?"

Colleen grimaced. "With the demon gone it can no longer maintain her youth."

"It was all an illusion?"

Colleen shook her head. "No, not at all. As long as the demon lived, it rewarded her with a bit of the life it took from its victims. She was truly young—as long as the demon lived and fed her."

Colleen took him by the arm and turned him away from the sedan. As they walked back toward McGowan's car he asked, "What'll happen to her now?"

"Walter and Vasily will put the two thralls down."

Paul stopped and looked her in the eyes. "You mean like . . . putting a pet down."

She considered him carefully. "That woman fed the demon life after life for God-knows-how-many years. Innocent lives, to feed its needs and her youth. Hundreds, perhaps thousands of lives over the years. She's worse than the worst mass-murderer you've ever read about in the news. So, yes, I mean putting her down like an animal, but more like a rabid dog. If we don't, who knows, she might find another demon to help."

She turned back toward McGowan's car, didn't let go of his arm and led him back toward Katherine and the midgets. They stuffed Paul into the back seat and the leprechauns joined him there.

Katherine sat behind the wheel and the hippie climbed into the passenger seat beside her. As Katherine started the engine the hippie turned back and looked at Paul. "Young man," she said sharply. Her harsh tone got Paul's attention and he looked into her emerald green eyes. "The name is Colleen," she said. "Don't ever call me an *old hippie* again."

Katherine looked at her, said cautiously, "But dear, you do look just the teensiest bit hippie-ish."

Colleen's eyes narrowed. "I don't care about the *hippie* bit; it's the *old* bit that really pissed me off."

Acknowledgements

I'D LIKE TO thank Durelle Kurlinski for fixing all my dotted t's and crossed i's, Karen for both supporting my dream and being my most valuable critic, and Steve Himes, and the whole team at Telemachus, for getting a quality product out the door.

Books by J. L. Doty

Series: The Dreadmark Covenants
Dread Child (available 3/1/2024)
Dread Spirit (6/1/2024)
Dread Soul (9/1/2024)
Dread Lord (12/1/2024)

Series: The Treasons Cycle
Of Treasons Born
A Choice of Treasons

Stand Alone Novel
The Thirteenth Man

Series: The Gods Within
Child of the Sword
The SteelMaster of Indwallin
The Heart of the Sands
The Name of the Sword

Series: The Dead Among Us
When Dead Ain't Dead Enough
Still Not Dead Enough
Never Dead Enough

Series: The Blacksword Regiment
A Hymn for the Dying
A Dirge for the Damned
A Prayer for the Fallen
A Requiem for the Forsaken

Series: Commonwealth Re-contact Novellas
Tranquility Lost

About the Author

JIM IS A full-time SF&F writer, scientist and laser geek (Ph.D. Electrical Engineering, specialty laser physics), and former running-dog-lackey for the bourgeois capitalist establishment. He's been writing for over 30 years, with 19 published books. His first success came through self-publishing when his books went word-of-mouth viral, and sold enough that he was able to quit his day-job, start working for himself and write full time—his new boss is a real jerk. That led to contracts with traditional publishers like Open Road Media and Harper Collins, and his books are now a mix of traditional and self-published.

The four novels in his new coming-of-age epic fantasy series, *The Dreadmark Covenants*, are scheduled for release beginning in early 2024.

Jim was born in Seattle, but he's lived most of his life in California, though he did live on the east coast and in Europe for a while. He now resides in Arizona with his wife Karen and Julia, a little being who claims to be a cat. But Jim is certain she's really an extra-terrestrial alien in disguise.

Visit the author's website at https://www.jldoty.com/
Contact the author at jld@jldoty.com

Made in the USA
Monee, IL
30 January 2024

51938632R00135